MW00680998

B

Briarwood Publications, Incorporated

THE HOPE OF TIMOTHY BEAN

RICHARD STEIGELMAN

Briarwood Publications, Incorporated

First Published 2001
Briarwood Publications & Sassy Cat Books, Inc.
150 West College Street
Rocky Mount, VA 24151

Richard Steigelman
THE HOPE OF TIMOTHY BEAN
ISBN 1-892614-39-1

Manufactured in the United States of America

Printed by
Briarwood Publications, Inc.

For my Mother and Father, and for my
wonderful wife, Donna

Chapter One

"Oh—for heavens sake, Fab, put that away!" implored Mrs. McWheeten. "Good God, why on earth do you have that out? Put it back where it belongs—this instant. The kitchen is no place to be displaying that. Goodness, what would a tenant think if he or she were to walk in here right now and see you clutching that filthy thing in your hand? Now away with it, man, before we are discovered."

Fab McWheeten, whose gaunt and angular figure was especially striking when contrasted against his wife's robust presence, seemed slow to comprehend; though, as the viscid grumblings of his uncertainty degenerated into a fit of coughing, he did turn and leave the room.

"Good heavens," said the landlady, with a wealthy sigh of relief. "If the tenants should discover a mop upon the premises—why, they'll expect us to clean."

Timothy Bean locked the door to his room, down in the shadows near the end of the little front hallway, and slipping the key inside his pocket, stepped out into the clear and cool October evening.

Lottie Daniels emerged from her room close by the house's main entrance. Awkwardly encumbered with an array of cooking utensils and ingredients, she crossed over to the nearby stairs and, with careful steps, followed them up and around to the second floor. Nearing the end of that hallway, she turned left, passing precariously by the head of another set of stairways, which led to the basement quarters at the back of the convoluted boarding house. There, she entered into the kitchen.

1

"Well, hello, Lottie. This is indeed a pleasant surprise," expressed Mrs. McWheeten, now quite nicely recovered from her husband's brief bout with absent-mindedness. She was setting places for herself and her spouse at the small kitchen table tucked up next to the window across the way.

"Going to do some cooking, I see," the landlady noted with a little button of a smile. "How nice. We like to encourage our tenants to make the most of our fine facilities."

And with an amused laugh, as she moved back towards the stove where her own meal was cooking, Mrs. McWheeten was compelled to segue onto another point.

"You know, I find it so entirely fascinating the great lengths to which people will go to devour a dead beast. Standing over a hot stove, with the flame dancing high about their quarry—well, not in our kitchen, of course; we are duly conscious of regulating our gas appliances for the safety of our tenants—

"Yet," she resumed her original thought, "with the smoke peeling from the carcass so thick, sometimes, as to literally choke the life from the preparer himself—well, not here, naturally. We have a more than adequate ventilation system, as I believe is evidenced by the present lack of even the slightest wisp from this dead animal's hide—

"But what I mean to say is that, isn't it so very intriguing the way we humans will cook and carve these poor creatures in order to keep ourselves going, with nary a care nor consideration for their plight? For instance, this cow which is providing Mr. McWheeten and myself our sustenance tonight—oh, that man!" squirmed the landlady in a sudden display of exasperation, as she peered more closely into the frying pan.

"Why, he forgot to turn the stove on. Honestly now. Why, sometimes, he just—well, never mind," the landlady would resist the temptation to delve into her husband's shortcomings. "He is not well. I'll just reach down here—" and almost simultaneously with her tending to the matter herself, Mrs. McWheeten cut loose a horrible shriek, for the flame had shot forth with such fury that she had been unable to prevent its catching hold of her sleeve!

She leapt upon her heels, before collapsing to the dingy linoleum floor where she quickly subdued the small blaze beneath a series of frantic maneuvers.

A mild breeze kicked up the fallen leaves along the sidewalk as Timothy Bean paced onwards, his hands settled into his coat pockets, his head bent in thought toward the ground.

The comparatively dull preparation of her own meal being concluded, Lottie was ready to transport it back to her room, when Mrs. McWheeten, sitting calmly now with her husband over dinner, bid her tenant to, "Enjoy your supper."

"Thank you, Mrs. M'Wheeten," replied Lottie, standing before the kitchen door. "I hope you all right."

"Oh, it was nothing, dear," said the landlady with a wave. "A little of that burn cream and I'm a new woman. I'm afraid it was just a matter of inattentiveness on my part. Let that be a lesson to you. Oh, by the way, Lottie, everything is all right down in your room, I trust?"

Lottie's pause was stark in its honesty, and she was clearly not comfortable in having to reply, "Well—'member, I tell you 'bout that light bulb burn out on ceilin' las' week?"

"Oh—goodness gracious, that's right," the landlady clasped her palm to her cheek. "I had completely forgotten. I'm so sorry, Lottie."

"Kinda dark in there, even if I got candle on."

"Why, we'll take care of that tonight, won't we, Fab?"

The husband, who had been contentedly focused on his dinner, glanced up from beneath his full, untamed brows, and issued a dull grunt of confirmation that seemed hardly to ease the mind of their tenant.

"A landlord's job is never done," quoted Mrs. McWheeten with a smile. "Well now, Lottie, you should probably run along before your meal gets cold. And I promise to send Mr. McWheeten down sometime tonight to replace your light bulb. All right? Fine. Now, run along."

From just inside its double-doors, Timothy scanned the room, but, of the dozen or so people who loitered about the neatly-aligned cots, he recognized no one. He realized that it was still early enough in the evening that those who would be spending the night at the ministry's shelter might not yet have arrived. And he was contemplating whether to bide his time or, perhaps, try the city shelter several blocks away, when he was heartened by the entrance into the room of a trim young man with scraggly blonde hair and a scratchy beard.

"Mike?" He advanced towards that individual with the tentative hope that he might be remembered. That was not seeming probable, though, as the other simply stared at him through eyes bleared by intoxication.

"Jesus Chris', what the hell're you doin' here?" slurred the young man, finally, in recognition.

It was an unexpectedly chilly reception, witnessed by two or three others who stood nearby, and made Timothy keenly self-conscious of his own contrast to the present environment.

Timothy's response was consequently made hesitant, and he tried to exclude those others by focusing only on his acquaintance. "I thought that—maybe I might find Hank here."

Mike snorted with disdain. "Why? That fat ol' landlady a yours send ya over to collect his rent money? Well, I got news for ya, he ain't got it! So, why don't you jus' go back 'n tell her fat ass—"

Timothy hadn't come on any errand for his landlady, he reported to a skeptical audience. "I just wanted to see how Hank was doing. And to see whether he might need anything."

"He don't need nothin' from you—or her," came the reply, "—'cept to be left alone! Got It? So, if ya really wanna help 'im, why don't you do your part by gettin' the hell outa here—"

Timothy tried to ask whether Hank was expected at the shelter that evening, but Mike would hear no more from him, and, turning his back, he swaggered off across the room.

Timothy returned home and, upon entering the house, became startled by Lottie's poking her head shyly out from behind her door.

"Hello," he said to her, and recalled her name from their first meeting a few days earlier.

That may have been a small gesture, but it brightened Lottie's face, and she moved out a little further from her door. "How weather tonight?"

"A little cool," answered Timothy with a shrug, still preoccupied, it appeared, with his visit to the ministry. "But not too bad." He had removed his eyeglasses and was wiping them off with his shirt.

"You jus' gettin' home from work?"

Timothy informed Lottie that he was returning from the shelter for the homeless at nearby Saint Augustine's Church. "I thought that I might find Hank." He motioned towards the next room down the hall. "But he wasn't there. I did run into Mike, though. I don't know if you remember Hank's friend . . ." Timothy's voice tailed off into a sigh, and he reflected on the meeting with a shake of his head.

"He certainly wasn't very helpful, though. Nor friendly. I don't know him very well, but the few times that I saw him over here visiting Hank, we seemed to get along well enough." And while continuing to ponder this evening's perplexing deviation, Timothy happened to glance overtop Lottie's five-foot tall frame, and asked her about the darkness of her room.

"Light bulb on ceilin' go out las' week. Only light I got, 'cept for candle."

"Have you informed the McWheetens?"

"Yep," Lottie replied with a big nod. "Say they be down to fix it tonight. Say that las' week, too."

Timothy had an idea, and he beckoned Lottie to follow him down the hallway. "I'll give you my bulb," he told her. "And you can just send the McWheetens down to my room."

"But then what you gonna do for light?"

"I have a candle, too," he said, smiling at her over his

shoulder. "You'll have to excuse my room, though." He was unlocking his door. "It's a bit of a mess."

Lottie grinned enormously. "Can't be as bad as my room. I got clothes all over place!"

"Well," replied Timothy, as he maneuvered through the darkness towards his desk—and lamp, "I'm finding that it's very difficult to keep such small rooms tidy."

"My room bigges' in whole house an' I still can't keep it clean!" Lottie beamed with peculiar pride over this accomplishment.

Timothy cleared some of his clothes and a few books off a sad little wicker chair that he pulled out from a crowded corner. "Careful that you don't fall through," he quipped in offering it to Lottie.

He then took off his coat and crammed it into an open makeshift closet along the wall, before stepping back over a hassock and seating himself at his desk.

"Did you know Hank from next door?" he asked Lottie, while pulling off his brown leather hiking boots.

"I saw him," she replied. "But didn' really know him. I stay in my room by myself most a the time—lookin' at mag'zines an' playin' games an' things like that.

"Heard him, though," she revealed with a sharp grin. "Ev'rybody heard him. That why he get kicked out."

Timothy sighed and nodded. He then removed his glasses and rested his chin in his hand. "Though I'm not sure I agree that evicting him was the best solution. There's no denying that he has a problem—with alcohol. But I just don't see how throwing him back out onto the street will do anything but compound the matter."

"He loud."

Yes, Timothy conceded that their former neighbor had, at times, been too loud, which only served to underscore Timothy's point. "He definitely is in need of some professional help. So why, then, would a woman like Mrs. McWheeten, who considers herself a good Christian, turn her back on such an obviously troubled individual, and by doing so, I'm afraid, only make a bad situation worse?"

Lottie giggled abruptly. "Mrs. M'Wheeten light herself on fire tonight."

Timothy was confused by Lottie's digression. "She did what?"

"She light herself on fire tonight," Lottie eagerly repeated.

"How?"

"You know how fire on stove jump up real high soon as you turn it on?"

Timothy had noticed that, yes.

"Well, fire jump up an' start her shirt on fire."

"Is she all right?"

"Oh, she okay," said Lottie, nodding. "She fall on floor an' roll 'roun' an' scream till fire go out."

"Was there much of a burn?"

"Only a little," reported Lottie, with a toss of her shoulders. "Wasn't much of a fire on her shirt. Couldn't roast marshmellows on it or nothin'."

Timothy expressed his relief that the landlady was not more seriously injured; though his guest seemed not to hear it, for her eyes had begun to wander about the room.

"So, you got job, right?" she inquired.

Timothy said that he had. "At the State Street Grill. Scrambling eggs and flipping burgers. It's all right," he shrugged, "for the time being. How about you?"

"Work in kitchen, too," Lottie smiled. "At ment'l han'cap center."

"Oh—"

"I ment'lly han'cap."

"Well—that's nothing to be ashamed of—"

"Oh, I not. It ain't so bad," she remarked with resignation. "State help take care a me. An' people at work are all older 'n me, but they like me. But they say I talk too much," her quick grin twinkled with mischief.

Timothy smiled, and confessed that his first impression painted her as quiet.

"It hard for me to get to know people," she freely acknowledged. "But when I do—look out!"

Timothy laughed, and told her that he was looking forward

to that pleasure; however, right now, he was rather tired and should probably be going to bed. "It's been a long day. And I have to be to work by six in the morning," he said, giving a weary sigh. "But before I forget." He lit a candle and turned off the desk lamp, allowing the bulb a moment to cool before removing it. Volunteering his six-foot height for the task of installing it into Lottie's ceiling, Timothy then returned to his room and was soon settled into an unsound sleep.

Chapter Two

"Oh, hello, Mrs. McWheeten. How are you this morning?" Timothy had entered the kitchen facilities, startling his landlady, who, across the way, was attending an old and very sickly dog which lay in a newspaper-lined cardboard box upon the floor.

"For heaven's sake, Timothy, what are you doing up so early? Why, the roosters aren't even up yet."

Timothy smiled tiredly and mentioned that he had to be to work shortly. "And I'm getting a little bored with the same old food at the restaurant," he explained as he moved up to the counter with his pot and his box of oatmeal.

"How's Sunshine today?" he asked after the dog.

Mrs. McWheeten returned a heavy sigh and reported that the indolent creature, with its deteriorating coat of grungy white hair perforated by generous swaths of diseased skin, was doing 'as well as could be expected.'

"Poor thing, though," she said, shaking her head with pity as she observed the dog struggle to simply lift its nose up to the edge of its box in response to Timothy's visit. "Can you imagine such an existence? Being both deaf and blind, and so dreadfully ill besides? I'm afraid she hasn't much time left, though I simply cannot bear the thought of having her put to sleep, as has been suggested to us. She's been with Mr. McWheeten and myself too long—nearly twelve years—for that even to be a consideration. Her Time shall be determined by the Good Lord, not some veterinarian who stands to cash in on her hardship."

Timothy empathized with his landlady. "Dogs are very special pets," he agreed, and, as he began recalling a favorite from his childhood, while mixing his oatmeal into the pot on the stove, he noticed, with a glance, that Mrs. McWheeten was not listening, having turned her attention back to her dog.

"I had a rather interesting experience last night," Timothy remarked after a few quiet moments of tending to his pot. He had an eye surreptitiously trained on Mrs. McWheeten's reaction.

"Oh?" came her half-attentive response. "And what might that have been?"

"Well," replied Timothy, deliberate in his manner, "I went and visited a homeless shelter on my own for the first time in my life, looking for Hank—" and he paused to observe as Mrs. McWheeten's face revealed a new and fuller attentiveness.

"Hank?" feigned detachment by the landlady. "Why, you don't mean Hank—Klegman?

Timothy did mean Hank Klegman.

"I'm sorry," she snorted, "but why? I don't understand; I mean—he was such a lout, if you'll pardon the expression."

Timothy chose, rather, to ignore the expression; and he lowered the flame beneath his fast boiling pot. "He has some problems, I have to admit—"

"Well, how could you not? My goodness! And will you also admit that he did a very capable job of turning them into everyone else's problems, as well?"

Timothy sighed, collectedly, with his eyes remaining on the oatmeal he continued to stir. He conceded to his landlady that, "Hank's dependence on alcohol did, at times, make him inconsiderate of the rights of others—"

"You're damn right it did!" Mrs. McWheeten was standing upright now, her hands placed emphatically on her hips. "And he seemed not to care in the least. I mean, the man's attitude was simply atrocious!"

Timothy did not disagree; rather, "Couldn't that be considered a probable sign of alcoholism? And is it not such an individual who is most in need of the help and support provided by a solid Christian sense of duty?"

"Well—good heavens!" cried the landlady in rebuttal. "What is one supposed to do when faced with such a hostile animal? Certainly, Timothy, you can find no fault with my evicting him? After I had so earnestly pursued a civilized dialogue, in my numerous warnings to him of the consequences should his roguish behavior continue.

"I mean, surely, you cannot argue that his constant and continued abuses of the other tenants' rights should have gone unchecked? Why, his music I could hear clear up to my room right across the hall here! And his wild two-man parties with that brute Mike—oh, what's his name—"

"Saunders."

"Saunders—right. Ooh, how that name haunts me. I mean you, yourself, admitted to me back when I approached you, upon receiving the complaints of other, higher-paying tenants, that the noise was frequently a nuisance even to you, did you not?

"Was I not acting, then, in your own best interest, as well as the interests of those other tenants, in responding to an increasingly hopeless situation by simply removing the problem from our midst? Certainly, an intelligent young man like yourself can see the logic behind the ultimate result?"

Timothy's response was measured. "I definitely understand your frustration over some of his behavior," he allowed. "I just don't see how removing it from our midst addresses the root of the problem at all. I really fear that it may only exacerbate it."

"Why, what would you rather I had done? Permit such a disruptive, inconsiderate and irresponsible tenant—who, incidentally, no longer felt the need to pay his rent—would you have had me, a barely subsisting landlady—with a very sick husband who requires a great deal of peace and quiet—keep this person on, regardless of his utter lack of any redeeming qualities? Now honestly, Timothy, put yourself in my place—"

"Well, Mrs. McWheeten, again I understand your anxiety over Hank's nonpayment of rent. That must be a landlord's nightmare, similiar to a tenant's losing his or her job, making payment of that rent an impossibility." This was a reference to his former neighbor's circumstance that the landlady chose not to acknowledge.

"I must take exception, however," said Timothy in continuing, "to your comment that a person—a human being—beset with a serious problem—a disease, really— has no redeeming qualities. That, to me, seems harshly judgemental and, certainly, nothing I would ever expect to hear from the lips of an erudite Christian—"

"Wait one minute, sir," she said, thrusting her forefinger remonstratively into the air. "I certainly do trust that this little sermon of yours concerning my compassion in the Klegman case is not intended to imply that I, a regular churchgoer who is not above a healthy pitch into the basket every holiday—that I am not a good Christian! I've been a Christian since long before you were born, believe me. And I can personally tell you that the difference between an erudite Christian and an ordinary Christian is that the former has the wisdom to know when to give up a cause as lost! And this Klegman is a lost cause—along with this Saunders character."

"Well, you'll have to excuse me for saying so," replied Timothy in finally turning to her, "but that does not sound like Christian sentiment to me—"

"It takes two to Christianize!"

"I don't believe that, Mrs. McWheeten," Timothy countered, respectfully. "Being the grandson of a minister, I was taught that Christian love comes from the heart of the individual—"

"Timothy, please. When I desire the religious bantering of a twenty year-old, I'll ask for it, thank you. You haven't been around for as long as I have. When you have, you'll find yourself gladly trading in your idealism for realism. And my vast experience tells me the reality in this case is, that there is absolutely nothing positive in the existence of those two hoodlums! They are not keepers. The Good Lord would be well advised to cast them immediately into the Sea of Eternal Damnation and rebait His hook!"

Timothy struggled to maintain his equanimity. "It surprises me, Mrs. McWheeten, to hear a believer in the word of Jesus Christ speak like that about another human being; for I cannot imagine Him ever doing so—"

"Jesus, my dear boy, did not have to tolerate the present day's fringe of humanity. Had He, and had He been more compassionate—fine. It's His birthday the world celebrates, after all—not mine.

"Experience, not idealism, will prove your enlightenment, young Timothy. Some people are bad apples, and shall always be bad apples. That, my fine fellow, is one of the preeminent laws of nature."

"Well, I can't accept that, Mrs. McWheeten," Timothy replied with quiet conviction. "And I would certainly hope that if one were to gain anything from the example of Jesus' life and from His teachings, it would be to never turn his or her back on any human being in need, no matter their plight or prospects."

"Timothy, dear, you're not Jesus Christ, in case you haven't peeked in the mirror lately. You're Timothy Bean, and you're a little out of focus if you cannot abide by the simple fact that some are born to lurk upon the fringe of humanity, beyond the bounds of reasonable acceptance—and redemption, and your buddies Klegman and Saunders are of this calling."

"Well, Mrs. McWheeten," Timothy wished now to be through with this conversation, "perhaps you are right when you tell me that experience shall diminish my idealism. I can only pray that it does not destroy it altogether; for I truly believe that to stop trying to help others is to have stopped caring about others. And I can think of nothing worse."

"Well, for heaven's sake, stop caring about others? And, pray, did your Mr. Klegman care a fig about me? Why, you saw what he, along with his good buddy Saunders, came back and did to that room next to yours after he'd been evicted! Why, they left it in an utter shambles during a drunken rampage!

"Now, my dear boy, what kind of caring, on his part, was that for this particular Other? Why, it'll take me a week—minimum—to repair the damage, before it can possibly be shown to a prospective tenant. Now, I ask you, where was his regard for the right of a landlady to make an honest living?"

Timothy shovelled his breakfast into the garbage can and walked out of the room.

Chapter Three

She was sitting on the edge of an old couch with an even older, and very faded, tablecloth for its ill-fitted spread. She sat heavily on the weary springs, her elbows dropped upon her knees, her palms cupped around her cheeks. Periodically, with hope struggling in her eye, she would lift her head back round to peer out her window to the front yard—and beyond.

Always, she turned back with a sigh steeped in disappointment and a melancholy glance for the clock on the little three-legged table in the corner.

Timothy was returning from an early evening visit with some friends, and, passing by a corner store near home, he recalled his need for a light bulb. Rather than rely on a visit from the McWheetens, he decided that he would take care of the simple matter himself.

He added a couple of food items to his short, impromptu list and headed up to the counter. There emerged at the same time, from the next aisle over, a tall, bespectacled young woman of plain appearance with her long brown hair pulled back, whom Timothy, with a curious double glance, could've sworn had once been introduced to him, in Hank Klegman's room, as the girlfriend of Mike Saunders.

She recognized him, as well—with a quick and pleasant smile, and even remembered his name.

Timothy thought he recalled hers as "Kate?" and was relieved not to've bungled it.

He asked her how she was doing, as they moved into line behind a mother and her small child.

Kate replied that she was doing fine, "except for this upset stomach I can't seem to get rid of," as she displayed for him over-the-counter medicine she had come to the store to buy. "Guess I haven't been eating as well as I should be," she remarked with a grin.

This, Timothy had no trouble imagining as he silently observed the twelve-pack of beer which was her other purchase.

He asked Kate whether she were still spending her evenings at Saint Augustine's.

She was.

He mentioned that he had stopped by there the previous night. "It was probably half an hour or so before closing," Timothy guessed. Their turn having arrived, he signalled Kate to precede him to the counter.

Kate had heard of Timothy's visit. "That was nice of you, showing concern like that," she told him. "But from what I heard from some people today, Hank's already moved back home to Cleveland. They said he was thinking about doing that even before he got evicted," Kate reported, as she produced for the clerk her identification for the purchase of the beer.

"He has a brother there who has a house with his wife and kids. When they heard about Hank's losing his job and how things weren't going so good for him here, they told him he could come stay with them, if he wanted—they have a room in their basement— until something turned up for him in the Cleveland area.

"It sounds like he just kept putting off doing that—partly, I think, because he kind of resents his brother for being successful and all," she said as she and Timothy exchanged places at the counter. "But, then, when he got kicked out of that house, I guess he figured he didn't have any other choice. He didn't have any place to stay here, except to go back to the shelter. And I know he didn't like doing that. Not even for that one night. And there just wasn't any reason for him to stick around here any longer. Especially since there were a lot of people, besides your landlady, who were after him for money."

Timothy received this last bit of news with something of

a grimace, before remarking how fortunate it was for Hank to have had such an option available to him.

"That is awfully nice of his brother," Kate agreed, though her voice trailed off into a sigh. "But I guess I just can't help but worry a little bit. I don't know how much his brother knows about Hank's drinking. And with three young kids in the house—"

That was certainly a legitimate concern, Timothy acknowledged—and shared; yet, "Perhaps that sort of environment, surrounded by the care and support of family, is what Hank needs most right now. I have to believe that that kind of living arrangement will be more helpful to him in overcoming his problems than living out on his own."

Kate's primary concern remained, quite clearly, with the nieces and nephews; though she conceded Timothy his point.

"I hope you're right," she issued but a dubious murmur, as Timothy turned back towards her, tucking his receipt into his bag.

"How's Mike taking the news of Hank's move?" he asked her as they made their way out the door into the chilly evening. "They seemed to be pretty good friends—"

Kate shrugged and replied that Mike was predictably despondent; though, "It's probably the best thing for him, too. I know I'm happy to see Hank go. Mike's got enough problems of his own without being around Hank's bad influence."

The candor of Kate's response caught Timothy very much by surprise, and he hung intently upon her every word when, momentarily, she resumed.

"I couldn't take being around Hank. That's why you only saw me over there at that house once. He was always on something—and it wasn't just alcohol, either," she disclosed with a grim nod of confidentiality.

"He'd go to work that way, too. And all the times I had to listen to him brag to Mike about the things he had stolen from work. It made me so mad sometimes, Timothy, I wanted to go right down and tell his employer all about it. But Mike, he just thought what Hank was doing was the greatest—and funniest—thing in the world. Even after Hank got caught and fired."

It was not exactly the story that Timothy had heard from Hank regarding his dismissal.

"And I didn't like the way he used Mike, either," her indictment remained mild in tone. "Letting him sleep on the floor of his room as long as Mike brought along enough booze for the two of them. Hank was the one with the job—not Mike. Mike couldn't afford to do it, but he kept right on supplying Hank, anyway.

"And when I tried to explain to him what was going on, that Hank was draining what little money Mike had, he just got mad at me. Said I was jealous because I didn't have the option, like he did, of sleeping somewhere other than the shelter.

"And then he went and told Hank what I was saying about him," the betrayal over which still haunted her voice and required that she pause a moment to collect herself.

"So, after that, Mike got to stay over there almost every night," Kate continued, "even when he didn't have the money to bring any liquor. That was Hank's way of getting even with me," she sighed with a glance to her listener. "By getting in between me and Mike. And, of course, when he had to, Hank came up with the money to set the two of them up with booze for the night. He even took Mike over to that strip club in Ypsilanti a couple times. And as much as I'm sure Hank liked looking at the girls, I think he even got a bigger kick from going around afterwards telling everybody all the details about it in front of me. Especially about Mike's behavior over seeing such pretty women wearing hardly anything. I could tell that Hank really enjoyed humiliating me like that. He would just stare at me the whole time and smirk.

"And Mike never stopped him. He just laughed along, and told me that my anger—and tears—were an overreaction.

"So, as you can see, I'm not going to miss Hank a whole

lot myself," she tried to pass off a grin; though, rather than humor, her expression was more indicative of a self-consciousness over having voiced such private matters to a relative stranger.

"But even with him gone," she whispered, momentarily, from her somber trance, "I'm not sure how much hope there is for the other. Not all of the blame was Hank's."

Her ceiling light was on now against the darkness. She sat reclined upon her sofa, her arms folded with resignation across her chest, while her ear stayed stubbornly poised towards the door—just in case. The board game spread upon the coffee table before her had been abandoned. She struggled with a head that was beginning to nod.

Timothy, having been so completely captivated by Kate's disclosure, failed to even notice that they had passed by the old stone church—and shelter—across the road, until Kate ushered them to a stop in front of a small high school just beyond.

Her explanation for this slight diversion centered around the beer she had bought at the store.

"Mike wanted more," she stated in a quiet voice, hinting at self-reproach, "even though he probably doesn't need it. But he just would've gone and gotten it himself," she reasoned with a shrug, "so I figured that if I volunteered to go get it, at least I could get the non-alcoholic kind, and, as drunk as those guys already are, they'd probably never know the difference. And with the lighting being burned out on this side of the school, they won't be able to see the labels, either."

There was a walkway, at the head of which they were halted, that led round to that side of the building where Timothy supposed Mike was waiting. It certainly seemed dark enough to Timothy to suit Kate's deceit, for he could distinguish nothing beyond the outline of the school.

Though not without some trepidation over the prospect of another encounter with his drunken antagonist of the night before, neither did Timothy feel comfortable, in light of the revelations just made, in allowing Kate to approach alone such a capricious character. He offered to accompany her on her delivery and, then, on her short walk back to the shelter.

Kate accepted with implied relief, and said that she hoped the visit would not be long.

They said nothing to one another as they made their way along the chain link fence that separated the path from the darkened house next door. On the right, extending up to the school was a hedge, from behind which, as they neared, could be heard indistinct dialogue.

They peeked around that shrubbery and along the cement wall that ran behind. Toward the corner, up against the school, they saw huddled three vague silhouettes, with the embers from their cigarettes dripping to the ground.

"What the hell took ya so long?" said Mike, beginning to move toward her, as Kate edged more fully into view. "Who the hell's that?" he stopped short at the appearance of a second figure. "Aw, Jesus Christ!" he said upon recognizing Timothy. "What's he doin' here?"

"I ran into him at the store," Kate hoped that in assuming a submissive tone she might defuse Mike's temper. "He was on his way home and offered to walk me—"

"Well, tell 'im this ain't his home—an' to jus' keep walkin'."

Timothy was braced against such a reception, but when Mike resumed his advance on Kate, it was with such heightened agitation that Timothy feared for her, and readied himself to intervene.

Mike's mission remained, however, to simply snatch the grocery bag from Kate's hands and to distribute its contents back amongst his circle. Neither Kate nor Timothy were included in the handout.

Kate anxiously signalled Timothy that they should go, but the latter found his fear temporarily repressed by an incredulousness that prompted him to step forward and demand of Mike an explanation for his inexplicable hostility.

"Tell me what I've ever done to you to deserve—"

Mike's eagerness to engage Timothy alarmed Kate, and caused her to try and move between the men. "Mike, please."

She was easily brushed aside. "Don't try 'n tell me you don't know what you done."

Mike's aggressive move in his direction confirmed Timothy's apprehensions. But he was determined not to back down, for he hadn't any idea as to what Mike was talking about—and was saying so, when a sudden sharp movement by Mike, coinciding with a violent shattering of glass, caused Timothy instinctively to flinch for cover. He peered back around only to find himself cornered against the wall with the jagged remains of a beer bottle squared to his chest.

Kate's shriek pealed through the small sideyard, and she begged that Mike throw the bottle aside. She was joined in her dire dissuasion by Mike's own companions, who were finally brought to life.

Mike was paying no heed, however. "Don't lie to me!" he screamed at Timothy. "I know you was one a them that complained 'bout Hank 'n me—an' got him thrown outa that house—"

"That's not true."

"Didn't I tell you not lie to me!" Mike's hysterical reiteration was accompanied by a seemingly unconscious thrust of the bottle that tore into the material of Timothy's heavy coat. "Why, that goddamn landlady of yours even said you was one of 'em!" Mike leaned in so closely that the beer, whiskey and cigarettes that colluded to foul his breath compelled Timothy to turn his head aside.

"An' so now you're feeling guilty, aren't ya?" Mike was reveling in his position of dominance over this despised prey. "An' ya wanna see if ya can help," he pawed at Timothy with an effeminate mimic of the sentiment that the latter had expressed the previous evening. "Well, it's too late for that now! You shoulda thought a helpin' out before you opened your goddamn mouth to your landlady! But you jus' couldn't keep your mouth shut for a change, could ya? An' tell me somethin' else—how come if you was over there a couple a them times, Hank 'n me was the only ones to get the blame? Explain that one to me, will ya?"

As anguished as he felt over the realization that Mrs. McWheeten had used his own reluctant, and even coaxed, confession over Hank's behavior to bolster her own case against her troublesome tenant, Timothy clearly recognized it futile, if not plain foolish, to further provoke Mike by trying to deny or explain anything.

His sole concern, now, was to safely extricate himself from his present situation, before Mike's mindless and recurrent jabs evolved, by some minute provocation, into a more aggravated assault.

However, Timothy's complete abdication of his own defense only served to accentuate, in Mike's rabid eyes, the depth of his terror, and inspired the latter's continued taunting of his captive.

He laughed at Timothy's detour outside his societal element and wondered whether he was planning on joining the others in making the streets, and the shelter, his full-time home. He mocked some more Timothy's sappy and naive do-goodism; but most enjoyable to Mike was, undoubtedly, his goading of Timothy to deny, again, any responsibility for Hank's and, in effect, Mike's own eviction from the McWheeten household.

Timothy, though, would not offer at the bait, and he maintained a still and sidelong vigilance of his tormentor—and his weapon.

Timothy's refusal to further participate disappointed his adversary and it didn't take long for Mike, like a young child, to tire of playing the game alone.

Mike did make it a point, as the bottle sagged to his side, to inform Timothy of Hank's move from town. "So there ain't no reason for you to come stickin' your damn nose round here no more." And, with a flick of his wrist, the half-bottle he had been brandishing crashed harmlessly against the building.

Still, Timothy did not feel free to move, until Mike had rejoined his relieved associates; whereat Timothy sidled along the wall to the path, and, with a watch kept over his shoulder, strode swiftly back towards the road.

He noticed, in his retreat, that Kate hastened to follow, and he slowed his course to enable her to catch up.

She trembled in fragmented apology for Mike's actions and for her own responsibility in having brought Timothy there. She should have known—

Timothy, however, would accept no blame from Kate, and his concern, as they resumed their way across the street towards the church, focused on whether such violent and threatening behavior was typical of Mike.

Kate looked away and her issuing of but a weak shrug served, for Timothy, as an appalling affirmation.

"Sometimes I don't know why I hang on," she met his own faltering glance. "There really isn't anything there anymore," she plainly conceded. "But I don't have anything else, either; and I guess," she sighed, "—sometimes, when you're lonely, you'll settle for anything. Even if it's worse than being alone."

The shame that she assumed for her predicament, and her apparent resignation to it, disturbed and disheartened Timothy. Yet, he did not know what to say to her; and his limp silence was broken only by their arrival at the shelter door.

Lottie rolled off the couch, landing softly upon her feet. She rubbed at her eyes and gazed wanly at the blackness out her window. She walked over to the door and opened it. A resonant silence—though, now, faint footsteps in some far off corridor of the vast, disjointed house.

She stepped up and peered out through the front door. A lifeless side street at this hour. She ambled down to the end of the hall, then returned to her door, pausing a moment before reentering. She turned off her light, with a sigh, and, making her way across her room in the dark, crawled onto her mattress in the corner; and was sound asleep, when, minutes later, the front door of the house creaked quietly open.

Chapter Four

"Good God," said Mrs. McWheeten, seething as she stood, hands on hip, surveying the surroundings. "Can you believe what that monster did to this room? That miserable wretch—ooh, how I'd like to strangle him. And that bleeding heart next door wonders why I pitched him out on his ass!"

Fab McWheeten had been working alone at the restoration of the small, irregularly configured room wedged like an inverted apostrophe between Lottie's apartment at the front of the hall and Timothy's near the back, and he paused, now, to observe his wife's entrance and cry.

"God," she steamed on with clenched jaw, her black hair tumbling into her face and she pushing it aside, "it might be days before this room is bringing in money again. I'll have to raise the rent just to pay for the cost of repairs! I tell you what we ought to do, we ought to take that degenerate to court and throttle some repair money out of his hide. And I would, too, if we had any other witness besides a poor little retarded girl.

"Of course, then he'd have no money left over for booze and, these days, no judge would allow for that. Heavens no!"

"Tape's not gonna hold," reported her husband in his short, gruff voice, having returned his attention to the room's desk, which, in truth, consisted of nothing more than a flimsy piece of black pasteboard tenuously attached to the top a wall-length cupboard. It had been torn asunder during the previous tenant's infamous rampage.

"Oh, for heavens sake, Fab, don't worry about that," his wife dismissed such piddling concern. "It looks fine. Should it fall apart under the next tenant, we'll simply deduct a small damage fee from his security deposit. He'll never know.

"Now, I'm thinking that we should probably throw a light coat of paint over these chips in the wall," the landlady had shed her debilitating disgust and was getting down to business. "Nothing too extensive, just a little cosmetic touch-up where needed.

"Fab! I said that's enough tape on the desk, for God's sake—and careful not to lean on that chair, please! It has a wobbly leg as it is.

"And, as far as the hole that those barbarians punctured in the wood panelling there, I think that would probably be as good a place as any to hang one of those odd little paintings of your aunt's that we have cluttering up the basement.

"Well, well," remarked the landlady, brightening, "I'm beginning to think that we might be able to put this little room back on the market much sooner than I had originally thought.

"These rugs should be cleaned, as a matter of course, but those minor tears in the curtains we can probably leave. They've been torn for years and nobody's seemed to care. I'll just continue to make a point of keeping the curtains drawn whenever I show the room.

"If I'm not mistaken, then," and she made certain that she was not, with a comprehensive look about the place, "that should do it for repairs. So, Fab, if you'll continue on with the chores I've just outlined, keeping moderation in mind, I'll go inform the newspaper that apartment two is back in the profit-making business."

Timothy had gotten up early that morning and, having examined more closely the rips left in his coat by the previous evening's encounter with the broken end of a beer bottle, decided it wisest to have them repaired immediately, for fear that they might otherwise expand. He counted himself fortunate, in this quest, to have a friend from college who earned for herself some extra money working in a tailor's shop, though he felt equally sheepish in having his long-promised visit materialize in pursuit of a personal favor. Neither was he pleased with himself for blaming the damage on his climbing over a fence; but the truth would have presented questions he was in no frame of mind to handle.

The visit, nevertheless, went well and, with a promise for the two of them to get together again soon, Timothy returned home, with Lottie tripping quickly across her room to greet him at the front door; just as Mrs. McWheeten was emerging, on her errand, from apartment two.

"Why—good morning, Timothy. Lottie."

"Good morning, Mrs. McWheeten."

"Timothy, perhaps you'd like to take a closer look at the condition of the room next to yours? I'd like for you to know that Mr. McWheeten and I have been in there most of the morning, unable to control our fret over the magnitude of the repairs that will be required before the room is made habitable again. Come, I'll show you both the residue of Hank Klegman's gratitude for my putting a roof over his head."

As Timothy needed to make the walk anyway, to reach his own room, he silently consented; with Lottie following as well.

Mrs. McWheeten, upon reentering apartment two, gladly proceeded, for Timothy's benefit, to delineate the monumental project lain before her and her husband, wrapping up her heavy lament with, "We'll be round the clock on hands and knees to make this room available just as soon as possible, so that some needy soul may have a place to hang his hat. We consider it our calling.

"This, I believe," and she turned specifically to Timothy, with her hands clasped gently together, "substantiates my claim that one Hank Klegman departed our closely-knit community not in the best of graces. I harbor no ill will. We are all God's children.

"Now, if you'll excuse me," and here Mrs. McWheeten made her exit from the apartment, as did Timothy and Lottie, the two of them loitering briefly out in the hallway, before stepping into Timothy's room.

Timothy sank into the chair at his desk, while Lottie assumed an upright posture at the edge of the hassock.

"You didn' come home las' night till late, did you?" she jostled him from a shallow trance; and regarding the inquiry a moment or two, he conceded that he wasn't sure exactly what time he had gotten home.

"I wait up for you as long as I could, but fall asleep," she flashed a small grin.

Timothy simply nodded, his thoughts having drifted again. "Did you ever meet Mike Saunders' girlfriend, Kate?" he turned back, momentarily, to his neighbor, providing her, by request, with a description.

Lottie was then able to confirm that, though she hadn't been introduced, she had, in fact, seen her once. "She say 'hi' to me—out on porch when she leavin' house as I come home. But Mike not with her. He still inside Hank room. I could hear him through my wall."

"I ran into her last night," said Timothy. "In that little store over at Division and Huron. It was the first opportunity that I've really had to talk to her much. She's quite a nice person."

Lottie agreed emphatically, for, "She say 'hi' to me when I don't even know her."

Timothy produced a smile, before subsiding into contemplation. "She tells me that Hank's already moved back to live with his brother in Cleveland," which made little impression on Lottie.

"It'll be a good move for him, I think," Timothy resumed, nonetheless. "He defintely has some serious problems and, in retrospect, Mrs. McWheeten probably had some justification in evicting him. But I have to believe that the stable environment, and support, provided by family would be the best thing for anyone trying to overcome their personal problems."

"Not my fam'ly," stated Lottie in unabashed rebuttal. "They sen' me 'way, 'cause I too much trouble. Not 'cause I bad," she quickly clarified, with something of a grin, "but 'cause I diff'rent an' they not know how to take care a me.

"So when I lit'le they sen' me to live with my aunt who live here. See, I 'rig'nally from O-ma-ha. That in Nebras-ka.

My fam'ly still there. Ev'ry Christmas an' birthday they call me an' sen' me card," the reference to which heartened her.

"My aunt a social worker, so they figure she take better care a me. An' she did! She didn' have any kids of her own, so I was her only one. We have so much fun together. She like havin' me with her. We was bes' frien's for all a my life.

"But she die over year 'go. I cry for long time," the emphatic nod that accompanied this revelation being hardly necessary in light of the reemergence of those old tears, struggling to remain welled in the corners of her eyes.

"An' I didn' know what gonna happen to me. I didn' really wanna go back to my fam'ly, 'cause I not really know them no more. An' it would be hard for them to take someone like me back, anyway, 'cause I so diff'rent.

"But when my aunt die, frien's a hers help me get job with some a them at Han'-i-cap Center, so I can stay in Mich'gan, like I want, an' can take care a myself. An' they like me at work, 'cause they know me from before from my aunt, an' they don't care that I diff'rent, 'cause that why they work there, to be with people like me."

Timothy's face, which had reflected such a quiet sadness through the course of Lottie's disclosure, was brightened now by her spirit; and he harked back to her having stayed up the night before, waiting for him. "Was there something you wanted?" he asked.

Lottie gave a small shrug. "Jus' to talk."

Timothy returned upon her a warm smile, before a thought suddenly flashed over his expression. Reminding Lottie that Halloween was only a couple of days off, he noted, with disappointment, that, "There's not a single jack-o-lantern to be be seen anywhere in this house."

His proposal that they alter that grave circumstance was met by Lottie with great enthusiasm, and, in a matter of only minutes, they were on their way to the Farmer's Market.

"Well, I've just placed an ad—oh, for God's sake, will you look at this?" Mrs. McWheeten was stopped short in her reentry into apartment two by the sight of her husband gazing absently out the window, amid a swirl of smoke easily traceable to the cigarette he was holding between the restive fingers at his side.

"What, is emphysema not quite enough for you? You'd like to throw cancer into the mix, perhaps? Good God, man! How can you continue to defy the doctors and persist with this habit that has taken from us, in medical costs, nearly everything we had, including our beautiful home on the river?

"I mean, look at you. Once one of the city's more prominent attorneys—and, now, a cumbersome old house rat, puffing his way to an early grave. Well, at least I've learned my lesson from your health insurance debacle and have not allowed your life insurance policy to lapse!"

By the time his wife finished her diatribe, Mr. McWheeten had extinguished his cigarette on the window sill, and was spreading a drop cloth as a prelude to his painting, when she interrupted him with, "That'll have to wait till later. I've just received another check from Walter for last month's rent, and I suspect that it isn't any more sound than the first one; in which case, he's on his way out. Therefore, I'll need for you to drive me over to the bank. It closes at noon on Saturdays, so we haven't much time.

"I've placed an ad in the paper," as she led her husband from the room, "asking for twenty dollars a month more than the Klegman lease. That might be a bit of a hike, but, fortunately for us, the law of supply and demand is on our side; so I don't anticipate it's being long before we fill the vacancy.

"Now, I've left Sunshine with fresh water in your sleeping quarters down in the basement. Much better there, I figured, since she has yet to pass last night's supper, than up in my room, so near to the kitchen."

Her husband absorbed her spiel with his customary series of abstracted nods, unintelligible mutterings and sickly coughs, as he trailed her up the hallway.

"Oh, no," murmured the landlady, coming to such a sudden stop that her husband could not help but bump into her from behind. "Here comes Hilgen up the front porch.

Hurry, Fab, back into the bathroom here, lest he should spot us and drone on about his broken window being replaced before the onset of winter. Hurry now."

Hilgen Drost, a slightly stocky young man of near average height, entered the house whistling a cheerful tune. He closed the door behind him and was set to embark up the stairways to his room above, but finding that his bladder urged he make one stop prior, he dutifully carried his happy song down the front hallway. To his dismay, he found the bathroom door locked.

"We're busy in here," came Mr. McWheeten's raspy response to the rattling of the door handle. "It'll be a while. Try the upstairs bathroom."

Mrs. McWheeten was heard hushing her husband.

"Aah!" Hilgen swiftly surmised, with considerable surprise—and approval. "A flash of that old romantic spark, have we?" he vollied back through the door. "Good to see that the spontaneity hasn't gone out of your relationship, as so often happens with married folks after a few years.

"I was a married man myself, until recently, and the former missus and I harbored a bit of a hankering for the nighttime rooftop rendezvous—you know, shake the heavens a little. Mimic the shooting stars," Hilgen rolled into a deep and contented chuckle. "Why, we even have two little girls as breathing tribute to our astronomical success. Orion and Vega.

"And to be quite frank," he leaned a little closer to confide through the thin wooden barrier, "if it hadn't been for such release of our own carnal instincts, our marriage probably would've disintegrated like an August meteor shower long before it did. The chimney was our inspiration, heh heh. A location of worship. A place to smoke, if you know what I mean, Mr. M. But this little bathroom here—nice touch. Would never have thought of it for such a purpose myself. You're a better man than I am, Fab."

There was obvious discomfort, and confusion, in Mr. McWheeten's voice as he grumbled in false reply, "We're only using the plunger, Hilgen."

"Oh-ho!" an abrupt chuckle marked with scintillation, and cupping one hand alongside his mouth to encourage the transmitting of his message, "Well, that probably won't land you any children, Fab, but it sounds like you're into exploring new horizons, and I'm a bit of a new horizons man myself— though, admittedly, through other manifestations. But the avenue to human pleasure knows no monopoly.

"Well, hey, don't allow me to interrupt any further. I'll just go use the upstairs bathroom. So, carry on—and I'll be seeing you two crazy kids later."

Only when they heard Hilgen's footsteps finally attain the second-floor above, did Mrs. McWheeten cautiously open the door and peek out. All was clear.

"God, how he goes on and on," she muttered beneath her breath, as they quietly emerged from the facilities. And, then, twisting upon her husband, "I trust that you're done opening your big mouth?"

He was done, and from the building they were now safe to depart.

"I recognize him," Timothy nudged Lottie and motioned towards a short man in an oversized plaid coat and a baseball cap who wandered, with a steady eye, along the perimeter of the busy marketplace. "He was at the shelter the other night."

Over one shoulder, the man (who, through the several days' growth that shrouded his pudgy cheeks, looked to be about thirty) had slung a large plastic bag, from which Timothy deduced that he derived a portion of his income from pruning garbage recepticles of their recyclable bottles and cans and returning them to the stores for the monetary refund.

Timothy called out to him.

The man received the greeting warily, however, and was inclined to move on.

"You don't recognize me, do you?" which Timothy fully understood, with a casual smile. "I was at the shelter, over at Saint Augustine's, a couple of nights ago—"

And, now, from the stranger a small nod of recognition

and an arched expression. "You wasn't there long, was ya?"

Timothy confirmed that it was a brief visit.

"Yeah—you was gettin' into with that one guy. What's his name?"

"Do you mean Mike Saunders?"

"Yeah, that's it. Well, let me tell ya, I don't like 'im, neither, an' as far as I was concerned, ya shoulda busted 'im one! The way he walks aroun', pickin' on people—he ain't nothin' but a punk—"

"By the way, my name's Timothy," as a means of diverting the conversation. "What's yours?"

The man seemed equally disinclined to part with hand or name, but, as he reluctantly advanced the former to meet Timothy's, it was quietly announced that, "MacKinnon's my las' name. Mac is what I go by."

"Well, Mac, this Lottie. Lottie meet Mac."

Lottie met Mac, with a rigid nod, from back round behind Timothy, where she had subtley edged when her friend first drew them into the company of this unrefined stranger.

"Ain't never seen you at the shelter before," said Mac to Timothy.

Timothy replied that it was the first time he'd ever been there.

"Why didn' ya stay? 'cause a that one jerk?"

No, that wasn't the reason, Timothy replied; rather, he had a place to stay and was only visiting the shelter that night.

"You got your own place?"

Timothy explained that he rented a room nearby, and then went on to give a brief history of his former neighbor Hank Klegman (with whom Mac stated that he was unfamiliar) and his consequent acquaintance with Mike Saunders.

"I don't know too many a them others," Mac reported with an air of disdain. "Like it better that way. Jus' stay to myself, know what I mean? Better for business, too," he jiggled his nearly full bag of returnables. "It ain't half bad money if ya stay with it," he imparted with a confidentially that betrayed his distrustful bearing.

"Most a them others don't bother with it; which is fine with me. The less people that do it, the more money for me," which brought to his implacable expression the vague hint of a grin. "So, do me a favor an' don't tell any a them others, 'specially that one guy—Mike," the name being spit from the homeless man's mouth.

Timothy promised to keep Mac's secret, and he complimented him on his resourcefulness.

They then parted ways, with Timothy and Lottie watching briefly after the misanthrope as he meandered diligently off in search of additional income, before they turned back to their own quest for the perfect pumpkin.

Reese Dingell resided in the fourth and final room of the first floor, tucked all the way down at the very end where the hallway curled slightly round behind the bathroom facilities and out of view. But rarely was he ever seen making use of that door situated in darkness beyond the paltry effect of the tiny bulb plugged low into the wall back up the way; for his room had access not only to the porch where it came round to that side of the house, but to the bathroom, as well.

It was at this third door that, presently, the tall and gangling young man with dark-rimmed glasses and wavy black hair biased heavily to one side applied, repeatedly, his gentle and courteous knock while simultaneously calling out for any sort of response. When finally satisfied with the probability of the room's being vacant, Reese then proceeded to enter, though maintaining all caution.

He paused, just inside the room, and listened, as above him the wooden staircase labored under a pair of descending footsteps. Standing there, in the very narrow neck of the facilities, Reese could not resist the impulse and he bumped his head out of the hallway door for a peek.

He received a bit of a start by finding, from up around the corner near the entrance, a pair of eyes peering right back at him.

Letting go of the front door, Hilgen turned his steps down the hall, a neighborly smile flashing wide beneath his broad moustache.

"Say, now," he called out in greeting, "I've seen you before. You live in the apartment off the porch here."

Reese was flabbergasted at being recognized. "But how did you know?" as he slid tentatively out from the bathroom. "I'm sorry, but I don't believe I've seen you before—"

Hilgen broke into a lively chuckle, and he extended his hand. "W-e-l-l," he said in a playful drawl, "I keep a pretty close eye on the goings-on in this building," before confessing, with a wink and a pat to Reese's shoulder, that, "Actually, I've seen you from my window approaching the house on a couple of occasions. I live right over the front porch. First door on your left when you get up to the second floor."

Reese only now relaxed into a smile, amid a nervous gush, and remarked that he knew exactly where the second floor was.

"Say, the name's Drost. Hilgen Drost."

"Oh—Reese—Dingell. I'm very pleased to meet you," which he sincerely was. "So, have you lived here long?"

"About a month," replied Hilgen with an easy shrug. "Blew into town on a couple of dollars, and this is what it bought me," he quipped, with a gesture to their modest surroundings.

"Just got divorced," he went on to explain," so I'm afraid that I'm starting from scratch again, a few years wiser, if a few dollars poorer. Aw, but I'm only thirty-two—still a young man, I like to think. My entire life ahead of me—like a vast field of rigorous challenges and golden opportunity, of great rewards—and, inevitably, some setbacks and sorrow.

"How about yourself, Reese—how many years have you been going toe-to-toe with this adventure called life?"

"Twenty-seven."

"Married?"

Reese blushed. "No."

"Ever been?"

Reese shook his head no.

"Any children on the side, perhaps?" winked Hilgen, with a mischeivous chuckle. "Any two-legged miscalculations

35

circulating around out there, wreaking havoc on the Friend of the Court?"

Again Reese blushed, and he denied any such responsibility.

"Well, someday you'll have them," Hilgen exuded a hearty optimism. "And you'll be a better man for it, my friend. A voice of experience here. I am co-author of the two sweetest little dumplings in this or any other galaxy. Orion and Vega, by name, the very apples of my eye."

Reese was affected by Hilgen's display of paternal passion. "You must miss them," it was probably not necessary to note, and caused Hilgen to dwell more deeply on the separation.

"I miss them dearly," he acknowledged, with his grimace trying vainly to mold itself back into a smile.

"Say, Reese," Hilgen would seek to steer them onto another subject, "I hope I'm not being too bold, but if you wouldn't mind, I've long been harboring a secret desire to take a gander into this room of yours—with the three doors. See how the upper half lives," he smiled, before falling in behind Reese, who was only too happy to oblige him with a tour.

"My my, that's quite a book collection," Hilgen's chuckle becoming wedged in his throat as he viewed the accumulation of texts that cluttered the surfaces of Reese's desk, dresser, two tables and nightstand, and filled the several boxes stacked high upon the floor across the way, rendering nearly invisible that door which led out directly into the hallway .

"I like to read."

Hilgen snorted so violently at the understatement that he nearly choked. "The man speaks an honest word," as he stepped closer to examine a couple of the older, and mustier, selections on Reese's desk. "I like to read myself, Reese, and it does my heart good to see such a voracious interest in the written word. The noble hobby seems to be on its deathbed in this country, but I think that, single-handedly, you've upgraded its condition from critical to stable."

Reese flushed over his prominence in such a crusade, before admitting to Hilgen that such a display was easy for him to amass, for he worked in a book distributor's warehouse and was given good deals on the merchandise, with some free copies thrown in besides.

"You're welcome to come down and borrow a book anytime."

Hilgen graciously thanked Reese for the consideration, though he joked that he might not know where to begin.

"Say, who's the chubby little fella?" Hilgen's squint falling upon the full profile etching that occupied a place of distinction over the head of Reese's bed.

"Oh—why, that's Martin Van Buren," answered Reese, pleased that the portrait should attract notice.

And so it was, as Hilgen maneuvered in for a closer look. "Are you a descendant?" he presumptively inquired.

"Not of the president himself," replied Reese, "but, rather, of an attorney named Francis Sylvester, who gave a young Martin Van Buren his first job in the legal world. In fact, I still have family in the Kinderhook, New York area, and we've always felt a great sense of pride in the small role our ancestor played in shaping American history."

Hilgen made a respectful nod, and, with a glance back towards the etching, remarked, "Who could blame you?"

"Are you off to work?" asked Reese, as Hilgen zipped up his jacket in preparation for departure.

"Just going out for a walk," replied Hilgen."I'm a walking man, Reese. Don't head out with any particular destination necessarily. Just allow my feet to carry me where they will; though, they do tend to show a partiality towards the parks down by the river, which is fine with me, for I'm a bird man, Reese. I like to observe the birds."

Reese expressed a similiar fascination. "I find birds quite pretty and their calls precious, though I'm afraid I do not know a great deal about them."

Hilgen smiled, and placed himself in that same category. "However, if you've an hour or two to spare, I'd take it as an honor to share with you the minimal knowledge I do have of the Michigan bird scene."

Reese gladly accepted and, shortly, they exited out onto the side porch, and were coming around to the front just as Mrs. McWheeten was stepping from the house with her poor, sick dog cradled in her arms.

"Good afternoon, Mrs. McWheeten," Hilgen startled his landlady. "Taking our little Sunshine out for a stroll, are we?"

"Oh—her. Yes—well—she just has to do her thing," Mrs. McWheeten laughed half-heartedly as she recovered her wits. "You know how dogs are."

"No different than us humans in that regard, I'm afraid," chuckled Hilgen, as he stroked, with a gloved hand, the mangy creature's head.

"Oh—and Mrs. McWheeten," Hilgen lowered his voice to imply intimacy, "speaking of human needs as they pertain to bathroom-related activities, I truly am sorry for my interrupting of services being conducted earlier today between yourself and the mister—"

"That was nothing," the landlady stiffened. "We were just—"

"Say no more," Hilgen waved her to silence. "I thinks it's nice. And I also think that it's very important, and healthy, for Mr. McWheeten to continue to display a vigor for life. I firmly believe that a positive attitude is critical in a battle such as his.

"And I quite realize," Hilgen continued, as he and Reese followed the landlady down the steps and into the tiny scrap of a front yard, "that, with Mr. McWheeten's illness hanging over your head, the daily maintenance of the building is likely to suffer due to a natural ordering of priorities. So, until a time which is convenient for you, my broken window can wait. A little late October breeze in the middle of the night is a rather invigorating delight that one does not typically get to appreciate. Rather reminds me of my days camping out in the mountains of Utah. Actually, a veritable heat wave by comparison. So, anyway—at your leisure."

The landlady smiled.

Chapter Five

Timothy smiled in noticing the basically-designed jack-o-lantern still flickering in Lottie's window at the front of the house, though Halloween was now a few days past. Too, it told him that she was at home, to which he would respond with a visit after completing the letter to his father that he had begun the night before.

He was hardly seated down to that task, when there came a knock at his door. He smiled to himself at Lottie's having brought the visit to him, and he asked her to enter.

But she did not comply. Perhaps, she hadn't heard him. Timothy repeated his polite command. Still, no response—until, momentarily, the door was drawn open just enough to reveal a cloaked forearm against the dark backdrop of the hallway.

Timothy craned his neck, perplexed by her tentativeness, and was coming forward from his chair, when, finally, there peeked into the open doorway a scruffy face tucked underneath a baseball cap.

"Mac?"

Mac couldn't tell whether Timothy's surprised tone welcomed his appearance, and was, therefore, very reluctant to confirm his identity, until the latter beckoned him to come in.

Still, there remained uncertainty in Mac's movement as he shuffled obediently into the room, closing the door behind at Timothy's request.

"I wasn't sure this was your room," stated Mac, warming his exposed hands before his breath.

Timothy dug the wicker chair out from the corner. "How did you even know that I lived in this house?"

"Followed ya," answered Mac with the simplest of

shrugs. "Cold out there, ain't it?" he observed with a shiver.

"Followed me?"

Mac nodded, before explaining that, "I was lookin' for bottles over on campus, an' was goin' back to the shelter a little early cuz it's so cold, when I seen ya walkin' up State. I was 'bout a block behind ya all the way from Ann Street. Thought I was gonna lose ya when you turned that las' corner there, but I come runnin' up, with my bottles an' everything (I left 'em hid in the bushes out front), an' I was just in time to see you go into this house here. Had to look at the mailboxes to find out which room number was yours. Even then, I wasn't sure, cuz ya can't see nothin' out in that hallway."

Timothy had been listening patiently, though he was anxious to know, "Why did you follow me?"

Mac hoped that Timothy was not upset, and he fidgeted in the face of his host's interrogation.

"I jus' thought that—maybe ya'd wanna know that that one jerk who was yellin' at ya las' week at the shelter—"

"Mike Saunders?"

"Yeah, him; that he got arrested—"

Arrested? "For what?"

"Tryin' to steal a bottle a wine."

Timothy sank back in his chair with a sigh, and said nothing.

"Hell, don't take that many bottles to buy cheap wine," volunteered Mac, in reference to the collection of returnables.

Timothy wasn't listening, however, and stirred from his daze only after several moments had passed. He glanced round to the clock on the desk behind and, pushing to his feet, asked Mac whether he were ready to accompany him over to the shelter.

"Huh?" Mac was startled to see Timothy set so suddenly into motion, and disappointed to be asked so soon to step back out into the cold. "I kinda like sittin' here instead," he frankly responded. "The shelter don't close for a while," he noted, with a nod toward the desk clock, and couldn't they hold off for half an hour or so before leaving?

But Timothy could not wait, and, though not completely comfortable with the proposition, he found himself occupied by a concern far greater than the notion that Mac, if permitted to remain behind to warm up, might help himself to the little of value that Timothy had in the room. And, certainly, Timothy would have no trouble in tracking down this potential perpetrator.

He reminded Mac that he had thirty-five minutes until the shelter locked its door; and, then, checking to make sure that he had his keys and wallet, Timothy grabbed his scarf from atop the dresser and hurried from the building.

It was not only cold, now, but drizzling, as well; and only the fact of the church's being close by dissuaded Timothy from turning round to retrieve his umbrella.

Kate's surprise over seeing Timothy's entrance into the shelter, which drew her up from her cot, was quickly transformed into alarm by the expression on his face when, momentarily, he picked her out from the rest and began moving towards her.

He had just heard about Mike, Timothy explained, and had come right over—

Kate made but a trifling grimace in response, with her glance then falling away.

Looking out over the premises, Timothy asked whether they were still holding Mike down at the police station.

Kate did not know, nor, she stated, did she care. "It'd serve him right," was her terse opinion. "It's not the first time he's done something like this and it won't be the last. And, to tell you the truth, Timothy, I know I'd be much better off if they just kept him in jail."

Certainly, given all that he knew of the character of Mike Saunders, Timothy should not have been surprised at the voicing of such sentiment, and was trying to express his understanding, when she interrupted him—

"Timothy," her voice faltering in exasperation and her face flush with self-consciousness over the dialogue she had entered into; but, finding reassurance in Timothy's concerned expression, she was able to gather herself, and with a long and quietly drawn breath, "Timothy, I'm pregnant.

"I haven't been feeling good for a while," she went on to relate, "my stomach and all. And after talking about it with one of the women volunteers here, I went and saw a doctor a couple days ago—"

Though Timothy had been rendered dumb by the incredible announcement, and heard none of what was said immediately afterwards, she correctly supposed his first question, and confirmed for him that, yes, "Mike's the father."

"Does he know?"

Her expression sank under the affirmative. "Of course he denies it, though he's the only one it could've been. And when I told him that, first he called me a liar, then a tramp and, then, he insisted that it had to be somebody else's because I wasn't pretty enough for him to sleep with. Then, when he couldn't think of anything else bad to say, he shoved me to the floor. That's why you won't see him here anymore. They kicked him out after that. Which, of course, he blamed on me."

Kate took a deep breath, at having completed this painful report, and blinking against a tear, she bowed her head in self-repudiation.

Timothy deplored his own sense of helplessness, and had come fully round to despise its incarcerated source. He placed his hand gently upon Kate's arm.

There was a glimmer of appreciation as she lifted her sad eyes. "Timothy," she softly pleaded, "even though I know for a fact that the baby's his, I don't ever want him around it. From now on, all I want from him is to be left alone. That's all. I know I'm better off without him—and I've known that for a while.

"I guess maybe I needed something like this to finally do something about it, but now that I have, I can truthfully say that I don't ever want to see him again. Ever. He scares me so much," she was quivering under Timothy's touch. "I know it sounds bad—and I can't help it, but, to tell you the truth, I just as soon he'd gotten caught doing something more serious

42

than stealing a stupid bottle of wine. I really do—as long as it didn't involve hurting anyone—so they could put him away for a longer time.

"I just don't want to have to worry about him anymore; but I know I'm going to have to, because he'll be out of jail soon, if he's not already. I guess my only hope is that he doesn't want any more to do with me than I do with him. But after listening to the way he talked about ending my pregnancy with a hanger if he had to, I don't know how realistic it is to expect him to just go away and leave me alone.

"I mean, if he wants to deny that the baby is his, that's fine with me. It really is. I'm willing to adopt his 'truth', because if my being a 'tramp' is what it takes to keep him away, then I'll do it." And the shame that had infected her earlier tone was no longer present. She sounded, instead, resolved—and unyielding.

And though her inference seemed clear, Timothy's astonishment required Kate to state plainly that she was indeed going through with the pregnancy—and keeping the baby.

Kate understood his apprehensions and acknowledged that, "It's not going to be easy. But that's not going stop me. Something like this will help me put a focus back into my life. I've been floating aimlessly long enough.

"Timothy, there's only one reason I haven't had a job in a while. It's because I haven't bothered looking. But I am now. And if I have to take two jobs to make up for it, I will.

"I don't blame anyone but myself for falling in with the wrong crowd of people when I moved here a couple years ago. But I was so lost then. My mother had just been killed in a car accident. My father was already dead. I was eighteen and felt that I was too old to go live with relatives," she said, letting out a sigh, "when, really, I was just too devastated and disturbed to appreciate the support they were offering. I just felt as though I was being crowded in by all these people wanting to help me; so, not knowing what to do, I ran.

"I came here, because I heard Ann Arbor was a great town to hang out. And that's all I did. With people who didn't know anything about me, with people who didn't ask questions, who didn't care.

"And for a while, it was kind of nice, drifting away from the pain and concerns of that previous life. But I just kept drifting, never trying to regroup and formulate an alternate plan for my life.

"And, now, I'm so mad at myself for wasting these last couple years, and especially this past one with Mike. Our relationship wasn't anything special to begin with. It was convenient, that's all. But it was never very romantic, or rewarding. It was just a trap waiting for a very confused kid to come stumbling along.

"And, frankly, the only good thing to come from it is right here," placing her hand to her stomach. "Now I have a focal point in my life. And now I'll have someone with whom I can have a loving and fulfilling relationship. I'm just so tired of being alone.

"Timothy, I won't deny that I'm very, very nervous about all this. God, I tremble thinking about all the responsibility— it's still all so new. But I'm very excited, too. Finally, I'm moving on with my life. It took a couple of years, but now I'm done with all those old excuses. I'm putting them behind me. And nothing's going to hold me back."

Timothy found his approval of Kate's new determination and brightened outlook on her life stubbornly tempered by his own many and deep misgivings. He kept those to himself, however, and voiced only his support.

Mac moved over to Timothy's chair for firmer seating than the wicker could provide. To expedite the thawing process, he withdrew from his bulky coat's interior a pint of the cheapest whiskey. Wiping his lips and chin with the sleeve of his coat after a sloppy swig, he placed the bottle on the desk behind.

He then settled back in the chair and gazed about the place. He was struck by the modest configuration of the room. Had he the inclination to verify it, he supposed that no more than six or eight paces would have carried him across the width of the apartment, with the length being essentially equal, but for the back corner, where a small wing conveniently allowed just enough space for a mattress.

Timothy possessed more belongings than could be comfortably accommodated by his dwelling; with those articles of clothing unable to be squeezed into either the open closet along the one wall or the small dresser next to his desk being draped over the books, record albums and other miscellaneous items tucked into the plastic milk crates that were stacked in the corner behind the wicker chair.

And, frankly, Mac found himself not entirely convinced that he was tasting a lifestyle so superior to his own, especially when the matter of rent and utilities was taken into consideration.

He turned back for another go at his liquor bottle, when, for the first time, he noticed the desk radio set back against the wall, outside the sphere of light provided by Timothy's lamp.

He drew it closer and auditioned several stations, before settling on one to his liking. He then slouched back in the chair, his bottle in hand.

With her head barely poking above the folds of her oversized bathrobe, Lottie popped from her room and was approaching the bathroom door, where, upon hearing the low transmission of an active radio she believed coming from Timothy's room, she allowed herself a minor pause.

Having completed her business in the restroom, she entered back into the hallway and proceeded across to Timothy's door, where she was prepared to knock.

Mac felt quite sure that it had been the flushing of a toilet, and it sounded, to his poised ear, as though it had come from just across the hall. This discovery came as a relief to Mac, for he was now in need of such a facility and, not daring an exploration of the house, had been contemplating a trip to the bushes round the side of the building.

He placed his bottle back on the desk and tiptoed across

the floor.

Lottie shrieked; Mac fell back behind the door; and Mrs. McWheeten, in a moment, came bustling down the front stairs.

"Lottie, what's wrong, child!" cried the landlady.

"Nothin'," peeped her tenant, shrunk into the corner. "I jus' feel like screamin'," she added, while striving feebly for a grin.

"Dear me, the poor child's delirious. You just felt like screaming the entire house into a frenzy? Is this some sort of joke? Timothy? I say, dear boy, open up," Mrs. McWheeten rapped vigorously on his door. "What's the meaning of all this? Timothy?"

"He ain't here," a strange and panicked voice blurted through the door.

"He ain't here? What—now, what's going on here? Open up! This instant, I say! Open up—"

The door yielded, slowly; Mrs. McWheeten screamed; Mac fell back behind the door.

"My God," gasped the landlady, "who was that?"

Lottie shrugged helplessly.

"Open up, I say! Who are you? Come out of there or I'll call the police!" Mrs. McWheeten had rebounded feverishly upon the door. "Who are you? Open up!"

And as her command was being gradually complied with, Mrs. McWheeten repositioned herself at a safer distance from the intruder.

"I say, who are you? And what do you mean by terrifying Lottie and me?" drawing that other frightened soul in under her arm. "Now, you come out of there right this instant!"

Mac stolidly obeyed and stepped, with drooping head, just outside Timothy's doorway.

"Where's Timothy? What've you done with him?"

"I ain't done nothin' with him, ma'am," Mac's eyes ventured meekly up. "He went to see someone, I think."

"To see someone? What on Earth are you talking about? Explain yourself."

"Well, ma'am, he tol' me he had a go an' talk to someone

(he didn' say who) after I tol' 'im some guy he knows, named Mike—Saunders, was in jail."

"What—Mike—ha! Well, good, good for the law enforcement department of our fair city. And he can rot in jail for all I care!" and by the cut in her tone, Mrs. McWheeten was obviously relishing her assumption that she had hooked before her a good friend of the nefarious Mike Saunders.

"Yes, ma'am," Mac would try to work with her. "An' so he wanted me to keep a eye on his apartment while he was gone."

"Keep an eye on his apartment? What on Earth for? Does he feel that we fail to provide adequate security for his property? Is that it? We do have a double lock on the front door, for his information—"

"Wasn't locked when I come in."

"And just who, might I ask, are you, anyway?"

"Friend a Timothy's," Mac skirted the truth with avertive eyes.

"A friend? From where?"

"Aroun'."

"Around where? Come, come, from where could Timothy know the likes of you?"

"Saint Augustine's."

"What? Saint Augustine's? The church? Why—I don't believe you. And I suppose that next you'll be telling me you're the pastor? Now, quit this fiddle-faddle, I want some answers."

"From the shelter there."

"The shelter?"

"There a homeless shelter at Saint Aug'stine's," injected Lottie.

"Is there, now?" rejoined the landlady. "Well, I hadn't any idea, though I suppose I should've guessed it was from a homeless shelter that you came—and to where, sir, I believe it is time for you to return. And you can inform Timothy, if you happen to see him, that Lottie and I'll keep an eye on his belongings until he gets back."

Mac realized that he hadn't any choice but to yield to the

demand, though he paused just up the way and, turning partly around, inquired as to whether he might be permitted to use the bathroom before leaving.

"They have facilities at the shelter, I trust?" the landlady was cool to the request. "It is but a couple of blocks off. Now, please be gone, before I am compelled to have the police come rustle you off to provide company for your compatriot Mike Saunders!"

With Mac's speedy departure, Mrs. McWheeten allowed a sigh of authentic relief, and she draped her arm again around Lottie's shoulders as, slowly, they made their way back up the hall.

"Lord knows what is going on in dear Timothy's head these days," mused the landlady to her tenant, "what with his peculiar choices of association and the inexplicable pursuits of his spare time. I fear, though, that his behavior is contrary to the best interests of this house and its occupants. So please, Lottie, for the good of us all, if ever you should see any more of these questionable street types in the house, come get me immediately. Understand?" said Mrs. McWheeten, as she made a point of locking the front door.

Lottie nodded, dismally, in reply.

Timothy remained so absorbed in his thoughts that the oddity of the front door of the house being locked failed to even register. He simply fished his keys out of his pocket and let himself in. What did wrest him from his concentration, however, was Lottie's stepping out from her room to meet him, though that was quickly developing into a sort of a custom.

"I gotta talk to you," she said in a very subdued manner.

Timothy shed his thoughts of Kate in light of Lottie's uncharacteristic behavior. He suggested they go down to his room.

"It about your room," her pitch rose sharply in anguish.

Timothy did not understand.

"Earl'er tonight," Lottie commenced her explanation with a grievous sigh, "I goin' down to bathroom an' I hear music come out a your room—"

"Music?"

"So, I go up to your door an' was gonna knock an' say 'hi', but door open firs' an' I see that one guy—"

"Mac!" Timothy had completely forgotten about his visitor and started for his room.

"He not there no more," Lottie corralled him.

"He's not there? What—"

"He open door an' I scream."

"You screamed? But why?"

"I didn' mean to," she pleaded with round eyes. "I jus' not 'xpect to see him. I 'xpect to see you. Mrs. M'Wheeten hear me scream. She come down an' kick him out a house."

"Why'd she do that?"

Lottie shrugged.

Had Mac done anything to warrant getting expelled from the house?

Again, Lottie shrugged, very much ashamed over her role in this development. "Nothin' I saw—'cept make us scream."

Timothy heaved a disconsolate sigh, and he worried for Mac's well-being, for the shelter was locking its doors even as Timothy was departing, and Mac had yet to appear.

"Where's he going to stay the night if he's shut out of the shelter?" he wondered. "It's just getting colder outside. And it's still raining," he offered his own damp appearance as proof. "At least I could've offered him a warm room and dry floor for the night."

"I sorry I scream."

But Timothy did not blame Lottie; rather, he cast a silent glare towards the upstairs of the house and shook his head in unproclaimed disgust.

Timothy found Mac's abandoned bottle on his desk and, after briefly examining the contents of its label, set it aside to return it.

"Mike Saunder in jail?" Lottie broke their short silence, and, having loitered about the open doorway awaiting her overlooked invitation, moved in on the hassock.

Yes, he was, but how had Lottie found out?

"Mac say it."

Timothy responded with but a nod, and he placed his radio back along the wall.

"Is that where you was?"

Timothy replied that it was not; and, then, divesting himself of his soggy coat and sitting wearily down to his desk, he proceeded to share with Lottie his conversation with Kate.

Lottie listened, transfixed, with a subtle expression of joy on word of the baby, and an unconditional look of disapproval for Mike's longstanding treatment of Kate.

"I don't blame her for not wantin' to see him no more," she stated unflinchingly.

Neither, of course, did Timothy; however, "She will encounter him again," for even with a second shelter in town to ensure the theory of nighttime separation, "It's not that big a city," he reasoned, and, therefore, it could not possibly be long before they would meet up again.

And what was there to prevent him from continuing his terrorizing of her? If he had shown no restraint before, when linked by the frail bonds of their relationship, what existed now that might curb any tempestuous impulse? Timothy feared deeply the wounded ego of a weak man, and could counterfeit little optimsim that Mike might obey her wish and simply leave her alone.

Nor was he convinced that Kate was doing the right thing concerning the pregnancy.

"I sympathize with her reasons for wanting to keep the child," he submitted, and expressed his belief in the sincerity of her determination to turn her life around, but, "It's such a big step," and one which he viewed with despair, "to go from being jobless and childless to becoming a working single mother. Just finding a job is going to be difficult enough," he fretted. "She's twenty-one years old—with no real work experience, no references, no personal address, no phone number.

"She's very bright, but who's going to even bother to listen to the explanation of her life when there are so many qualified applicants from whom to choose?"

Lottie remained calm in the face of her friend's gloom. "One a our employees where I work at Ment'l Han'cap Center retirin'. Kitchen service. I put in good word for Kate tomorrow."

Lottie had made it sound so easy. But did she really think that she could get Kate the job?

"I try," she replied with a shrug; and, then, breaking into a smile, "I got lotta pull. They like me there."

Timothy was dumbstruck at the overwhelming simplicity and obvious nature of such a scheme, and his resulting preoccupation while at first flattering Lottie came to disappoint her, for it virtually excluded her from the room.

Chapter Six

The drizzle did not subside until the following afternoon, leaving sleek and slippery the drear November day. The pavilion that had sheltered them from the rain could offer little protection, however, against the relentless wind, whose icy fingers pried into and around every crevice and nuance of the park's lone building.

The three men, to an individual wrapped in dark, ill-fitted clothing of poor quality and long wear, were favoring the partly shielded passage leading to the men's room, undeterred by the foul fragrance left behind by those whose bladders were denied, by the dead-bolt, access into that facility.

They stamped their feet and shook their limbs to encourage the blood's circulation, and kept their hands cupped close to their cigarettes or socked away against the torn lining of their coat pockets. They appreciated every reprieve from the shifting winds, no matter how slight or brief, and busily insulated themselves against its return with rapid turns at either of two bottles, which periodically emboldened them to stray out from their brick barricade to rest their stiff, aching joints upon the near end of a picnic table drawn under the pavilion.

"I was gettin' sick 'n tired of havin' her around, anyway," grunted the young man taking a step back from their tight huddle for a drag at his cigarette. "Hell, she used to be kinda fun—at the beginnin'. Did whatever I said. But, then, she turned into such a goddamn nag after a while. Jesus, I got tired a her way back. It just took her till now to figure that out. I guess a person can only be so dumb."

His two comrades shared in his leering grin, but as the one turned to spit against the wall, the other, crouched low in the corner, offered the light-hearted observation that the woman being picked over was, nonetheless, "kinda cute."

"Yeah, right," snorted the woman's former companion, resulting in a messy drink from the bottle. "Maybe after six beers," he smacked his lips and then ran his sleeve across his mouth. "But six-beer beauties get kind of expensive to be around on a regular basis. I'd rather go find 'cute' over on Fourth Avenue when I'm in the mood for it. Prob'bly don't cost as much in the long run, an' they don't come aroun' pesterin' ya afterwards.

"But if ya don't wanna take my word for it," said Mike to the crouching man, "an' wanna go ahead an' complicate your life, you're welcome to her. Me 'n her been done for months, really."

And as Kate's secret admirer seemed to quietly ponder his unlikely prospects, the other listener concurred with the art of nagging being a prominent shortcoming of the female character and offered Mike an ardent toast to freedom.

The inflexible November sky that promised more rain, if not a blend of snow, was snuffing prematurely the wan daylight and rendered indistinct the lone figure shuffling its way towards them through the long grass and wet brown leaves.

It stirred amongst the trio an instinctive alarm. Another city ranger, they assumed, slogging out to carry on the perennial and mechanical harrassment of those who spent their evenings at the nearby city shelter, and to command them to move on, at the behest of those homeowners who lived close by the park.

But why, on a day like this, when their retreat against the impending nightfall, and its harsher elements, could've been presumed imminent?

The bottles got tucked away, carefully balanced within the slipshod pockets, and they wondered, as they awaited the confrontation, why this individual had uncharacteristically come alone to discharge his duties. His independence stoked their resolve and defiance, and they drew in tight to oppose him.

"Jesus Christ, what're you doin' here?" Mike squinted

hard against the dusky afternoon, and his cigarette nearly fumbled from his mouth.

Timothy glanced past Mike, however, with a rigid nod of greeting for the two strangers, who were, at once, relieved and disappointed that he represented nothing official; and though continuing to eye him with an insular distrust, they nonetheless felt safe in returning their bottles into the open.

Timothy, his cool outward demeanor at odds with his spleen, explained to Mike that he had just stopped by the city shelter, from where he had been directed to the park.

"You came here intentionally lookin' for me?" Mike gaped in amazement toward his friends, who seemed unaware of the significance. "Jesus Christ, I thought I scared you away for good the other night—"

"I came here to have a word with you," stated Timothy.

"Well, I ain't got nothin' to say to you."

"All you have to do is listen."

Why, the audacity—

"Look, Mike, all I want is a couple minutes of your time and, after that, I just as soon never see you again. But I'm not leaving until you hear me out, so, the sooner you cooperate, the sooner you'll be rid of me."

Mike was silently astounded by Timothy's expressed determination, and not nearly so drunk to attempt to resist it through tried histrionics. He looked, with a sort of vague supplication, to his friends, who still did not comprehend the scene; and sighing, in resentful acquiescence, he flicked his cigarette to the pavement and lagged at a short distance as Timothy guided them against a brisk crosswind towards a baseball field that lay nearby.

"I talked to Kate last night," Timothy had paused, so that Mike might join up.

So, that's what this was all about, was it? Mike stopped short. "Well, then, I'll tell you the same thing I told her—"

"Mike, I'm not interested in hearing your denials," rejoined Timothy. "All I want to hear from you is your promise that you'll stay away from her from now on. That's all she wants from you—"

Richard Steigelman

"Yeah, right," snorted the other. "An you jus' wait till that damn kid's born an' see if she don't come 'roun' lookin' for somethin' more from me. Like money! So, why don't you jus' go on back an' tell her to forget it, 'cause that kid ain't mine—

"What money?" exclaimed Timothy. "You don't have any, Mike. You have to steal just to get a cheap bottle of wine. I'm here, of my own accord, to tell you that Kate doesn't need your problems in her life anymore. Nor does she need, or deserve, your physical and mental abuse. And I promise you," declared Timothy, squaring up to his antagonist, "your stay in jail last night will be nothing compared to the one you'll receive if you ever touch her again. I'll see to that personally."

"Hey, you don't come out here threatenin' me!" Mike broke into a strut, wagging his finger as he circled halfway round his opponent, then back again.

"Listen, Mike, you don't scare me. You're nothing but a coward," Timothy's hands were lifted free of his coat pockets as a precautionary measure. "You demonstrated your bravery behind a broken bottle the last time I saw you and I wouldn't put it past you to do it again. But I'm still not afraid of you. So, I'm telling you again, you leave Kate alone or I'll be out here with the police next time."

"Well, fine," sneered Mike, showing an inclination to end the dialogue right here and return to the pavilion. "Ya got what ya wanted, as long as you tell her to leave me alone when that kid's born. So, there's your deal. An' now ain't either one of ya ever got to see me again. So now you can get the hell outa here. An' let me jus' say that I hope you have a good time playin' the daddy."

"I'll help her any way I can," Timothy raised his voice to cover the distance that Mike was gradually putting between them. "She's moving on with her life, Mike. You can be a punk for the rest of yours, if that's what suits you. She has bigger plans for herself.

"She has a good lead on a job, and it probably won't be long thereafter that she has a place of her own to stay. She'll

56

no longer have to worry about being shut out of the shelter at night or rustled out of it first thing in the morning. She'll be in control of her own life. But I don't suppose that appeals to you, does it? You'd just as soon—"

"Hey, ya got what ya came here for, now leave me alone. That was the deal. An' I sure as hell don't need any a your goddamn lectures—"

"No, not as long as you have your cheap wine, I know. Do you even realize how little it takes to get your own room in a house somewhere, like the one that Hank had? Judging by how often you stayed over, you certainly seemed to prefer his accommodations to those of the shelter. Didn't having a similiar situation ever appeal to you? All it takes is a job— and not necessarily a great one. I'm only a cook and you've seen how small my room is, but it's better than nothing. At least I can come and go as I please."

Mike made a sort of scoff, and tossed his head to one side, clearly uncomfortable with the topic, though he had delayed his slow retreat to listen. "An' I suppose next you're gonna tell me ya have a job to give me?"

Timothy had no such offer to make; however, "We're always in need of dishwashers. They seem to come and go so fast sometimes—"

"Must be a great job," retorted Mike with a harsh laugh.

Timothy shrugged, and postulated that, "A lot of college kids probably think it's beneath them—"

"An' I guess nothin''s beneath me, is it?"

Timothy would not be baited, however. He simply sighed in minor exacerbation. "Mike, I'm not going to beg you to come down and apply at the State Street Grill—or anywhere else, for that matter. It's not my concern. I'm just trying to show you, by way of example, that there are jobs to be had in this town, if you ever decide that you want to advance yourself in life—"

"You mean all the way up to dishwasher?" said Mike, cackling.

"It pays five-fifty an hour," said Timothy. "How's that compare with what you make now?"

Mike responded with an expletive directed back at his inquisitor. "An' don't think I don't know what you're up to," he added. "You get me makin' some money an', then, next summer—boom! mommy comes along with some judge an' takes most of it away to raise juinor!

"Well, nice try, but no thanks. I don't need that kinda help. Now, why don't you go off an' pester the real father," Mike continued to ply his weak line. "I'll even give ya a hint: you'll prob'bly find whoever it is back at that church shelter, 'cause there ain't but one or two a them guys that come through there that she ain't slept with."

Timothy willfully tuned out the false and malicious accusations being vented against Kate. Nor was there any truth to Mike's suspicion that Timothy's talk on employment was part of any scheme to aid Kate and her child.

Timothy recognized, however, that it would be futile to contest the former or deny the latter. He simply shook his head at the pitiful figure railing before him, as, quietly, he took his leave, refusing even to acknowledge Mike's profane exhortations never to bother him again.

Timothy observed with relief the bleary porchlight of the McWheeten residence, and could only wonder, as he entered the house, how anyone might spend such a day almost entirely out of doors. His own walk home from work, with its brief sidetrip to the park, had left his hands aching with cold, and caused him to chastise himself, as he sat down to his desk, for having recently lost his gloves and not immediately replacing them. It was a circumstance he pledged to correct the next day.

With fingers stiff and bent, Timothy struggled with a maddeningly flimsy book of matches before finally managing to light the candle on his desk. He rubbed his hands together overtop the flame for a while, then stripped off his wet coat in favor of a dry, heavy sweater from his dresser. He was in the process of replacing his damp socks, as well, when he heard Lottie's bashful tap at his door.

"It cold out, huh?" as she sat herself down on the hassock. "I jus' get home little while 'go, too. I still cold," and simulating a shiver, Lottie drew her large robe more tightly around herself.

Timothy soberly concurred that it was a day better spent inside, as, leaning forward from his chair, he draped his discarded socks over the rim of the small, plastic wastepaper basket set around the corner from his desk.

"You go see him today?" Lottie had been made aware of Timothy's intentions.

Timothy's nod was slight, and despairing, and he reclined heavily in his chair. "Found him out at West Park," he said with a sigh.

"You tell him not to bother Kate no more?"

Timothy recounted his meeting with Mike. "He still denies any responsibility," Timothy quietly marvelled. "But I suppose Kate's right, that if running from the truth is what it takes for him to stay away . . . then let him run. He does seem very willing to do that.

"My main concern now is, how will he react once he sees Kate noticeably pregnant? He fears that once the baby's born, she'll come after him seeking financial support for the child. I'm afraid that I failed to convince him that she wants nothing more to do with him—ever. Period." And it bothered Timothy that he had been unable to make that point clearer.

"Kate come in for interview at work tomorrow," Lottie piped up, momentarily, partly in the hope of cheering Timothy from his somber reflection. "I put in good word for her today an', 'cause they like me, they say, 'Bring her in tomorrow," Lottie issued her report with a spirited nod.

And it did please Timothy to hear this news, though he could not conceal his anxiousness that all would go well in the interview. "She's not too familiar with this process," he remarked. "I just hope they like her as much as they like you."

Lottie's radiant expression bore her own confidence over the matter. "They can't help but like Kate. She so nice. They will hire her—easy."

Timothy was charmed by Lottie's bold presumptiveness. Receding, then, into a sigh, he revealed, in a chagrined manner, his own unsuccessful attempt to borrow Lottie's blueprint for Kate and transfer its prospects to Mike.

"We're frequently in need of dishwashers," he explained with an open glance, "and I just sort of blurted that out to make a point. I had given it some consideration beforehand," he admitted, "but decided against it because I really didn't want to be responsible for bringing someone like Mike into my own workplace. I've just never seen anything in his behavior to indicate that he's trustworthy. Or dependable. And I just saw no point in jeopardizing my relationship with my employer on behalf of somebody like him.

"So, I was rather relieved when he expressed no interest," though Timothy appeared somewhat ashamed of that sentiment. "And perhaps I could've gotten him a start there—at least part-time. But he just seems so beyond hope. And what's the point of trying to help somebody who's helpless?"

The thunderous clap that came, just then, at Timothy's door nearly rattled the hassock out from beneath Lottie.

"Where is he!" it was Mrs. McWheeten, who, as she barked this command at Timothy's opening of the door, edged upon her toes to peer over her befuddled tenant's shoulder, under the apparent supposition that 'he' was to be found here.

"Where's who?" Timothy glanced after her search.

"Who!" cried the landlady, further annoyed by Lottie's not being 'he'. "Why, that little—troll you had in here last night!"

Timothy begged her pardon.

"Come, come, don't deny it!" she waggled her finger. "Why, I caught him in here myself—"

Timothy realized, now, that she was referring to Mac.

"Timothy, how could you! After all the trouble we just experienced with those other two street hoodlums, how on Earth could you leave this other fellow in the house unattended!"

But what had Mac done, Timothy inquired, other than to startle her and Lottie—

"What's he done?" squawked the landlady. "Why, how does missing rent money strike you as 'what's he done'!"

Timothy was staggered by the charge.

"Nearly eight hundred dollars cash!" reported Mrs. McWheeten, "in late rent payments from the usual handful of laggards we shelter here—"

But how?

"Well, quite obviously, after I banished him from the premises last night, he lingered about the shadows outside and when, shortly after the incident, I took the dog out on her pre-bedtime errand—Mr. McWheeten having already repaired to his quarters downstairs—the rascal made his move up the fire escape, which, as you know, runs right past my room—"

Timothy asked whether Mrs. McWheeten had seen anyone lurking about while she was outside with the dog.

The landlady stiffly replied that she had not; but—

"Then what makes you think that it was him?"

"What! What makes me—why, Timothy—honestly, who else could it have been?"

Timothy had no other suspects in mind, certainly; but neither was he convinced that Mac was capable of such enterprise—or ingenuity. He offered, in this belief, a carefully and uncontentiously worded opinion that, as it was his first visit to the house, Mac would have had no way of knowing which room belonged to the McWheetens.

Moreover, "He was in my room all that time and I haven't noticed anything missing."

The landlady scoffed. "Well, Timothy, may I first recommend that you thoroughly inspect your room, and, secondly, may I suggest that you likely had nothing quite so valuable as eight hundred dollars cash laying around?"

Timothy resigned himself behind a sigh, aware that no response would do.

"But not to worry," remarked the landlady in contrast to her previous manner, "for, as we stand here and speak, the police are out tracking your grubby little guest—to the shelter, I presume. And, furthermore, I haven't the slightest bit of doubt that the police investigation of this case shall reveal that it was under the specific instruction of his good friend Mike Saunders, who is familiar with the location of my room within this house, that that fellow was here last night, to scrounge up whatever bail money he might be able to heist—

"Yes!" Mrs. McWheeten cawed, with a twisted smile, "I heard all about Mr. Saunders' legal troubles. Well, at least for a little while he had a place of his own to call home. I only hope that, now, you are convinced of his general worthlessness.

"Timothy," the landlady then sighed, her evil expression quickly dissolved, "I must confess to you my growing concern over your conduct. And I regret the necessity that I feel in explicitly imploring—no, make that demanding—that no longer do we allow such 'guests' as Mike Saunders or this other fellow to contaminate our common dwelling. I haven't the desire, nor the patience, to play 'house mum' to all society's misfits.

"So, please, Timothy, in the name of communal harmony. I truly believe you to be a bright and decent young man," expressed with sincerity, "and simply do not understand why you choose to waste your time with such riff raff when it could be spent so much more productively."

Chapter Seven

The young man approached the house and, pausing before the porch, referred again to the scrap of newspaper he held in his hand. There was no mistaking the match between the address of this residence and that of the 'elegant older home' whose 'spacious and well-appointed accommodations' had caught his eye.

He gazed, for a moment, up along the facade to the gables of the dull, charcoal structure, set against a like sky, then ascended to the porch. He peered in through the window pane of the front door, before poking his head in. Finding himself far too self-conscious to obey the instructions of a note taped to the wall directly before him, imploring that he call out 'Mrs. McWheeten' by name while standing there alone in a strange and silent house, he settled instead upon a more reserved search for the landlady.

Turning his ear up the adjacent stairs, he caught the distant rattle of a pot or pan, and determined to pursue the source of this small clatter to assist him.

He had just begun his ascent of the stairs, when there came another slight commotion, this time from behind. Returning to the first floor, he peered around the corner of the hallway, where he observed a husky, middle-aged woman running her hand through her black hair as she stared back into the room from where, it appeared, she had just come.

And when Mrs. McWheeten momentarily detected, through the corner of her eye, an eclipse of the small pocket of daylight that filtered down the gloomy hallway from the window of the front door, she turned in surprise at discovering herself with company.

"May I help you?" she squinted against the soft glare that outlined the young man's partial silhouette.

"Yes," replied the stranger, gratefully, as he stepped forward. "I have a three o' clock appointment to see Mrs. McWheeten—"

"Oh—why, you must be James—James—"

"Conlin."

"Why, of course—Conlin," and, wiping her hands upon her sweatshirt, the landlady eagerly approached the visitor.

"I'm Mrs. McWheeten, the woman to whom you spoke over the phone. How very pleased to meet you." They shook hands.

"Please, come along," she beckoned as she began back down the hallway. "I was just doing a few last minute touch-ups on your room—or, rather," with an affected chuckle, "your prospective room. Are you currently living in Ann Arbor?" she asked over her shoulder.

The young man replied that he had a brother in town, with whom he had been staying while looking for a job in the area.

"I see," said the landlady. "Any luck?"

He reported that he had found a job just the day before.

"Well, good for you," with hardly a thought.

"So, naturally, the next order of business was to find a place of my own to live."

"Naturally," echoed the landlady, paused, now, at the room's entrance. "Have you looked at many places yet?"

He had not. "This is only my second stop."

"With a good many others on your list, I presume?"

"A couple more," answered the young man, with a shrug. "Hopefully, I'll find something I like today. I've been imposing on my brother and his roommates for a week now—and I'm sure they'd just as soon see me off their couch," he smiled.

The landlady smiled, too. "Well, now, this room—provided you like it, of course—is available as of today. Shall we take a look?"

The entranceway to apartment two was rather a tight fit, being pinched between Timothy's room on the right and a crudely constructed wooden wardrobe to the left. Having squeezed past that piece of furniture, Mrs. McWheeten ushered her three o'clock appointment down a brief corridor that let out into the tiny square which was the room.

The landlady moved to the center of this cubicle and turned back round with a charged smile upon her lips and her arms induced wide by the special grandeur in which they were now immersed.

"Well, what do you think?"

James Conlin did not respond, however; rather he was glancing curiously about the room, for something seemed quite wrong. "Is there a bed?" he felt rather embarrassed having to inquire.

"But of course, dear boy," how dare he suggest that she might let a room without a bed? "Why, look above you," and as Mr. Conlin stepped out more fully into the room and craned his neck to behold the loft which, in fact, formed the ceiling of the little passageway down which he had just travelled, the landlady directed his attention to the ladder attached to the wall nearby.

"Your guide to deep sleep," she said, cooing. "Ingenious, isn't it? I'd like to take the credit for it myself, but, actually, one of our former tenants here built it to increase his space and comfort. And all the renters who have subsequently occupied apartment two have fallen in love with this room for that very reason. What do you think?"

It was a nice touch and "does make for more room down here," Jim Conlin casually assented, while pondering how those tenants who had preceded the loft could possibly have found the room livable.

"And don't you like the way we've made a desk out of these cupboards over here against the wall, by putting this nice pasteboard atop them? Why, look how long and spacious it is, so that you can spread yourself out in case you have any work to do."

Jim Conlin gave a vacant nod as he ran his hand lightly along the delicate black pasteboard, while his wary glance was reserved for the decrepit plastic and chrome chair that apparently accompanied it.

"And the piece de resistance!" hummed the landlady as

she flitted over and made sure that the curtains were drawn to their fullest, "—at least according to a good many of the room's past occupants, the abundant window space!" with an equally abundant hedge brushing up high against it, providing, at any rate, Jim Conlin observed, an increased sense of privacy from the two-story house that loomed just beyond.

"And beneath you," she said, twirling him back around, "as I'm sure you've already noticed, we've included these nice rugs. Just back from the cleaners." And, then, tossing in under a heavy sigh, "I'm afraid they'd been left quite a mess by the previous tenant. We had to evict him several days ago," she edged into this confidence.

"He didn't turn out to be one of our kind of people. A bad sort, really. He was lazy, for one thing—refusing to pick up after himself, either here or in the kitchen. He was grossly inconsiderate to the rights of others, playing some god awful excuse for music at any volume or time of day that suited himself. He was self-indulgent, spending more time inside the bottle than he could tolerate outside it. And, simply put, he was just a downright bad person, falling behind two months—two months! mind you, in his rent, without so much as an indication that he might pay, or even an expression of remorse over his failure to do so.

"You look like an upstanding young man, Jim—which I've no doubt you are. Now, tell me, isn't two months an awfully patient period of time for a landlord to wait for some indication that a tenant intended to fulfill his contractual obligations?"

Jim Conlin instinctively balked at lending an opinion on a matter so new and unconnected to himself, but, finally, acknowledged that it sounded patient to him.

"Why, certainly it is," asserted the landlady. "And this— no-good, who hadn't paid his rent for two months, grew increasingly hostile whenever we approached the subject with him, that the point soon arose where we—my husband Fab and I—felt our physical well-being genuinely threatened.

"And, therefore, we also came to feel as though we had

been left no alternative but to seize the opportunity of his being out—probably off stealing liquor somewhere, you know the type—to enter into his room and carefully box up all his belongings, which we then set neatly out along the street curb; and whereupon my husband immediately changed the locks to the front of the house, as well as the one to the apartment here.

"And though we certainly would've been justified in calling in the authorities and, probably, even having him jailed, we simply felt this to be the more Christian-like resolution of the matter and more consistent with our natures."

Jim Conlin paid them vague commendation, which Mrs. McWheeten graciously accepted.

"But then!" she clenched up tight, somewhat startling Jim, who had hoped the topic closed, "that very night, while Mr. McWheeten and I were out, this—rascal gets back into the house and, along with a lowly friend of his—I have it from a reliable source—breaks into his old room, this very room in which we now stand, and utterly destroys it! You've no idea, Jim, the time, money and energy spent to restore this room to its former glory.

"But even with such exemplary effort on our part, I would feel criminal to ask even the rent that was charged, though long not received, from that last scoundrel. Why, I'd sooner join his ranks of ne'er-do-wells than to ask a penny over one hundred and ninety-five dollars a month for this room.

"So, you see what he's done to me, Jim?" she wound down with a sigh, and a slight and saddened smile. "Not only does his memory get my blood to boiling, but he's forcing my conscience to markedly restrain the price appreciation of this room. Ah well," with another beleagured sigh and a mopping of her brow, "we are all God's children, are we not? So, now then, what are your thoughts on the room?"

Jim Conlin was rendered momentarily dumb by their return to the matter at hand.

"You said that it's available as of today?"

"With a security deposit consisting of a month-and-a-half's rent, in addition to your pro-rated rent for November, I could let you have the key as of this very moment."

The prospective tenant glanced intently, if a bit wistfully, about the room, and though the accommodations were not nearly so lavish in his estimation as she had let on in hers, it did fall within his limited financial resources. And for this price could he realistically expect to do much better? Moreover, was a protracted search to achieve some small improvement in comfort or space truly worth the effort or was it preferable to simply take this room, while it was still available, and be done with the headache?

Jim Conlin would accept the room; but then discovered, to his dismay, as he dug through his every pocket, that, "I must've left my checkbook in my car when my brother dropped me off at the corner." However, with the landlady's permission, "I could bring it by tonight, with my belongings—"

"Splendid," replied Mrs. McWheeten, sealing their verbal agreement with a glad hand. "It'll allow me the opportunity to do a bit more tidying in here."

Lottie agreed to the diversion, for, even with dinner already factored into their plan, they would still have plenty of time before the movie began. Night was not completely fallen when she and Timothy emerged from the house.

It was but a brief sweep that Timothy wished to conduct through the nearby Kerrytown shopping district. His aim was not to actually enter the triumvirate of old converted warehouses, but rather to circle round the premises, including the neighboring commercial enterprises that branched out from this vital centerpiece.

Timothy guided his obedient companion, whose struggle to keep apace his brisk step was but a minor distraction compared to the conflicting streams of early holiday shoppers who obstructed their search.

As Timothy's expectations had been modest, his disappointment over what was evolving into a luckless venture was minimal. They had traipsed twice around the complex and through its courtyard, while having covered a broader arc, as well. That would be enough for this night.

They abandoned their mission amid the vacant stalls of the farmer's market, taking their leave through its long shadows. They cleared, with a late burst, the impatient traffic clustered about the first corner, landing upon the opposite curb just ahead of a horn. They were laughing with the success of that adventure, when Timothy stopped quite suddenly.

Lottie was perplexed by his lagging behind, until her glance caught up with his across the tiny plaza into which they had entered.

There, with his illumination by the street lights shaded by a small stand of trees and shrubbery stood, with his back to them, a short man made recognizable primarily by the large plastic bag he had resting on the pavement next to him as he made an exploratory peer into a public garbage retainer.

Mac was startled by the calling of his name, for he had few acquaintances, and he braced himself with suspicion as he detected the two figures advancing towards him in the dusk.

He recognized Timothy, now—and Lottie as she labored up behind—and seemed the more terrified for it. He tried instinctively to back away from them, but came up flush against the cement planter that cradled the trees.

"Mac—"

"I didn't take no money. I didn't take nothin'! The cops was already by to hassle me about it. So, there ain't no need for you to do it, too."

Timothy grimaced that Mrs. McWheeten had actually gone through with the calling of the police.

"They even take me down to the police station an' fingerprint me! I told 'em I didn't know nothin' 'bout no money, but they still take me down!"

"Mac, I'm really sorry," Timothy said with a sigh.

The homeless man, however, seemed little interested in apologies, and quite clearly held Timothy partly accountable.

Timothy moved to explain that, "I told Mrs. McWheeten that it couldn't possibly have been you—"

"I wasn't doin' nothin' but mindin' my own business in your room," with a swift and narrow glance back to Lottie, who ducked in further behind Timothy.

"I don't know why she go off on me like that," Mac quailed still, in recalling the encounter. "But, Jesus, I run like hell outa there, an' even left my bag behin', an' didn't stop till I got back to the shelter. But it was already closed, so I had a sleep outside the church, behin' some bushes where the wind ain't so bad. It was still pretty cold, but I slept outside in worse. An', at least, I was away from that mean lady."

Timothy tried to calm Mac, who still resisted any closer approach on the part of the former by sidling along the planter towards the sidewalk, with assurances of his own belief in Mac's word commingling with apologies for his landlady's rash behavior.

"I ain't never been in no serious trouble before, and now because—"

"You're not in any trouble if you didn't do it," Timothy made a point to remind him, which seemed hardly to soothe Mac.

"I don't want them pinnin' nothin' on me. I didn't do nothin'."

And though he again appealed to Mac not to worry, Timothy was beginning to accept that Mac's anxieties over the matter would likely endure until well after the case was solved and most of the principals died off.

Observing that Mac was probably near the end of his work day, what with his bag mostly full and night fast upon them, Timothy tried to shift the subject and volunteered Lottie and himself to escort Mac to the store where he would convert his empty bottles into money.

"Don't need no company," Mac flatly declined. "An' tell that lady I didn't take her stupid money." Then, securing his bag over his shoulder, Mac moved slowly away, remaining vigilant all the while of their movement, in case they should try and follow.

They hadn't any intention of doing so, and when Mac had crossed over to the far side of the street, Timothy turned back round to Lottie.

"Who you think take the money, if not Mac?" she asked, hesitantly.

Timothy shrugged and said he really didn't know. "I suppose it may have been an inside job," he glumly suggested. "I guess we'll have to start being more careful about locking our doors when moving about the house," and the need to begin eyeing their fellow tenants with such suspicion cast over them a somber pall.

"Do you still wanna go see movie?" Lottie hoped against her apprehension.

Her friend stirred from his preoccupation with a gentle smile, and brought relief to her expression by making it plain that he planned on seeing their evening through.

"Where should we go to eat?" he asked her, as they turned from the plaza.

"I want big hamburger," was Lottie's voracious response, as she displayed her hands around that imaginary item.

"Me, too," chimed Timothy. "Anywhere but the State Street Grill," he made this condition with a grin.

Lottie understood. "You there 'nough," she acknowledged with an empathic nod. "It will be nice for change to have somebody make food for us, won't it?"

Timothy relished the notion as much as she; though they discovered themselves not so pressed by time, or hunger, that they could not peruse the shop windows of Fourth Avenue as they went, especially with the spectre of Christmas shopping already rearing its head.

And openly speculative that most of the items that caught her eye were better suited for herself than for any other, Lottie's playful avarice prompted Timothy to wonder whether the labor laws of the North Pole would accommodate the overtime hours required to fill his friend's requisition.

Lottie vowed to take her case directly to Santa Claus, if need be; in which event, Timothy begged a good word for himself.

* * *

She had a little more space and, perhaps, a bit more luxury than the other residents of the house, but all such advantage was conspicuously diminished by the tools, materials and many boxed forms and other miscellaneous papers that clutter the life of a landlord.

There was hardly an open space to be found upon the perimeter of the floor (with even the heating vents partially obscured) or atop the cramped furnishings of her quarters. Every nook seemed assigned its practical purpose to the exclusion of nearly all decoration—a couple of trinkets serving as the exception upon the top shelf of the cabinet that stood adjacent the hulking wooden desk at which Mrs. McWheeten, with her reading glasses resting far down towards the tip of her nose, was assiduously running her pen over one of the many pieces of paper that rustled about beneath her fingertips.

Across the way, upon the low-riding couch that pulled out to form the landlady's bed, her husband was quietly at work, tinkering with a malfunctioning clock radio, whose precise defect seemed troublesome to pinpoint. He rested his tiny screwdriver intermittently upon the coffee table to glare and grumble at the uncooperative article before taking up arms and charging back in.

The missus, being deeply indulged herself, paid him no heed, nor was she especially cognizant of her own periodic pats for the dog Sunshine, resting drowsily in her box next to the desk. The landlady soon concluded her scribbling and, with a sigh, removed her glasses as she turned to address her husband, who was only too willing to put aside his chore to listen.

"We're looking at thirty dollars a month more out of Mr. Conlin's pocket than we would've been collecting had that slime Klegman been paying for his room.

"One hundred and ninety-five for rent," the landlady slipped her glasses back on to consult her calculations, "—twenty dollars over the previous lease. And, seeing as how our young Mr. Conlin neglected any inquiry into his share of the utilities, I'm quite confident that we can adjust that fee from a mere twenty-five dollars a month to a more suitable thirty-five dollars without his ever knowing," whereupon the landlady again removed her glasses and gazed thoughtfully off towards the floor.

"He appears to be such a fine, upstanding young man," she reflected. "A little inexperienced in the ways of the world, obviously, given the manner in which he imprudently tipped his hand this afternoon, by revealing to me the urgency with which he desired to secure lodging. It was an opportunity for financial gain that I could not, in good conscience, pass up.

"Still, he seems quite a bright young man, and I feel that we're very fortunate, especially in light of that room's previous tenant, to have such a—why, that might be him right now," in response to a knock at the door, which the landlady moved quickly from her chair to answer.

"Why, good-evening, Jim," she put on a smile. "Ah, you've brought your checkbook, I see. Good, good." Mrs. McWheeten then took a moment to introduce her husband from across the room, before backing her new tenant out into the hallway.

"Our room's a little messy, as you can see," the landlady sheepishly explained her maneuvering, while closing the door behind her. "What do you say we tend to our business in the kitchen just across the way here. Why, you didn't see our wonderful kitchen facilities when you were here this afternoon, did you? Dear me, what a neglectful hostess I've become," the landlady tittered.

"Well, we're about to remedy that," and crossing over into the small passageway—and past the back stairwell, they were soon entering through the kitchen door.

"Why, good evening, Zimfou," Mrs. McWheeten smiled in greeting the young black gentleman standing before the stove, whose colorful and beautifully emboidered native African shirt cried out in bright contrast against his otherwise dull and yellowed surroundings.

He smiled broadly in return and gave a small, polite bow. "Good evening, Mrs. McWheeten," he said with the deliberate enunciation of a foreign tongue.

"Zimfou, this is James Conlin. He's the newest member of our happy family. James, this is Zimfou. He lives just down the hallway here, and is a graduate student from—Nigeria?"

"Kenya."

"Why, of course—Kenya. Well, we've established that it's one of those countries with elephants, haven't we?" Mrs. McWheeten snickered all around in good humor, then casually signalled Zimfou that he may return to his cooking.

"Well, Mr. Conlin, the table here awaits our business, so we may as well oblige it. Have a seat, please." The two participants in the transaction then proceeded into the computation of that first check to be paid Mrs. McWheeten in exchange for the key to apartment two, the occupation of which was to commence that very evening.

With the sum being easily attained and agreed to, Jim Conlin was signing his money over to Mrs. McWheeten, when the pen was stricken from his hand by a chilling shriek that had come from Zimfou, whose shirt sleeve had dipped amid the flames that he was raising about his pot.

Mrs. McWheeten reacted instantly, and with amazing collectedness, seizing Zimfou by his other arm, as he flapped about in his pain and shock, and pulling him quickly up to the sink, where she extinguished the smoldering sleeve under a torrent of cold water.

She asked him how his arm felt, as she gingerly sought to peel the wet and burnt garment back from the wound. He replied that it hurt.

But of course, nodded Mrs. McWheeten. "Come with me," she instructed her writhing tenant. "I have plenty of ointment over in my room," and, excusing herself from Jim, she led Zimfou across the hall.

When Mrs. McWheeten returned, shortly, Jim asked whether Zimfou was all right.

"He'll be fine," she shooed away any need for worry. "Mr. McWheeten is tending to him. You know the Africans, give them a pot to put over a fire and, inevitably, they feel the need to roast somebody, be it even themselves at times. Is the check ready?"

Jim handed it to her.

"Ah, good. All your t's crossed and i's dotted, and just the right number of zeros at the end." She smiled to indicate a jest.

Noting Zimfou as an example, Jim then asked, as his new landlady designated their respective copies of the lease, whether, "you have many students living here?"

"Some," replied Mrs. McWheeten, rather absently as she folded her copy of the lease into quarters and, along with Jim's check, tucked it into the breast pocket of her shirt. "And some are just young people with a different story.

"For instance, down on your floor, in the room nearest the front door, you have Lottie. A very sweet girl, but—well, how does one put this delicately? Well—she's mentally retarded, which, naturally, means she's not very bright. She can be rather difficult to figure out, at times. One can never clearly read what's going on in her convoluted mind. Usually, the answer's nothing. But she does possess that aloofness which is the wont of her people and that, naturally, sparks a certain uneasiness amongst the general populace.

"And in the room that occupies the other side of the bathroom—well, you remember I showed you that one door this afternoon? In that room, you have Reese. A very nice and polite young man, though not especially noteworthy. Works in a book warehouse—the graveyard shift; so you probably shan't see much of him.

"And right next door to you, in apartment three, is Timothy. He's a suspect in a house burglary—"

Jim begged her pardon, for certainly he could not have heard her correctly—

"Well—" the landlady considered, "I suppose, perhaps, that it might be more accurate to state that he's suspected of harboring and, consequently, abetting the burglars. Or at least the one burglar, I should say, whom I suspect of having entered into our room across the hall and making off with over eight hundred dollars in rent money!

"Do you recall this afternoon when I told you of the destruction heaped upon your room by the previous tenant? Well, the friend I referred to then as having assisted in the demolition is a low-life fleabag named Mike Saunders.

"Well, it is a friend of his, whom I discovered Timothy having left unattended in apartment three on the night of the burglary, that is the prime suspect in the case; the motive quite clearly being to scrape up enough bail money to get his buddy Saunders out of jail on the charge of the attempted theft of a liquor store.

"Timothy, himself, I sincerely believe to be innocent of any criminal intentions. I believe quite simply that he was duped by a pair of seasoned conniving minds, which is inevitable when one of good heart comes to involve himself, as Timothy has done, with such a dubious cast of characters.

"He's actually quite a bright, clean-cut young man—and, really, has no business bothering with that lot—but, anyway," the landlady hadn't meant to sermonize. "Please, Jim, do me a favor and keep your eyes and ears open down in that corner of the house, and if you should see or hear anything suspicious—for heavens sake, come report to me immediately!"

Jim Conlin's blank expression faltered upon the table and his copy of the lease spread before him, with his signature so prominent at the bottom.

"Well, now," said Mrs. McWheeten, brightening, "let's go get you that key so that you can get all moved in by bedtime. And, again, a most heartfelt welcome, Jim, to our warm, if humble, home. I trust you'll find your stay here with us to be a memorable experience."

Chapter Eight

Jim Conlin hadn't much to move into his new room. His shirts and coats, along with his belts and the very few ties that he owned, were hung in the wardrobe by the door, with the remainder of his clothes being tucked away on the shelves of the pale green cupboards that formed the base of his wall-length desk.

Standing on tiptoe and steadying himself by means of his left hand being clutched to the edge of the loft, Jim slung, with his free arm, a bulky mass of blankets and sheets up to his mattress, before climbing aboard to properly install them. He soon came to fear, as he maneuvered clumsily around beneath the low ceiling, for that occasional bad dream that might incite him to sit abruptly up in bed.

His collection of books, both in soft and hard cover, filled nicely the small bookcase provided just below; and his few decorations and personal momentos, as well as a half-dozen candles sprinkled about the room, lent a homey flavor to a strange little place.

Having closed his curtains to any of the curious who might dwell in the house hovering next door, Jim surveyed with approval, and from as many angles as the limited surface permitted, his modest new residence; for, certainly, it beat sleeping on a stunted sofa in somebody else's apartment.

With time to spare before bed, Jim thought that he might have a closer look around the premises, beginning with a visit to the bathroom just across the hall from him.

He found himself instantly struck with dismay by the cantankerous old fan that revved up in collaboration with the light switch, and was puzzled as to how he could have failed to regard it during his brief introduction to the facilities earlier in the day. Perhaps it came to his attention only now, with bedtime near, for the disrupting influence it might wreak upon his sleep whenever the bathroom should be called upon in the small hours of the morning.

This sudden and unsettling concern rendered almost absent Jim's observation of the large black ants that cantered along the room's many surfaces; for the ants could be brushed aside, trod upon and generally adapted to, but the harsh clatter of metal reverberating through ones sleep, night after night after night—

Jim decided it urgent to run an experiment, absolutely determined, that should he be able to hear the hue and cry of the fan from his loft, to bring it immediately to Mrs. McWheeten's awareness.

Thus, leaving the bathroom light on (and the fan clanking), Jim was entering back into his own room, when he heard the front door of the house being opened. Pausing in his doorway, he peeked back out, only to find himself being approached by two silhouettes of greatly disparate heights.

"Hello," nodded the taller person, who led the small troupe—a young man whose smile was revealed as moved into the realm of the tiny nightlight outside Jim's door.

"Hell-o," replied Jim, uncertainly.

"Are you the new tenant here?" the young man asked.

Jim said that he was, while silently wondering just what business it was of this fellow's. "I moved in tonight," he stated concisely, with a sharp suspicion of this stranger's companion choosing to remain hidden behind.

"Well, then," returned the young man, his smile breaking wider, "that makes us neighbors. I live in the next room here. My name's Timothy."

As Jim had begun to suspect—and somewhat fear. Bracing himself accordingly, it was a moment before he recovered to stiffly meet Timothy's extended hand and introduce himself.

"And, Jim, this is Lottie. Lottie, say hello to our new neighbor Jim. Lottie lives in the first apartment there. We're just getting back from a movie," Timothy explained; to which Jim responded with a vacuous nod, neglecting, in his present apprehension, even the standard inquiry into which film they had seen.

"So, Jim, what do you think of your new place?" Timothy peered closer to observe the complete work of the McWheeten restoration.

Jim subtley squared himself to more fully obstruct the entrance to his room, and, not daring to take his eye off this boldly encroaching stranger, replied, "Oh . . . it'll do."

Timothy smiled at the tenor of the response, as he stepped back. "Heck, it's bigger than mine," he quipped. "Lottie has the biggest room on the floor, though."

Lottie grinned, bashful before the newcomer's glance. "Pay mos' money, too," she directed her peep towards Timothy. "'cept Reese. He got three doors."

"Say, Jim, Lottie and I were just on our way to my room. May we welcome you to the house by asking you to join us?"

The lack of a ready acceptance, as Jim's blank glance bent from the one to the other, went uninterpreted by his new neighbors, and though not fluid in his recovery, Jim momentarily agreed—and was expressing gratitude for his inclusion, while allowing for the others to precede him so that he might bring minimal attention to the locking of his door.

"Please, have a seat," Timothy offered his new acquaintance the wicker chair with the smiling caution, "Be careful, though, there's a bit of a hole in the middle, underneath the cloth."

"Chair more like toilet," chirped Lottie.

Jim managed a flat grin as he lowered himself to the edge of the chair. "So—" he began, before realizing that he hadn't anything particular to say, and concluding simply with, "How long have the two of you lived here?"

"Well, let's see," said Timothy with a sigh, pulling one leg up to rest across the other as he eased back in his chair, "Lottie's been here—what is it, now, a little over a year?"

Lottie verified, with a big nod from the hassock, that it was, "Year 'go Augus'."

"While I've only been here about a month and a half."

And how did they like it?

Tossing his shoulders, Timothy replied that, though the accommodations were unremarkable, he found that there being "some very nice people who live here" more than compensated for that which was materially lacking.

Having acquiesced to the modesty of his new home by signing the lease, Jim was pleased to learn of this counterbalance. He then leaned further into their circle, and, delayed by a hesitance that included a glance between the two, he inquired with an air of intimacy, "What kind of landlords are they?"

Timothy met Jim's cocked expression with a reflexive grin, before shifting his eyes to the floor. "Well—Mrs. McWheeten's . . . a rather interesting woman," as he gathered Jim had perceived, "and is pretty much in charge of the household," he further remarked, adding that Mr. McWheeten was quite ill.

Which sustained Jim's initial impression of the husband.

"Emphysema, I believe," said Timothy. "He was a heavy smoker for a number of years, from what I'm told. And between his illness and the medical treatment he never seems to be all there; though I have to admit that I've never really gotten the opportunity to talk to him much."

"She yell at him a lot 'cause he still smoke," injected Lottie, with a strong nod.

Timothy sighed and regretably confirmed Lottie's observation. "I can understand her pain and anguish," he granted, "and her sense of loss over the life they once had together. But I guess I can't help but feel that, in general, she could be a little more sympathetic towards others and their weaknesses," whereat Timothy, with a casual shrug, was inclined to dismiss the topic, except that—

"She don't like people who live at shelter, neither," Lottie's further contribution causing Timothy chagrin, for it was he who had to field Jim's inquisitive glance.

So, Timothy sat forward in his chair, a hand set upon either knee, and looking up from his contemplation, he wondered how much, if anything, Mrs. McWheeten may have told Jim about his room's previous tenant?

Jim would reveal only that she had mentioned to him that there had been trouble of some sort.

Concerning which, in an attempt to clarify, Timothy proceeded to give his account of the Hank Klegman case. And though he was sure that the method of Hank's eviction was illegal, Timothy certainly could not condone the vandalism that it provoked.

"Had I been home, I would've tried—somehow—to stop it—"

"I was in my room when it happen," Lottie interjected, her eyes wide with the horror of this vivid memory. "Soun' like thunder nex' door!"

"Now, is it this guy Mike whom she suspects of stealing some money—" the inquiry flowing so naturally that it was already voiced before Jim caught himself divulging this bit of gossip that Mrs. McWheeten almost certainly had shared in confidentiality.

Timothy could profess no surprise at Jim's having been tipped off by their landlady, though he did glance with some disbelief; and he found himself with yet more explaining to do.

"And I suppose it's logical that she would suspect Mac, given the timing of her discovery of him in the house and, then, of the missing money. But I also can't help but get the feeling that she sees his personal situation as making him a convenient scapegoat.

"Because not only do I find her re-creation of the crime a little implausible, but I believe Mac when he tells me that he didn't do it. I could see it in his manner tonight when I talked with him," and he glanced to Lottie for her tepid corroboration (for she hadn't witnessed much from behind Timothy's back).

Jim listened passively, the fingertips of one hand now tapping lightly together with those of the other, as he was leaned forward with his forearms resting across either leg. His curiosity, however, was irrepressible, though he strained to veil it in a casual approach when asking, "So, who do you think did it?"

Timothy grimly acknowledged that it very well could have been one of their fellow residents of the house, though he hadn't any particular suspicion, nor could he confidently say whether the incident was motivated by a personal vendetta against Mrs. McWheeten or merely monetary gain, with the landlady's quarters perhaps singled out as a profitable strike near the first of any month. Just the same, Timothy cautioned Jim against leaving his room unattended and unlocked.

"I more careful now," declared Lottie, nodding her head vehemently. "But it not stop me from havin' people over. I like havin' people over. I trust ev'ryone I know here."

Lottie's ingenuous testimony coaxed a soft smile from Jim, which encouraged Timothy to jokingly assert that Lottie was the house's social director.

And with such delight did Lottie embrace her new title, offering up for its justification the placing of the house jack-o-lantern in her window as opposed to any other.

Jim replied that he looked forward to experiencing Lottie's hospitality; which she assured him would come soon.

"I will let you know when."

And while Lottie settled silently into scheming for that anticipated event, the men proceeded to converse, with Jim giving a brief account of himself, discovering, to the surprise of neither, that he and Timothy had in common time and money spent at the university; though unlike his host, who was suspending his studies "To find myself" (submitted with an easy smile), Jim had finished with a liberal arts degree and had moved for a short while back home to the western side of the state before his recent return to Ann Arbor.

"I'd rather be underemployed here as a bartender than underemployed there," he explained the move.

Timothy could certainly understand that. "It is a great town in which to hang out," he warmly concurred, "regardless of whether your life has direction."

They chatted a while longer, and when, shortly, it was time for Jim to go to bed, he did so quite at ease with his two new neighbors, his sleep not once disturbed by images of their designing against his wallet; nor, for that matter, by any off hours caterwauling by the fan across the hall.

*   *   *

It was not long before Jim was to again sample his new neighbors' goodwill. He was sitting at his chair by the window, some couple days later, with a heavy blanket draped across his lap and a newspaper spread open before him, when he heard their knock at his door.

Having bade them to enter, he watched as Timothy preceded Lottie into the room.

"Listening to the game, I see," said Timothy in a smiling reference to the radio on the portable stand next to the chair. "Whom are we playing today?"

"Purdue," replied Jim, his legs now tucked up under him and his newspaper folded aside.

"Ah," nodded Timothy. "But the big game's next week, right?"

It was. "Down in Columbus."

"Ohio State's always a good game," remarked Timothy. "Say, Jim, Lottie and I were just on our way up to the kitchen to try our hand at some pancakes," which answered Jim's wonderment over the collection of utensils and ingredients they had with them. "Care to join us for the experiment?"

"It my idea," Lottie piped in, to underscore her role as the house social director.

Jim responded with hesitation, however, and a glance to his radio.

Timothy assured him, with a smile, that there was an outlet in the kitchen. "We can listen to the game while we have our pancakes."

In which case, Jim was happy to accept their invitation. "I'm afraid, though, that I haven't much to contribute to the meal," for he had yet to get to the grocery store.

Timothy dismissed Jim's cause for concern. "It's our treat. We extended the invitation. All you have to bring is your appetite."

"An' your radio," added Lottie, drawing a smile from the two men.

Timothy placed his load on the kitchen table, with Lottie doing likewise.

"The outlet's sort of hidden, just behind the refrigerator," Timothy assisted his anxious neighbor, who was having no luck with his own search.

"All right, let's see here," Timothy examined the directions on the box of mix. "Looks simple enough. Lottie, why don't you get three cups of water, to begin with, and I'll start pouring the mix into the bowl here.

"Jim," responding to a request from that person for assignment, "you can just sit there and keep us informed on what's going on in the game. There you go, Lottie, just dump the water in there like that—good. And I'll let you take the spoon to continue mixing the batter while I butter the pan."

"Are you sure there's nothing I can do to help?" Jim was feeling rather shiftless in his simple and sedentary duty of keeping his ear to the radio.

They assured him, however, that they needed his assitance in nothing but learning the score of the game.

"Still twenty-one to nothing, Michigan," he obediently complied.

"I should probably get a burner going," remarked Timothy, though pausing to advise Jim that, "You want to be extra careful whenever you turn the stove on. The flame has a tendency to shoot up rather high at first."

"People burn 'selves if they not careful," said Lottie.

Jim nodded, but said nothing of having been a witness to that fact.

They were soon surrounding their late afternoon feast.

"These pancakes are yummy, Tim'thy," Lottie issued her compliment with a full mouth.

Jim agreed with her assessment and, again, thanked them for including him.

"Do you have such 'cook-outs' often?" he asked.

Timothy responded with a quick nod and, washing down

a swallow with a glass of milk, explained to Jim that, "As the house has no living room to serve as a community meeting-place, Lottie and I have decided to start taking as many meals up here as we can—as opposed to eating in our rooms—in order to meet some of the tenants whom we otherwise might not see much."

Jim thought it a splendid strategy.

"It's just the best way to meet people in this house," maintained Timothy, with a shrug. "Even now, for instance," as he turned round towards the door, "it sounds as though someone's coming this way."

"Well, well, what do we have here?" Hilgen Drost cracked a pleased grin as he entered the kitchen carrying a plastic water pitcher in his hand. "An early supper club? Pancakes—ooh, nice and thick, too. And stuffed full of blueberries. Do I sense the work of master chef Timothy Bean here before me? A little demonstration of one of the world's more satisfying arts? Say, whom do we have here? I don't believe we've met before. The name's Hilgen. Hilgen Drost. And yours?"

"Jim Conlin."

"It's a pleasure to meet you, Jim," as the newest house member rose to shake Hilgen's hand.

Timothy ran his napkin over his mouth, before letting Hilgen know that, "Jim moved into Hank's old room a couple of days ago."

"Ahh," said Hilgen with raised eyebrows, "a room with a past."

"He's been briefed," Timothy noted with a smile. He then urged Hilgen to join them in their meal. "There's plenty here."

Hilgen declined the offer of food, for he had eaten not long before, but, "I'll gladly join you for a little conversation."

"Hilgen like to talk," Lottie playfully divulged behind another forkful of pancake.

"Now, Lottie," rejoined Hilgen with assumed propriety, as he brought forth an extra chair that had been along the wall, "is that a nice thing to say about a person—to his face, no less—and in front of a new acquaintance?"

"But it true an' you know it!"

"Well, now," Hilgen retreated into a ready chuckle, "I certainly do not, for one moment, dispute the veracity of your statement. I guess I do tend to exhibit a sort of allergic response to any lull in a conversation and am, by nature, disposed to step forward and eradicate such voids with a wee bit of banter. By the way, who's winning the ballgame here?" Hilgen gave a toss of his head to indicate the radio atop the refrigerator.

"Michigan's up, twenty-eight to nothing," Jim informed him.

Hilgen was impressed. "A machine," he nodded expertly. "But we'll see exactly what kind of machine next week, won't we? I don't like playing 'em down there."

As the other men nodded in sober accord, Lottie darted a mischeivous little grin around her circle.

"Mich'gan gonna lose!" she boldly proclaimed.

"Whoa, now," Hilgen reacted with pretended offense. "What do we have here, a traitor amongst the ranks? A closet Buckeye, perhaps? And just what colors, may I ask, are your underwear, Judas?"

"Hilgen!" Lottie was shocked, in spite of her giggling.

"Ah," went Timothy. "Sensitive about her underwear. A dead giveaway of a Buckeye supporter. What shall we do with her?"

Lottie was thoroughly enjoying the game, and stirred it up further by cackling, "Mich'gan gonna lose—by hundred points!"

"A hundred points!" echoed Hilgen, with a chuckle caught in his throat. "Why, I'd like some of that action. I've got five dollars here that says Michigan doesn't lose by more than ninety-nine. So then, Lottie, what's it going to be, are you going to put your money where your mouth is or are you just going to spout off the top of your head?"

Lottie grinned impishly. "Spout off top a my head," she decided.

"In which case," said Hilgen, giving her a look of feigned disapproval, "I'll just stick this five dollars right back here in my wallet and will expect to hear no more from you on the subject, young lady."

Lottie responded by making a face at him, which he did not observe, and, then, buried her fork into a fresh stack of pancakes.

"Refreshing the plants a bit?" Timothy noted the pitcher.

"Indeed I am," replied Hilgen, "though I know not what chance they might have with nothing more than a plastic covering to intercept November's nasty chill. I'm resigned to the probability of having to replace that window myself," he said with a sigh. Then, with a glance at his watch, he rose from his chair.

"I have plans for the evening," he explained, "and need to get ready."

"He goin' out drinkin' tonight," Lottie suggested with a lurid grin.

"As a matter-of-fact, Lottie, I am," Hilgen laughed in response. "But how did you know? Have you been intercepting my phone calls?"

"No, that ain't it," she shook her head firmly. "Ev'rytime I see you go out at night, when you come home I hear you stum-ble through front door an' run into wall."

Hilgen erupted into a hearty chuckle. "I'm afraid that's sometimes true," he conceded. "I promise to try and be quieter tonight, Lottie. Real good to meet you, Jim. Looking forward to seeing you around." And with a good-bye for all, Hilgen, with his pitcher filled at the faucet, left them to their meal.

As they had no individual plans for that evening, the three of them decided, following dinner, to catch one of the movies shown at discount down on campus. Afterwards, they stopped for a couple of drinks at the bar, which quickly accentuated the giggly side of Lottie's nature, not withstanding that she found herself the frequent target of the men's light-hearted jests.

She retaliated with the frolicsome threat of practicing upon them her powers of witchcraft (learned from a book she kept at home), vowing to saddle the men with a menagerie of curses they could not hope to break any time soon.

Timothy immediately brought it to their waitress' attention that there was a practicing witch upon the premises, which provoked from Lottie a howl of embarrassed alarm, and reaching over to sock him on the arm she upended a nearly full glass of beer.

The waitress, in turn, brought it to her manager's attention that she believed the party at table six had had quite enough to drink.

Any potential conflict over that evaluation was fortunately avoided when table six asked for nothing more but their bill. Returning home, then, they gathered in Timothy's room for more silliness and conversation, before, in about an hour's time, calling it a night.

Chapter Nine

The cold burned. It lashed across his face and could not be shaken, or alleviated, by any number of defensive manipulations of the head. Already, it had stripped most of the flexibility from his exposed fingers, curled as they were into fists and, alternately, dropped into the pockets of his coat or pulled up inside the frayed cuffs of its sleeves. The flawed zipper of that second-hand article of clothing drooped haplessly before the chill that scarfed his neck with an itch no rub would relieve.

He cursed the lateness of the hour, as he stumbled along an alley in the center of town, his chin in a protective tuck against his chest, his breath billowing from beneath his loose collar with every profane syllable. The exact time of night he did not know; nor did it matter to him, now, for the shelter was locked shut whether it five minutes past closing or five hours, and was inaccessible even to his frantic knocks.

He cursed, too, the meteorlogical forces that had conspired to drive such an improbable front through town, accelerating by several weeks February's phantom.

He angled towards the familiar crevices and nooks that had served him before, wedging himself in behind stacked crates and fragrant garbage cans, beneath fire escapes and up into forgotten doorways. He could find, however, no immunity from this cold, and only slight and unsatisfactory relief at any stop.

He was beginning to fret that to fall asleep in the grasp of such elements might be his last earthly act and he struggled against the drunken somnolence pulling irresistably over him. He bundled forward down the alley, trying, now, the back and side doors of every business that lined the three blocks of this dismal avenue. Every last door was locked—

and soundly.

The alley finally let into to an open parking lot that, at the present hour, was reduced to less than a quarter full. A thought, then, came dimly upon the despairing man, but how quickly it blossomed, and, with hope rekindled, his purposeful stagger broke into a near jog as he approached the nearest parked car and began pulling systematically upon every door handle.

The first half dozen cars compounded his disappointment, as well as his panic. The seventh car, however . . . a run-down scrap of dinted metal whose passenger-side door sagged so dramatically upon its hinges that it seemed unlikely that it could lock even upon command.

He piled in, groaning with immense relief, then crawled into the back seat so that he could lay down. He found himself further buoyed by a heavy, albeit cold, blanket that he quickly drew over himself, before passing almost immediately into sleep.

He felt his body vibrating and awakened to the foggy fear that he was becoming sick to his stomach. He pawed the blanket away from his face, to the gradual realization that the car in which he rested was idling; and that there was somebody in the driver's seat, searching the radio dial for an acceptable station.

The homeless man dare not move, except subtley to retreat back beneath the blanket, lest his face should be spied through the car's rear view mirror. It was a predicament that, in his desperate quest for shelter, he had not conceived.

Alongside his concern over being caught, the man, in his awakening, found himself again quite cold, for, really, the car possessed minimal warmth, and his muscles and joints tightened and twinged against every minor, involuntary movement.

In another moment or two the car was backed into motion. And though hardly soothed by the turbulent rhythm of the malfunctioning engine, the invisible passenger was grateful for the perforated muffler that, along with the radio, might conceal any little noise he may inadvertently make.

But—where were they going? And who was this person behind the wheel? Moreover, was there anything here in the backseat that this driver might need to fish out once his destination had been reached? From beneath the blanket, the man could detect nothing that he might be laying on, nor was there anything on the floor within his arm's limited reach.

Any fledgling peace of mind, however, was immediately checked by the frequency of the streetlights that passed overhead, regularly illuminating his inordinately bulging cover in the backseat.

The ride was short. The dip and bump of a driveway, followed by a veer to the right and the brakes fast applied. The ignition was turned off, with a bit of a whine. The engine hiccuped and sputtered, before petering out.

The internal drama built, now, as the driver forced open the stubborn door on that side of the car. The homeless man clenched beneath the blanket in breathless anxiety. What would he—or could he—do, were the driver to discover him now? Certainly, a shout would go out for someone to call the police—and, good God, not another visit with them! Would he, laying as he was stiff and prostrate beneath this unwieldy blanket, be able to spring forward and overpower the driver and make a successful run for it? But where would he go? And where was he?

The car door closed. The driver's footsteps he could hear fading into silence. He was left alone.

He listened, still. Nothing, but the passing of a car some little ways off. He poked his head cautiously out from underneath the blanket, but would not risk raising it for another moment or two. With great care, then, he edged upward, enabling himself, at first, no more than an obstructed peek at his surroundings from overtop the backseat. He pivoted his head smartly around for any human presence, and was relieved, though no less leery, when there was none detected. Even his chauffeur was gone from view, though he had been unable to ascertain in which direction the man had parted.

He sat up a little higher to further investigate and observed that the car was parked up near the sidewalk at the head of a gravel drive that ran back past a house and a small apartment complex, in one of which the owner of the car certainly must live.

Given the relatively brief duration of the ride, as well as the close alignment of the traffic lights along the way, he guessed that he must be in a neighborhood not far from the center of town; though precisely where he still could not determine.

A gently sloping side street out front, running dead into a crossroad nearby. A stone church on the far corner, the silhouette of its belltower almost indistinguishable against the night's sky—in fact, looked very familiar. Why—

He turned his head fast around, his eyes darting with apprehension across the street—until there! just opposite, with its porch light illuminating that familiar facade, he recognized, with a shudder, the McWheeten house!

He dropped quickly back down in the seat, his troubled glance more concerned, now, with the spectre of Mrs. McWheeten than the possibilty that the owner of the car might return to retrieve something out of the glove compartment.

It did occur to him, though grudgingly, that it was rather unlikely that the dreaded landlady of that house across the street would be able to detect his hardly visible presence from her home, even should she be in the window with her eyes concentrated towards him. And there was no evidence of this.

His experience with her was still fresh in his mind and he remained steadfast against any renewal of their acquaintance. Yet, it would be a very harsh night spent outside. The shield of the car and the insulation of a single blanket were treacherously insufficient. His extremities tingled towards numbness. His ears were already there.

It was an option that he would have regarded as unfathomable just an hour earlier (had it come to mind), but, now, he could think of no other. The risk involved made his heart tremor. But if he could safely negotiate the glare of the porchlight and make a stealthy entrance, his tenuous hope was that within this house he would be able to impose upon one whose nature he knew to be more open and understanding than that of the volatile proprietor.

He would have to take this chance. The reduced dexterity of his joints rendered his movement slow and ungainly, and made it a chore simply to extricate himself from the car.

Once this had been accomplished, he was careful to close the door quietly behind—with the door, in fact, failing to completely latch—so as not to disrupt the stillness of the evening and touch upon the curiosity of anyone near to a window in one of the surrounding dwellings.

His approach across the street was made with a tentative spirit that induced him along a small arc and away from the full influence of the porch light.

He came up on the sidewalk near the neighboring hedge, where he staked a temporary position. There was a light on behind the closed curtains of the window directly above the porch, though he did not believe this to be the room occupied by the landlady. Keeping his eye fixed on it, nonetheless, he tripped quickly across the small front yard, moving himself up close to the house, just beneath Lottie's darkened window.

He, then, slipped along the house towards the porch, with the light shining there giving his mission restive pause. An interior light allowed for a glimpse up the stairways. All seemed clear.

There was no sense in delaying any further. He was careful not to rattle or, in any way, mishandle the door; and, once inside, his surreal terror evolved instantly towards a suffocating crescendo in which he half anticipated all the doors of the house being thrown open in synchrony to proclaim his whereabouts to the predatory swoop of the landlady.

But there came no action, nor sound, that did not emanate from his own trepid respiratory system. He anxiously relocated outside the light of the landing way, inching himself along in his intended direction, down into that shadowy little hallway with the dusty bulb. He did not recall the wooden floor creaking so on his previous visits.

He paused, and pondered, with his eyes straining, trying to discern any signs of light escaping the closed doors ahead. For what if this person whose assistance he sought had already gone to bed? It certainly must be late enough for the possibility.

He supposed, with some disinclination, that he would have to try and wake him—and quietly enough so as to awake no others—for his only other option of the car had already been discarded. And how he began to resent the need to seek this person's help.

Nevertheless, he moved forward. He hesitated as he crept past the second apartment along the way, due to the quiet activity he heard inside. His apprehension amplified when he stepped even with the following room and detected the light from within that outlined the mismatched door of its frame.

Timothy sat bent over his desk, tapping the end of a pen lightly against his chin as he paused in weary contemplation. He had taken up the practice of keeping a journal, to which he liked to address his thoughts on any number of topics and on as many nights of the week as he could find the time. This having been one of those evenings, Timothy was discovering that, presently, the predominant thought coming to his mind was that of sleep. And there was no use fighting it.

He stared drearily at the incomplete reflection scrathed on the paper before him and was struggling to bring it to a prompt and satisfactory close. He thought he might have something, now, and, consequently, was only dully cognizant of the light rapping that seemed refracted from some point upstairs.

The knock being duplicated, however, Timothy realized it coming at his own door and, glancing back over his shoulder, he bid entry, fully expecting to see Jim, whom he had heard arrive home from work only a few moments before.

But there came no response, which puzzled Timothy, for, surely, from such a close range he must have spoken loudly enough to be heard. Putting down his pen, he rose from his seat and with an air of curiosity went over and opened up the door himself.

Timothy fell back upon his heels, his tired posture now bolted upright, his fading eyes pried wide in speechless disbelief—and alarm!

The pose struck by Mike Saunders was every bit as qualmish, with his stark expression seeming to indicate a belief that, perhaps, he had made a serious mistake in coming here. He was backed off along the far wall.

"What're you doing here?" Timothy's fingers were kept poised upon the edge of his door, should there come sudden cause to close it.

But the figure sunken before him, cold and humble in appearance, evinced no intent, nor the capability, really, of moving swiftly in mischief (as Timothy, though with intractable wariness, was beginning to sense). And with a docile and supplicating manner that could not but confound Timothy in its unusualness, Mike asked whether he could come in.

Timothy hesitated against some sort of ruse, though again all signs were to the contrary, before yielding passage to this visitor, who, with his arms wrapped about himself, received Timothy's grace with a silent wariness of his own.

Mike dropped himself into the wicker chair, huddling forward so that he might, by applying feverish rubs, stimulate the circulation in his legs and feet.

"Jesus Christ, it's cold out there," he muttered, his evasive eyes stealing a peek at his benefactor as he passed by to the corner. Timothy emerged with a heavy blanket that he placed around Mike, who marked the act with a gruff nod of appreciation.

Timothy moved back from the unkempt figure whose heavy breath was now directed at trying to rehabilitate the pliability of his fingers.

"Why aren't you at the shelter?" Timothy remained on alert, standing, now, before his desk.

Mike had expected the interrogation, though that made

him no less annoyed by it. An unquestioned approval of his use of the floor for the night had been pure fantasy. And though Timothy's tone was not at all judgemental—still, it reeked to Mike of paternalism. But he must keep his tongue or be returned to the car and the cold. He leaned even further forward in the chair, ostensibly to tend more easily to his feet, though, in truth, it made more natural the averting of his eyes by bringing them closer upon the floor.

Timothy asked the question again, and, looking to the clock on his desk, noted that, "The shelter closed over three hours ago."

With a sniffle, Mike drew his head back, his eyes glancing off Timothy's, before quickly falling away again. With a sigh, he acknowledged that he had been late in getting himself to the shelter.

"I was over at some guy's apartment havin' a few beers," he confessed with his throat sore and raspy. "Then all of a sudden the son of a bitch tells me that he's goin' to bed an' that I gotta go!" while searching for sympathy in his listener. "Hell, by that time it was too late for me to get into the shelter an' I told 'im that, too!

"The dude I went there with, who was the one who really knew this guy, had already took off to go meet some woman. But I figured, what the hell, this guy didn't seem to mind me stayin' behind with him, so he prob'bly wouldn't mind neither if I crashed on his couch. Hell, I was just 'bout fallen asleep as it was, when, all of a sudden, he throws me outa there!

"Christ, I was drinkin' beer with this guy all this time, laughin' it up with 'im, then—boom! he turns nasty on me an' starts treatin' me like I was some sort a criminal, when I ain't even done nothin'! Says the only thing he knows about me is that I just got busted for tryin' to rip off a liquor store— an' says that he's been ripped off by people before, too. Hell, I jus' wanted to sleep there. An' when I tell 'im that, he threatens to call the police on me if I don't leave right away! He jus' freaked out on me. I couldn't believe it.

"I tell ya, I shoulda gave 'im a reason to call the police, by takin' a poke at 'im, the son of a bitch," Mike grumbled in regret at this oversight; and, shivering again, he drew the blanket more closely around himself.

"So, you came here?" Timothy was dubious of the possible logic that had rewarded him with being Mike's next option.

Mike shied from Timothy's penetrating stare, and rejectinging any disingenuous puffery of Timothy's good nature, he momentarily confided the coincidence that had landed him at Timothy's door.

"Scared the hell outa me, man, when he started that car up," shaking his head in bewildered recollection. "I figured, with my luck, he's gonna drive me straight to the police station for breakin' into his car, ya know? But, I swear to God, that door wasn't even locked. Honest. So, I jus' climbed in. I had to, man, I was freezin'," showing another shiver for effect.

"Then when he got out, I waited a little bit—till I knew, for sure, he was gone— before I took a look aroun'. An' when I seen that Saint Mark's church on the corner there, I knew exactly where I was."

The car to which Mike alluded, Timothy realized, was that of his neighbor Jim, made evident not only by the timing of this evening's events, but also by Jim's prior references to the faulty state of both his car doors, the one being reluctant to budge and the other occasionally popping open around even the gentlest of corners.

Timothy kept this knowledge to himself.

"So, I figured, what the hell," shrugged Mike, as Timothy's focus returned upon him. "I know we ain't always—got along so good; but I also know you ain't the type to let a guy freeze to death, neither." Mike sponsored this opinion with a hopeful eye kept coyly upon its objective.

Timothy saw through the artful praise and found himself in a private quandary. No, he could not willfully send somebody out to spend the night in such a cold, though neither was he comfortable with the notion of allowing Mike to stay with him.

"An' I got to wonderin', too," Mike momentarily

interrupted Timothy's deliberation, "if, maybe you guys—was still lookin' for a dishwasher down at that place you work?"

Timothy made no attempt to veil his instant skepticism, and his scrutiny caused Mike to fidget.

"You want to know if we still have a job opening?"

Mike made a short nod.

"I see," responded Timothy, folding his arms across his chest. "And why the sudden interest, Mike? So that I'll let you stay here tonight, only to discover, come morning, that you've had a change of heart?"

"Hey, listen, I ain't makin' this up," Mike's snap was absent its usual fight. "If ya don't wanna give me that job, that's your business. I didn't know ya changed your mind so fast about givin' a guy a chance or I wouldna asked. But I guess you're allowed to change your mind an' I ain't—"

"And, tell me, Mike, just what reason do I have to believe you've changed?" Timothy rebutted sharply. "You come here, asking me to stick my neck out for you—first, by letting you stay here the night—which Mrs. McWheeten would never permit—and, secondly, by risking my reputation and good standing at work, when you've never given me a sensible reason to do either.

"What evidence regarding your nature do I have to go by? Your swinging a broken bottle at me and your fists at Kate," the second charge making Mike squirm in his chair, "so you'll have to excuse me if I happen to think that your proposal is nothing more than a con job brought about by present circumstance."

(The sudden rise of voices from next door, only one of which he recognized, piqued Jim's concern, and he kept his ear trained upon the thin wall between the two rooms, prepared to act if he felt necessary).

And though he bristled with resentment at the accusation, and was obviously astonished by the uncharacteristic tone in which it had been levied, Mike could not deny its basis. He steered his glance away to the floor, as he worked to gather both thought and emotion, before inclining his head only partially to address his antagonist.

"Listen—" a harsh whisper emerging from an exasperated sigh, "I don't blame ya for not believin' me. An' for not likin' me, either. I don't blame anybody for feelin' that way about me, all right? But the reason I'm askin' about this job ain't so you'll let me stay here tonight. It's because I'm flat-out tired of livin' like I am. I'm sick 'n tired a worryin' about findin' myself in this kind a situation 'cause I didn't get to the damn shelter on time. This sure as hell ain't the first time I found myself locked out. I've slept in them alleys an' parks in some pretty nasty weather, an' I'm jus' tired of it.

"I guess I always kinda liked the thought of not havin' any responsibilities, ya know?" Mike went on. "Do whatever I want all day an' not worry 'bout nothin', 'cept just gettin' over to the shelter before it closed. But that is a responsibility, an', in the winter time, a damn important one.

"An' nights like tonight just make me think I'd rather have the responsibility of answerin' to a job than to that stupid shelter. At least I'd be makin' money doin' that. An', ya know, it ain't like I do much with all my free time, anyway, 'cause I can't afford to do nothin'. That ain't freedom.

"You was right that day out at the park when you was tellin' me 'bout the advantages of havin' your own place. I was jus' too angry at you then to listen. An' if I can't afford nothin' else, I'd at least like to afford not havin' to worry about tryin' to stay warm behind some garbage dumpster all night.

"Man, I tell ya, I was so cold tonight crouchin' down in that alley that I could hardly get up after a while my legs was so stiff. An' all I could think about was that someone was gonna find me in the mornin' frozen to death behind some garbage cans. An' if not this time, then the nex' time, or the time after that.

"I just can't keep goin' like this, man," Mike's beleagured expression was highlighted, now, by a welling in his eye. "I jus' can't. I'm so worn out from livin' like this. I mean, look at me, man, I'm twenty-six years old an' I look like I'm forty-six. An' I feel like I'm fifty-six. 'cept I ain't ever gonna see fifty-six if I keep goin' like I am. I gotta break outa this somehow. An' I'll take anyway I can."

It was a forceful appeal, and left Timothy mute. He gazed upon the bent figure with the familiar features, whose own eyes drooped back to the floor, and he could not suppress the hope that these proclaimed sentiments would awaken with this stranger in the morning.

And though there could not help but be some lingering doubt in Timothy's mind—for he had witnessed too much of the 'other' Mike to be completely proselytized by a single meeting—if this person before him now were to have any chance at making good on his conversion, there might come no better opportunity.

Timothy prefaced his guarded response by clarifying for Mike that he, Timothy, had no power in the hiring practices of his employer, and that any decision would be made by another; but that, yes, there was a part-time dishwashing job yet unfilled, and that if Mike were truly interested, he could accompany Timothy to work early the next morning, where the latter promised to advance his case.

Mike's face reflected a genuine sense of appreciation that his mouth appeared too uncomfortable to translate; and he was relieved when, momentarily, Timothy turned his attention to clearing a space on the floor for his guest.

Timothy provided an additional blanket, to serve as insulation against the wooden floor, as well as a pillow; and seeing Mike into place, Timothy then climbed upon his own mattress and slept hardly a wink.

Chapter Ten

Mrs. McWheeten had had enough. Enough of stumbling over hidden boxes; enough of having so much of her small quarters made inaccessible; and enough of not being able to readily call up certain papers and other miscellaneous objects for which she had been compelled to search.

It was due to one such maddening hunt that she finally decided something must be done. And so there she knelt, along with her husband, in the center of the floor sifting painstakingly through each of those boxes that had been moldering in the corners, along the walls and beneath and behind the furniture, separating their yellowed contents by virtue of whether they should continued to be saved or pitched, at last, into the garbage.

Old receipts, deemed no longer relevant, were stuffed by the score in amongst the disposables. Faded copies of leases for tenants no longered remembered seemed extraneous—and unimportant.

Brochures, maps and guides to exotic travel destinations that no longer held any real hope of ever being visited were discarded by the landlady with reluctance. Trinkets and other keepsakes from the happier times at their former house were pared by sad resignation to the modesty of any future domicile.

Too, so much of it now seemed like nothing but junk to the landlady, and had her puzzled as to why it had ever been allowed to make the move with them. She disparaged every last scrap of this pile. Mr. McWheeten, to the contrary, sorted quietly, feeling nothing upon either side of the emotional divide.

And the landlady's vindication was won against this cardboard empire, when, near the end of their mission, she came upon the single form whose elusiveness had incited this entire operation. She placed that paper atop so many others already on her desk; and, feeling newly inspired, started marching the outgoing boxes down to the garbage cans alongside the house.

It was with the gratifying relief of an arduous task come to an end that Mrs. McWheeten reentered the house, wiping, first, her dusty hands upon her pant legs and, then, her shirt sleeve along her brow, when she was very nearly popped in the nose by Lottie's door as it was opened from within.

"Oh, I sorry, Mrs. M'Wheeten," Lottie grabbed the door short of her landlady's face. "I didn' know you there."

"Oh, that's quite all right, Lottie," replied Mrs. McWheeten, pleasantly. "No harm done. Why, I see you have a visitor," with a glance into the room. "How nice."

"Uh-huh," nodded Lottie. "Her name Kate."

"Well, hello there, Kate. It's very nice to meet you. I'm Mrs. McWheeten, the landlady here."

Kate very politely returned the greeting, and, having been in the process of following Lottie out the door, shook Mrs. McWheeten's hand as it was offered.

"Are you an old childhood friend of Lottie's, perhaps?" inquired Mrs. McWheeten.

"No, ma'am. Actually, I've only known Lottie a couple of weeks."

"Oh—"

"Kate work with me."

"Well—how nice," the landlady stammered in response. "Though, of course, Kate, like every citizen, I'm sorry to hear of your mental deficiencies. I want you to know that we're all behind you—"

"Kate not ment'lly han'-i-cap like me."

"Oh—I—" and with a short laugh induced by her own embarrassment, "Why, I'm so sorry, Kate. I just assumed that to secure such employment, one, to some extent or other, had to be without normal cerebral capabilities. I'm sorry to mistake you as such."

"That's all right," replied Kate with a soft smile of

understanding. "The reason I'm working there is that Lottie got me the job," she explained. "I wasn't having any luck finding a job on my own, and when Lottie found that out she helped me get this one at the Handicap Center."

"Why, Lottie, how very—Christian of you. Looking out so for your Fellow Man. But, you poor child," Mrs. McWheeten turned back to Kate, "without any means of income, how on earth have you subsisted? Perhaps, you live at home with your folks?"

"Well, right now, I'm staying at the shelter."

"The shelter? Oh—"

"But, hopefully, now that I have a job, I won't be there too much longer. The first thing I want to do is save up enough money so that I can get a place of my own as soon as possible. I'm very tired of staying at the shelter."

"Well, good for you," Mrs. McWheeten struck an encouraging note. "You appear to be making an honest effort to improve your station in life and deserve our unyielding support. How simply god awful it must be to lead that base lifestyle. To go without a bath or fresh clothing must be such a dehumanizing experience—and one," with special emphasis, "that most of the street people in this city don't much seem to mind. Really, they seem not to care a fig about the opinion that decent society holds for them and their ways.

"That is why it so truly gladdens my heart to see one like you lifting herself up and onto the road to respectability. Most in your predicament are quite more than willing, I must tell you, to live off the poor, overburdened taxpayer—such as myself. You'll be one fewer mouth I'll have to feed and, for that, you have my blessing."

"I was thinkin'," Lottie had waited anxiously for the landlady to conclude her oratory, "that when Kate got 'nough money saved up, maybe she could move into house here."

"What? Lottie, a streetpers—oh, I don't—"

"Maybe she could have C'ssandra room. She movin' out at end a nex' month."

"Yes, don't remind me," snipped Mrs. McWheeten. "But,

Lottie dear, Cassandra's room, with its spacious accommodations, angled ceiling and lovely view, is quite expensive to rent. I don't think—"

"Maybe you can make it cheaper to help Kate."

"Lottie dear—"

"You say she deserve all the help she can get."

"Well—yes, Lottie—certainly Kate here deserves all the help that she can reasonably get. But, dear, what you propose is simply not how the renting game is played, as you'd know had you been in this business for seventeen years, as I have. We do not rent out according to ones needs, but, rather, in strict adherence to the objectivity of the market; for, as it is imperative to remember, the more money that we collect in rent, naturally the more money we then have for the appropriation of repairs in and of the structure.

"It's all quite simple and basic, and, even without us, I'm sure Kate will find a very nice place in which to live. Do stop in and see us—on occasion, Kate, and good luck with your new life."

And upon the bestowal of these good wishes, the landlady beat a hasty retreat up the stairways, near the top of which she encountered Hilgen leaving his room.

"Good afternoon, Mrs. McWheeten," he said routinely in passing, before abruptly halting and calling back to get her attention.

"Yes, Hilgen, what is it?"

"Nothing too important, really," he replied, as he stepped back up to the second floor. "I just wanted to let you know that I took the liberty of replacing the broken window in my room."

"The broken—oh, right. Why, of course—your window. You went ahead and replaced it, did you?"

"It wasn't any big deal," Hilgen assured her. "It's just that—well, I know you've been preoccupied with other things. And the plastic covering your husband installed worked fine for a while, but with November's nasty breath beating incessantly against it, I'm afraid it had outlived its usefulness. So, instead of pestering you over the matter, I just went ahead and did the job myself."

"Why, of course," came the landlady's flat response. "Quite understandable. And thoughtful of you not to bother us, if I might add."

"I have the receipt right here," Hilgen pulled it from his wallet, "with the hardware store's estimate for the labor required. I was thinking that I might just deduct the total cost from my December's rent, if that's agreeable to you?"

Mrs. McWheeten cast an absent glance over the receipt now in her hand. She muttered something about "studying the precedent" and told Hilgen that she'd get back to him on his proposition.

He thanked her for her time and they parted ways.

Mrs. McWheeten reentered her room, peering rather blankly still, through her reading glasses, at the receipt. Her husband was off in one corner of the room rearranging some of the boxes that were to be kept.

Mrs. McWheeten sighed in mild despondence as she placed Hilgen's receipt on her desk. "Well," she said, removing her glasses, "I'm afraid we're finally going to have to make the time tomorrow to go and price windows for Hilgen's room. The plastic covering has failed. And he actually took the initiative to go out and replace the window himself," which she seemed not to've expected. "His bill strikes me as a little high," gathering it up again, "which leaves me a little concerned that Hilgen may've taken the opportunity to provide himself a top-of-line product on our credit, and, perhaps, even turning a small profit for himself on the labor." She set the receipt back on the desk, with another little sigh, before returning her attention to their task.

She remarked, with bland approval, of the noticeable increase in floor space. It, then, occurred to her that since they were already driven to such industry, they should probably complement their tidying with at least a light effort at some true cleaning.

She would dust and assigned her husband to sweep.

"Oh, Fab," she interrupted his pursuit of the broom and

dust pan, "before we get started, what do you say we clean out the dog's box and replace the lining with fresh newspaper. We haven't done that in a while and it's beginning to show.

"Here, I'll lift her," Mrs. McWheeten slipped her hands down and around either side of the startled dog and, cooing into the deaf animal's ear—and with a kiss atop its head, she raised her beloved pet gently from its box.

Her husband, meanwhile, pulled the empty box out from the shadow of the landlady's desk, and tugged from its folds the old newspaper that had long padded the dog's rest. And when he loosened and removed the final sheet there fell from its crease to the floor a large white business envelope.

Mrs. McWheeten was absolutely dumbstruck as she gaped down at it from overtop the dog. Her head twitched in its stricken disbelief towards her husband, who was crouched near the envelope and who reflected a more vague incredulity than that which had temporarily incapacitated his wife.

She let the dog tumble from her arms and swept down to grab the envelope (nearly knocking heads with her husband) and fumbled frantically for its flap.

"Oh—for heavens sake," she murmured, having finally pried the envelope open and running her fingers now through its contents. "Why, it seems to be all here," she reported, with a quiet groan, of the nearly eight hundred dollars in rent money. She collapsed into her chair.

And it was a long moment or two, as she pulled herself upright at her desk, before the landlady feebly surmised, with a listless glance at the scene, that, "It must've fallen out through the side of the drawer and into the dog's box. Why, for heaven's sake," with her head falling again into her hand.

"Well," she whispered, as, momentarily, she reached for the phone. "I guess I had better call the police and tell them— that the thief's conscience compelled him to secretly return the money; and that we just as soon the matter be dropped." And with that call being completed, Mrs. McWheeten returned the envelope to its former place in the drawer.

Early that evening, Mrs. McWheeten, still somewhat bedeviled by the late afternoon's rapid succession of events, stood lost in her thoughts at the kitchen sink, scrubbing some dishes.

She greeted Timothy's appearance with as much geniality as she could artificially muster, as he carried into the room the ingredients for his dinner.

He returned her greeting and placed his pot atop the stove, near to the sink.

The landlady could not help but notice that her tenant seemed to be in a mood equally pensive to hers, and, after a couple minutes of observation, verbally noted as much, with a request to be let in on what was troubling him.

Timothy was surprised, and embarrassed, at having been found out; and ducked for cover behind the limp reply that nothing was wrong.

"Very well, then," responded Mrs. McWheeten, though not in the least believing him. She went back to drying off a platter.

"What would you say, Mrs. McWheeten," he returned to her after a moment, and was eyeing her with keen anticipation, "if I were to tell you that I helped get Mike Saunders a job?"

She glanced through the corner of her eye, and let it be known that she did not find his joking humorous. She rigidly advised him "to stop the practice of such deceit."

He told her that there was nothing deceitful about it. "It's the truth."

"Oh come, now," she answered in sharp retort. "Why, who in their right mind would hire that worthless scrap of humanity? In a legal enterprise, mind you. I am more than certain that that shiftless vagabond would pay infinite dividends to one engaged in activities on the dark side of the law. Oh, I am well sure of that."

"I helped him get a job as a part-time dishwasher, and janitor, at the restaurant where I work," Timothy plainly interjected.

"What? Why—you're quite serious, aren't you?" The platter was set down on the counter.

Timothy was serious.

Mrs. McWheeten found herself at a temporary loss for words. "What on earth—and just what sort of trickery, might I ask, did you employ to procure such an inhumane deed? Obviously, you touted him as something he is not."

"Mrs. McWheeten, I was completely up front with them about —"

"And did you inform them that his last occupation was as a jailbird? Ha! I still crow over that—"

"They know all about that."

"What! They know—and did they not at least demand to take a look at him first? For God's sake, one look at such a wretch would've told them—"

"He had a personal interview with them this very morning."

"And, still, they hired him?" the landlady steadied herself by gripping the edge of the sink.

"Yes, they did," Timothy retained his perfect calm. "They decided to give him a chance. With the blessing, I might add, of the liquor store owner, who happens to be a regular customer of ours, and who is willing to drop the charges so that Mike can start clean—"

The landlady scoffed at the notion.

Timothy did not seem to quite understand her response. "I thought you'd be pleased to learn that Mike was trying to turn his life around and become a 'respectable' member of society?"

"Monkeys," she muttered beneath her breath, as she grabbed haplessly for a dish in the sink. "Boy, are they in for a surprise with Mike Saunders. So, he'll be cleaning toilet bowls for a living, eh? Well, that's appropriate enough, I suppose. And just how long do you think it'll be before he's got his filthy little mitts in the till, huh? I give him maybe two weeks—"

"There's plenty of supervision," countered Timothy on the defensive.

"Ha! you'd better call in a whole squadron once he hones in on where the cash is kept. Good God, Timothy," she addressed with a sigh and a grave shake of her head, "what have you gotten yourself into?"

"Certainly nothing for which I have any regrets."

Such youthful naivete, expressed the landlady with a simple roll of the eyes. "Well, dear," she remarked rather flippantly, "if he ends up getting you both fired, please remember to use your savings to pay your rent first. Any other debts can come after. We've already had enough trouble with our rent collecting for this year, what with Saunders' buddy Klegman. We needn't any more of that."

Timothy replied that she need not worry herself over that—to which Mrs. McWheeten reacted with but a mildly reassured smile—and touching upon her lead-in, he inquired about the progress of the investigation into the missing rent money.

Mrs. McWheeten shed her crooked grin in dealing him a suspicious sidelong glance, before recovering herself and, as casually as was possible, asserting that they had probably seen the last of that money.

"Apparently, the burglar was wearing gloves and left no fingerprints anywhere on the premises. Fortunately, though, we do have insurance to cover such a loss; so, as far as I'm concerned, the case is closed. I hope the burglar, whomever he may be," with a deliberate glance at her tenant, "enjoys the fruits of Mr. McWheeten's and my labor."

Timothy was tempted to respond with a blanket defense of Mac—and Mike (and any and all of their associates), but, as Mrs. McWheeten appeared content to let the topic rest, Timothy resisted. And when the preparation of his light meal was completed, he returned to his room to dine.

Chapter Eleven

Kate had quickly developed into a regular visitor to the McWheeten house, for she and Lottie had struck up an immediate camaraderie on which both women, having been so starved, now gladly gorged.

They might simply sit around Lottie's room playing either a board or card game—or both, in turn; or, if tired of them, eagerly shift their attention to their magazines, through which they would browse together, seeking out the most up-to-date fashions, as well as the handsomest male models.

They would go for walks, too, which inevitably entailed window shopping; though, as neither woman had much money—and with Kate desperately trying to save up to get her own room—they seldom peeked inside.

When they did indulge themselves, it was typically to see a second-run movie, with a hardly coincidental partiality being shown those flicks whose male stars rivaled, in appearance, the models from the magazines.

It always made Lottie happy whenever her new friend would stay the night. And that had fast become a custom. In the morning they would go off to work together, where both, especially as a pair, enjoyed considerable popularity amongst their generally older coworkers.

Lottie incessantly quizzed her new friend on what it was like to be pregnant, to which Kate would ordinarily reply that it was too early in the process to chronicle any extensive alteration in her general condition; though she always felt obliged to feed Lottie some little morsel of intrigue.

On one such occasion, Lottie could not contain her envy, confiding to Kate how very much she would like to become a mother herself. Kate responded in great length, advising her friend against rushing into anything, and reminding her that, at her age, she had plenty of time to begin a family.

Lottie promised Kate that she would do nothing rash. But she could not help but hope, someday, for a family of her own, preferably shared, she added, with one of the actors they had seen in the movie the night before; whereat the two women giggled heartily amongst themselves and proceeded to divvy up the on-screen prospects with vows not to encroach upon the other's territory.

The evening at hand the two women decided would be a 'cookie' night' and, stepping from Lottie's room with their bowls, pans and ingredients en route to the kitchen, they encountered Timothy, who was entering through the front door of the house.

He was apprised of their plan and conditioned his acceptance of their invitation to join them on his receiving his fair share of the final product.

"We think it over," replied Lottie with an air, before relenting into a giggle; whereon Timothy concluded that his sole means of guaranteeing his fair share would be to join them, which he did, momentarily, after dropping his coat off in his room.

"Oatmeal 'n raisins," Lottie satisfied Timothy's inquisitiveness as he peered over her shoulder into the mixing bowl.

"My favorite," came his pat reply. He offered to help Kate butter the pans.

Timothy joked about the curiosity of three food service professionals choosing to spend their spare time in a kitchen, and he asked Kate how things were going at her new job.

Kate answered, quite honestly, that she could not have been any happier with her work arrangement, and that she enjoyed the company of all who worked there, "especially Lottie," which made the head baker color with good feeling.

Timothy imagined that "they are as happy with you as you are with them."

Kate gave a blushing laugh, and said she didn't know about that, but that she hoped so.

"They like Kate a lot," Lottie earnestly declared. "She a good worker. An' good person!"

And having cleared up that issue, to Timothy's satisfaction, Lottie said that she was ready for the pans. As Timothy and Kate looked on, she carefully dabbed the dough in neat formation.

Try as she did, in was nearly impossible for Kate to sound nonchalant when, after a moment, she asked Timothy how things were going down where he worked?

"He's doing all right," Timothy presumed her angle with a steady nod. "It's still all so new to him, though. He's dragged in a little bit late these first couple of mornings, but that's not any big deal. And doesn't make him any different than most of the the dishwashers we've had. I imagine it'll take him a while to get used to having to be someplace by six-thirty in the morning. That's not easy for anyone to adapt to.

"But, as far as his performance," Timothy went on, as Lottie carried the pans over and slipped them into the oven, "I haven't heard any real complaints, other than he moves a little slowly. But, again, he's new and doesn't have the routine down yet. And his attitude's been fine, as far as I can tell. He really doesn't talk much to anyone. I think it'll probably take him some time before he feels comfortable in such a new and different environment. He just goes quietly about his work and really does seem to be making a decent effort."

Kate's expression could not conceal the surprise to which she presently confessed, though she softly added that she was "glad to hear that he seems to be trying to change his life around." Yet, "I still can't help but think of him as the Mike I know, and I just hope that he doesn't do anything that'll get you into trouble with your bosses."

Timothy told her that it was a matter she need not worry over. "They know as much about Mike's history as I do. My immediate supervisor was willing to take the chance because that's the type of person she is. So my only concern, should this somehow backfire on us, is that she not experience any negative repercussions. That would bother me far more than anything they could do to me.

"But she understood the risks, and acknowledged the same apprehensions that I had. She went ahead and hired him, anyway," he remarked with admiration. "And if Mike turns out badly—well, he wouldn't be the first dishwasher to fail us. That's long been accepted as a part of this industry. We'd just go out and hire another.

"And I really don't believe that Pam or I would be held accountable if Mike doesn't work out—barring, perhaps, some extreme occurrence. And even if we were," Timothy shrugged with unconcern, "what's the worst that could happen to us? They might fire us. Either one of us could easily land another job in town. Mike probably doesn't have that luxury and I think he knows that. And, judging from what I've seen so far, I think he's determined to make the most of this opportunity he's been given."

Kate simply could not sign on to Timothy's guarded optimism; which Timothy understood.

"Whatever happens," she spoke near a whisper, "I still don't want anything to do with him. And I hope he feels the same way about me," as she searched Timothy's face for a hint.

Timothy, however, could provide her no information, conceding with discouragement that, "He pretty much ignores me at work. I guess I'm hoping that eventually he'll open up to me—at least a little bit. But, for the time being, I think that it's probably best just to allow him to get himself acclimated to his new surroundings. Maybe then, I'll get the chance to know the real and complete Mike Saunders. I have to admit that I'm rather curious."

Kate's eyes, having been cast gloomily towad the floor, were lifted again. "Well, I can tell you what I know—that he and his dad didn't get along very good. His dad's . . . a lot like Mike," she revealed with a dismal shake of her head. "Real bad temper. Made worse by drinking. And drunk or not, he just as soon make his point with threats and violence.

"And Mike being a screw-off in school, he was always getting into trouble with his teachers and principles. Which got him into trouble at home. And he even hit one teacher," said Kate, etching a grimace. "His dad pounded him pretty good after that one.

"And I guess his mom never did anything to stop his dad from hitting Mike. Usually, she took his dad's side, and thought that physical punishment was as good a way to teach a lesson as any.

"Then, one time, Mike hit back. Hit them both. Really cracked his dad hard. And didn't stop when he had him down. He still has the scars from where his mom scratched at him to try to get him off his dad. That scar on the right side of his face is from that.

"That was nine years ago and he hasn't been back home since. He hung around Flint for a while after being kicked out of the house, then came down here."

"Has he spoken to his parents at all since then?" Timothy asked in quiet dismay.

Not that Kate was aware. "I finally got him to get in touch a little bit with one of his older sisters who was married and moved away. But, you know—I guess I really can't blame him for not wanting to have anything to do with his folks anymore; even though, having lost mine, it makes me especially sad to see such a rift between parents and their child. Someday, if they're not already, they'll all be sorry for it, but I'm afraid that it's probably too late to do anything about it. And, for all his faults, I just can't blame Mike on this one."

Lottie had listened to their discussion in a respectful silence, and, when there occurred now this lull, she took the opportunity to redirect their attention to the cookies, which she thought ready to come out.

Timothy volunteered to taste them for doneness, and, with their receiving his approval, the trio grabbed the milk from the refrigerator and went down to Lottie's room for a spirited game of Monopoly, during which, to the growing delight of the others, Lottie's personal liberty seemed placed under the continual constraint of the jailkeeper. In response, she soon resorted to bribing her exultant competitors with cookies for her early release, which, by evening's end, had cost her dearly. Then, only by prostrating herself before their mercy was Lottie able to retire that night on a full stomach.

Chapter Twelve

"Our ball!" Jim leapt from the wicker chair to his feet. "That'll do it—this game's over," and the football that he held in his right hand he slammed into his left.

Timothy smiled at his friend's demonstrativeness, as he remained calmly seated close by the radio on his desk. "That was Ohio State's last chance," he agreed. "Now, all we have to do is just run out the clock."

Jim knew that it'd be a tough game, "but we did it," with a very relieved sigh. "And, what's more, Lottie's wrong, aren't you?"

"Oh, hush, you," Lottie shot back with a grin, as she rocked herself on the hassock.

"That's right," remembered Timothy. "Didn't she predict that Michigan was going to lose this game by a hundred points?"

"I believe she said, 'by at least a hundred points'," Jim tossed the football casually into the air and caught it on its way down.

"And didn't she bet five dollars each with you, Hilgen and myself?" Timothy then inquired of his next-door neighbor.

"I believe that it was ten dollars each," Jim played along.

"No! it was nothin'!" Lottie came bubbling to her own defense. "I didn' bet nothin'! I jus' say Mich'gan gonna lose by hundred points," she was pleading her case to Kate, who sat quietly by, with a smile for the developing exchange. "So, I was wrong," she shrugged with her palms turned upward, "—big deal. But I didn' bet on it!"

Timothy and Jim looked at one another with assumed consternation and gravity, and, then, trading brief nods, turned back to Lottie.

"Lottie," it was Timothy who addressed her, "do you know what we do around here to people who renege on their bets?"

She shook her head with a giant giggle, as Jim moved round behind her.

"Well, first, we present them a football," Timothy explained, as Jim reached around and dropped the ball gently into her lap.

"What you guys gonna do to me?" she chortled as she observed Timothy move to the edge of his chair. "You guys!" she rocked back in an unconscious maneuver that simply facilitated Jim's gripping of her shoulders.

Timothy pounced, almost simultaneously, from his chair; and as Lottie squawked and giggled her way through a series of protests (and unheeded requests to Kate for some help), her assailants hoisted her squirming frame atop their shoulders and, with Lottie clutching futilely at door frames and knobs and all else to impede their progress, they marched her up the hall, through the front door and down the porch steps into the gray November afternoon, not feeling their sense of retribution satisfied till they had tucked her away, bottom first, into a rusting garbage can left out by the side of the road.

Their last laughs, enjoyed as they were retreating back toward the house, were interrupted, however, as the football, which Lottie had clung to throughout her ordeal, came sailing back at them from behind, taking a piece of either's leg; upon which, Lottie crowed hysterically and jostled her container until it tumbled safely over, and to her feet she won with a bounce and a smile.

"That'll teach you: don't mess with me!" she delighted in taunting her two stunned abductors.

The men conceded at having been bested, whereat Jim went over and retrieved the ball off the sidewalk, prompting Timothy to send himself gliding out into the street on a fly pattern.

Jim rolled to his right and, finding a clearing amid the trees and their branches, lofted a beautiful spiral long down the gradually sloping street.

Timothy leapt in full stride, as Jim's throw was just off the mark, only to have the ball deflect off his hands and sail back across his upturned face, and, eluding a second frantic and twisting grab, the ball then bounded across the hood of a car alongside the curb, before caroming off the trunk of the one parked before it and disappearing somewhere in between.

"Should've had it," Timothy consoled his quarterback, who had now taken a position high up the road.

Timothy groped beneath and between the two cars until he found the ball, and springing to his feet he let go a wobbly pass that seemed to have slipped from his hand, with the ball landing on the pavement closer to him than it had to Jim.

Laughing at his own woeful attempt, Timothy fetched the ball himself and exhorted the two women, who lingered up by the porch, to come join them in a game of two on two.

But the women weren't much interested and, instead, plunked themselves down on the steps to watch.

Timothy turned back up the road with a much prettier pass that bounced off a windshield to Jim's right.

Timothy grimaced at his aim, but was soon recovered and mapping out the deception of the imaginary defenders swarming in his vicinity.

And when Jim, who had romped around to the other side of the car to get the ball, lifted his head, Timothy, in breaking to the far side of the street, barked out the old footballer's cue, "Sideline!" And off with a flurry Jim sought to meet this immediate demand on his marksmanship.

Timothy came skidding to a halt atop the loose pebbles and dry leaves gathered at the head of the McWheeten driveway and, reaching back round against his rudderless momentum, tried desperately, with one arm, to haul in the misfired pass, only to have it glance off his fingertips and bang into a radiator grill before rebounding back out into the road.

"Have to get loosened up a little," Jim hollered down as he swung his right arm around in relevant exercise.

The door behind the women was opened, presently, and

out onto the porch came Reese.

"What's going on here?" he asked them.

But before the ladies could answer, Timothy, who noticed Reese from the street, called up and inquired of him whether he'd like to join their game and experience the same fun that he and Jim were having?

Reese, not being at all athletic, graciously declined, opting instead to remain on the porch with the women.

Lottie looked up at Reese, as he continued to stand, leaning against the wooden post at the top of the handrail.

"Your car not parked on road, is it?" she asked him.

It seemed, to Reese, a rather odd question, but, "No—it's not. It's in that small lot across the street there."

Lottie said that she was glad to hear that.

Out in the street, Timothy was chasing down an overthrown pass that had bounded nearly down to the crossroad.

"Hey, look who's coming around the corner!" he shouted back to the others. "Here, Hilgen, catch!"

With a sporting grin come readily to his face, Hilgen struck a sturdy pose to receive the ball. And though the pass was perfect, the reflexes were not, and the ball squirted through his hands and staggered him with a blow to the chest, before dropping at his feet.

Hilgen simply chuckled and shook his head in shame. "Must've been those last four beers," he quipped, and he picked up the ball for an eventual toss. "How 'bout our Michigan boys, eh? Did you watch the game?"

Timothy informed Hilgen that they had listened to it on the radio in his room.

"And where's—ah, there she is. Hiding out on the steps, I see! Well, now what do you have to say for yourself, Lottie? A hundred points, huh? Jim, go deep!" Hilgen waved Jim even further up the road, and then, from the sidewalk, fired a rapidly rising pass that exploded into the brittle branches of the nearest tree. The ball, along with a good many twigs, dropped to the ground not far from where it had been launched.

"So, Lottie, if my memory serves me correctly, did we not make a modest little wager on the game?" Hilgen continued at her expense, as he strolled down into the street, his eyes following the flight of the ball being thrown by Timothy to Jim.

"You owe me money!" she waggishly rebutted. "I say Mich'gan gonna win."

"Oh—no, no, no. You said Ohio State—by a hundred points, you little devil. Now, pay up. Jim! I'm on the fly here—"

And from his elevated position up the road, Jim let go with what was easily the most impressive pass of the day— a majestic spiral, deep and sailing.

Hilgen strode confidently under it, his eyes fixed as the ball approached. But in adjusting his body ever so slightly to welcome the pitch into his chest, he inadvertently nicked the toes of one foot across the heel of the other, stumbling for a couple of paces before spinning out in a spectacular scrape along the pavement.

Timothy and Jim rushed instantly to his aid. The three spectators stood in concern upon the steps.

Hilgen was able to rise, slowly, under his own power. He remained bent as he rubbed the side of one knee. Jim went after the ball that had squibbed away under a car.

"Damn," muttered Hilgen, "will you look at that, I tore my pants."

"How's your knee?"

"I just bought these Tuesday.

"Your hand's bleeding. Maybe you should go in and wash it off."

"Nice toss, Jim. Right there. Should've had it. Guess I should've stopped after six beers."

"Maybe you should go in and clean up that cut."

"Nah, a little blood doesn't stop the great ones," Hilgen chuckled at the presumption. "And it shan't stop me, either. Here ya go, Jim, give me a little sideline number this time."

They proceeded to throw the ball around between themselves a while longer. Short of breath after an especially deep route, during which he had sought, unavailingly, to dupe Timothy into a defenseless posture of flat-footedness, Hilgen bent over and, resting his hands on his knees, declared his day's exercise at an end.

Timothy and Jim called it quits, too, and together the three men dragged themselves up to the porch, where they languidly collapsed. It was becoming too chilly, however, to simply idle outdoors for long and, soon, the entire clan was filing back inside, where Timothy began promoting the idea of a dinner party.

The suggestion was warmly endorsed by all. Reese volunteered his car and, along with Jim and Hilgen, went off to the store to purchase the proper provisions for a robust spaghetti dinner.

Timothy and the two women would remain at the house arranging the kitchen for the feast. To provide adequate seating space, they coaxed a table from Lottie's room (grabbing a couple of chairs, as well) up along the winding staircase to the second floor.

Timothy dug through the collection of communal cooking utensils kept in the cabinet space between the stove and the sink and filled a couple of large pots with water, which he began immediately to heat. Kate and Lottie set the tables.

The candles were Timothy's idea and, with the overhead light turned off, added a splendid, if improbable, coziness to the drab McWheeten kitchen.

Their hunger had grown great during the course of the meal's preparation and, when finally seated, they wasted little time, or fanfare, in vanquishing it. Lottie displayed a disproportionate interest in the meat sauce, with the unintentional effect of disguising whether or not there were any noodles on her plate beneath. Jim gladly passed the massive salad bowl on down the line without allowing so much as a single leaf of lettuce to blemish his own plate. Hilgen had insisted on including in their fare three loaves of garlic bread, to ensure, for himself, a minimum of one half-loaf, with his eye vigilant of any of the remainder being neglected around the table.

The feast moved along in full gear, with the red wine disappearing as quickly as anything. Hilgen, in fact, was already persuing a refill.

"Say, nice bib there, Lottie," he snorted as he grabbed the bottle nearest him. "Looks a lot like your shirt."

And though her head had maintained a constant pose low over her plate, the wriggling noodles she was slurping ambitiously up into her mouth were indeed leaving an abstract pattern of chunky meat sauce down the front of Lottie's shirt.

"Oh, hush, you," she said, with a stray noodle straggling up her chin.

Hilgen's consequent chuckle made his pour a little shaky, but he avoided any spillage and, setting the bottle back down, continued with, "So, Kate, tell us, when at work does Lottie actually serve the food—or does she just wear it? Sort of a walking menu, going from table to table with the day's specials magnificently displayed from ear to ear and nose to tummy?"

The loudest burst of laughter, of all the loud laughter that echoed round the table, came from quiet Kate, who thought she might choke on her food if Hilgen didn't stop. And Kate could not help but feel a sense of guilt over laughing so at her friend's expense, as Lottie absorbed the jesting with mute embarrassment. She quickly remarked, with due sincerity—and gratitude, that she thought Lottie the best worker they had.

"Well, I do not, for a moment, doubt that," replied Hilgen, laying it on a bit; adding that, "If she works with the same zeal with which she eats, I do not believe any of us could doubt that." He chuckled quietly into his glass, before keenly observing, "Kate, you don't like your garlic bread?"

She liked it well enough, she said. Just not half a loaf's worth. It reverted to Hilgen.

Lottie beamed at this transaction. "If you work like you eat, I sure you best worker at your job, too!" she cackled with her mouth half full and dripping meat sauce to the table.

Hilgen saluted her wit with a chuckle. "Touche, Lottie,

touche."

And when all the others were done with their helpings, their plates being pushed away and their postures drawn deep into their chairs by the fullness of their bellies, there was Hilgen seduced forward and scarfing down, with consent, a forsaken end of bread from Reese's plate. Finishing up there, he, too, sank back, with a sigh.

"Reese, my good man," Hilgen struck up, momentarily, from overtop the glass of wine he rested near his lips, "I trust that I can expect your enthusiastic company on any one of my winter walking expeditions, when though the bird's are not nearly so plentiful, their distinct silhouettes against the stark winter landscape and their lonesome calls pining through the frosty air are a spiritual reward more than commensurate with the modest risk of pneumonia."

Reese was easily sold. "I quite enjoyed our first walk."

"As did I," whereupon Hilgen made the invitation general to all the party.

"So, Reese," Hilgen resumed, presently, smacking his lips after a sip from his glass, "tell me, was the president a bird man?"

"The president?"

"Mister Van Buren."

"Oh—" but, of course. "Why—I don't—really know," for which he apparently felt some shame.

Hilgen chuckled over Reese's assumed ignominy. "Well, being the Red Fox of Kinderhook, I suspect he may have hunted a bird or two in his time. Chickens, anyway—"

"I thought he hunted Indians," remarked Jim with a quick smile, his arms folded casually across his chest.

"Scourge of the Seminoles," confirmed Hilgen with a nod, while in admiring contemplation of his wine.

Reese acknowledged, with chagrin, that, "Mister Van Buren did continue the prosecution of President Jackson's campaign against the Seminole Indians, yes—"

"Prosecution or persecution?" rejoined Jim, with no hurtful intentions.

Reese, however, was silently wounded. "Mister Van Buren

was in a difficult position," he wanted them to know, "having attained the presidency, in large part, due to the influence of his friend—and mentor, President Jackson. To have reversed course on Mr. Jackson's crusade would've been a public repudiation. President Van Buren's loyalty would not have permitted that, even on an admittedly questionable campaign as this.

"Besides," proceeded Reese, having warmed, now, to the task of defending the nation's eigth commander-in-chief, "I think that, on the matter of human rights, President Van Buren, when able to act upon his own conscience, showed his moral supremacy, as well as his political courage, by breaking from his own Democratic Party, as it waffled over the slavery issue, to serve the cause of the anti-slavery Freesoil Party as its presidential candidate in the campaign of 1848—"

"But," Jim moved forward in his chair to contest the point, "was his joining forces with the Freesoil Party truly born out of moral supremacy—for he later opposed the candidacy of Abraham Lincoln, nominee of the anti-slavery Republican Party that was evolved from the Freesoilers—or was it merely political expediency, for had not the Democrats already turned their backs on him, both in 1844 and 1848, by defeating his bid to again become their presidential nominee?"

"I think Jim has a point here, Reese," injected Hilgen with appropriate sensitivity. "For if compelled by a sense of moral supremacy to join with the Freesoil Party, how do you reconcile that with his earlier refusal, while president, to interfere with the institution of slavery as already practiced in the southern sates, as well as his refusal to even seek its abolishment in the very District of Columbia in which he lived?

"Frankly, one cannot help but suspect the impetus of political expediency," continued Hilgen, "when observing what very much seemed like the private coddling of the southern members of his Democratic Party—by downplaying the issue—in hopes of gaining their support for his bid to be nominated for re-election at the Baltimore convention of 1840, while, at the same time, publicly opposing the expansion of slavery as immoral, which, presumably, would placate the northern tier of his party."

"Naturally, I agree that the practice of slavery was abhorrent," Reese soberly prefaced his defense, "but I think when discussing this issue, one has to take into account that times were different then, and that slavery, as mysterious as this may be to our modern sensibilities, was not universally condemned. And, too, I think we must recognize that any politician was politically hamstrung to simply abolish such a widespread practice, by any means short of a civil war.

"I believe that, at the time of Mister Van Buren's administration, the best one could hope for was to prevent the expansion of slavery into the territories, and then work for its gradual demise in those states where it already existed.

"And, also, in regards to the question of political motivations, I think one should remember that a key component of Mister Van Buren's defeat for the Democratic nomination of 1844 was his firm, though unpopular, opposition to the annexation of Texas from Mexico, when it was generally presumed that Texas would be admitted as a slave state. I don't believe one can plausibly argue that there was any political expediency in such a stand. Quite to the contrary, for it was the clearly inevitable backlash from the powerful southern bloc of the Democratic Party that doomed his chance for the nomination, giving it and, ultimately, the presidency to Mr. Polk.

"So, I think that what you witness," Reese was concluding his thesis, "from the practical uncertainties of the 1830's to the Freesoil pulpit of the 1840's is the spiritual and moral evolution of a man cast amid the divisive torrents of an adolescent nation."

Which was certainly good enough for both Jim and Hilgen, who, nodding in homage to the case made by their neighbor, brought their cooperative cross-examination to an end.

"I would hereby like to propose a toast," proclaimed Hilgen as he conducted their glasses toward the center of the table, "and to declare founded The Martin Van Buren

Society, with its Ann Arbor Chapter to be presided over by our distinguished friend and colleague, Mr. Reese Dingell—and, in his absence, by his own vice-president—Miss Kate!"

Hearty cheers and shouts of recognition for the history being made accompanied the fervid clinking of glassware, beneath which could be faintly heard Kate's incredulous laughter and her confession that she "didn't even know who this guy was."

Such noisy festivity was more than a passer-by might ignore and, momentarily, Hilgen was surprised to observe none other than Mr. McWheeten's face poked tentatively round the kitchen door.

Those of the party made immediate and sincere calls for him to join the company. And there could be no mistaking his temptation.

As Hilgen filled a glass with wine, Timothy got up to retrieve an extra chair from the corner. Mr. McWheeten teetered towards acceptance of their invitation.

"What's the occasion?" he cleared his heavy throat and, having tenuously commanded the discomfort with society that had evolved from his dilapidating illness, he edged within the full effect of the candlelight, which unveiled an unusual alertness in his generally cloudy features.

"Friendship and camaraderie," answered Hilgen with a gentle toss of his shoulders. "And we would not count the night a success unless you agree to take a glass of wine with us." The others concurred.

Mr. McWheeten coughed, amid the mumbling of his gratitude over this sentiment, and moved, with some lingering hesitancy, to occupy the chair that Timothy had wedged between himself and Lottie.

The original revelers, though they had encouraged, and welcomed, his inclusion, were now uncertain as to how to interact with their customarily aloof landlord. They watched, as one, while he swirled his glass studiously beneath his nose in prelude to sampling the wine. They expressed their pleasure that he liked the vintage, then fell silent again, not knowing in which direction to guide the conversation.

Mr. McWheeten seemed completely oblivious to their predicament (he looked to be more interested in the wine), when, presently, he lifted his glance with a melancholy satisfaction and working it deliberately round the table— which made some of the party uneasy—he paused at one figure to offer his, "Congratulations, Reese, on your appointment as president of the local Martin Van Buren Society."

Hilgen smiled at his landlord's eavesdropping. "And, Fab, I think I speak for the entire group when I say that we'd take it as a supreme honor if you'd join our fledgling organization."

It was with the eerie smile of a waning face that Mr. McWheeten accepted the privelage, "despite Mr. Van Buren's handling of the Seminole Indian affair. He was hardly the first American politician to mistreat the Native American, nor the only to smite at a minority to appease his Southern base."

"But to play the devil's advocate here, Fab," rejoined Hilgen, "could not one reasonably contend that the Indians were a threat to the white settlers and, as a public official elected as a representative of those settlers, was he not bound by duty to act in their interest?"

"There is a Higher Authority than the electorate, Hilgen," the landlord rebutted, "to which we all must ultimately answer. And I would be willing to bet that the Little Magician, among a good many other elected officials, has been doing some pretty fast talking to explain himself."

Hilgen yielded the point with a chuckle. "Well, Fab," he drawled, "I suspect you're right."

It was but shortly afterwards that Mrs. McWheeten's curiosity followed her husband's into the room. She seemed surprised, though not necessarily displeased, to find him among the gathering. Her concern, as expressed, lay in the interaction of the wine with his medication, and, too, she took to remind him of the exaggerated effect that even the slightest intake of alcohol might have on one who had been medically consigned to virtual abstinence.

Her husband cared not to face her, and received her

admonition with bowed head. Hilgen promised to serve as monitor, or if she cared to join them—

She was not up to accepting their invitation, however, for she was not feeling completely well. And she good-naturedly dismissed Hilgen's facetious claim of red wine being the elixir of all ills, both mental and physical. Nor could she be persuaded to join them in a toast to Martin Van Buren, explaining her steadfast refusal, on this account, as a general policy "not to honor Democrats, no matter how dead they are."

She had merely stopped by out of intrigue, she said; and, then, relayed her wish that her husband, when finished "with his one glass of wine" take the dog out before bed.

Mr. McWheeten took his time in finishing the glass. Still, it was not long before the party was coming to an end, due mainly to the drunken drowsiness that was beginning to afflict most of the others. It was the newcomer who was most disappointed by this break-up, though he bore it silently. And while the others set indolently about the task of cleaning up after themselves, Mr. McWheeten was left to take Sunshine on her errand.

Chapter Thirteen

Jim hoped that it was the knock he had anticipating. Pushing from his lap onto his hassock the two blankets under which he'd been curled up, he rose from his chair to answer it.

"Why, good evening, Jim," said Mrs. McWheeten, feinting at a smile (while her husband could be heard coughing in the dark background). "We got your note. Is there something wrong?"

Yes, there was, replied Jim, and he went on to explain to his landlady that he was finding his room far too cold for comfort.

"I was wondering whether, with December here, the heat in the house had been turned on for the winter?"

Mrs. McWheeten's resulting glance addressed her tenant sharply, for what might he be insinuating? "But, of course, it has, Jim. Now, what precisely is the problem?"

"Well—it's just that I don't seem to be getting any heat coming up through the vents. Almost none at all."

"May I come in," said the landlady, implicitingly admonishing her tenant for neglecting his manners, "and take a look?"

Jim certainly obliged this request and, leading the McWheetens to the center of his small room, lamented to them that, "I've yet to feel any heat coming up through this vent here—"

And what a relief this revelation was to the landlady, for, "Jim, the purpose of that large vent there is to suck any cold air out of the room," she articulated with special emphasis. "It's the small vent over here which is responsible for sending heat up into the room. In fact, I can feel its flow right now." She was bent over it.

"Perhaps, though, the duct has become partially clogged," she submitted. "That does happen on occasion. Mr. McWheeten and I would be glad to take a look. Now, you just wait here next to the vent and listen for our voices."

Jim bided this time crouched down and passing his hand discerningly over the tiny vent, from which, presently, there escaped the usual wisp of air that only the most fixed mind could construe as heat.

It was three or four minutes before Jim heard, through the vent, their voices beckoning him to reply. He complied. He, then, heard some clattering of metal, another call (responded to) and nothing more, until the McWheetens came trudging back into his room.

"Well?" he said.

The landlady sighed from her recent exertion, and she smiled. "We checked everything out and I'm happy to report that there was no blockage and that all seems to be in proper working order."

Jim's heart sank so swiftly that the landlady asked him if he were all right?

And, of course, he was not. "I'm afraid," he droned quite miserably, "that the cold air duct is overmatched by the constant draft that filters in through the cracks in the wall here—"

"Cracks in the wall?" Mrs. McWheeten edged upon her toes to gaze down past the chair to the baseboards.

Jim was now hunkered in the corner, running his hand along a plainly decaying section of wall (generally concealed behind the floor-length curtains). "It's especially cold on the feet and shins," he said of the air current. "Feel it."

"Well—Jim, I've no cause to doubt you; but you should've come directly to the point, dear boy. I mean, for you to initially imply that the problem lay in the heating system, thereby prompting my husband and I to battle our way down along the dark, dirty and cold reaches of the basement in order to rectify your discomfort, when it turns out that the problem is not in the heating system at all, but, rather, in some fundamental aspect of the structure, which, after all, is nearly sixty-five years old and is allowed, I should think, some modest degree of deterioration. And, Jim, certainly I think you'd agree that the fair rent and low utility fee that attracted you to us in the first place more than compensates for any minor inconvenience due to some limited structural degeneration.

"Might I suggest, Jim, that you dip into the market for some heavy woolen socks? And, too, I see that you've brought along your own footrest—so may I further recommend that you keep your feet propped toward the ceiling, where, science tells us, you'll find the air to be warmer."

Having thus assured herself that all was remedied, Mrs. McWheeten, along with her husband, then left the cold room to its rightful occupant.

And the room only proceeded to get colder with the advance of night, scarcely less so away from the wall as next to it. The room was simply too small to escape the conditions. Even up in the loft, heat gathered only by stray molecules and were inadequately detained by Jim's two heavy blankets, two sweatshirts, long johns, sweatpants, winter gloves and two pairs of socks.

Jim had lain awake in bed for some time, alternately peeping his nose above the blankets for air and beneath them for warmth; when, having come up for oxygen, he detected, through the slipshod carpentry, a sliver of light from Timothy's room next door.

Unable to fall asleep, Jim thought that he may as well visit and, dragging his two blankets along with him, he stepped out into the hallway.

He was astonished to find Timothy sitting in comfort at his desk in a light sweater and blue jeans. Timothy, conversely, was somewhat bemused to find his neighbor traipsing around the house wrapped in several layers of clothing and draped with ponderous blankets, and he voiced his concern when hearing of Jim's woes.

"It is a very drafty house," Timothy acknowledged with a nod; and, momentarily, he was rising from his chair in yielding to Jim's impulse to show any sympathetic person his crumbling wall. But 'drafty' was not a stern enough description for the condition of Jim's room, his neighbor agreed, and that Mrs. McWheeten refused to satisfactorily redress the problem dismayed Timothy nearly as much as it had Jim.

And Timothy could not help but feel some small sense of guilt, for not only were his exterior walls intact, but with his own quarters being that much closer to the furnace below, his floor benefited from an influence that seemed to peter out at the boundary of Jim's room.

Timothy had a couple extra blankets that he was happy to let Jim have, and even went so far to offer the accommodation of his floor for the evening.

Gratefully declining that invitation, but being in no hurry to climb back into his cold loft, Jim would return to his neighbor's for a short visit.

They chatted, first, of Kate—and Lottie, and all the time they seemed to be spending together.

Jim thought they made a cute couple, given their complementary natures and disparate heights.

Timothy could not've been more pleased over the development of that friendship, for the sake of both, noting of Kate that, "I don't think she ever felt comfortable in the street circle. I don't believe that was ever really her crowd. She just kind of got caught up in it, and having nothing else—

"But now that she's gotten a break, I know she's determined and will make the most of it in moving away from that scene altogether—

"Mike, on the other hand," Timothy went quiet with a sigh, "—I honestly don't know how easily he'll be able to break from those associations. Or whether he'll even try; for even if he no longer desires that lifestyle, as he maintains, I still think that it's the only group of people around whom he feels comfortable. And I guess I'm a little bit concerned that he'll be unable to distinguish between the good people of that group and those whose influence might sabotage his progress.

"And he is making progress," Timothy auspiciously noted. "Not only has he improved his work habits—though he probably still needs to move a little faster—but with one of our other dishwashers failing to show up for work yesterday, Mike's moved up in seniority—and into full-time.

"What's more, Pam's been pleased enough with Mike's performance that she came to me to see whether I knew of anyone else in Mike's situation who might be interested in picking up his part-time hours."

Jim was not only impressed with Mike's development, but, also, with Pam's willingness to scour the streets for her labor force. "I don't know of many employers who would actively seek out homeless people."

Timothy smiled in response. "Well, she does plan on getting her master's degree in social work; so maybe she looks at this as her first project, which is what I was hoping when I first approached her on the matter. And, so far, it's been a successful experiment."

Jim asked whom Timothy had in mind for Mike's old job.

"The only person I could think of was a guy named Mac, but he wasn't interested. Doesn't like too many restrictions placed on his life," Timothy explained with a shrug; and, then, breaking into a grin, "But I'm really not too worried about Mac. He seems very independent and quite capable of looking after himself. I think he'll be all right, as long as Michigan keeps its bottle deposit laws.

"But, anyway, when I couldn't help her," Timothy continued, "Pam addressed the matter to Mike himself. So, he's going to check amongst his friends and acquaintances— and I really pray some of his better ones. But I think that might be the most remarkable development of all," suggested Timothy. "Not Mike's having lasted nearly three weeks on the job—which, I suppose, might be cause for amazement— but that Pam trusts him enough already to seek his recommendation. I think even he was surprised by that."

Timothy certainly was, and pleasantly so; which, in turn, pleased Jim.

The relative warmth of Timothy's room had the effect of making Jim drowsy and he declared his intentions of returning to his loft. And if, before, he could not quite believe his own sleeping attire, it seemed all the more ridiculous when Timothy handed over to him a spare ski cap. Jim said thank you—and good-night—and tramped back to his room.

Chapter Fourteen

The city's holiday spirit burned brightly on display, with the festive white lights of the season strung along the barren branches of the trees that lined the main thoroughfares of both the downtown and campus areas. Beneath, the sidewalks teemed, with so many daytime workers flooding into the settling dusk, driven thither-and-yon by the merchants' extended hours.

Against the stress of such serious-minded pursuits, there glided more easily those whose chatter signaled an objective more convivial—the indulging in a yuletide libation with friends—humming along with the Christmas music that softly emanated from some nearby shop and tipping their hats and, more welcomely, their wallets to the volunteer ringing the bell for charity on the corner.

In common, the two breeds of walker, in both turn and unison, exacerbating the rush hour motorist, his grip white on the steering wheel, as he impatiently waits out the unmindful pedestrians straggling against the traffic light.

Down in Liberty Plaza, just off the sidewalk and a couple of steps below the surface of the street, the scene lay much quieter, with all the metal seats being unoccupied, save for the last of one row, in which there sat a young man, unconcerned, it seemed, with the deepening chill of this December eve. Occasionally, from the interior of his coat, a bare hand would come forth to manipulate the cigarette hanging from the side of his mouth, before slipping back into a pocket.

Not even the sniffles that were beginning to inflame his nostrils nor the coughing that periodically choked his breath were sufficient stimuli to spark him on his way. Any glance he paid the street scene was void of keen observation. And those who scurried through it were equally heedless of him.

His next cough drew both hands from his pockets, up to cover his mouth, where he took the opportunity to blow on them for warmth. He then slouched forward in the chair, resting his elbows on his knees, with his absent gaze fallen upon the dying embers of the cigarette he had just flipped to the pavement.

There was a store close by whose only access was off the plaza and from which there presently emerged a young woman with a small brown shopping bag in one hand. She moved vigilantly through the lonely and darkening square, with the spirited corner above, kindly illuminated by a bank clock, serving as her beacon.

She did not see the young man sitting behind a concrete planter. Her footsteps, though, had alerted him to her approach, and how his heartbeat quickened as he honed in on her passing unsuspectingly by—

"Kate?"

She let out a quiet cry and staggered round in sidelong retreat. "Mike?" she called out, breathlessly, as her eyes squinted towards that voice she surely knew.

Perhaps it was peculiar that they should've been so surprised to come across one another when the movements of each were confined to a limited and common part of town. Yet, it was their first encounter since their final falling out, and neither knew exactly how to proceed.

"What're you doing—sitting out here in the cold?" she wondered, rather oddly—with an anxious glance about to assure herself of the availability of human interference should it be required.

He shrugged off the inquiry with a sniffle. "Ain't that cold," and he seemed to follow the track of her eyes up to the sidewalk.

"So—what're you doin' out here?" he turned the question back on her, for the lack of anything more remarkable to say.

She had just bought some Christmas cards, she said, indicating the bag in her hand. "For our Christmas party at work next week."

Mike made no response, other than a small nod, until, "So—how do you like workin' at that kinda place?"

She loved working there, she strongly emphasized in the face of his dubious tone. "It makes me feel good to help those people," she let him know. "Even if I am only serving up their food—and doing other little things, which isn't anything anybody else couldn't do. I guess maybe it's just that, having been on the other side of it and having other people help me—when it really shouldn't've been necessary—it's kind of nice to be the one doing the helping. And for those who really do need it.

"And to see the appreciation in their faces—" there was no need for Kate to relate any further, for her reward was quite evident in her own face, nor did it seem that Mike was much interested in hearing about it.

He had simply been nodding along, with his eyes beginning to wander. He was hunched forward again, to reduce his exposure to the elements, with his hands tucked deeply into his pockets; and he stamped his feet lightly on the ground to aid circulation.

"Not to mention that it's kinda nice gettin' that first paycheck, ain't it?" he remarked.

Kate would not deny that.

"Jus' got mine today," declared Mike, without any effort to subdue his air of accomplishment, in case she had been skeptical of his ever making it through to this milestone.

Quite naturally, she had been; but keeping that to herself, she asked, "So, everything's working out okay?"

"Yeah, it's all right," he answered. "Ain't the greatest job in the world, but prob'bly ain't the worst, neither. Don't like havin' to be there so damn early in the mornin'," he snorted, "but I'm kinda gettin' used to it, I guess. An' if they're gonna pay me to get my ass goin' in the mornin', then I'll get it goin', that's for sure."

Kate was a little leery to broach it, given Timothy's earlier report, but she was curious to hear from Mike how he was getting along with his co-workers.

"All right, I suppose," he shrugged as he considered it.

"Don't talk too much to the wait people," he conceded. "Bunch a snooty, know-it-all college kids. A couple of 'em are all right, I guess. I jus' ain't got nothin' in common with any of 'em.

"But I get along pretty good with the cooks. Some a them guys are pretty cool. Just regular people. Don't put on no airs. Hell, even smoked pot with a couple of 'em already, out behind the restaurant—"

"Oh—Mike—"

"After work, for Chrissake! Jesus, do you really think I'm that dumb, to do somethin' that could cost me my job? Maybe it ain't the greatest, but now it's full-time, an' I'm gonna be makin' more money than I've ever made before. An', believe it or not, I am smart enough to know I ain't gonna find nothin' better right now. Besides, if it wasn't all right to do it, then them cooks wouldn't be doin' it. They been there long enough to know what's okay an' what ain't."

There had been more to Kate's reflexive remonstrance than merely the venue in which Mike chose to engage in such an activity, but, having had a moment to collect herself, she recalled, with relief, that it was no longer her concern; though she was quietly encouraged by Mike's expressed determination to keep his job.

"Hell, ya know who's gonna start workin' there?" he disrupted her reflection. "Barry! He's takin' over the job I had."

Kate nodded in vague approval, for she did not know Barry well.

"Yeah, I pretty much got 'im the job," Mike went on. "When I moved up to full-time they came 'n asked me if I knew anybody who'd want my old part-time job," there was no mistaking Mike's pride at having been consulted, nor was there any confusing Kate's lingering incredulity, for she had heard of this developing situation from Timothy.

"Well, tell Barry that I'm happy for him," she eventually replied.

Mike nodded to imply that he would. "Yeah, it'll be kinda nice havin' someone I know workin' there. Like I said, I like some a the guys in the kitchen all right, but I know Barry, so that'll make it even better—even though we ain't gonna be workin' the same shifts, of course. But we'll still see each other around the place."

Kate told Mike that she was glad things were working out for him. "Have you thanked Timothy?" she then asked.

It was obvious that he had not, given the manner in which he fidgeted about his chair and twisted his face askew. "I should prob'bly say somethin', shouldn't I?" he was addressing the planter more directly than he was her.

Kate was clearly disappointed that he hadn't already.

"Guess I just ain't gotten 'roun' to it yet," he lamely submitted.

Kate shook her head at such a sorry explanation.

"I'll try 'n remember next time I see 'im," it sounded a hollow promise.

But, to Kate, there seemed no point in pursuing it.

"So—he says you're spendin' a lotta time over at that house?"

Kate could not see what business this might be of Mike's; nor was she comfortable with the thought that his infrequent dialogue with Timothy might center around her.

"Lottie and I have become very good friends," she said rigidly, "and we spend a lot of time together away from work. Sometimes, she even lets me stay overnight, which is kind of nice—and makes me even more determined to get away from the shelter for good. A couple more paychecks and I figure I'll be able to start looking for a room of my own."

Mike said that he had the very same intention. "I can't wait to get the hell outa there. I been there long enough—livin' by their rules. Ain't as tolerant of that as I used to be, let me tell ya. Timothy thinks I should open up some kinda bank account to sock away money until I got enough saved up to get my own place—"

Kate suggested that it was a good idea, and said that it was exactly what she had done.

Mike mumbled something about looking into it. They had fallen silent for a couple of moments, when Mike, with a hitch in his voice, very reluctantly inquired, "So—you still plan on goin' through with it?"

"Yes, I do," her firm response belying the anxiety she felt over his raising of this topic.

Mike's sigh blurted forth with such distress, for he simply could not understand!

"Mike, I'm not asking you to understand," she countered his outcry. "And I'm not asking you to help. It's my decision—"

"An' you're gonna be able to take care of a baby all by yourself an' work full-time, too, are ya? What, you gonna leave it in a crib by itself all day long? Why the hell're you rushin' into a family for, anyways? Christ, you got twenty years to start one a those! when you got yourself in a better situation. This jus' don't make no sense—"

She informed Mike, with her emotion flexing against all restraint, that she need not be reminded as to the difficulty of the task before her; nor would she permit it—or him—to deter her.

"And I really don't want to discuss it anymore," she preempted his starting up again, and to ensure that this exchange was indeed over, she said that she must be going.

Mike chided her for allowing their difference of opinion to propel her on her way, but she was not to be dissuaded.

She repeated, albeit flatly, that she was happy that things were looking up for him, before turning away and quickly assimilating herself into the street scene above.

Chapter Fifteen

"What's all this?" asked Jim when he answered the knock at his door to find Timothy wishing him, "Good morning," while presenting him with what appeared to be a roll of some sort of clear plastic.

"We were passing by a hardware store," explained Timothy, and he indicated with a nod up the hall that 'we' included Lottie and Kate whom, somewhere out of view, could be heard engaged in some activity or other that was causing a slight commotion, "and it's being that time of year, this was being advertised in the window," with Jim having immediately come to mind.

Timothy then offered his assitance in installing the insulating sheets of plastic and brandished a role of adhesive tape he had bought for the purpose.

Jim gladly accepted and, allowing his friend to pass by, he ventured a peek out into the hallway to see what the women were up to, only to hear Lottie's door closing behind her.

"We knocked at your door earlier," Timothy remarked, but aware that Jim had worked the previous evening, they had knocked lightly in case he were still asleep (which, indeed, had been the case).

"We went out and bought a Christmas tree for the house," announced Timothy, "and we're going to put it in Lottie's window," which answered Jim's curiosity concerning the women. The plan was to decorate it when the two men were done with their present task.

Thus, they set about sealing Jim's room off from the inhospitable draft that so readily passed through its decaying outer wall, as well its disproportionate window space, by attaching the wide strips of plastic from up near the ceiling down the full length to the floor, from the very leftmost end of that one wall all the way round to the partition that divided their respective rooms on the right.

The women, having successfully planted the tree upright in its stand before Lottie's window and having time to bide until its decorating, stopped by Jim's room to see how the men were doing. They found themselves unable to resist a tittering critique of their work-in-progress, focusing their smiles on the several loose flaps—which the men would then remedy—as well as the peculiar angle at which the plastic was taking shape on the wall.

Timothy good-humoredly suggested that the women might better expend their energy in going upstairs to the kitchen and preparing a pot of hot cocoa for their tree-trimming party. The ladies obliged.

The result of the men's hard labor was to rob from Jim his much ballyhooed view of the imposing structure next door. It also muffled even further the sparse daylight that ever did slip so obliquely into his quarters. The improved insulation from the cold, however, Jim already found to be well worth these drawbacks.

Jim chastised himself for not having thought of this solution himself, and he asked Timothy how much money he owed him for the materials.

Timothy checked him on this concern, however, and simply wished him a Merry—and warm—Christmas.

The Christmas tree was rather small—intentionally so, given the restricted dimensions of its predetermined site. As such, it did not take long for the four of them to fully dress it. They draped it, first, in gold and silver tinsel. The few candy canes that Lottie hadn't gotten into were, then, hooked onto some of the smaller branches, while the larger limbs were bowed by the weight of hearty bulbs of red or green. Lastly, came the two strings of Christmas lights, multi-colored and blinking (Lottie's favorite).

The decorators had taken to the front yard to more fully admire their work, when there turned into the driveway an old, pale brown car, whose drooping underside scraped lightly over the bumpy entrance. It was the McWheeten vehicle.

"My goodness," said the landlady, having gotten out on the passenger's side and now approaching, with her eyes having followed the plane of their attention, "is that a Christmas tree I see?"

They confirmed the observation and said that they had just bought it that very morning.

"Why, how pretty. Fab, come take a look. Isn't that something? Why, really. And, Lottie, what a coup for you, dear, having the honor of displaying it in your room."

"My room bes' for it," Lottie explained. "At front of house."

"But of course. And makes your lovely room all the lovlier, I am sure. And, certainly, it does make our humble little abode all the more Christmasy. Why, indeed. My, Fab, how lax we've become these past few years. Why, I'm afraid that our own Christmas decorations never seem to make it out of storage anymore," rued the landlady to her tenants with something of a sigh.

"Fab, why don't you go see if you can at least find the wreath for the front door. For heaven's sake, yes. And, if I'm not mistaken, there really ought to be some outdoor lights down there somewhere, too. And while you're going about that, I'll retrieve the dog from your room and take her out on her business."

To witness the front porch of her house being decked out in Christmas lights furthered the landlady's holiday spirit, so much so that she was rendered lenient of—or, more likely, oblivious to—Sunshine's marking her territory in the usually forbidden realm of the walkway leading up to the front steps.

It tickled her tenants to see her so giddy, and they responded to her expressions of gratitude for this minor cosmetic transformation by remarking that they felt this their home, as well; which made the landlady swell even more.

And how delighted and ready was Mrs. McWheeten to exude upon a fresh pair of ears, when Hilgen's broad smile was seen coming up the sidewalk.

"Merry Christmas!" she greeted his intrigued advance.

"Well, well, what do we have here?" the lighted tree in the window putting an added twinkle in his eye. "A stopping station for jolly old Saint Nick?"

Lottie, from her position of assisting with the lights up on the porch, replied that it was—and that, further, she was going to hog all the presents that were left at the house for herself.

Hilgen chuckled at her avarice. "Well, Lottie, given what I've witnessed of your behavior over these past couple of a months, for you to receive any presents at all would require such thievery."

"That not true!" she squawked at his inference. "Okay, maybe some time true," she momentarily allowed with a mischeivous grin.

Timothy, from the top of a step ladder placed upon the porch, asked Hilgen whether he'd like some hot cocoa.

Hilgen appreciated the offer; however, "I'm afraid that I don't have the time. Just stopping back here briefly before I'm off again."

"Goin' out with 'nother girl, huh?" drolled Lottie.

"A woman, Lottie, a woman. I father girls, I date women. A brunch date today; made all the more seemly by the fact that the lady is buying—"

"I have date tonight, too!" boasted Lottie, knocking Hilgen's chuckle flat in his throat; and having permitted herself a moment to revel in the silent surprise of all, Lottie blurted out, "Tim'thy takin' me to his Christmas party at work!"

Hilgen grinned at her guile, and, winking aside to Timothy, "Best keep an eye on her, it's your reputation at stake."

"I know it will be hard," Lottie giggled, "but I will behave myself. I not make Tim'thy shamed to take me places."

Timothy only wanted for her to have a good time, and commented that individual bad behavior would not likely stand out at this function.

"Well then, Lottie, it sounds as though you can just be yourself after all," Hilgen gave her a playful nudge as he passed her on his way inside.

"He mus' think I awf'lly bad," reckoned Lottie, not completely displeased by the image, after Hilgen had entered the house. "But I only preten'," she confided to the others, who received her assurances with quiet smiles.

The McWheetens, too, were soon on their way upstairs, after all had been completed outdoors. The four who remained then went back into Lottie's room where, turning the sofa full around and rearranging a couple of other chairs, they gathered cozily about, with their hot cocoa, and admired the Christmas tree with its tinsel sparkling and its lights blinking against the dreary gray sky beyond.

Chapter Sixteen

With the very obvious exception of the red shag carpeting that, at a glance, strongly discouraged any closer inspection, it probably was not as shabby as a diner should be, with only a few of the vinyl booths torn and the wooden tables and chairs looking spiffy and new.

Timothy, along with a half dozen others, had arrived early to help convert the modest eatery into something a little more Christmasy for the occasion of the staff party.

Small cardboard cutouts of Santa Claus and most of his reindeer were the first things to go up, in no sequential order, along the restaurant's vast front window, an endeavor which piqued the fleeting curiosity of some of the passers-by out front. There were snowmen mixed into the scene, as well; while strips of crepe paper, in red and green, began appearing from the ceiling throughout the interior.

A sprig of mistletoe was hung, suspiciously, from above the passage that led from the large main dining room into the long and narrow annex that constituted the smoking section, near the front of which, at the window, was placed the small and sparsely decorated artificial Christmas tree.

The most compelling ornament of all, to no one's surprise, proved to be the pony keg of beer that the restaurant had purchased for the affair, and which had been placed alongside the tree.

Lottie had accompanied Timothy on his early arrival and clung shyly to his side during the setting up; and, though having been introduced all the way around, when, infrequently, she did speak, it was directed almost exclusively at him.

She became even less comfortable in her strange surroundings when the party's commencement, at six o' clock, ushered in another round of arrivals and introductions. Remaining always near to Timothy, Lottie listened to his conversation with others only as intently as her drifting gaze would permit, and joined in the dialogue but monosyllabically whenever Timothy tried to include her.

It was perhaps inevitable that the Christmas music playing over the stereo system was soon replaced by a sound more contemporary and popular—and completely independent of the holiday. The change was almost universally endorsed.

It was about six-thirty when Mike Saunders made a quiet and unheralded entrance. He was in the company of his friend Barry, who, having just begun his employment at the restaurant, seemed no more at ease than did Lottie with any of the assumed social demands of the function; and with his conspicuous stomach and swayed back, Barry looked natural in taking up his station next to the beer keg. From time to time, with his cup freshly topped, he would catch up with Mike, moving in his shadows as the latter mingled, chiefly amongst the kitchen staff.

And if the music was an important matter to those who had come, the mistletoe, on the other hand, apparently was not, much to the good-natured chagrin of Jerome, an amiable cook of forty-some years who had positioned himself strategically so that no female could go from the one room to the other without simultaneously passing both by himself and beneath the mystic plant. He never failed to point out the coincidence.

His behavior prompted from his female co-workers, mostly college students less than half his age, warm smiles and laughter, as they politely declined. He greeted each rejection with a show of surprise—and a chuckle, along with a declaration of the offending party's loss.

Though largely unsuccessful—one waitress did oblige him with a peck on the cheek—it was clear that Jerome's indiscriminate geniality made him a very well-liked figure amongst his fellow workers.

He appeared a favorite of Mike's, as well, which was simply another reason for Lottie to try her best to avoid him, his unseemly advances towards the other women being the first.

It was Mike, however, who frightened her most, though they had rarely ever crossed paths—and despite Timothy's positive reports of his progress. She knew too much of, and had personalized too deeply, his mistreatment of Kate. And anybody who could so terrorize such a sweet being as Kate—

It had been Lottie's hope, in her accepting of Timothy's invitation, that Mike would skip this event altogether, her belief finding its basis in Kate's firm supposition that Mike possessed none of the spirit of the season and would likely be repelled by its premises and pretensions.

Lottie regretted her dear friend's error. And though Mike had not acknowledged her since his arrival, she felt his frequent glance, which always turned her head in another direction.

There, presently, arose for Lottie a dilemma, with her beer having run dry and Timothy gone to the restroom facilities downstairs. For, to replenish her cup just then would mean to move alone past Jerome—and Mike—and beneath the mistletoe. The resulting apprehension over this predicament simply exacerbated Lottie's sense of thirst, soon convincing her that she would be unable to wait out Timothy's return. Thus, seizing the opportunity to fall in with two other women, Lottie hoped to pass by without notice.

"Make way, here comes Timothy's lady!" announced Jerome with a roar, causing Lottie to cringe under his sudden spotlight.

"I not Tim'thy's lady," she rebutted, blushing. "We jus' live in same house an' are frien's."

"Hey, d'y'all hear that!" bellowed Jerome, "She talks!"

Lottie's color deepened, and her grin came off poorly. "Sometimes," she tried to play along.

"Sometimes?" echoed Jerome skeptically. "Like when? Before now, I ain't heard a word from you all night."

"Like when I know people, I talk more," Lottie blurted out what she felt must surely be a universal axiom.

"Well, all right, then," nodded Jerome agreeably, and popping his cigarette into his mouth and transferring his drink to his left hand, he presented his right. "My name's Jerome. This here is Mike, the new fella there is Barry. He don't talk no more than you do—"

Lottie was shrinking from these latter introductions—

"I didn't think it'd be long before I found you setting up shop underneath the mistletoe."

Lottie was far too relieved by Timothy's return to blush anew over his smiling insinuation.

"I ain't touched her, Timothy," Jerome drew both hands back to underscore his innocence. "Though, as you can see, she don't seem to be movin' none from beneath that there mistletoe. An' I do want y'all to know, it's all I been able to do to keep these other cats from misbehavin'; but, unless she gets a move on, I can't promise I'm gonna be able to hold 'em back much longer."

Timothy and Jerome seemed the only ones fully enjoying the joke, though Barry added something of a grin.

Mike, on the other hand, seemed much bedeviled by her lingering presence, and was relieved when, momentarily, she continued with Timothy on up to the beer keg.

It came time, shortly, for the volunteer (and anonymous) exchange of gifts to be conducted between the participating members of the staff, with all the partiers gathering towards the Christmas tree to witness.

The slender and cheerful young woman who addressed their mostly undivided attention nominated Timothy as her helper, in as much as he stood nearest, and who, in turn, enlisted Lottie into his service, as a further means of drawing her out.

Timothy would receive the packages from Pam and distribute them himself to those within arm's reach. For the others, further to the back of the crammed gallery, he would hand their present over to Lottie and point her in the right direction. Always, there would ensue a pause in the proceedings for the gift to be revealed and, naturally, commented upon by the congregation.

Lottie was enjoying her role, with its increased, if quiet, interaction, though she became a little unsettled when

Jerome's name was called out.

She, nonetheless, bore his gift back to the perimeter amid the considerable hooting and hollering that, predictably, accompanied his moment.

"Don't' y'all go bein' nice to me now," he chortled in reference to their manifest desire to share in his present, which, plainly, was some sort of bottle, appropriately wrapped in the same brown paper bag in which it had been purchased.

"Blackberry brandy!" He let out a disbelieving howl, for he could recall but rarely having ever drunk the stuff. "All right, now," he addressed his amused audience, "I know we ain't 'posed to be tellin' who got what for who, but we gonna make an exception right here. Was this you?" to Mike, who stood with a wry grin nearby.

Mike denied the charge, however. "Hell, I woulda gotten ya something that I like, too—like bourbon," which incited Jerome to issue a public damnation of Mike for not having drawn his name.

Jerome then let it be known that his protest of the brandy was only in jest, and he proceeded to thank the anonymous donor and vowed that not only would he drink it, but that he would enjoy it, as well. He was already making good on his promise by the time the next name was called.

Lottie was relieved to have survived the delivery of Jerome's gift unharassed, but, with an explicit glance to Timothy, she subtley refused to collaborate when, near the end of the exchange, Mike's name was called—and, with it, Barry's.

Both men were visibly confounded as they blankly observed Timothy's approach, for not only hadn't they entered into this event, but the drawing of the names had taken place before Barry had even begun his job.

They were uncomfortable under the consequent attention and opened their packages tentatively, as though anticipating someone to step forward proclaiming that a mistake had been made and that these gifts were actually meant for others. But they were not interfered with, and whomever their sole benefactor was, he or she appeared to have exceeded the designated spending allowance; and there was produced an admiring gasp from the others when the two men displayed their identical pair of sturdy winter gloves.

The articles were certainly much needed—and appreciated, but neither of them knew what to say—nor to whom, as Pam announced that all the gifts had been given; whereupon, the party slowly fanned back across the restaurant.

Mike came first to suspect Timothy, which caused him an anxious pang, and then, perhaps, Jerome; but was convincingly refuted on both fronts.

The proper answer occured to Mike only when his gaze fell back towards the Christmas tree, to where Pam was picking up after some of the recipients.

He felt obligated to approach, though, as a rule, discomposed around even such a kindly figure of authority; and inarticulately presuming that the gifts were her doing, he extended a very disjointed expression of thanks.

She appreciated his sign of gratitude all the more for its humble, and sincere, presentation, and assured him that he need not worry, when he disclosed unease at having received while not having given.

"It wasn't expected of you," she explained, "since you and Barry had just started work here. But it did not seem right to me that the two of you should be excluded because of that, either. And I thought that you might find them useful with winter already here."

"I'll tell ya what I'd find useful," Jerome butt in, just then, his cigarette being waved about with inebriated flare. "My man Irvin there done brought hisself some gin, but ain't no one brought any tonic water. And ain't none a the ladies gonna partake unless we get some tonic water to go with it. An' we don't wanna disappoint the ladies, now, do we?"

Pam sighed and could not help but release something of a smile at Jerome's routine. She agreed to fund the mission and asked Jerome if he'd like to run the errand himself.

Jerome balked, however, pleading a drunken inability to negogiate the moving traffic that separated them from the store on the corner opposite, and suggested that it might be wise to substitute for him.

"Besides," he added, "I wouldn't feel right about leavin' the ladies alone with Irvin—a young buck like that don't know how to behave hisself properly."

Pam simply shook her head, before turning to Mike and asking whether he and Barry, who had come by, would be willing to assist Jerome in his bidding.

The two dishwashers agreed to the opportunity to break in their new gloves and Pam handed them a twenty dollar bill with the instructions to add to the grocery list the replenishing of any snacks that they saw fit.

It was not long after their return that the gin, never cut by any more than a dribble of tonic, began showing signs of its influence. Female giggling could be heard to grow louder—and more lasting, prompting the young cook Irvin, who fancied himself dashing, to openly join Jerome in his lascivious pursuits underneath the mistletoe; with their greatest success coming in drawing laughter for their efforts, which, nonetheless, were readily buoyed by that occasional triumph.

Mike had resumed his place on the periphery and gladly took to quietly needling the two men for their general futility. They returned, with false offense, a challenge for him to prove himself any more irresistable. Mike replied that a strong sense of reality prevented him from even trying; for which the other two razzed him, before returning their full attention to the ladies.

Mike noticed Timothy standing alone nearby, leaning against a table and sipping at his beer as, with a smile, he watched his two fellow cooks presiding over their court.

Mike started, after several hesitations, in his direction.

Timothy greeted the unexpected company with a look of mild surprise.

"Ain't too bad a party, huh?" offered Mike, his gaze diverted back towards the others.

Timothy thought it a success, and said he was pleased that Mike was enjoying it, too.

Mike insipidly confirmed that he was, despite what Timothy observed as a restless manner. Timothy's eye was then drawn to Mike's hand, that seemed to be searching around for something in his coat pocket.

Momentarily, Mike withdrew an envelope, with some of its corners bent, and pushed it into Timothy's hand as though hoping not to attract any outside attention to his action.

Timothy received the Christmas card with a curious look.

"Listen, this kinda thing ain't easy for me," Mike's voice bore the evidence, as he preempted Timothy's making any sort of issue out of it. "I guess it's jus'—my way of sayin' thanks, ya know? I still don't completely understand why ya even gave a damn about me —I know I wouldna if I was you—but, it turns out I'm glad ya did.

"You're the only one here I got a card for—though, now, I'm feelin' kinda bad that I didn't get one for Pam, too," he alluded, with a pat, to the new gloves in his pocket. "But I guess I still got a couple a weeks till Christmas. So, anyway—."

And not able to focus on, nor, perhaps, much interested in hearing, Timothy's own expression of thanks, Mike immediately excused himself to the restroom. Burning with an acute sense of self-consciousness over what, for him, had been an outpouring of sentimentality, he sped through the kitchen towards the basement, insensible even to Jerome's call for him to come join in the gin. He was bounding down those back stairs without a single regret for his deed, however, when he ran straight into Lottie at the bottom.

It gave her such a horrific start that she was unable even to retreat.

The small shriek that came to her throat terrified Mike, for what would anyone think—

They both peered, with their desperate and disparate hopes, to the top of the steps, and whereas Mike found faint relief, Lottie seemed drawn into a silent panic.

Perhaps some sort of greeting—which came out garbled— might work to settle her; though not nearly so much as his incidental yielding of access to the stairways, towards which

Lottie slid along the wall.

He startled her from this escape by abruptly asking how Kate was doing.

"She doin' fine," came Lottie's curt reply, as she delayed with a sidelong glare from part way up the stairs.

There was no mistaking, by Mike, of the deep-seated ill-feeling that Lottie held towards him, and it weakened his own glance.

His only appeal, before watching her go, was that if Lottie were to see Kate later in the evening that she might pass along Mike's regards—

The peculiar submissiveness of the request would've given Lottie special pleasure in refusing outright, except that, "I ain't gonna see her tonight. She stayin' at shelter," and wanting nothing more to do with this animal, Lottie made a dash up the stairs without looking back.

When he reached the top of the stairs himself, Mike paused and pondered his presumed return to the party that now reentered his consciousness from the left; before dismissing its claim upon him and making a sudden and unannounced departure from the building through the back door to his right.

It was a calm and starlit winter's night whose notice was subdued by the contemplations that carried him on his way.

He did not return to a concrete recognition of his physical surroundings until the silhouette of a church loomed silently before him. And though he had been often by its old stone walls, and had remained in contact with several of its transient lodgers, since his expulsion those few weeks before, he experienced a sharp sense of unwelcome standing in its shadows now.

But it was not the response that his planned breaching of the ban might provoke amongst the volunteer workers that caused his resolve in carrying out his objective to begin to waver. They were only a secondary concern.

He still had available to him the option, as he loitered upon that street corner, of returning to the Christmas party, though to the myriad questions his extended absence would surely raise. Or, he could simply turn his steps toward the city shelter, under the future guise of having suddenly taken ill at the holiday gathering.

This latter alternative was proving quite tempting. His eyes already wandered along in that direction. Yet, if ever he meant to act upon his present purpose, and he was convinced that he did, why not now that he was so near?

It was with more anxiety than had ever accompanied his illicit lifting of a liquor bottle from a store shelf that his infirm legs tottered forward, round to the side of the church. He came upon that door through which he had so often admitted himself to the shelter and he dared not hesitate, for the sake of his mission.

His determined entrance was made against a shortness of breath. Inside the foyer, his weltering glance skipped across a couple of familiar faces, with whom he exchanged hazy nods.

He did not linger—or speak—and tried to convey a straightaway motive. He crossed over to the doors of the large conference room that served as the facility's sleeping quarters. He entered quietly, disdaining notice.

She sat upright on a cot, her back against the wall, indulged in a magazine; and only looked up when a shadow settled into place between she and her reading light on the ceiling. Kate nearly screamed.

Mike's beleaguered expression begged that she remain composed. And she did so, though mainly by virtue of her momentary recognition of their being in a well-lighted room along with several other people. She swung her legs round to the floor on the side of the cot opposite him.

Having undertaken this entire enterprise very much on edge, Mike bumbled now to explain his visit. He was further suffocated by the delusion that all eyes had come round to examine his behavior—and his past; when, in fact, he was being paid little heed at all. He managed to ask Kate whether he could speak with her in private.

Having collected herself, Kate offered the foyer as a semi-private compromise.

No more able to mobilize his tongue coherently in the lobby than he had been inside the sleeping quarters, Mike finally plunged a hand fitfully into his coat pocket, which prompted Kate's eyes to flash round for the nearest help—

"I was gonna give this to Timothy tonight an' have him give it to you for me," Mike's downcast eyes hadn't picked up her alarm, nor her present curiosity, as he withdrew from that pocket an envelope, which he held towards her. "But, then, when I learned you was stayin' here tonight, I figured— I could prob'bly get over here before close—an' give it to you myself, like I should. Even though I know I ain't supposed to be here."

It was a Christmas card, of course, which Kate, quite dumbfounded, received hesitantly into her hand. The only word inscribed inside by Mike was his signature.

Kate didn't know what to say to this improbable act, other than, of course, to thank him by rote.

As with his delivery to Timothy, Mike seemed embarrassed by his gesture—and the moment, and threw his shoulders into an awkward shrug.

"I guess I just figured—it was the least I owed ya," he could hardly bring himself to look her in the eye, "for rilin' ya up the other night—when I shoulda jus' kept my mouth shut about your own personal bus'ness—an' for some a the other things I put ya through these last few months—" tailing off into a disconsolate sigh. "An' I jus' want ya to know, I don't blame ya for nothin' ya did in regards to me. Hell, ya probably shoulda tol' me to shove off a long time before ya did. Ya had every right to."

Kate's subtle expression revealed a similiar opinion that, just as well, went unperceived.

"An' I guess I wouldn't blame ya, neither," Mike's voice quivered up an octave, before releasing into a deep breath, "if ya don't feel like forgivin' me for some of them things I did—an' said. Hell, I don't know if I would if I was you. I don't know why I said some of that stuff I did. An' if I thought I meant it then, I know I didn't mean it now. I was just angry—an' stupid. Takin' out on you things that weren't your fault.

"But, ya know, despite all that—an' despite the fact that we ain't together no more—it jus' don't make sense to me that we should be complete enemies—"

"We're not enemies, Mike," she gently emphasized, though," There might've been a time when I thought different. I was mad at you for the way you started treating me, but I was also mad at myself for not doing anything about it. I felt as though I couldn't change your behavior and attitude, but I knew that I needed to change mine.

"And I think—and I hope—that what I did was really in the best interest of both of us. We just weren't going anywhere before," she had concluded. "And I don't necessarily know where each of us is going now," she remarked with a small grin, "but given where we've been, it's got to be up."

Mike concurred, though more sober in manner, that they probably had hit bottom together; and he expressed a similar, if ambiguous, optimism regarding the future, a main tenet of which, he hoped, would be that, "somehow, we can at least get along with each other."

As unlikely as the notion would've seemed but twenty minutes earlier, Kate was moved, not only by the sentiment, but, also, by the fact that Mike had summoned up the courage—and the humility—to propose it.

"I think I'd like that," she replied; and, as it had come time for the shelter to close its doors—and for Mike to go, she thanked him again for the card and wished for him a Merry Christmas and an even happier New Year.

Chapter Seventeen

It was only a few days later that the two women, Lottie and Kate, were to have their own workplace Christmas party (with the patients naturally included) and there was never much question in their minds that their contribution to the affair would be cookies. It was what they felt they did best.

Thus it was that on the night before the party, they set out for the McWheeten kitchen on their project. Once everything had been transported into place, Lottie volunteered to mix the first bowl of batter, so that Kate could engage in some preliminary browsing of the classified ads to get a feel for what was available around town in terms of lodging.

Kate was not bent long over her paper on the table before commenting on the disconcerting trend towards "everything being so expensive," and she plaintively declared that, "I'm probably going have to wait till after the first of the year before I have enough money saved up to start looking at even the cheapest places around."

"I help you look," Lottie announced with a decided nod. "But it gotta be someplace close to here," a stipulation that caused Kate to smile; and not wishing for her spirits to be depressed again, Kate folded up the newspaper and removed it from the table, thereby clearing a space for Lottie to set down the bowl.

Kate was rising from her chair to assist her friend in pouring the dough onto a cookie sheet, to be then molded into various yuletide symbols, when Lottie, with a yelp, suddenly let the bowl drop from her hands to the table, which sent some of the dough splashing up and over the sides of the plastic container.

"What's wrong?" Kate came quickly to her friend's side.

"I seen one a them bugs in there," a shrill reference to the bowl.

"One of what bugs?" as they both closed back in over the bowl, with Kate taking up a spatula to sift through the mixture.

"There!" Lottie spotted the object dragging along in the undercurrent of Kate's stroke. "Did you see it?"

Kate had, though it was now disappeared again. "It looked like a cockroach," she noted uneasily.

"It look like cockroach," Lottie surely agreed, "but Mrs. M'Wheeten say they not cockroach, they only ''merican water bug, 'cause we live close to river."

Kate had never heard of such a thing, though she was certainly in no position to refute it.

"She say they ain't nothin' to worry 'bout," reported Lottie, her eyes still watchful over the bowl, "even though we got lotsa them."

Kate momentarily dredged up the offending insect with the spatula and carefully lifted it out of the muck for closer inspection. "It sure looks like a cockroach," was all she would say, with a shrug. Then dumping all of the contents into the trash can, they rinsed out the bowl thoroughly, before starting over, much more keenly vigilant, this time, of the motives and movements of the American water bugs with which they were sharing the kitchen.

Despite this delay, it was not too terribly long before there could be seen emerging from the oven angels and snowmen, Christmas trees and Santa Clauses, all then dutifully sprinkled with red or green sugar. Lottie and Kate could not decide which ones they thought tasted best, and had it not been for a visit into the kitchen by Mrs. McWheeten, who came to refill the dog's water dish, they may have scarfed down the entire stock before rendering their verdict.

"Why, Kate, it's a pleasure to see you—as always," said the landlady in cordial greeting. "It's almost as though you live here after all, isn't it? And what do we have here—why, I'd venture to say Christmas cookies. How nice."

Lottie nodded, with the crumbs accrued at the corners of

her mouth. "For our Christmas party at work tomorrow."

The landlady commended them on their thoughtfulness and their labor, but, "take care not to eat them all yourselves. Why, you certainly wouldn't want Santa coming down your chimney with an empty bag, now, would you?" she supplied her moral with a little laugh, before moving on to the sink.

Lottie felt a bit ashamed over this appearance and promptly placed the lid back on the cookie tin; before recalling her manners and removing it again to offer a sample to Mrs. McWheeten (and her husband), with the landlady graciously accepting, while snapping up an extra one in the name of Sunshine, as well.

The two young women were returning to Lottie's room, shortly thereafter, when they encountered Hilgen entering the house.

"Well, well, good evening, ladies," he met them with a smile, and a bow, as he closed the front door quickly against the cold.

"You home kinda early tonight," noted Lottie with a sparkle fast in her eye. "How come you ain't out with girls?"

"Because, young lady," responded Hilgen with affected propriety, "I was out with girls all day today. A couple of very young—and very dear—ones, in fact. I'm just getting back from a visit with my daughters in Detroit. And am quite exhausted, though pleasantly so."

"Well, you mus' be hungry, then," reasoned Lottie with peculiar logic. "Would you like to join us in my room for Christmas cookie? We jus' bake them for Christmas party at work tomorrow."

Hilgen observed that the cookies looked quite scrumptious, and that he could hardly refuse. "Lead the way, temptress," and following after the women, Hilgen remarked how much tidier Lottie's room was than when he had last seen it; to which Lottie rightfully cited Kate's influence, as she handed out cookies to her seated company.

"We better not eat too many more," Kate gently reminded Lottie, just as the latter was asking Hilgen about his daughters.

"They're doing quite well, Lottie," he answered her inquiry

with a nod, as he took a bite from his cookie. "I thank you for asking. It was wonderful to see them again," with a swallow and, then, a sigh. "It'd been nearly two weeks—and I don't like going so long between visits. I try to get over there at least a couple of times a week, but, sometimes, my schedule just doesn't permit it.

"I must admit that I am quite fortunate," he acknowledged, "that the former missus is very good and obliging about visitation; for a fear far greater than that of death, to me, is to be separated from my two little girls and have them growing up not knowing me—nor me, them—and perhaps even coming to know someone else as their 'father'.

"And I do truly believe that whatever shortcomings that the ex felt I might've had as a husband, she realizes I make up for in terms of being a father. I'm a damn good father. And though I moved here to find employment, they're still less than half an hour away—especially given the way I drive when going out to see them," and, finally, there returned to Hilgen's face that broad, familiar smile.

Kate was moved by Hilgen's testimony, and she asked him the ages of his daughters.

"Orion is three-and-a-half and Vega just turned two. Plenty old enough, I think," with a burgeoning smile, "to be placed atop a pair of ice skates, which is where I took them today. A sight to behold, truly. And it's left me no doubt whatsoever that they shall be ready, if not for the next Olympics, then certainly for the one after. It's merely a matter of founding a competition tailored to their particular skills; which is to say that style points must be omitted," Hilgen's fond, paternal chuckle pleasing Kate to witness.

"How's your ex-wife able to take care of them?" she wondered.

"It would probably be very difficult indeed," Hilgen soberly conceded, "were she not from such a tightly-knit and well-off family. We're very fortunate to have that support system for the children. They're very good people, her family. And I feel doubly fortunate to still be on good terms with such a group and to be welcome in the home of those whose company I so enjoy. In fact, today the old man and I made plans to do a little fishing together next summer at his cabin up north."

Kate's expression had turned dismal with an envy she could not suppress, and she murmured absently, "I wish I had the same kind of support system available to me," a comment that had Hilgen begging her pardon.

Kate hadn't meant to be heard, and felt very awkward to discover that she had been. She apologized for her ambiguity, and, following an initial hesitation, she then quietly confided to Hilgen the matter of her own pregnancy, which he absorbed in rapt empathy.

"And I just don't know how I'm going to do it," she bluntly assessed her prospects at single parenting. "I don't have any family to fall back on, not even a poor one. And the father of the child wants no part of it—and just as soon I abort it; which I wasn't even considering before, but now, the more I think about it the more I wonder if, maybe, that wouldn't be the best thing, after all—"

It was the first time that Kate had publicly revealed a doubt or declared a reservation about carrying the pregnancy to term. And these unexpected intimations were especially alarming to Lottie, who had been looking so forward to being an 'aunt'.

"You ain't gonna have baby?"

Kate cast her glance tenderly round to her friend, and she confessed that, "I'm beginning to wonder whether I should. At first, I was pretty determined—but, now, I think a lot of that was just because I was scared of being alone. But, really, I'm not alone anymore. I've got you as a friend, and we go out and do so many things together and have so much fun. And there's Timothy—and you," to Hilgen. "And the people at work.

"I would love to have a baby—some day. I just don't know if now is the best time for it. I mean, what kind of life is that baby going to have, being so poor—and who's going to look after it—"

"I help!" Lottie desperately volunteered.

Kate was touched by the fervor of her friend's offer, but reminded Lottie that, "You work the same hours that I do. And I know I'm not going to be able to afford baby-sitters or child care—or anything like that. Besides, I don't like, either, the idea of my child growing up thinking of someone other than me as its mother."

"Kate, as far as the baby's being born poor," Hilgen addressed her in a caring and confidential tone, "as long as you are able to give him or her your full love you will provide it with all it'll ever need. And as a daily presence in its life, the child will never mistake who it's mother is, for no baby-sitter nor child care worker can give it a mother's special love.

"I'm not trying to persuade you in one direction or the other, for this is far too important a decision to be swayed by any outside influence. But, Kate, I think you should be aware that there are social services established for people in your predicament, and before you make your decision I believe that you owe it to yourself to thoroughly investigate all your options.

"Children are certainly a delight—if you want them, and are ready to introduce them, with their endless demands and constraints, into your life. And whether you decide that that time is now or better left for somewhere down the road, I can guarantee you that when the time does come it'll be accompanied by a certain self-doubt about whether you truly are ready. That question is always present when you assume responsibility. And there is no greater responsibility than that of being a parent; and no greater reward than in being a good one.

"But you are still quite young, Kate—though very mature for your years. You have plenty of time in which to start a family and presumably under conditions you'd find more favorable for the child's upbringing. When I gush so over the joys of parenthood, it is as someone who waited until he was close to thirty before welcoming, with a great deal of apprehension, that experience. And who did so while involved in what he believed to be a long-term relationship.

"You are pressed by more difficult circumstances, though with the wisdom, I am very confident, to choose and travel the route presently best for you."

Kate did appreciate, deeply, Hilgen's kind words and encouragement—and was silently returned to her contemplation, when Lottie abruptly announced, "I wanna have babies!"

"Well, now, Lottie," Hilgen responded, momentarily, with delicate surprise, "—I'm sure that someday you shall; though the question for you obviously will not center around going through with the birth, but will pertain, rather, to which of the town's many eligible young bachelors you shall choose to privilege. Or, perhaps, you'd desire to bear a child from each?"

"No! not that many," Lottie blushed over such industry, as well as the probable stain upon her reputation. "Jus' some a them!" she ammended with a giggle.

Hilgen could not help but chuckle at her moderated designs. "Well, then," he said, "I'd better send up a smoke signal and warn my unencumbered brethren that Lottie's on the prowl—and to run for cover."

Lottie's outburst of giggling betrayed her exaggerated exception to the barb, in which she took up a pillow from the couch and dealt Hilgen a series of blows, most of which he managed to fend off while ever maintaining his humor.

And only as it neared time for bed did Lottie come to recognize that, over the course of the evening, their stock of cookies had been depleted by nearly one-half. Thus, with Hilgen excusing himself to his room, the two women were compelled, by guilt, to return to the kitchen, where they were busy replenishing their tins until the hour of midnight.

Chapter Eighteen

Jim held the telephone receiver limply in hand after the party on the other end of the line had already hung up. He set it blindly back down upon its mount, with some initial inaccuracy, and sitting in a heavy silence stared ahead at nothing before him.

It was a chore, of which he appeared barely capable, to lift himself from his chair, and his posture bent under his low spirits as he dragged himself out into the hallway. The dark little corridor felt even drearier on this night—and how desolate and undisturbed the structure, except for the creaks that he provided. He ambled listlessly through its halls, with an eye towards any sign of life that might help alleviate his sudden burden of loneliness.

He lingered several minutes up in the kitchen in the hope that, perhaps, someone would pass through. But not even the McWheetens emerged to supply him company. Jim was quite alone in the house. And on Christmas Eve.

Returning to his room, he burrowed back beneath the blankets that he kept in a perennial heap upon his chair, and began to read. It was a struggle of concentration at first, but, incrementally, Jim was able to move from his solitary world into that of the novel, and had become so engrossed that he likely would've missed them altogether, had the footsteps which entered the house proceeded on upstairs rather than down his hallway.

Jim lowered the book into his lap as they passed by his door, and he listened with suspended breath as they came to a halt just beyond.

The book was readily abandoned, and Jim arrived at his door before Timothy was fully through his.

"I thought I heard you," there was loud relief in Jim's

voice.

And clear surprise in Timothy's eye. "I thought you were going home for Christmas?"

That had been his plan, Jim answered with a sigh, and he went on to tell Timothy of the telephone call from home advising him of the heavy snowfall battering the west side of the state, in particular the Lake Michigan shoreline that Jim called home.

"The roads are pretty much closed down," he reported, adding with an important emphasis, "Even the highways." Jim's hope was that the situation would be better by morning.

Timothy was sorry to hear of his friend's unfortunate news, and he asked Jim into his room, where he offered him a glass of red wine.

"I really liked that wine we had with dinner after the Ohio State game," Timothy remarked with a smile, "so I went out and bought a few bottles of it for the holidays," the first of which he was now opening.

And though the wine tasted every bit as good to them on this evening, their mood could not help but be markedly less convivial than on that previous occasion.

It was midway through his first glass before Jim quietly acknowledged that, "I suppose I should stop feeling so sorry for myself for being stuck here and be a little more thankful that my mother got a hold of me before I left Ann Arbor. I was nearly out the door. Can you imagine driving into a blizzard? At night? In my car?" and he shook his head in grave consideration.

Timothy, too, reflected somberly on the closeness of the call.

Led by Jim, the men then proclaimed their resolve to exhibit more cheerful frames of mind, an evolution they found facilitated by the arrival home of Lottie and Kate.

"Where've you two been?" Timothy came sauntering up the hallway to greet them.

"We been at a dinner," said Lottie, gloating. "One a the ladies we work with had some a the people at work over."

Timothy asked them whether, for a nightcap, they'd care

to join he and Jim back in his room.

The women were glad to accept, expressing, first, surprise at Jim's still being in town and, secondly, sympathy over his misfortune.

And though he did not have a Christmas tree to match the ambience of Lottie's room, Timothy attempted to compensate by drawing forth a pair of candles, in their brass holders, as well as the radio from the back corner of his desk, on which, with little search, he was able to focus upon the sound of the season.

His efforts met with approval.

And while his friends were sincere in extending to Jim their hope that he would be able to make it home in the morning to spend the holiday with his family, if such were to prove not possible, "We gonna have Christmas feast here tomorrow, ain't we, Tim'thy?"

Timothy confirmed for Jim that they were planning to pick up a ham the next day, along with all the proper accompaniments, adding that, "Naturally, you're welcome to join Kate, Lottie and I—"

Kate politely interjected here, that she would not be able to make it, as planned, for, "I volunteered to help serve Christmas dinner at the Center tomorrow. So, I'm afraid I'm going to be there most of the day and probably couldn't get here until kind of late."

Timothy was impressed with Kate's impending good deed and commented that she could not be missing their own little dinner party for any better reason.

"I vol'teer las' year," Lottie pointed out.

Timothy smiled and commended her, as well.

"The very essence of the season," he profoundly maintained, with a gentle swirl of his wine glass. "Not simply the fleeting display of kindness towards others, but the desire and willingness to actually reach out and help those who are truly in need. And what impresses me most," he said to the women, "is that for the two of you it isn't just a seasonal transformation. You practice it every day at the Center, year round; whereas, for the majority of us, thoughts of the disadvantaged never occur until we see somebody ringing a bell on a street corner in the middle of December." Timothy reflected society's shame in the shaking of his head, and had some personal embarrassment added to his mood when, in noticing Jim's need of a refill, he was reminded that he had forgotten to pour for the ladies a first offering. He apologized for the oversight and quickly moved to correct it.

Kate, however, preempted his pouring her a glass, with the soft addendum, "It's probably not good for an unborn baby."

It was the first indication that Kate had given since her talk with Hilgen, those few days earlier, that she had come to a decison on this delicate matter, and she absorbed, uncomfortably, their quiet stares.

"I'm not sure I'm going end up keeping it," she clarified for them, before they could begin to question, "but since I really don't know exactly how I feel about all this right now— except for realizing that I just can't bring myself to abort it after having spent all this time thinking of it as a real person— I figured the best thing to do is to go ahead and have it, and, then, when the time comes, if I don't feel I'm up to it, I can always put it up for adoption," though she conceded, "I don't know how easy that'll be, once I've had a chance to hold it. But," in concluding with a deeply drawn breath, "if giving it away to someone else is what's best for the baby, then that's what I'll do."

Her friends offered their prompt support, and they praised her reasoning.

Timothy suggested that the baby was bound to be much loved in either circumstance.

"I hope you keep it," Lottie wasted little time in lobbying. "I think baby better off with you raisin' it, 'cause you it's mother an' you so nice to ev'rybody. An' I promise I will help you with baby. I serious," she pressed on, to the warm smiles of the others.

"I show you," Lottie was turned completely around on the hassock, now, and facing her friend. "You almos' got 'nough money saved up to rent a room a your own, right?"

Kate, a little confused at the line of questioning, replied that she thought she was near to that goal.

"Okay, then," Lottie said. "Well, why not move into my room with me instead? That way you already got 'nough money, 'cause it cos' you only half as much as rentin' whole room by yourself. An' the extra money you can save up for baby things. An', also, here you will have frien's who help you take care a baby, so you don't hafta do ev'rythin' yourself." Lottie was pleading with such passion that Timothy and Jim watched in silent awe, not objecting in the least that she was volunteering them for baby tending duties that they, themselves, may not have felt qualified to offer.

Kate was even more amazed, and overwhelmed, by the proposition; for what an ideal living situation it seemed to her. But did Lottie really want to incur the inconvenience of sharing her room?

"You already stay over here a lot anyway!" was it really necessay to remind Kate? "So, it won't be any dif'rent than now—'cept I will only hafta pay half rent, too!" Lottie delivered this sudden afterthought with elfish glee.

But were Kate to decide to keep the baby, "it's going to be awfully crowded in there with three of us—."

"Me 'n baby small! You the only big one. There plenty room for all of us," Lottie was adamant.

Kate smiled with affection upon her friend, and acknowledged, with guarded optimism, that, "If it's okay with Mrs. McWheeten, I think I'd really like that."

Timothy stated, as the two women twisted together in a clumsy embrace, that he saw no reason for the landlady to object.

Lottie and Kate, eagerly assuming Timothy's prognosis for the proposal's acceptance, already began making plans for the permanence of the move, rearranging the furniture, in their collaborating minds, to maximize their space, with Lottie keeping prominently in her view the contingency of a baby joining the equation in just a few months' time.

Lottie promised, as her most exacting concession, a faithful attempt at being more tidy than was her natural inclination.

The men found immediate humor in this dubious vow, and joked of the high probability of the newborn's turning up lost beneath the contents of Lottie's floor-length laundry hamper. And there was Lottie laughing right along with them.

"Then I give it bath—'long with my clothes," she shrugged. "But I promise not to put into dryer, 'cause then it will shrink an' be even harder to find on floor nex' time."

"She'll just hang it out on a clothesline instead," suggested Jim.

Kate was able to smile at Lottie's fictitious abuse of her unborn child, and quipped that it was compelling her towards adoption.

Lottie protested that leaning, and blamed it on the men. "Santa ain't gonna visit you two if you keep talkin' 'bout hangin' babies on clothesline!" to which Timothy countered that Santa no longer visited him anyway, speculating that that omission likely stemmed from the Christmas, sixteen years earlier, when he tried capturing Santa Claus by rigging his father's fishing net at the bottom of the chimney the night before, not with the intent, Timothy emphasized, of commandeering more than was his fair share, but simply to steal a glimpse of the preeminent celebrity in action (not the least consideration for which was the impression that it would make amongst the neighbor kids). Timothy recalled, with laughter, his mystification upon awakening that Christmas morning on the couch and discovering the living room filled with presents and, yet, not so much as a string of the net disturbed.

Lottie, on the other hand, at age four was far more interested in her take than in the mechanics surrounding it, and had to be removed by her aunt from Santa's lap before the recital of her extensive list was completed, lest the wriggling line of restive children—along with their parents— should perform the manuever less gently.

Such a threat of lynching was not at issue with three-year old Jim when he tempestuously refused his mother's encouragement to take part in the custom and enter into the line to see Santa; stubbornly demanding to be taken, instead, to visit the Easter Bunny. (Rather, he found himself taken home).

Timothy then asked Kate, after a silence, whether she had a Christmas story to share.

Kate reflected—sadly, it seemed—before remarking, with a smile, that though she had a few favorites from childhood, she preferred to place her focus on the present holiday and her good fortune at being surrounded by such friends. "Especially one who's done so much for me. First, in helping me get a job and, now, maybe, a nice place to live. I just don't know how I'm ever going to repay her."

Lottie promptly provided her own idea for fair compensation. "Let me be father to baby!" which brought the warmest laughter from her friends, and from Kate a promise that if, in the end, she did decide to keep the lady, Lottie would be the father.

*   *   *

The phone call came early the next morning and dashed Jim's tenuous hopes. There had been no letup in the snow to the west, nor, more importantly, was there any improvement in road conditions. He would be spending his Christmas Day at the McWheeten house.

Jim sat slumped in his chair, with the weak daylight of the gray morning straying in overtop the tall hedge outside his window. A light accumulation of snow seemed the entire extent of the easternmost remnant of the weather system that would keep him put.

It was not long, before the first stirring of his neighbors disturbed Jim's moping. It was Timothy next door getting ready for church.

Jim glumly apprised him of the situation, for which Timothy expressed his empathy, noting, however, that, "Western Michigan's loss is Lottie's and my gain. It'll be a pleasure to share Christmas supper with you."

Jim was grateful to have this alternative; and while

Timothy went off to church, and Lottie slept, he walked the quiet streets to the deserted and windswept marketplace nearby to purchase a morning paper from its box, and patiently bided his time back in his room until the Christmas Day operation should begin.

Jim offered his car, when that time finally came, for their trip to the store. The centerpiece of the meal was to be a ham that was certainly larger than three people could eat, but, as Timothy pointed out, it would provide each of them with lunch meat for days to come.

Timothy, being the most veteran culinary professional among them, was put in charge of the entree. Lottie went to work on the vegetables. Jim peeled potatoes. All contributed to the drinking of the red wine (the early afternoon hour notwithstanding) and either hummed or sang along with the Christmas music that played, at good volume, on Timothy's radio, transported to the kitchen for the occasion. Timothy had brought up his candles for the table, as well.

Jim was determined not to allow the disappointment of his plight to dampen his holiday, and was as merry as the Day in his teasing of Lottie, who seemed to be fumbling as many vegetables onto the floor as she was pitching into the pot.

Lottie giggled under his observation, and jokingly blamed it on having already consumed too much wine.

Timothy was not buying the excuse, however; rather, "I've heard, from reliable sources, that it's a standard practice of yours to make the people at the Center eat off the floor—"

"That not true! I put food right on plate!"

"And then the plate on the floor—"

"No! You guys—"

Their rollicking good spirits were bolstered, just then, with the surprise entrance of Reese into the kitchen.

"Are you here for the day?" Timothy hoped, as Jim instinctively filled a spare glass with wine.

How thoroughly delighted was Reese at this effusive reception, and how happy to be able to report that, yes, he was here for the day and, further, that he woud be pleased to join them in their Christmas celebration.

While slipping the ham into the oven, Timothy asked Reese why he hadn't gone home for the holidays.

"I had to work yesterday," came Reese's reply, as he leaned casually against the wall next to the table, his glass of wine in hand. "And I have to work again tomorrow."

"Well, I'm sorry to hear that," said Timothy, double-checking the temperature of the oven. "I know how much you must've wanted to get back to New York."

Reese shrugged, and said that it certainly would've been nice, but that, actually, he had volunteered to work those two shifts, "so that some of the other workers who are married and have children could spend that time together. Besides, I was able to get time off to go home over Thanksgiving, so I can't be too disappointed. My only concern was that I might be spending Christmas alone. I feel quite fortunate to have discovered you up here."

Timothy proposed a toast to their collective good fortune at being able to spend Christmas Day "amongst such good friends."

When there came a point where nothing on their menu required immediate attention, Timothy enthusiastically suggested a romp outdoors in the snow.

"No pickin' on me today!" Lottie demanded, as a conditon for joining them.

Timothy tried to persuade her that such behavior would be incongruous with Christmas Day.

Lottie remained skeptical. "Santa gonna be watchin' you for nex' year," she warned, as she trailed them out of the kitchen.

Lottie was hardly down in the yard before Timothy and Jim were reneging on their implied promise, and began pelting her with handfuls of snow. Reese jumped in to aid Lottie, who, between her giggles, howled about using her influence with Santa Claus to ensure for her two attackers a very sparse Christmas the following year.

The threat, however, brought her little relief from the barrage and, in the matter of but a very few minutes, Lottie was nearly cloaked over in snow.

"I gonna get you guys!" her giggling declarations being drowned out by the whoops and laughter of her vanquishers as they trudged back indoors and up the stairs.

Lottie required a change into dry clothing before rejoining them in the kitchen.

The red wine worked quickly to rekindle the warmth in their bones, assisted by the toasty oven around which they gathered.

Cheers went up when Timothy proclaimed the ham nearly ready. Jim and Reese turned to setting the table. Lottie reached for the vegetables atop the stove.

When, shortly, the ham was removed, Timothy slipped the dinner rolls into the oven to warm. Jim had grabbed the wine and was pouring a round—

"Why, hello there!" came the startling greeting from behind them. "And Merry Christmas to one and all."

It was Mrs. McWheeten, at the entrance to the kitchen.

"Why, what do we have here—a bit of a Christmas feast?" she was moved into the room in front of her husband, who peered around the door with the boxed dog in his arms.

The tenants, glancing among themselves in blank surprise, came presently round to inform her of their holiday plan.

"Well, how nice," sparkled Mrs. McWheeten. "My, look at the size of that ham—goodness. Come, come, Fab," she beckoned him in for a look. "Why, I think it's absolutely splendid that four of the more esteemed members of our household would come together and celebrate the spirit of goodwill—and sharing—that mark this joyous season.

"Oh—why, look here, red wine—and egg nog, too. Why, of course. My, this is such a production—I mean, compared to the modest little meal of leftovers that Mr. McWheeten and I have planned for ourselves; but this, my goodness—why, this is Christmas!"

It was an offer he recognized having been led to, yet it was with an affable smile that Timothy remarked, "Well, this ham's certainly big enough to accommodate two more."

"Why, Timothy, are you sure? I mean, we wouldn't be

imposing?"

"Not at all."

Whereby, Mrs. McWheeten promptly accepted.

Jim went with Mr. McWheeten to round up another table and a couple more chairs, while Reese serviced two wine glasses for the newcomers.

And for the McWheetens, their arrival could not have been more fortuitously timed, for no sooner was the additional furniture arranged than the dinner was lain, in full, before them.

Mrs. McWheeten insisted they say grace, and nominated Timothy to lead them.

Timothy was glad to conduct that brief ceremony, and, when concluded, assumed the further honor of carving up the ham and divvying the slabs amongst the company. Round, too, went the rolls and potatoes, the peas and the carrots—and, not least significantly (nor rapidly), the wine.

"Why, thank you, Jim," said the landlady, as he took the liberty of topping off her mostly drained glass. "Oh—Jim, by the way, did you happen to see in the morning paper where Sorenson's department store is running an after-Christmas sale on woolen socks? Unless, of course, you've already remedied that situation—"

Jim deflected his subtle grin towards Timothy, and thanked Mrs. McWheeten for the information.

"My, my," the landlady glowed, "this is quite a tasty ham here, Timothy; though I suppose that I should not be at all surprised, should I, over the quality of the preparation, what with your being a professional cook and all. Please do pass the potatoes along, Fab—you're not renting them, you know."

"So, Lottie," Mrs. McWheeten bantered merrily on, as, taking the bowl from her husband, she shovelled a disproportionate lump of the potatoes onto her own plate, "where's your friend today, the young street person, oh, goodness, what was her name again—"

"Kate."

"Yes—Kate," nodded Mrs. McWheeten from the end of a celery stick. "As frequent a visitor as she's been to the house, I'm rather surprised to find that she's not taking Christmas dinner with us."

"She workin'," explained Lottie.

"Working?" echoed the landlady. "On Christmas Day? Why, how unfortu—"

"She vol'teer to help serve patients Christmas dinner at Han'cap Center."

"Why, the dear!" exclaimed Mrs. McWheeten, pausing with a piece of ham at the tip of her fork. "How very thoughtful—and Christian-like—of her. What a dear, considerate child."

"I vol'teer las' year."

"Why, it sounds as though our young friend Kate is doing quite well for herself," asserted Mrs. McWheeten. "How heartwarming to hear of the triumph of the human spirit over adversity—and on Christmas Day, no less! I've always maintained that, armed with nothing more than a little resolve, even those slumped at the bottom of the human ladder could evacuate themselves from the rancid bowels of that underworld and forge a respectable—and even honorable— path in life. And may I offer a toast in honor of my living proof!" and leading the others in tribute to Kate's accomplishment, Mrs. McWheeten moved boldly towards her third glass of wine.

"Kate has made remarkable strides," Timothy respectfully allowed, "but I don't think one could say that her triumph is complete, or even irreversible, as long as she is forced, by financial constraints, to continue residing at the shelter, which is hardly an ideal living environment for any human being."

"You shall receive no argument here on that point," snorted Mrs. McWheeten, contemptuously. "Jim, old boy, please do pass the salt."

"A place of ones own," Timothy deliberately resumed, "be it just a room in a nice house somewhere, is essential, I think we'd all agree, in helping to create for one a feeling of dignity and self-respect, as well as introducing into their lives a sense of stability—"

"Why, Timothy, now you're coming round, dear boy," lauded Mrs. McWheeten. "And if the good-for-nothings of our society would ever get out of Uncle Sam's wallet long enough to find a job and earn their own way they might be better able to afford such stability."

"And, as you know," her tenant methodically pursued, "Kate has taken that important first step of finding a job, and has begun saving up money in hopes of soon finding a place to live—"

"Why, I certainly cannot imagine a dear heart like Kate should have any trouble in securing quarters of her own. I'll gladly serve as a personal reference. I do know a few people in this business, mind you."

Timothy acknowledged the graciousness of the offer; however, "Some of us were thinking that—perhaps—Kate might be allowed—to move in with Lottie—"

"I beg your—move in—here?"

"It would be a much more affordable situation than Kate could ever hope to find on her own. And Lottie's room is fairly big."

"Hmph," went the landlady, bringing her knife and fork to a perpindicular rest atop the table, as the others anxiously observed her pensive pose. "Why, I must confess that such a double occupancy had never occurred to me. And, Lottie, you've no qualms over sharing your room?"

Lottie let loose with a vehement shake of her head. "It my idea!" she proclaimed. "I be happier with Kate livin' with me. An' she be happier, too. She like it here—a lot. She like all the people an' will be livin' in house with her frien's. That 'portant for person, too!"

"Well, she certainly is a charming and deserving young person," granted Mrs. McWheeten with a quiet nod. "And I do heartily concur that the benefit she would reap in residing under such a roof as this would likely assist her considerably in her progress.

"Well, then!" burst the landlady from her soliloquy. "I can conjure no argument against it. I do not know, right off hand, what sort of arrangements will have to be made for this accommodation of Kate. I do believe that we have an extra mattress in the downstairs storage," looking to her husband for confirmation. "And, naturally, we'll need to get another key made—and to get Kate's name on the lease, of course. The security deposit arrangement you can hash out between the two of you.

"Well, well," exulted the landlady, sitting erect in her chair and spreading her happy glance around the table, "this certainly does add to the cheer of the day, does it not?"

Her tenants, not a little surprised by the swiftness and zeal with which she had adopted their proposal, could not have agreed with her more; nor could they drink a sufficient number of toasts to their landlady's personal embodiment of the very spirit of the season.

Chapter Nineteen

As Lottie had suggested, when making her proposition to Kate, the latter's formal moving in did not represent such a significant change from the days when Kate was merely a frequent visitor to the house. The transition, in fact, was made all the more minimal by the McWheetens, whom, it seemed, had forgotten about the promised mattress, thereby landing Kate right back on the old familiar couch. Kate, however, whispered not a complaint to anyone, nor intimated a reminder to her new landlords, for she was simply—and truly—happy to be a paying tenant anywhere (though especially here).

Happy, too, were those in the house acquainted with her case, and none outwardly more so than Mrs. McWheeten herself, who could not refrain from broaching the subject with Timothy some few mornings after, when he entered the kitchen to prepare his breakfast, as she sat at the table doing paperwork over a cup of coffee. The dog, Sunshine, was tucked away in her box on the floor nearby.

"Kate's extremely grateful to you," Timothy wished to reiterate, for his landlady's consumption.

"Well, I should say so," replied Mrs. McWheeten with a pleasant little laugh, recalling, as she removed her reading glasses, the emotional embrace bestowed upon her by her newest tenant. "Why, it gave me quite a jolt, I must say. A delightful jolt, mind you."

Timothy smiled over his landlady's display of such sentimentality, and, having partially filled his pot with water, he placed it on the stove.

"Well, I know that it meant a great deal to her," as he added the oatmeal to the pot, "that you found her worthy of this opportunity. To be honest with you, she was somewhat concerned that her coming directly from the shelter may have inhibited many prospective landlords from leasing to her. For you to look beyond that and welcome her without reservation has done as much for her self-esteem and confidence as anything I can think of."

"Well, Timothy, I appreciate your kind words," the landlady dipped into a genteel nod. "And, as a Christian, I cannot tell you how grateful I am, in return, that the Good Lord chose to direct Kate here, to our closely-knit establishment, to spend the formative period of her rehabilitation. I think it quite evident that she has already prospered by it, and, I am confident, will continue to do so. And I believe that we, too, shall benefit equally from her inspirational story."

Timothy expressed his whole-hearted agreement.

"And as much as anything," resumed Mrs. McWheeten, deep in her thought, "I am impressed by her seemingly complete break with her previous lifestyle. I must confess," though without remorse, "that, when I agreed to become Kate's benefactor, there did arise within me, after some reflection, a slight apprehension that—perhaps—the house might experience—an unwelcome infestation of some of her—prior acquaintances, looking for a handout or simply a respectable place to come warm themselves at all hours of the day and night. I am much relieved to find this to have been an unfounded fear; for I think Kate well understands that to reacquaint herself with that class would be to severely undermine her evolution. She must not look back."

Timothy said nothing, other than to declare his oatmeal ready, and, bidding his landlady (and her dog) good-day, he returned to his room to eat.

*   *   *

It was, under the relative terms of January, a fairly pleasant late afternoon. At least there was no breeze to nip at them. From between the silhouetted two-story houses across the alley the soft orange glow of the receding sun reflected weakly in their eyes, as Jerome and Mike settled upon the edge of the loading dock for a post-shift cigarette.

"Don't care none for these damn slow days we always get after the holidays is over," Jerome bemoaned the vexing seasonal pattern. " Gimme more damn orders than I can handle in a week," exhaling his smoke into the winter air, as he tucked his pack of cigarettes back into the breast pocket of the flannel shirt he wore beneath his unzipped overcoat, "instead a payin' me to twiddle my thumbs for seven hours. Lord, I hate that."

Mike nodded, amid his own swirl of smoke, and with a cough, he agreed that time seemed to go by much faster with tasks to perform than when there existed nothing to do.

" 'course, Pam always finds somethin' for the dishwashers to do, even when the restaurant ain't busy," he added without resentment. "Ain't always a lotta fun at the time, but I guess, on the other hand, it beats standin' 'roun' doin' nothin'.."

Jerome let out a quiet chuckle and glancing aside to his companion, "Yeah, well, let's see how you feel 'bout two months from now—after scrubbin' them same damn walls day after day after day."

Mike simply shrugged off that future concern.

"Hell, only thing I got outa standin' roun' today," Jerome recalled, momentarily, with a sharp grin, "was a chance to go on with that little blonde waitress Pam jus' hired. Ooh—hoo—wee! Did y'all see that little bright-eyed college girl? Mmm-mm!"

Mike couldn't help but laugh at Jerome's lustful exhibition, and replied that, naturally, he had noticed her; and though agreeing with his friend's appraisal of her physical charms, he musingly summarized that, "She ain't my type. An' I'm sure I ain't hers."

"Shoot, prob'ly ain't neither one of us her type," suggested Jerome with a rueful laugh; before turning a cocked expression round. "So, brother, tell me, what is your type, if cute, young an' blonde ain't?"

"Hell, I ain't got nothin' 'gainst cute, young 'n blonde," Mike clarified, with a corroborating leer that fell blank upon the small cellophane bag that Jerome had just removed from an interior pocket of his coat.

"So, you're positive it's all right for us to be doin' that here?" Mike inquired, displaying a wariness as scanned the alley for witnesses.

"I told ya before, ya ain't got nothin' to worry about. Hell, I even smoked out here with the guy who owns the place; an' if that don't tell ya it's all right—" and having lighted and sampled the drug himself, Jerome passed it over to Mike. "So, tell me again, what is your type a woman?"

Mike choked on his first puff over his friend's supposition that he had a specific 'type'. "Hell, I don't know," with a toss of his shoulders and a regenerative thump at his chest. "I jus' know that that waitress ain't it, is all I'm sayin'."

Jerome found this response unsatisfactory and was set to razz Mike over it (as soon as he, Jerome, had completed his turn at their shared cigarette), when the back door of the restaurant opened up behind.

Pam was surprised that anyone should be idling outside on such a day, stating that she could not wait to get home, where it was warm.

"Aww, it ain't so cold out—hell," Jerome dismissed such concern as that solely of a woman. "Now, why don't y'all come sit down here 'n join us?"

The offer first brought to her attention their illegal activity, which threw Mike into a genuine fright; but, to his relief, Pam's initial response was merely to roll her eyes in resignation. She declined the invitation and pleaded with them to take proper precaution to ensure that they did not get caught.

"The police do occasionally patrol this alley, in case you were not aware."

"Now, don't y'all go worryin' your pretty little head off none, Pam, dear; we wouldn't think a doin' nothin' to get you into any trouble."

Pam took her solace in their relatively obscure location— as well as in the impending dusk, rather than in Jerome's light assurances; and with a lenient smile for his patronizing tone, she again urged that they, "Please make sure," before wishing them both good-night and descending the steps to her car.

"Now, that there is a nice lady," remarked Jerome, with a

respectful nod, as, with a wave, Pam turned her car out of the lot. "I like ol' Pam. She knows how to treat people good. I been aroun' a little bit an' believe me, you don't always find that in a boss. An' damn! if she ain't pretty, too," extolled with a poor chuckle and wistful shake of the head. "Now see, y'all, that's my kinda woman there."

Mike smiled, and agreed that, "She is awfully nice."

"Thing 'bout Pam, though," which Jerome found troubling, "she probably ain't the type to go for my foolin' 'round with others; which is a shame, 'cause I really think I could do that girl some good. But I ain't one who likes to be tied down. No matter how pretty a girl is. I enjoy samplin' the spices a life too much for that. So, if a woman don't mind bein' jus' one a the mix, she's welcome to jump into the bowl with me; but, then, if she comes back nex' time wantin' to clear out the whole damn rest a the cupboard, I ain't lettin' her back into the kitchen! Know what I'm sayin'?" and with his philosophy plainly laid out, Jerome finally relinquished the cigarette back to his companion.

Mike's smile was feint as he held the cigarette in neglect at his side. "Well, I don't know much 'bout all that," he conceded with a limp shrug. "What I do know is, the las' bit a samplin' I done is gonna make me a daddy—"

Jerome's surprise over this revelation made him temporarily oblivious to Mike's offering back to him the last of the joint. "You—a daddy? Why, who'd you—"

"My old girfriend," supplied with an anguished sigh and grimace.

Jerome hadn't known of Kate's existence, and was inquiring—

"No, you ain't never met her," remarked Mike, before dryly adding, "Least as far as I know."

Restraining a chuckle as best he could, Jerome maintained his innocence, before addressing the question of Mike's. "An' she's sure it's you, is she? How long ago—"

"It was me," Mike confessed to it, "though I wish like hell I could say it wasn't."

"When'd you find all this out?" and inhaling the remaining

life from the cigarette, Jerome flicked it to the pavement below.

"Couple months ago," said Mike. "Before I started here. It's one a the reasons we broke up. I wanted her to get an abortion. She didn't want to. An' there jus' wasn't no way I was ready to play daddy; so—"

"An', now, she comin' after you?" Jerome assumed, with a nod.

And to his friend's incredulity, Mike replied that she was not. "Says she don't want nothin' from me. No money—nothin'."

"You ain't believin' that, are ya?"

Mike shrugged and, glancing stoically back across the darkening alley, "Guess I couldn't blame her if she changed her mind on it. Hell, why shouldn't she? I'm partly responsible for this stupid mess. An' she can't be makin' the kinda money it takes to raise a kid. Hell, if I was her, I'd come after me. 'course, if I was her, I wouldn't be havin' the baby in the first place."

"Well, before you go 'n do somethin' foolish," instructed Jerome, "let me jus' say to you, if she don't wanna make this whole thing your problem, then let it be. You sure as hell don't want the government comin' after your paycheck every week like they come after mine. I finally got the sense to have the doctor make sure I was done leavin' my mark on this world. Five kids by three different women, from here to Detroit. Let me tell ya, that don't leave much of a paycheck left over for me. But if that's the price a freedom, I'll pay it, brother—believe me.

"Couple of 'em comin' of age soon, so I ain't gonna be payin' for them much longer; 'cept maybe through my taxes, if them boys don't straighten up. I hear they's gettin' themselves into trouble all the time over there in Dee-troit. Little stuff so far, but if they ain't careful—"

"Do you ever see them?"

Shaking his head, while reaching into the pocket of his flannel shirt for a conventional cigarette, Jerome replied, "Ain't seen either one a them boys in a long time. Ain't ever seen much a them, really, even when they was young. 'cause

I was young back then, too, an' didn't like it anymore than you do now that the mother let herself get pregnant. It took me two a those mistakes before I finally got myself a clue an' got the hell outa there.

"The government found me, a course, which is cool, 'cause I done my part in makin' them kids, jus' like you done. An' I wasn't gonna deny it, neither. An' as long as they didn't make it so I had to stick aroun' an' have anything to do with bein' a daddy, I was okay with jus' sendin' along some money. Hell, that was easy enough," and with a hollow laugh, "Especially when the government took over doin' that for me."

Mike remained quietly observant of his reflecting colleague, until, "Any a your kids still aroun' here?"

Jerome answered with an abstracted nod. "The third one I don't know about. I ain't heard from him or his mother in a long time. She never came after me. But the two youngest ones—twins, a little boy 'n girl—live over in Ypsilanti. I'm told they's really taken to school. An' I ain't gotta tell ya they didn't get that from me," Jerome's small laugh becoming a cough.

"Do you ever get to see them?"

Not really, said Jerome, keeping his eyes fixed straight ahead. "Once in a while, I'll run into them an' their mother on the street. But not that often. I thought at first, when they was babies, I might be old enough finally to handle bein' a daddy, but . . . I jus' wasn't never cut out for that. So, I kinda split on the mother. Then when she started takin' up with another man, I figured it was probably best that I stay outa the picture altogether—even though I still had a thing for her—an' let them kids grow up thinkin' of only one person as their daddy. So . . . I jus' let the government send 'em some a my money an' ain't nobody got any complaints.

"Cute little rascals, though," with his paternal pride showing through. "An' I sure do hope they turn out good. Better than them older ones. An' I think they will. They have a 'father' roun' them now an' I think that's good for 'em. An' it makes it easier on the mother, too. That's a whole lotta hard work, raisin' kids. Even for two people. An' like you, brother, it just ain't for me."

The two men then fell quiet, each in contemplation over a cigarette. Night was near and how tranquil the eve, save for the clattering from the dishroom that grew prominent in their silence.

The fatigue of a long day seemed finally to be setting in, and, with a breeze beginning to build momentum through the alley, perhaps it was time to go. As they moved toward this conclusion, the metal door behind was shoved open, this time by Barry, who had been unaware of their presence on the dock.

"We're jus' hangin' out," explained Mike as he rose to his feet. "But, now, it's time to get outa here."

Barry wondered, as he lighted a cigarette for himself, whether Mike, before he went, might take a look at the dish machine.

"It's startin' to make some loud noise, an' the dishes ain't comin' out so clean now."

Mike agreed to investigate and, having said good-bye to Jerome, preceded Barry back into the building. Mike turned the machine on and, upon hearing the awful grinding sound described by Barry, immediately shut it back down again. He then drained the dishwasher of its water and, donning a single rubber glove from a shelf overhead, he searched in and around the filter at the bottom of the machine for the broken glass he correctly suspected as the culprit. After some few moments of scavenging, Mike peered in with a flashlight and was satisfied that all the significant pieces of glass had been removed. Finally, having secured the filter back in place, Mike turned the machine on to ensure that the problem had been righted.

Moving, then, from the perennial steam of the dishroom, made doubly uncomfortable beneath a winter's wrap, back out onto the loading dock, Mike found the night air especially embracing. And leaving Barry behind, leaning against the building with arms folded together and a cigarette hanging from his mouth, Mike began his way up the alley toward the homeless shelter.

Chapter Twenty

It seemed improbable on a night such as this, with the establishment enjoying a business which overwhelmed its seating capacity, that the prime table over in the corner would be vacant. Yet, the glassware looked drained and the chairs were certainly empty. The foursome whom had just entered through the front door, not quite trusting their good fortune, set off slithering and twisting aggressively through those who idled near the bar and the many others who mingled between tables, lest any one of them should become aware of the opportunity behind them and stake a preemptive claim.

The large round table, with its wooden surface crafted into a relic by so many penknives over the years, not only comfortably accommodated their party, but provided them, as well, with an enriching view of the snug tavern and its unequivocating soul of curious clientele; where, on any given night, there might be seen, and heard, the perennially downtrodden swapping pithy insight into the irreversible decline in the benevolence of Man with the grim-faced university professor who owed his living to the study; while, just down the counter, the common laborer chatted it up with his new friend, the avant-garde artist, with nobody marking the difference and their bond firmly, if transiently, established at the bottom of a shot glass.

The brick walls all around traced the building's ancient lineage as a public watering hole, dating back more than a century, with obsolete maps of barely recognizable regions, framed posters and playbills from theatrical and musical productions no longer remembered and plenty of antiquated photographs of long dead fraternity brethren and now defunct sporting associations, as well as many other period portraits of unknown subjects—save for one near the front of the house that bore a much commented upon resemblance

Richard Steigelman

to Andrew Johnson, president of the Union at the time of the bars's inception.

From the beautiful, meticulously forged black tin ceiling a pair of wooden fans could do little to disperse the ubiquitous smoke of a prospering tavern. And, in contrast to the bustle and banter of such a scene, the snow fell peaceably outside the window next to them, shimmering against the streetlight above and salting the hair of whose who passed along the sidewalk just below.

Obscured behind a continuously refortifying, and shifting, wall of human revelers, the quartet may ordinarily have been pressed to attract the attention of the waiter, but for the fact that Jim was employed at the restaurant right next door, which operated under the same ownership. Their order for a pitcher of beer—and a glass of water for Kate—was, therefore, quickly tended to.

They inaugurated their own festivity, as was their custom, with a toast to friendship, and followed it up with an equally sincere salute to being in from the cold.

Before the toasting could become too accelerated, however, Jim mentioned that, like Kate—though Kate was not drinking at all—he, too, should monitor his alcoholic intake, in regards to both quantity and pace, for he needed to be up early the next morning. Timothy promptly proposed a toast to Jim's being finally able to go home to stage with his family the Christmas ceremony that the inclement weather of the previous week had forced him to miss.

Lottie made a quip that she and Timothy would likely end up having to drink all the beer; whereupon Timothy informed her that he had to work in the morning, and he slid the pitcher and also his glass—with Jim contributing his, as well—over in front of their giggling friend.

"I ain't drinkin' all!" she blurted out, before even drinking that which she had already in her mouth.

Thus, under a poor pretense of reluctance, Timothy and Jim agreed to assist Lottie and began by toasting the impressive portion of drink that she had dribbled on her chin, which caused her to laugh further and spit up even

192

more.

"Hey, Jim!" Lottie chirped as she finished mopping her face with the palm of her hand, "that junky car a yours gonna make it all the way home tomorrow?"

Jim raised a droll eyebrow upon her, which incited additional laughter, and asked her just what she thought deficient about his car.

"It got holes all over it—on both sides an' on bottom—an' on muffler, which only not fall off 'cause you got coat hanger down there keepin' it on! One door can't open an' the other one don't stay closed an' people almos' fall out onto street when you turn corner!" Lottie was panting by the conclusion of her spirited evaluation.

Jim replied that he hoped she had learned her lesson and suggested that, the next time she ride in his car, she wear the seatbelt.

"Them don't work, neither."

"Oh—"

"Nothin' on your car work, 'cept engine—sometimes—"

Which was all he needed, Jim cheerfully summarized, and he drank a solo toast to his singular vehicle.

They had not ordered another pitcher of beer, which accounted for their surprise and their effort to correct the waiter when he placed a full one before them.

He waved them down, however, and, with a wink, explained that, "This one's on Walt," (the owner), which prompted Jim's companions to express envy at his good standing in such a reputable place and to avow their own good fortune at knowing such a person.

And while such preferential treatment, as well as his friend's enviousness, naturally gave Jim considerable satisfaction, he reiterated, with mild dismay, the necessity of exercising constraint over his drinking, for a clear drive home in the morning.

They had nearly made it through that second—and final—pitcher, when Jim came up from his beer mug barking something about seeing Hilgen across the room. Timothy spotted him, also, and battling forth from his chair, he flagged down their housemate and the friend whom he was with, as they bumped along in an unsuccessful search for vacancies anywhere.

The friend, a square-jawed man of Hilgen's age with straight sandy hair and a day's growth pitched up around a sour expression, was introduced to the McWheetonites as Conrad. Having made their collective acquaintance with a single terse nod, Conrad, then, made himself known to the waiter across the way as, "Two more pitchers!" to which Hilgen imperatively added, "Shots of whiskey all around the table, please!"

"How come you ain't out with girls!" Lottie chortled, momentarily, under the effect of her beer.

Conrad snorted in quick disdain at the subject, and was unable to restrain himself from making a snide, and hardly subtle, comment regarding liberation, before turning his head away under the guise of taking in the crowd.

"A gentleman's night out, Lottie," Hilgen loudly proclaimed, in order to attract the focus away from his disconsolate friend. "Giving the ladies a much deserved break," he added with a chuckle, and, hoisting his glass of whiskey when it arrived—which spurred the others, excepting Kate, to do likewise, "To the ladies," a general tribute to which even Conrad tipped back his glass, with a grunt; before emptying Kate's, as well—with her permission.

"Now, Lottie," struck up Hilgen, in the afterglow of his liquor (while across the table Jim contorted feverishly amid the lingering vapors of his), "you seem to hold such an abiding interest in my romantic endeavors; so, how about your sharing with the rest of us the lurid details of some of your own carnal escapades?"

And though intended entirely in good fun, Hilgen's request had the uncalculated effect of making Lottie acutely self-conscious of the mental retardation that had hindered her compiling any such list.

"Too many to talk 'bout," she tried gamely to rebound, but her grin was false and transparent, and clearly disclosed to the others the pain of her predicament.

Hilgen was every bit as sorry for having brought up the topic, and, with a smile of compassion rising warmly from his remorse, he lifted his glass in her honor and pronounced that he had no doubts that, "such a personable young lady would attract her fair share of discriminating suitors," before adeptly changing the subject to Kate's recent move.

"So, tell us, Kate, what's it like living with this little devil here?" Hilgen was seeking to distract Lottie from her desponding introspection, and succeeded in pricking a mischeivous grin from his target. "Does she still lay her entire week's wardrobe out on the couch? The past week's, mind you."

"I don't no more!" Lottie took up her own defense, before sheepishly conceding, "I can't, 'cause that where Kate sleep."

"Only until Mr. and Mrs. McWheeten bring up the mattress they have stored down in the basement," Kate explained.

Hilgen apologized for his consequent burst of laughter, but, "I hope you've grown accustomed to that couch."

Kate smiled at his inference, and she shrugged. "Beats where I have been sleeping."

The waiter, in Jim's increasingly convoluted estimation, was jeopardizing his tip by presently poking his head back into their circle; thereby making it both convenient and irresistable for Conrad to order two more pitchers of beer, with Hilgen tacking on, over Jim and Timothy's slurred objection, another round of shots for all except Kate.

The instantaneous rush of cold air that braced his face and forehead as he stepped outdoors was a startling but very welcome boon to Jim's struggling sensibilities. He tugged dully at the zipper of his coat to promote the reinvigorating qualities of the night air, as he tottered, with casual help from the handrail, down the steps to the sidewalk.

The original foursome had left Hilgen and his friend Conrad with yet another two pitchers of beer, and did so without regret; for they suspected that the two men were bent on drinking till the knell of closing time, and better that it be without them.

And better that it had been without them much sooner, thought Jim to himself; and he was silently ruing the probability that his drive home in the morning would not start quite as early as planned, when one of the fuzzy trees planted alongside the street encroached upon his path and sent him stumbling across into Timothy.

Lottie howled uproariously over Jim's drunken misstep, until finding herself dashed across the bow of an oncoming group of pedestrians, whom, after some minor jostling, discharged her, giggling, into their wake a half-dozen steps or so behind her comrades.

The four regrouped at the opening to a service alley and were enjoying a general laugh at each other's expense, when interrupted, from up that corridor, by an alarming crash of metal that resounded through its narrow confines.

Drawn close together, they peered up the vaguely lighted way for the source of the ruckus, but saw nothing, until an upturned aluminum garbage can trickled down from next to a building.

An improperly placed can, they deduced with relief, and were set to hurry on their way, when Kate, with a diligent and sober gaze, remarked that she thought she saw a foot extending from the jumble of cans and crates that remained stacked against the building.

And there was a foot laying still in the midst of the pile, Timothy confirmed with a few small and trepid steps in that direction.

The possibilities, already unsettling, were made especially so by the figure's complete lack of response to Timothy's calls.

Timothy continued his advance, with the others in cautious tow behind. Nearing, he could hear the quiet moans of pain, compelling him to cast a keener glance about for any lurking accomplice in this man's misfortune.

"Are you all right?" Timothy asked, as he knelt over the figure lain amid the long shadows of the alley. With Jim's help, he assisted the short, disheveled man to his feet.

"Didn' even see 'im comin'," remarked the drowsy figure, his voice swayed more by astonishment than rancor.

"Mac?" Timothy had turned him round to the faint light of a high and distant street lamp.

This identification seemed only to startle and further confound the victim, and his glazed eyes strove unsuccessfully to reciprocate.

"Mac, what happened?" and in lieu of anything better being presently available, Timothy removed his scarf and began to wipe at the blood that was revealed on the homeless man's temple and cheek.

"Some guy jumped me outa nowhere," Mac related, with a surge of vim, though his initial steps, as they began a return to the sidewalk, were dependent upon their continued assistance. "I was jus' mindin' my own bus'ness, lookin' for bottles, ya know. Sometimes, these rest'raunts 'roun' here put whole containers of 'em outside to be picked up for recyclin' an' then I come by 'n take 'em. There wasn't none tonight, which was okay, 'cause my bag was mostly full anyway. But, then, someone grabbed my bag from behin'," and here, Mac let out a sharp yelp, as Timothy had dabbed too hard, for the second time, at the stained temple.

Timothy apologized, again, and turned the scarf over to the careful hand of the injured.

"He spun me roun' an' I didn't really get a good look at 'im, 'cause it happened so fast an' it was dark—an' I was a little bit drunk too, maybe—an' he was pullin' at my bag tryin' to get it away from me an' I was tryin' to hold on, when all of a sudden—blam! he hits me in the face with his fist an' knocks me off balance. Then he takes my face 'n shoves it into the side a that buildin'! Pretty much knocked me out, 'cept I heard my bag fall to the groun' an' some a the bottles break. An' I heard 'im pick up the bag an' take off, too. Then I think I passed out. I ain't got no idea how long I been layin' there."

Long enough for the blood to have hardened to the point of being difficult to remove with a dry scarf. They dipped it in snow.

With the gradual gathering of his faculties combining with the increased illumination of the lamppost under which he was now being examined, Mac was able, finally, to focus in and identify his rescuer as Timothy. It gave him quite a start.

"Jesus Christ, it's you—"

Timothy suggested they get Mac's wounds cleansed and bandaged, and he asked whether Mac were still staying over at Saint Augustine's.

There was a wary reluctance, now, in Mac's manner, and he responded with but a slight and tight-lipped nod for his interrogator.

Timothy checked his watch and, as he had suspected, it was too late in the evening to be admitted into either of the downtown shelters.   "Why don't you come home with us—?"

"Un-uh!" Mac recoiled at the mere thought, and seemed quite ready to bolt if they dared move to apprehend him. "Ain't no way I'm gonna go back to that house."

The episode that so riled Mac had slipped Timothy's mind, and he recalled it now with chagrin. He apologized to Mac for what ocurred that night.

"That fat lady went off in my face an' I didn't even do nothin'! An' I didn't take that money, neither!"

Timothy acknowledged that Mac had done nothing wrong that evening and that Mrs. McWheeten had overreacted—

"You ain't gettin' me to go back there—un-uh—"

"But, Mac, then where are you going to stay tonight?" Timothy delicately reasoned. "It's too late to get you in anywhere and it's too cold for you to sleep outside. You'll freeze to death out here."

"But what if that lady sees me again?" uttered Mac under the fearful recognition that he might have no other option.

"My room's right near the entrance," Timothy pointed out. "We'll be in it before the front door closes behind us."

The prospect of again meeting up with The Lady of the House was a staunch deterrent even when balanced against the certainty of hypothermia; though through gentle encouragement, especially that received from Kate—with whom he felt a sort of kinship—Mac acquiesced, and his dismal figure fell in with them on their trek home.

But how strong was his reconsideration when he gazed, with round eyes, upon that old haunted house again. He was insistent that they run a sweeping reconnaissance to make absolutely certain that the path was clear.

Once safely within his room, Timothy set Mac down on the hassock, which he had drawn near to his desk lamp for a better look. He then dug out some clean white T-shirts from his dresser drawer and asked that Lottie and Kate go dampen them in the bathroom across the way while he prepared the bandage.

Jim loitered about briefly, but, with Mac well attended, he expressed the necessity of preparing for his drive home with some sleep.

"Get these nice 'n wet," directed Lottie, throwing herself with vigor into the task, as Kate waited behind for her turn at the sink.

"You know, I've never seen that guy do anything mean to anyone," sighed the latter in soft dismay. "But look what somebody did to him anyway. He was just minding his own business on the street—"

"They pound him pretty good, didn' they?" Lottie concurred with an emphatic nod. "But I still think he kinda cute—even with cuts," and her twinkling eyes and suddenly blushing cheeks Lottie would have succeeded in shielding from her friend, but for the mirror, through which Kate caught her radiant reflection.

Kate hadn't any premonition of this attraction, and it brought a smile to her face. "Well, then," she said, as she reached in to help Lottie in the cramped sink, "we'd better hurry up with these shirts and go patch up your new boyfriend for showing."

"Who say anythin' 'bout boyfrien'!" pealed Lottie with an enormous laugh. "Me 'an him go out first—then play it by ear!" With the ground rules laid down, it was now time to start the chase. Stepping gaily back across the hall the women delivered the supplies to Timothy.

The pressure required to remove the stubborn scraps of dried blood, though causing Mac some minor discomfort, earned no mention in his lamentations, for those were centered exclusively on his loss of revenue.

"That bag was almos' full as it was," he said, flashing a wince under Timothy's hand. "I was jus' gonna go down that last alley, since it was on my way, an' then go get my money for 'em at the store. Then I was gonna go off to that church for the night. I don't know why that guy jus' don't find his own bottles. It took me all day to get the ones I had. That was a big bag, too—ya shoulda seen it."

Inching uncertainly forward to console Mac on his financial setback, Lottie sought to reverse his spirits by letting him in on the fact that, "You can make money givin' blood at clinic, too. An' it only take a little while; then you can go collect bottles after. It extra money—an' it easy," added with emphasis. "Make eight dollar each time. An' it help people, too—who are hurt."

Eight dollars per visit caught Mac's interest. Why, that calculated out to eighty bottles and cans, certainly not an insignificant percentage of any bagful of income. And though not at all fond of needles, Mac was set to inquire after more details when Timothy, having sufficiently cleansed the wound, sent Lottie and Kate back to rinse the shirts out in the sink, while he began applying the bandage.

The women were hardly entered back into the hallway, when they were startled by the silhouette of Mrs. McWheeten looming before them at the bathroom door.

"Why, good evening, ladies," she gave them a cordial greeting, as the two bumped to a halt. "I'm afraid that the upstairs toilet isn't work—good God, what's happened! Has Timothy had an accident?"

The flush of light provided by the bathroom door being swung open had revealed the bloody garments in their hands. And having been, in their sheer surprise over this meeting, too slow in hiding the shirts behind their backs, the women were at a loss to explain them now.

"Timothy, my dear boy!" the landlady rushed past her

two stammering tenants and, without even a knock, straight into Timothy's room.

Timothy had heard the encounter developing in the hallway and, as a precautionary maneuver, had sought to usher his bewildered patient back around the corner to the tiny annex where his mattress lay. They had not quite reached it when the landlady came bursting through the door.

"My God! what's he doing here?" she demanded of Timothy, though her glare was reserved for the offending presence; and, in her alarm, having drawn back fully into the doorway, she inhibited Lottie and Kate's re-entry to the room, forcing them to peek over and around her from the hall. They were joined by Jim, who had been brought tumbling out of his loft by the commotion.

Timothy portrayed a guilt he certainly did not feel, and with his head bent solely in anguish, he returned, alone, towards the center of the room. In an affecting tone, he then recounted for Mrs. McWheeten how they had come across Mac "beaten unconscious in an alley—"

"Beaten unconscious in an alley?" echoed the landlady with abhorrence.

Timothy confirmed it, with a grave nod, adding that, "He had been mugged—and robbed."

"And robbed?" of what? her expression curiously inquired.

"By the time we discovered him, just a short while ago," continued Timothy, "all the shelters were closed for the night; so—I persuaded him to come here."

From her distant surveying of the wounds, exposed by the bandage having been only partially attached when Timothy was alerted to her proximity, Mrs. McWheeten could find no basis for doubting the truthfulness of Timothy's story. Though far from revealing any pity for the victim, her expression, instead, seemed to intimate that the wretch probably got what he deserved for choosing to lead such an existence.

Her breath now calm, the landlady requested a private word with Timothy, up the hallway. Glumly acceding, he followed her round the corner to the foot of the stairways, from where their muted voices were rendered indecipherable to the ears poised yearningly against the interior of Timothy's door.

"He had nowhere else to go, Mrs. McWheeten," Timothy aimed to pre-empt her castigation. "And it's well below freezing outside—"

"I understand, Timothy," she said, stilling his passionate plea with an august motion of her hand. "You did as the good Lord would have any of us do, given the circumstances. I have no quarrel with your actions, especially since I can tell you've been drinking. My concern here is over a pattern developing, in light of my understanding and compassion regarding Kate. I do not expect to have my manifest goodwill exploited on this—fellow's behalf. In other words, I do not expect to see him moving in with you. Rather, I expect him gone, for good, by morning. Am I understood?"

Timothy was so relieved to discover that Mrs. McWheeten had no intention of turning Mac out into the cold that he readily submitted to her conditions.

The others were much relieved, also—and Timothy opted not to sour their moods with any mention of the landlady's stipulation. He finished bandaging up Mac's cuts and, insisting that Mac take the mattress for the night, Timothy then arranged for himself a pile of blankets on the floor, courtesy, in part, of his three neighbors. After a brief bull session, it was time for all to go to bed.

Chapter Twenty-One

It was a painful call back to consciousness, a piercing stab that caused Jim's body to uncoil in the fiercest agony, with his right arm sent grappling forth to quell the muffled trill of the alarm clock buried somewhere beneath his many strata of blankets.

The clamorous mechanism finally silenced, Jim collapsed back into his pillow, his heavy eyes unable to focus in the blackness of the hour. What a fool he had been—what an utter damned fool! He had been under no obligation to consume that second shot of distasteful whiskey, nor to participate in the fourth through sixth pitchers of beer. And for his lack of restraint he lay now prostrate and dim, fading under the strong temptation to sleep off the hangover now clanking along in full gear.

But they were expecting him back home at a reasonable hour, and were he to yield again to sleep, he realized that his family's make-up holiday plans, like the original, might pass without him.

With a flat and fledgling bit of energy, Jim reached back over his head and grasped blindly for the top rung of the ladder. He pulled himself out from beneath his blankets and dropped clumsily down to the floor.

A shower provided some minor benefit, and was supplemented by a quick cup of coffee and a tentative go at some food up in the kitchen. Filling his thermos with the remainder from the coffee pot, Jim, with his suitcase in the other hand, plodded out to his car, just as dawn was breaking.

Timothy hadn't survived his own early morning rise much better and was extremely grateful, as his shift was now winding down, that it had been a slow day at the restaurant. It had allowed him many idle moments in which to seek the support of a wall or chair, while trying to revive himself with a seemingly endless stream of coffee.

He was enjoying such a respite on the loading dock out back, when, presently, word came that he had some visitors in the dining room.

"So—how you feelin' today?" Lottie boomed, as Timothy entered into view, his cup of coffee faithfully in hand.

Timothy smiled and remarked that he was making a rather slow recovery. But why, he wondered, was Lottie apparently so unaffected by the previous evening's imbibing?

"I not drink as fas' as ev'ryone else," came her sprightly response, "—an' I leave secon' whiskey on table."

Timothy regretted not having followed her sensible course. He led Lottie and Kate to the nearest vacant booth and, slumping down across the table from them, asked what had brought them in.

"We in neighborhood an' thought we stop by 'n say hi to you," Lottie's simple reply bringing an incredulous glance from her roommate.

"Lottie wants to ask a favor of you," Kate directed them towards the truth of the matter, which caused Lottie to squirm and color completely over in red. As an afterthought, Lottie delivered a light elbow into her friend's arm.

Timothy smiled at their peculiar behavior and asked Lottie for an explanation.

Lottie, however, was unable to find her tongue—or, at least, her courage.

"Lottie would like for you to bring Mac over to the house again—soon—"

"Kate! Stop—"

Timothy was not quite comprehending, until—

"Lottie's in love."

"Kate! I gonna sock you." The emptiness of the threat was betrayed by the burst of laughter that accompanied it.

Timothy was dumbstruck. "Is this true?" he asked of his shrinking friend.

Lottie shrugged, in a poor attempt to play coy. "He kinda cute," she tossed off casually.

Timothy hid a smile in his coffee cup, and admitted that
he had not been aware of this attraction. And almost
immediately upon promising to promote Lottie's ambition,
Timothy recalled, with a grimace, his pledge to Mrs.
McWheeten on the previous evening.

The women asked him what was wrong; and Timothy
saw no alternative but to confide in them the terms upon
which Mac was allowed to stay at the house the night before.

The women voiced their surprise, and mild displeasure,
and were beginning to formulate an alternate plan of attack,
when Timothy quietly wondered about the possibility of
Mac's being found acceptable by Mrs. McWheeten as a
guest of Lottie's rather than of his own. Especially should
the visits be conducted under the auspices of romance.

The women were eager to test his theory.

"She ain't gonna tell me I can't have boy over," Lottie
defiantly proclaimed.

Timothy had an idea. He told the women of his
arrangement to meet up with Mac after work that day, over at
the public library, where he was to replace the old bandage
with a fresh one. Timothy's thought was to hand that new
bandage over to Lottie now and to explain to Mac that he
had somehow misplaced it at work; but for Mac not to worry,
because Timothy had another one back at home.

As he was laying out his plan, it occurred to Timothy
that, for the sake of appearance (should Mrs. McWheeten
be there to intercept), it would probably behoove them to
have Lottie, alone, escort Mack up to the house. It was
therefore agreed upon that Lottie would bump into them at
the corner of Division and Liberty streets at four o'clock,
shortly after which Timothy would drop off on an 'errand',
which would entail nothing more than meeting up with Kate
at a coffee house, and thus allowing Lottie full privacy to
pursue her objective.

The scheme was very positively received; and, as Timothy
should probably be getting back to work, he would hand
over the bandage now. He beckoned for the women to follow
him.

Between the enduring debility of a hangover and being enraptured by this cupid's plot, it had escaped Timothy's mind that leading Kate back through the kitchen to the basement, where his coat lay, would be to lead her right up to Mike. Timothy had them nearly to the dishroom before recognizing his oversight, and his abrupt stop led to Lottie's plowing straight into his backside.

It was too late, though, to issue a retreat, for Mike was already observing their advance with stone-faced surprise. The fear that Timothy held for Kate's discomfort over this encounter, though she had made him aware of Mike's small step towards a truce, was assuaged when she gave a modest wave up to her former boyfriend, who received it with a rigid nod.

Timothy, however, could not help but be amazed when Kate announced that she would wait for he and Lottie upstairs. She gave him a smile of reassurance.

Mike, too, was surprised that she had chosen his company. It was left to Kate, consequently, to start the conversation, which she did by asking him how his holidays had gone.

He responded with a shrug and, turning round to her after sending a load of dishes through, remarked that they had been "okay," informing her that rather than taking Christmas dinner at the shelter, he had been invited over to Jerome's.

"He's one a the cooks here," Mike clarified. "He ain't here today—or ya prob'bly woulda heard 'im whistlin' at ya when you was walkin' through the kitchen." With a grin, he went on to explain Jerome's nature, which made Kate relieved that her visit had coincided with Jerome's day off; though her only comment was to commend Jerome for his kindness in having Mike over.

"Barry was there, too," as he pulled the rack of steaming dishes from the machine. "An' a couple a others that you don't know. Yeah, it was all right," Mike reiterated with a nod, and he started to stack the hot plates atop one another.

"So—" he resumed while transferring the dishes over to a shelf behind where she was standing, "how you puttin' up with that landlady now that you're actually livin' over there?"

Kate flashed him a look of mild admonishment. "Now, Mike, please don't start."

"Well, hell, I was jus' wonderin' if she treats anybody good, is all. I know she didn't—"

"She's been very wonderful to me," Kate interposed with such emphasis that Mike understood it prudent to drop the subject; and not immediately conceiving another, he announced his intention to take a cigarette break out back, with an invitation for her to join him if she'd like.

As Timothy and Lottie had yet to reappear, Kate accepted, and she suggested that they move Mike's break from the cold shade of the loading dock out into the thriving sunshine below.

"That's one thing I don't like 'bout workin' here in the wintertime," remarked Mike as they descended the steps of the dock. "Every time that door gets opened, I freeze in the dishroom. An' it gets opened a lot, with all them delivery guys comin' in an' people takin' cigarette breaks."

Kate raised a concern over the effects of this constant exposure to the contrasts of the steamy dishroom and the biting Michigan winter. She wondered whether anything could be done to alleviate the potential health risks.

Mike shrugged and said that he didn't know what they could possibly do; besides, "It ain't as big a deal as it used to be, 'cause now what I do is help the delivery guys unload everything from their trucks onto the loading dock first. An' when we get that far, then we prop the door open an' kinda get everything inside as fast as we can, so we can close the door again. Before, they jus' propped it open first thing an' started wheelin' everything inside from the truck one load at a time. Took for goddamn ever! I had to put my coat on to do dishes."

They sounded like horrible conditions to Kate.

"But, what the hell," sighed Mike, "startin' next week it ain't gonna matter so much to me anymore, 'cause I'm gonna be farther away from the back door, up in the prep area, which is what you walked through just before ya got to the dishroom."

Kate wasn't clear on this reference to the prep area.

As he coolly withdrew the cigarette from his mouth, Mike explained that, "I'm gonna start trainin' as a prep cook nex' week. Still do some part-time dishwashin'—but some part-time preppin', too. I'm hopin' it turns out to be more preppin', though."

It sounded like a promotion to Kate; an interpretation that Mike could not resist confirming with some smugness.

"More money," he emphasized.

Kate absorbed his good news with a silent wonderment that he thoroughly enjoyed.

"Hell, I can't believe it myself," he let on with a smile. "I guess what I really can't believe, though, is that it took me so long to get aroun' to something like this. But, ya know, everytime I start gettin' mad at myself over it, I think, hell, I'm only twenty-six, an' better to get goin' a little late than not get goin' at all. An' I realize this place ain't paradise, but you can make a pretty decent livin' bein' a cook."

Kate said that she had heard that; but—what did he know about working in a kitchen?

He smiled at the doubting nature of her inquiry. "Hey, I cooked in a restaurant a little bit back when I was sixteen," he revealed his credentials. "An', believe me, I'm ready to learn it all over again; 'cause I'm sure as hell ready to get outa that dishroom, let me tell ya."

She could imagine.

"An' I'll tell ya somethin' else, I'm so anxious to get outa that shelter, too, that as soon as we get paid on Monday I'm gonna take the money I got saved up in that bank account Timothy helped me open an' I'm gonna start lookin' in the paper for places to live. An' I ain't gonna be that picky, neither. Not that I can afford to be."

Kate voiced her belief that he should be able to find an accommodation, and a price, that suited him.

He wanted to share her optimism, except that, "I ain't too good at dealin' with those types a people—landlords 'n them. An' even though I wanna get a place as quick as I can,

I don't wanna get took either. That's why I was kinda thinkin'
of—maybe askin' Timothy if he wouldn't mind takin' a look
at some a these places with me. But—I don't know—" with
a sigh.

"I'm sure he'd do it."

Mike thought that probably so, as well. "He's helped me
out a lot," he acknowledged. "I guess that's kinda why I
hate to bug 'im even more. It's prob'bly time I learned to
start takin' care of some a this stuff myself."

"But there's nothing wrong with getting help from friends,
either," countered Kate, "especially when it involves
something you're not familiar with. Lottie was going to help
me search, until she came up with the idea of us sharing her
room together. But I was nervous, too, about looking for a
place all by myself, because I hadn't don't it before, either.
And I tell you what, I was happy when she offered to help
me look, because even though Lottie didn't have much
experience at it herself, it would've been nice just to have
somebody else there with me."

Mike openly related to that sentiment.

"I mean—if that's all you're looking for," responded Kate,
though awkwardly for the position that she was putting
herself in, "I suppose even I could do that. I don't know how
much help I could be in actually dealing with the landlords,
but at least you wouldn't have to face anybody alone."

It was a very unexpected offer. "You wouldn't mind?"
Mike needed to hear it repeated.

Kate said that she would be glad to help, though again
warning him against setting any high expectations for her
input. "I'm not any more experienced at this than you are,"
she reminded him, "but—"

Mike accepted. They decided that, though it preceded
his paycheck, the following day, Sunday, would grant them
ample time to conduct a preliminary search, under the theory
that Mike's course of action would thereby be expedited
when the money was finally in hand. Their plan to meet was
settled, just as Timothy and Lottie poked their heads out the
back door.

* * *

"So, now I gotta go back to that nasty old lady's house?" Mac's irritation over this drastic development attracting the collective arched brow of the front reading room of the public library, where he had been feigning interest in a newspaper while awaiting the arrival of his medical attendant.

This unwanted attention prompted Timothy to coax Mac towards the exit, while trying quietly to reassure him that there was no need to worry.

But how, in God's name, could Timothy possibly have lost the bandage that Mac had witnessed him zip into his coat pocket prior to their leaving the house that morning?

Timothy blamed it on his hangover, suggesting that perhaps he hadn't zipped the pocket completely shut. He apologized for any inconvenience.

"Well, this one ain't so bad," Mack lobbied on behalf of his present bandage, as he displayed, now, a hard reluctance to pass through that final door of the building's exit.

Timothy, however, was quick to stress the importance of regularly replacing any bandage with a clean one, to avoid infection, specifically gangrene, "which can lead to amputation. Besides, Mrs. McWheeten turned out to be very understanding last night once your situation was explained. And this is really just a continuation of that circumstance."

Mac was not to be soothed, though, by any pitch invoking the benevolence of Timothy's landlady. And likely preoccupied with those unflinching doubts—and fears— he was completely unaffected by Lottie's joining up with them at the street corner; at least until Timothy excused himself from their company under the pretense of suddenly remembering an errand that not only could no longer be postponed, but that would also require some time to complete. He announced the necessity of turning over the care of Mac to his accomplice.

Mac went unconsulted in this matter, and he silently, though expressively, witnessed his transfer. His uneasiness at being bound over to this odd little woman lingered only until his approach, in broad daylight, to the McWheeten house.

He paused alongside the neighboring hedge and peered intently upon every visible window for the landlady's baleful apparition. Finding every sill unattended, he concluded that she must be lurking upon the landing way, ready to pounce on him once his broken boots edged over the threshold of her domain. He declared his intention of turning back.

"I don't care if my head becomes infected an' they gotta chop it off! That still ain't no worse than seein' her again."

Lottie, however, stepped up as his comrade and comfort, and she cajoled him safely inside to her room.

The relief of this uneventful entry endured only until Mac realized himself now entirely alone with Lottie, inside her apartment.

Lottie did not share in his awkwardness, as was made evident by her smile, which slightly leered; and almost immediately, she set about the business of weaving her web, the first step of which involved leading her docile prey over to the couch.

"Don't worry, I take as good a care a you as Tim'thy," she nodded with assurance, as she gathered up her medical supplies from the end table next to the sofa. She knelt very nearly in his lap to reach the old bandage that needed to be stripped away.

Mac did not survive this initial phase of the operation without some loss of temple hair, marked by a series of small yelps that would unfailingly produce a pause and an apology from his private practitioner.

"I try be more careful," she would promise, to his ever wary eye.

The old and discolored bandage finally discarded on the floor, Lottie proceeded, with a damp cloth, to clean the wound, before plastering a fresh bandage so low across his temple that it partially veiled one eye.

"There!" she proclaimed, and, quite satisfied with her performance, Lottie popped to her feet and began the post-procedural clean-up.

"You want apple or cookie?" she asked him, having finished her task and now wiping her hands with the towel that hung from the handle of her refrigerator door.

It had not occurred to Mac, this entire time, to inquire as to how one of Timothy's bandages had gotten into Lottie's possession or, furthermore, why it had been laid out on the table as though in anticipation of such a case as his. With the bandage now in place, those questions drifted even further from his mind, for he had taken up the contemplation of his departure.

Thus, Lottie's unexpected offer of food confounded him, though only momentarily—and with a shrug, he admitted that, "I guess a cookie sounds kinda good."

Lottie brought the entire package over and, plopping herself back on the couch, she placed the cookies between them.

While Mac nibbled, a restive glance fixed sidelong on his provider, Lottie gobbled, with her eyes plainly yearning for discourse.

They remained in their respective poses only a short time, before Lottie spotted her vehicle to lure him into fuller communication.

"How you like flowers on table?" she pointed them out with a great motioning of her half cookie. "They for you—to make you feel better."

Flowers? For him?

"I pick 'em out at store myself."

Mac glanced back at her with some unease, but said nothing.

Her first attempt at drawing him out having failed, Lottie sighed, and, slouching yet deeper into the couch, she made a listless grab for another cookie. She was crunching it around in her mouth, when suddenly she announced, "I sorry I scream that one night."

Not nearly so sorry as Mac had been. "I don't know why she went off on me like that an' threw me outa the house," he honestly maintained. "I wasn't doin' nothin' wrong—"

"She prob'bly think you stealin'," Lottie assumed, and,

breaking another cookie in two, she offered half to Mac.

"I didn't steal that money," he adamantly retorted. "I didn't take nothin'. She jus' don't like me for some reason. But that's okay, 'cause I don't like her, neither. She gives me the creeps."

Lottie broke into such a giggle that it sparked a glance of resentment from her confused guest, who thought that, somehow, it came at his expense; until Lottie gurgled, "You should see her dog! It even creepi-er!"

Mac's expression lightened, at last, into a grin. "Nothin' can be creepier 'n her," he insisted.

"Ask Tim'thy! He tell you. Dog ugly 'n smelly—"

"An' she ain't!" countered Mac with a hoarse laugh, and he dipped his hand into the package of cookies.

"Still ain't as bad as dog, though," contended Lottie, breathless from her laughter. "Ask Tim'thy."

"Then there ain't no way I wanna meet her dog," he grinned even wider, with she, in return, giggling up into his eyes.

There arose just then, from the hallway, some slight commotion that, presently, produced a knock at Lottie's door. She could hardly believe the poor timing of this intrusion and, trudging mechanically across the floor, wondered why Timothy and Kate would have returned so soon and foiled her skillfully developed plot. She opened the door with sad, pleading eyes—

"Why hello, Lottie," said Mrs. McWheeten, edged right up close into the doorway and panting at the near end of an old mattress steadied upon its side. Her husband was providing the balance from the other end. "As you undoubtedly can see," with a smile and presentative sweep of her hand, "we're here to deliver Kate's mattress. Is she in?"

Recovering from this dreadful surprise, Lottie alertly pulled the door round behind her as best she could given the landlady's forward advance. "She out," with a very emphatic shake of the head; so, perhaps, they could come back some other time?

"Well, no matter," replied Mrs. McWheeten dismissively.

"We'll just leave it here with you—and trust that she gets it," tossed off with a little laugh.

"All right, now, grab hold, Fab. Lottie, dear, you'll have to move out of the way."

Lottie dear had to be told a second time, and even then only reluctantly complied, in the face of being run over.

The McWheetens wriggled the ungovernable mattress through the doorway and across the floor, round the backside of the couch, to the far corner of the room where a space had been reserved for several days now.

Wiping her palms clean against one another, at the completion of this accomplishment, Mrs. McWheeten turned around, with a labored sigh, to address Lottie, when, "Good God, what's he still doing here!" nearly sent her tumbling backwards atop the mattress.

With the McWheetens held at bay in the doorway, Mac had been adequately concealed by the interceding lampshade, as well as the spread of the floral arrangement. As the McWheetens moved across the floor behind him, he remained obscured by the distraction of their toil. With a moment's respite at the end of their work, however, and in a room so small, Mac's presence was difficult to disguise, no matter the desperation with which he tried melting beneath the cushions of the couch.

Poor Mac stared straight ahead under the fierce glare of the landlady's inquisition, and he dared not budge even a glance of acknowledgement back her way.

"I ask him over," Lottie tried to assert.

"Lottie—you? But—why—"

"Because—because—he my boyfrien'!"

"Your what?" begged the heart-stricken landlady.

Boyfriend? Mac peeked up amid the crossfire.

"My boyfrien'!" resounded Lottie. "So I ask him over to see me so I can take care of his cuts."

"Oh—good lord," swelled Mrs. McWheeten with dismay and casting a vague look of betrayal at her uncomprehending tenant, she limply signalled her husband that they had better go.

Pausing at the doorway, Mrs. McWheeten had regained enough of her manner to submit, with hollow inflection, that, "We're quite sorry to've disturbed you. And please extend to Kate our apologies for the delay in the delivery of her mattress," before closing the door behind herself.

"See!" Lottie cheerily proclaimed, as she jounced back upon the sofa, "I take care a you. You ain't gotta worry 'bout her no more!"

Rather, Mac's apprehension was now fixed on Lottie.

"I gonna be bes' girlfrien' you ever had. From now on, I go an' help you pick bot'les from garbage cans so you make even more money, 'cause with me then we will have two full bags! An', also, I protect you from anyone who try an' take them 'way like las' night. An' I take you with me nex' time I go give blood. Make eight dollar ev'ry time. An' get free doughnuts, too!

"An' I don't care what Mrs. M'Wheeten say, whenever it cold out you can come over an' stay warm here—an' eat cookies. If she don't like it, I will tell her to min' her own bus'ness, like I tell her tonight."

Mac was trying to absorb this dramatic alteration of lifestyle being proposed for him, when, "You a cute boyfrien'," completely addled his thought process and returned him to a state of blank bewilderment.

"But you would be even more cute," Lottie bounded from the couch over towards a dresser, "with a haircut. I good at haircuts, too. Not only bandagin'."

The prospect of a haircut at Lottie's hands could hardly have made Mac less uneasy than an encore visit from Mrs. McWheeten.

"But my hair ain't that long," he rightly contended, and, doffing his cap, he drew a couple of his unkempt locks upward between his fingers for reassurance and proof.

"It need trim," Lottie just as rightly countered, swinging back round, snapping her scissors playfully. "Mrs. M'Wheeten mistake you for her dog if you don't keep your hairs nice 'n straight; an', then, she might try pick you up 'n hug you."

"My hair can't be that bad."

"Almos'!" pealed Lottie gleefully, while taking her positon behind the sofa.

Pondering her comparison in silent horrification, Mac found himself acquiescing to the blade, and he now simply asked that she be careful.

"I will, silly," she gave him a light pat on the head, as she surveyed her project. "You not need to worry."

If Lottie were cutting as designed, and she appeared to be, then her concept of 'nice 'n straight' seemed to deviate somewhat from the standard definition. The complexity of layering was completely beyond her grasp. Nonetheless, as she stood inspecting her work afterwards, Lottie could not have been prouder of the result.

And despite having no mirror at his disposal, Mac, too, exhibited a sense of satisfaction, though his likely stemmed from nothing more than the traumatic event being over. While gazing back at his examiner, there came a gleam in his eye.

"Your hair's more like a ugly dog's than mine!"

Far from being offended, Lottie burst into a giggle and, giving her shaggy locks a rambunctious shake, she claimed, "It 'posed to be like this, I a girl!"

But even a girl should have presentable hair, declared Mac in rebuttal and, under his command, Lottie willingly relinquished to him the scissors and assumed his former spot on the couch.

"Only take off little," she requested with a lively fidget that well may have endangered an ear, had Mac not been hesitating in deliberation over exactly where to begin.

Mac proceeded tentatively, having never done this before, and he did take off only a little in his sporadic course through her hair.

Lottie pronounced her happiness to no longer resemble the McWheeten's dog, and she thanked Mac for his role in this improvement. He, likewise, expressed a similiar gratitude to her.

They celebrated their mutual liberation from such comparisons with more cookies, and by flopping themselves upon the floor where, for the next couple of hours, they threw dice and flipped cards over various board games. And whenever there arose a reference to anything evil or frightful, they never failed to share a laugh at Mrs. McWheeten's expense. Neither was the dog spared. Nor each other, for that matter, for whenever either of them unfurled a run of good luck, the other was quick to levy good-natured charges of underhanded tactics as the source of that success; which were met, always, with howls of denial.

They went through every cookie in the room. Three bags. And nearly three-quarters of Mac's bottle of whiskey, explaining the state in which Timothy and Kate found them, with Mac slumped back and snoring against the couch and Lottie sprawled out and sleeping atop the gameboard.

Chapter Twenty-Two

The waitress made little effort to mask her displeasure over their occupying one of her prime booths with a simple order of two coffees, what with a thirty minute wait having now developed in the restaurant's foyer. She had no recourse, however, except perhaps to speed them along by assisting in their search for whatever it was that had lured their attention to the classified section of the Sunday paper, spread upon the table between them.

The waitress was showing no such inclination; rather, "Is there anything else I can get for you?" and, "I'll take your check up whenever you're ready," were the subliminal routes she plied in her attempt to move them on their way.

Her offers were politely acknowledged by Kate, but were to no avail, for the only movement they triggered was the positioning of the coffee cups to facilitate their refilling.

One advantage to Mike's residing at the low end of the income scale, they quickly discovered, was that it dramatically reduced the focus of their search by weeding out nearly every listing in the paper.

There were, however, six or seven rooms being advertised that fell within his projected means, and with these circled in ink, Mike, upon Kate's purposeful refusal to do his work for him, slid irresolutely from the booth and went in search of the public phone, with the aim of setting up some appointments for later that day.

Their waitress, while in the middle of taking an order at the next table over, detected his motion, and could not help but swing her head hopefully round. The false alarm recognized, she turned her churlish expression back to the father, who was rather puzzled by this mysterious diversion that required his, "Two eggs over easy with hash browns and whole wheat toast," be repeated.

Mike succeeded in getting through to four of the numbers on his list and, under Kate's advisement, scheduled appointments one hour apart, with the first, as it happened, taking place in just fifteen minutes.

"Now, remember," Kate instructed him, as they gathered together their coins—under the suspect glare of their waitress, bussing the table opposite—"if you don't like any of these rooms, you don't have to commit." The search could be resumed another day, she reminded him. "But if we do look at one you think you want, it's perfectly okay to say you'll take it, and then we can make an appointment to come back tomorrow, after you get paid, and sign the lease."

The bill was all set, Kate informed the waitress, to whom the fifty per cent tip did nothing to allay her contempt for them and their stay.

It did not matter to Mike that he would probably have to settle for a basement room. He was resigned, also, to the likelihood of shared bathroom and kitchen facilities, though it would thrust him into the awkward position of having to make acquaintances, which he acknowledged he did not do easily.

Still, it would be a vast improvement over the communal living arrangement of the shelter; and as eager as he was to make the move from there, he did concede the wisdom of Kate's advice not simply to grab the first room they came across.

Mike's apprenticeship in this order of patience was aided by the first two rooms they viewed, owing to the one's peculiar odor and the other's lack of heat.

They moved on toward their two o' clock appointment, which brought them back up North Main Street, and past the restaurant from where they had started their expedition. They continued on for another two or three blocks that brought them around a bend.

Marking the advancing numbers on the houses, they observed that their quest would land them in the last stand of modest little homes that lined the right side of the road on the way out of town.

They paused before the address that matched the one they had scribbled down in the margin of the newspaper, and noticed in its driveway an old green station wagon idling amid the swirl of its own exhaust.

The two of them proceeded up the steps of the short and steep front yard. The automobile was turned off, with the driver stepping out of the vehicle before the engine had sputtered completely to a halt.

A tall, wiry man bundled in a short parka, he came round the front of his car towards them. He tread carefully along the icy walkway of his property, approaching with a tight smile stitched across a face nearly as creased as his crusty tan corduroy pants.

"You the fella I talked to earlier?" he asked with his hands remaining tucked in his coat.

Mike said that he was; at which point Kate courteously initiated the introductions.

"I'm sorry," the landlord interrupted her with some confusion, "but the room I have advertised is a single occupancy. I didn't know there was two of you—"

Kate cleared up the misunderstanding, presenting Mike as the sole interested party.

It was obvious that, in the landlord's eye's, Kate cut the more agreeable first impression, and though it had been Mike with whom Mr. Broderick had made the present appointment over the phone, he could not completely hide his disappointment that he would be pitching the one and not the other.

As expected, Kate and Mike again found themselves being led down a flight of stairs, into a hallway that seemed hastily forged of nothing but plywood and glue.

It was to the third and final room that they were conducted and they exchanged hopeful glances as Mr. Broderick sifted through his crowded key chain.

The room being small, it essentially spoke for itself, while the landlord devoted his presentation to matters such as the security deposit, utility rates and the Laundromat "conveniently" located just over the river.

The room was clean and tidy and, as far as Mike could tell, heated. The mattress and box spring seemed firm enough. There was a dresser over in the corner near the foot of the bed, with a table and a chair along that far wall, as well. The small closet behind the door would certainly be sufficient for storage.

The room's one window, located high along the wall, provided an oblique perspective of the backyard and the sky above it.

A tour of the house came next and, as it entailed but the bathroom and kitchen, was finished shortly.

At this time, Mike requested a moment alone with Kate. Mr. Broderick, with a consenting nod, sat himself down at the kitchen table where he began tapping his fingers along the surface and whistling a tune, while Mike drew Kate out into the hallway and quickly expressed his desire to take the room.

Kate smiled in empathy, and, as she had sensed his interest growing through each succeeding step of the interview, she was not surprised at his eager declaration. She conceded that the accommodations might be as well as he could expect to find on his present income; though the location would mean a bit of a walk to work each morning, and with its being winter—.

Mike had taken that into account. "But if I see one I like, why risk losin' it to someone else? Besides, anything closer to campus—an' work—I ain't gonna be able to afford, anyway."

Mr. Broderick's smile, on hearing of Mike's intentions, revealed a smugness, rather than relief, and mechanically from his coat pocket he withdrew a rumpled application for tenancy, a requisite procedure that clearly threw Mike.

"Most importantly," Mr. Broderick directed his long and bent forefinger midway down the form, "I'll need the names and phone numbers of your most recent landlords—as well as those of your past employers and three unrelated personal references."

Recent landlords? Mike turned helplessly to Kate, who also had been caught unsuspecting of these requirements.

"Well—" she recovered, momentarily, to address Mike's blank gaze, "I'm sure Timothy will give you a good reference. And your boss, too—she just gave you that promotion," for Mr. Broderick's information.

But Mike's concern was not about the personal references. "I ain't got no recent landlords," did he really need to remind Kate? as he flicked at that portion of Mr. Broderick's document, before turning away in his frustration.

"Is there a problem?" Mr. Broderick feigned ignorance, though he had a comfortable grasp of the situation.

Kate moved to preempt the emotional response she sensed building within Mike. "He's been staying at the shelter most recently," she stated matter-of-factly. "So he doesn't have any names of landlords to give you. He's been working at a restaurant to save up money so that he can move out of there and into a place of his own. With the promotion he just got he now has that money—"

"I see," drawled Mr. Broderick pensively, as his forefinger scratched unconsciously along the surface of the application, seemingly as a prelude to gathering it back up. "Well—I ain't afraid to be up front with you folks an' tell ya that I've got some reservations about leasin' to anybody who doesn't have any landlord references. See, I don't want no trouble here. It's a peaceful—"

"He's not going to cause any trouble," Kate's rebuttal coming so reflexively that she hadn't allowed herself to consider her own knowledge of Mike's past . "Call the people at the city shelter, if you don't believe me. Call the place where he works and see what kind of an employee he's been. And he's got the money, Mr. Broderick—"

"Whoa, now, slow down there, young lady," the landlord chuckled over the fervor with which Kate was advancing her plea. "I'm sure he does have the money, or he wouldn't be here, right? So, I'll tell ya what I'm gonna do," as a favor, was clearly the implication. "If your friend's interested in the room, as he says he is, I'd be willin' to take a good faith deposit of, say—two hundred dollars, to put a hold on the room while I at least check out his personal references—"

"I ain't got two hundred dollars on me!" squawked Mike in further exasperation.

"I thought he had the money?" responded Mr. Broderick with a hint of displeasure towards Kate.

"He gets paid tomorrow," she replied.

"I see," sighed the landlord, rubbing at his chin. "Well, fine," turning up a faint grin. "You're more than welcome to stop by tomorrow, if you'd like. That'll give me the opportunity I need to check his references. And, if the room's still available, we'll talk. I just can't make you any guarantees that it'll still be on the market, you understand. I got some other folks comin' in later today to take a look at it, an' if any one of them likes it—an' has the money to put in my hand, well . . ." the room, naturally, would become theirs, he implied with a widening smile.

Kate had begun rummaging, almost frantically, through her purse. "That's okay," she retorted, while producing the checkbook she had just located. "Because we have some other appointments today, too, sir; and we've got the money right here and we're going give it to the first landlord who wants it—all of it, meaning the security deposit plus the first month's rent, pro-rated, in exchange for the key today. So, are you interested?"

Mr. Broderick no longer viewed Kate as such a charming young lady; for, how dare she corner him into either casting his lot with this scraggly, suspect character or committing his faith to the probability that his single other appointment for that day would yield an equally interested party with more impressive credentials—as well as a recent haircut and shave?

How tempting for him to advise this impudent young lady to take her checkbook—and her homeless friend— elsewhere. And, quite probably, that would have been his flip response, had the room not been on the market nearly two weeks now; and with January's leasing prospects ordinarily dim, he suppressed, as best he could, his disdain and he supplied Kate with a pen—and a correct spelling of his full name.

With the technicalities disposed of—primarily, the signing of the lease, which the landlord had had in his other pocket, and the exchange of the check for the key—Mr. Broderick gladly took his leave, with the sober reminder that, in accordance with the just signed document, it was the personal responsibility of each tenant to maintain a conduct agreeable to all his or her neighbors. Specifically, an acceptable degree of quiet. Good day!

So, now the room was Mike's, and he didn't know what to say. He stared at the key he held in his hand as though it did not belong there. He tried expressing his appreciation for the considerable favor that Kate had just done him, and approached coherence only when marvelling at her tact.

Kate blushed at the mention of her behavior, not quite believing it herself. "I guess he got me a little worked up," she admitted, though with a desponding sigh, "I just hope I didn't get you into a bad situation. I'm kind of wondering, now, if it wouldn't 've been better to've just gone somewhere else, because I really don't think he wanted to rent the room to us. I just hope he doesn't give you a hard time."

Mike seemed far less concerned over that possibility; in fact, even managing a grin. "Well, at least he don't live here."

Kate presumed his comment to be another shot at Mrs. McWheeten, but she let it pass. As her impromptu check to Mr. Broderick had nearly liquidated her checking account, she was very thankful when Mike turned the subject back to her good deed and his intention to repay her, in full, the following day.

Kate did, however, have a few dollars in cash on her—as did Mike, though he wasn't convinced that he wanted to spend them on 'sprucing up the room.'

"What for?" he asked.

Because, insisted Kate, the addition of a few decorations would greatly enhance the small room's hominess and give it character. "It'll make it your room instead of just any old room," she explained.

225

Richard Steigelman

But 'any old room' was cheaper, Mike casually replied, though he was to be malleable on the point and allowed himself to be talked over to her perspective.

Their first stop, at the Salvation Army store up the road, was devoted to the room's one glaring need, the acquiring of adequate bed linen, with a precautionary emphasis being placed on heavy blankets.

Returning these items back to the house, they then embarked on what Kate clearly found to be the more appealing segment of their journey, as she paced them to a nearby second-hand store.

Mike showed little initial interest in—and seemed quite overwhelmed by—the clutter that, at times, made him leery of following Kate down the narrow aisles, for fear that he might inadvertently knock something to the floor and be made to pay for its collective pieces.

It was decided that their first purchases would be practical houseware items such as kitchen utensils, a table lamp and a radio alarm clock, with each final selection being reached by easy consensus.

It was only when the decorative items moved to the fore of their agenda that Mike began to display signs of life and individuality.

A painting of "some dumb flowers next to a fruit bowl?" Why, she couldn't be serious—.

Instead of this one over here depicting a great battleship encounter, with the cannons blasting away at close range and men disappearing into the frothing sea?

"At least there's some action here. If I wanna look at flowers I can jus' go outside," he reasoned.

But, the flowers would lend a more favorable effect to the room's overall ambience, Kate countered; and, besides, the superior skill of its artist was plainly apparent—

"You gotta be kiddin' me," Mike's expression of disbelief piquing the critical interest of a browser nearby. "Hell, any artist can paint flowers. Ya got 'em there right in front of you to look at. But this guy here painted this battle scene from imagination. You're tellin' me that's easier to do?"

But it was such a horribly done painting, Kate couldn't help but remark with a laugh.

"An' since when've you become such a expert on paintings," he was amused by her pretension.

"I'll tell you what," she said to him, "I'll buy you that painting of the flowers out of my own pocket. That'll save you money for whatever else you would like to buy—except," a firm stipulation, "that other painting."

"You're gonna buy it for me?"

Yes, she would; provided he promised to adhere to her stated precondition.

It was certainly an inexpensive proposition for Mike, though he did not consent to it without a forlorn glance for the foundering ships and luckless souls that he was leaving behind.

"Hey, this fat guy's kinda neat, don't ya think?"

Kate retreated to the nook at which she had lost Mike, and her expression indicated that she did not share his rapture with the large wooden Buddha that he was examining with such a gleam. Really, how could he prefer that to the nice clay pottery on the table right next to it?

"Hell, what'll I do with that stuff, except break it into a million pieces?" he argued. "I ain't gotta worry 'bout that with this guy. Look at that gut on 'im! Hell, I thought I drank a lotta beer—"

Kate's cheery suggestion that they had enough money with them to buy both the pottery and "the fat guy" worked to achieve Mike's acceptance of the package deal.

And while Kate was contemplating the appeal of a pair of brass candlesticks, Mike was arming his Buddha with a quart-sized German beer stein; the observation of which subtly dissuaded Kate from encouraging live fire anywhere in the room, and the candlesticks were placed back on the table.

With their cash supply running low and the room's wall space still largely unaccounted for, they picked up a few posters cheap and proceeded with their quarry up to the counter.

Mike took more pleasure in decorating his room than he

ever would've imagined, and he found himself wishing for more space to house the many trinkets left behind that had gradually captured his intrigue.

He made do with what he had, though, with the pottery being signed over to the corner table and arranged around the newly acquired lamp. The imposing wooden Buddha, meanwhile, was issued a place of prominence atop the dresser, attended, naturally, by the ornate ceramic stein.

The finished scene was surveyed by its tenant with much satisfaction, and Mike regretted that not enough money was left over to celebrate with even a cheap bottle of champagne.

It was just as well, replied Kate, with a glance out the window into the fading afternoon.

Mike acknowledged the impending darkness, also, and understood that she should probably be on her way. But before she went, he wanted to reiterate his appreciation for the favors she had done him.

"I think you were right," he commented. "That Mr. Broderick didn't seem real gung ho about givin' this room to me. I guess maybe I can't blame 'im. An' I'm pretty sure, too, he prob'bly woulda found a way to give this room to anybody else but me. An' I kinda like it, 'specially now with all this stuff we bought."

Kate, too, was pleased with her deed, as well as Mike's response to it. "Beats the shelter, doesn't it?" to which Mike replied with but a muted nod. After a brief silence, Kate announced that it was time for her to be going, when he abruptly asked if she could wait a moment.

Kate complied, pausing before the door, and was made all the more curious by Mike's stubborn inability to come out and say whatever it was that had prompted him to request that she delay.

His eyes shied from her quizzical gaze and he sighed. "So—" finally, and with his voice cracking, "when's the baby due?"

Kate could not have been taken completely by surprise that he might raise this issue so central·to their relationship, but no degree of preparedness could prevent a rush of the old fear from coming over her. It had all been too recent, and the experience too disturbing and tangible. Had she erred, Kate could not help but now wonder, in being a willing party to this reconciliation that he had engineered?

She replied, with that apprehension punctuating her tone, that it was not due until July.

Mike nodded, remotely, before remarking, "That ain't so far off, really."

She granted that the date would probably come upon her fast, though, "Once I start getting big, it's probably going seem like it's taking forever," and there was some relief in that her own insipid smile was matched by him.

"Well—" he released an anxious sigh, and with his voice still infected with uncertainty, "if there's anything ya need— you know, if there's anything I can do to help out—before or after it comes . . ." and there was no need to complete the offer, for the inference was clear. And astounding.

Kate was positive that she had heard his quiet words correctly, but she could not be prevented from seeking out some sort of confirmation, and sincerity, in his limp gaze.

Mike was shamed by her doubt, though he could not fault her. "I guess I was kinda scared when you first told me 'bout the baby," he tried to explain. "Still am," with a weak grin she could not be coaxed to share. "Didn't want no part of it—as you know. An' I guess—I jus' thought that not havin' no part of it woulda been made a lot easier if you didn't go through with the pregnancy.

"But you made your decision—an' I still can't say that I agree with it," he confided. "An' I thought I made my decision on the matter, too. But I guess the more I've thought about it the more I can't get aroun' the obvious, that your bein' pregnant is as much my doin' as it is yours. An' I know I told ya this before—an' I meant it when I said I was sorry for some a them things I said an' some a the insinuations I made about your pregnancy. There was never any excuse for any a that. Disagreein' on things ain't a good enough reason. An' bein' jus' plain stupid don't count, either.

"An' even though it was your decision to go through

with the baby—an' not mine, I know I'm still partly responsible for how that kid turns out, whether I choose to help it as much as I can or totally ignore it. Whatever choice I make, I have an impact. An', ya know, for once I think, if I can, I'd rather have a good impact.

"I don't pretend to know the first thing about bein' a good father, mainly 'cause I never had the privilege of seein' one at work. But I learned what bein' a bad father's all about, so at least I know a lot about what not to do.

"So, I guess what all this ramblin's about is jus' to let ya to know that you don't have to go into this alone. I know that's gotta be hard on a person, an' it ain't really fair to you or the kid. An' I know I ain't ever given ya any reason to trust me, an' I won't blame ya if ya don't, but—I'm jus' lettin' ya know—if you want, I'm willin' to help out, like I shoulda been from the first. Financially, as much as I can, but also as far as spendin' some time—an' takin' care a the kid itself.

"If there's one thing I've learned from my own life—an' from talkin' to other people, too—it's that it's important for a kid to have a good father aroun'. An' even though this all still kinda scares the hell outa me—it really does—I know it's scared the hell out of a lotta people before me, an' they got used to it; so—" there was his offer relatively clarified.

Even had she a clear head, Kate likely could not have conceived of a proposition more unimaginable. She sat herself down on the edge of his bed, from where she gazed back up at him with a sort of melancholy wonderment.

He sought to ease her predicament by recommending that she simply think over his proposal. "You ain't gotta decide nothin' right now—"

"Mike," her soft sigh drifting away from his obedient stare, "—I'm probably not going to keep the baby," with her glance turned back upon him. "I'm thinking of putting it up for adoption."

Adoption? "I thought you wanted—"

"I did want a baby, Mike. And I still do—eventually. I just don't think I want one right now. I'm only twenty-two. And

I don't think I'm ready for it—anymore than you are.

"I thought I was ready, and I thought that's what I really wanted, but—I think, now, that that was nothing more than an emotional reaction—to you, to us. To my circumstance. I didn't have anything else to turn to," she lifted her shoulders into a hapless shrug. "The baby was going give me that something else.

"But things have changed so much for me in the past couple of months. I have a job—and a place to live. I have friends, now. I didn't have friends before. I never felt comfortable around those people we used to hang out with together. I didn't like them at all.

"Now, I'm going out and doing things, and I'm enjoying myself more than I have in years. I'm just starting to live again—and if I have a baby now—"

Mike certainly empathized with this perspective, though he was still surprised by its admission, and, gazing down at the sunken figure with the tear welled in her eye, he smiled gently. "It's about time you came over to my way of thinkin'."

Kate blinked up at, with a smile of her own. Sitting down next to her, then, Mike placed his arm loosely around her shoulders.

"Well, I'm gonna start savin' up money, just in case," he stated. "You know what they say about women changin' their minds."

She responded by giving him a nudge. "Well, saving money is a good idea, anyway," she suggested in a manner that caused Mike to laugh and remark that for someone who had just proclaimed herself unready to be a mother, she was sure sounding like one.

They went quiet, then, their eyes struggling, before Kate rose from the bedside. She commented on the advanced state of the twilight and said that she really must be going.

Mike offered to walk her home, but, as she hadn't far to go, she graciously declined it as unnecessary.

"I'll go to the bank after my shift tomorrow," he informed her, as she adjusted her scarf. "So, if you wanna stop by on your way home from work—"

Kate approximated that she would be by around quarter to six and she thanked him again for the prompt repayment. She, then, bade him good-night, which she followed with a moment's hesitation.

Mike had begun to ask whether something was wrong, when she leaned forward and surprised him with a kiss on the cheek, before slipping quickly out the door.

Chapter Twenty-Three

Like nearly any other night of a Michigan January, it was far too cold out for ceremony; and Mrs. McWheeten was earnestly imploring that her dog Sunshine get on with it. The landlady had already endured the dog's routine examination of the hedge, from where that bit of greenery began up at the sidewalk to the point where it cozied up alongside the house, and beyond which the landlady was unwilling, if even able, to squeeze. So it was, at Mrs. McWheeten's prompting, that they had reversed their course back towards the sidewalk, with the dog pausing repeatedly for all but its purpose.

The complete exhaustion of Mrs. McWheeten's patience was revealed by her mordant suggestion to the animal that if it failed to commence operations immediately, it very well might find itself passing the remainder of the evening—and whatever else—in the dreary downstairs sleeping quarters of Mr. McWheeten; for the landlady had far better things to attend to than the capricious return of the dog's regularity.

This passionate oratory, however, fell impotently against the dog's deaf ears, and it was only upon the subsequent display of the landlady's intentions—made with a hearty jerk of the chain towards the house—that the stubborn animal complied with an impressive spread lain out in a swirl very near to the center of the sidewalk.

With the production completed—and favorably reviewed by its author—there failed to follow the anticipated submissiveness to the directive of the chain; and the landlady cursed the dog's independent streak as she charged down after the creature, with the snow and ice threatening to undermine her every step.

Scooping the waggling animal up from underneath its

front legs, Mrs. McWheeten labored to keep it held out at arm's length, as she carefully negogiated the slippery terrain back up to the house. She hoisted the dog, with a grunt, upon the porch, just as around the corner of which there came Reese, adjusting his gloves for his own foray into the cold.

He greeted the landlady—and her dog, with a pat on the head for the latter.

"Off to work rather early this evening, aren't we?" observed the landlady, still panting from her exercise, and offering a poor smile ridden with an abiding consternation for her just-completed ordeal.

Reese had the night off from work, he was happy to report; rather he was on his way to the university's graduate library "to meet up with a friend and peruse the stacks. We like to bring a thermos of hot cocoa and make a night of it."

Mrs. McWheeten returned a vacuous smile, with an equally absent remark regarding the benefit of an interest in books; and, too, what a pleasure it invariably was to run into Reese and would that she had more time to chat, but that she had better get the dog (whose wanderlust she was keeping in check with her boots) back inside, and that certainly her tenant would understand.

So, Reese wished them good-night and was descending the steps, when he interrupted the landlady's escape into the building with, "Say, Mrs. McWheeten, who's the new tenant I've been seeing around the house recently?"

New tenant? The landlady was nearly over the threshold, with the front door ready for closing. "Oh—why, you must mean Kate—"

But, no, for Reese was acquainted with Kate; besides, it was "a short fellow whom I've encountered leaving the house these past couple mornings—rather early, as I've arrived home from work—"

A short fellow? Now, who could—"Why, you don't mean—" with sudden alarm. "This—short fellow—was he wearing one of those red and black plaid coats you see worn by the hunters?"

That was precisely the short fellow.

It required a moment, but Mrs. McWheeten rebounded from this positive identification by bluffing an expression of nonchalance, even feinting at a smile. "Oh—I believe that merely to be a short-term visitor to the house," she replied. "Very short term. But nothing more, I can promise you," and bidding Reese good-evening, the landlady guided her roving dog back into the house. She glanced out through the window to make sure that her tenant was on his way, before levying a stern double knock at the door of apartment one.

There came no answer, however, and, indeed, through the crevices about the door frame all seemed dark—and quiet—within. Mrs. McWheeten picked up her dog and transported it upstairs.

Kate hoped that she were not interrupting anything.

Timothy's warm smile immediately relieved her of any such concern, as he asked her to please have a seat. He had been at work on a letter to his father; but there was no urgency in completing it, he told her, and certainly none that a friend wasn't entitled to intrude upon.

In fact, Timothy was pleased by the visit, for he was eager to share with Kate as to how he had spent the early part of his workday hearing all about Mike's new accommodations and the generosity of a certain benefactor.

Kate, of course, was well aware of Mike's gratitude towards her, but she blushed that he should be telling others.

"He mentioned that you would be stopping by tonight," which, as Timothy suspected, was from where Kate had just returned.

She had paid the visit, she said, to be reimbursed—and, as it turned out, to help Mike celebrate with a bottle of champagne, with the drink being evident in her twinkle.

"I only had half a glass," as her head sank into her hand," but I haven't had a drink in so long that I'm afraid even that was too much. I wouldn't've had any, but he's pretty excited about his new place, so . . . And I figured that half a drink in nine months probably wouldn't hurt any—"

Timothy sought to assure her that the health of the child would probably be completely unaffected by her half a drink.

"It was—nice," she reflected on her evening as a whole, it seemed, with some minor surprise. "And he only had one glass of champagne himself. I guess I was a little bit concerned about that," she confided, to Timothy's empathetic nod. "He said he's going to bring the rest to work tomorrow to share with the cooks."

Timothy commented that he hoped it would be after their shift was completed.

Kate smiled at the joke, though it could hardly conceal her preoccupation. "I just can't believe how different he seems," she shared with Timothy her quiet incredulity. "And I keep watching—and waiting—for a return to his old self; but—these past couple of days . . . It's been like discovering a new friend.

"In fact, I think I can honestly say that I like him more as a person now," she revealed with a bemused smile, "than I ever have before. And I think we both realize that we're better off as just friends. We never got along anywhere close to this well when we were seeing each other. It was pretty horrible—as you know. That's what makes this all so unreal. I mean, a month ago I wanted him out of my life forever. I wanted him kept in jail. Now, I'm lending him money and helping him get his feet back on the ground. And I couldn't be happier."

"He's made a pretty remarkable transformation," said Timothy, nodding. "And I'd be lying if I told you that I wasn't a little bit surprised by it myself. I'm sure I would've put my money on his failing," he stated quite frankly. "I'm very pleased to have been wrong."

Chiding herself for having assumed Mike's ultimate failure in this venture, only now was Kate able to confidently declare that no longer did she believe his change to be a mirage.

"I apologized tonight for doubting him," she said. "He told me that he didn't mind me doubting him, because that finally gave us something that we had in common."

Timothy smiled with her; and he suggested that they

arrange a housewarming party in honor of Mike's move.

"It'll have to be an awfully small party," she lightly replied. "There's not room in there for too many people. Especially if Barry comes."

They decided, then, to wait until spring when they could conduct the festivity out in the yard of Mike's residence.

"But no more champagne for me," Kate wearily pledged, "until after the baby's born." And feeling the need for a short nap before dinner, Kate excused herself to her room.

Mrs. McWheeten was seated at the edge of her chair, eagerly punching her right index finger at the calculator that lay flat on the desk. The pen she held in that same hand busily recorded on a scrap of paper the numbers that flashed bright before her eyes.

She seemed quite engrossed in her task, and it sounded more of mere fancy than sincere lamentation when, momentarily, she sighed, "It is times such as these that I do wish our rooms were uniformly configured, for how much simpler it would be to have a seventeen per cent rent increase calculated across the board rather than have to figure out several distinct sums everytime a set of leases is due to expire. Ah well," with bland resignation, "it is the individuality of each accommodation, I suppose, that gives the house so much of its character," whereupon, she gallantly returned to computing the imminent appreciation due the uniqueness of apartment eight.

Mr. McWheeten lifted his head to audience his wife's musing, as he sat across the way on the low couch with the inner workings of a door lock laid out on the coffee table before him. He had been assigned his present project, for there seemed to have developed amongst the tenantry the increasing use of the basement utility room for their personal storage space; and the resulting clutter, Mrs. McWheeten had come to conclude, was impairing her and her husband's ability to properly function as landlords. Therefore, it had been decided to repair the long disabled lock, allowing then only the McWheetens access to the space. It was also planned that whenever entry was subsequently requested by any of the offending parties, it would be met, first, with a lecture against the ignoring of such notes as had been taped to the utility room door forbidding their trespass and followed by mildly-worded instruction to seek storage elsewhere.

"Seventeen per cent?" sounded like a bit of a hike to the husband.

And the landlady conceded it, perhaps, a tad high by conventional measures; however, "I feel it imperative to take into account, when assessing such things, the rent income forfeited by our occupying two of the rooms ourselves. Seventeen per cent, therefore, in my estimation, seems just compensation for that loss. And, certainly, it would have to be viewed as a fair tradeoff by the tenants, to have us upon the premises and attendant upon their various needs round the clock, rather than to have us detached from their concerns in some far away place."

Her husband made no rebuttal and returned his screwdriver to the rehabilitation of the lock.

With the calculator finally having earned its rest, Mrs. McWheeten turned to her notebook to dash off half a dozen or so individual notices regarding the following lease's rate adjustment.

It was easy, while so engaged, to ignore the faint voices and laughter coming presumably from the kitchen. Such sounds were routine when one dwelled just across the hall. But increasingly, upon the louder exclamations, the landlady found her ear distracted; each such eruption serving, consequently, to speed her hand along, to the point where the information she wished to convey to the occupant of apartment twelve was nullified by almost complete illegibility.

The pen, then, leapt from her hand to the desk, with her eye-glasses placed hurriedly beside and under the silent and confused stare of her husband, the landlady stepped quickly toward the door.

Poking her head into the kitchen, Mrs. McWheeten observed for a moment, before clearing her throat to make her presence known. It was perhaps inexplicable, given that the landlady's room was so close by, but Lottie and, to a lesser degree, Kate looked somewhat startled by her appearance. Mac was downright horrified. The landlady asked for a word with Lottie out in the hallway.

Chapter Twenty-Four

Lottie was naturally disappointed over her landlady's edict forbidding Mac's spending of another night at the house, under any circumstance, but she would not allow it to defeat her.

If Mac could not come to her, then she would simply go to him; beginning that very evening when, after their quiet meal was finished, she bundled herself up to accompany him back to the shelter, where she would join him in spending the night.

Kate thought the gesture cute and very romantic. Mac, on the other hand, was just plain confused, not cluing into the ardor behind Lottie's sacrifice.

"You gonna leave your own house to go sleep in a shelter?"

That was Lottie's steadfast plan all right, and not even a poor night's sleep spurred any regret.

"I gonna go back tonight," she reported, with a determined nod, to Kate the next day at work. "I ain't gonna let Mrs. M'Wheeten come in way a me 'n Mac. We like each other too much. My back will hafta get used to sleepin' there," she maintained with good humor.

So, from passing a great deal of their spare time together at the McWheeten household, it abruptly developed that Lottie and Mac were spending virtually no time there; for if the landlady wished to ban him for the nighttime hours, Mac would willingly boycott the waking ones, as well, inasmuch as the loathing was mutual.

Thus, when her work was done for the day, Lottie would seek him out and, in the early evening hours before the shelter stopped admitting, they might bide their time together on Mac's bottle collecting enterprise or, perhaps—if the weather were too cold, warming themselves at the public library, where Lottie took an immediate fancy to the glamour magazines, while Mac generally lost himself elsewhere.

And though they still spent their entire days together at work, Kate missed her friend's companionship in the evening, and certainly the house did not seem the same to her—nor to Timothy and Jim—for the absence of Lottie's animated spirit was not easily adapted to.

They, nonetheless, could not help but feel happy for Lottie, for they knew the importance of this relationship to her. Though, while the others appeared to passively accept Lottie's increased absence, Kate was soon compelled to hatch an idea that she hoped might readmit herself onto the pages of Lottie's social calendar.

It was Friday morning when Kate revealed her plan at work, informing her friend of a downtown club that in the early evening would be featuring free live country-and-western music, as well as reduced beer prices.

Lottie enthusiastically endorsed the idea. Kate then phoned the State Street Grill and found Mike also receptive to the proposal. Timothy, however, had previous plans and Jim, he believed, was scheduled to work that evening.

Nothing much seemed to inspire Mac, least of all paying bar prices, even at discount. He groused to Lottie that, if he had to go, at least they stop by a liquour store first, so that he might buy a bottle of something cheap to smuggle in and keep himself occupied while maintaining his budget.

"Don't worry—I treat!" and it seemed that nothing could've given Lottie any greater satisfaction; and slipping her arm through his, she bounced merrily along at his side as they started off towards the club, where they were to meet up with the others.

"Lucky I fin' you tonight, huh?" she patted him on the hand. "I not think that poss'ble when you wasn't at lib'ary. I look all aroun' downtown for you. Then, when I see you go 'roun' that corner so fas' an' you not hear me when I call out, I not know if I able to catch up with you. But I try as hard as I can to catch up an' it worth it," with a big smile and a stroke of his arm. "But I will hafta rest up at bar, 'cause I not used to runnin' like that."

They found Kate and Mike having just joined the line at the front door of the establishment, and within but a few moments the four of them were gathering in about a high round table with barely the surface space to accommodate their drinks.

It soon became evident that the ladies had come to dance, and every bit as clear that the men had not.

"Nuh-uh, you ain't gettin' me out there to dance," Mac recoiled so at the mere suggestion that Mike couldn't help but smile at the degree of his colleague's abhorrence.

The women were disappointed, but not surprised nor deterred. Giggling that they should be paired together, the two of them advanced upon the dance floor under the curious watch of their male companions.

The loudness of the music relieved the men of any perfunctory attempt at conversing, which suited them both; and only Mike was moved to display any appreciation of the band or any interest in being in the building at all.

The women were not especially fluid dancers, nor did they care. They very much enjoyed their three or four song stint upon the moderately crowded floor.

They returned to the table to tend to their thirsts and to good-naturedly implore the men to at least give dancing a try.

Mike was able to match their humor in his declining of the bid; whereas Mac seemed silently convinced of a conspiracy to drag him out onto the floor. He maintained a defensive posture low upon his stool.

The ladies were entertaining no such scheme, however, and appeared happily resigned to carrying on in partnership with one another. When they started back towards the floor, Mike informed them that he and Mac would be vacating their chairs, too, in favor of the pool table downstairs.

This came as a surprise to Mac and, though he really did not play pool, he was prompted to accept Mike's plan by virtue of his speculation that the basement of the joint had to be less crowded—and less threatening—than his present surroundings.

And he was right, for away from the burst of the band and the prattle of the patrons, down in the comparative quiet of the basement there stood a single, unattended pool table and very little else to draw a crowd of any size. There was a small table over against the wall nearby, atop which they placed the beer, and a couple of wooden chairs to support their coats. The restrooms were in the basement, as well— tucked down a dim corridor in the far back.

It was a perfectly dismal setting, with meager lighting and the air fouled by stale beer and old smoke. Overhead, the infirm ceiling seemed to bow under the heels that clicked resoundingly along the wooden floor of the bar.

Mike racked the balls and invited Mac to break.

The match proved quickly to be one of minimal skill, with Mike possessing the wee bit that might be impled.

It developed as a quiet game, as well, with the talk consisting mainly of Mike's analysis of the action and the shots available when his turn came around.

Mac's eyes moved dully between the table and his opponent, being unfamiliar with the former and not terribly fond of the latter, and he would not yield even a groan, or a curse, whenever a shot squibbed off the side of his cue.

Mike, despite his rudimentary command of the game, was very intent on its progress, and it was several minutes—as he stood back lighting a cigarette—before he took note of Mac's peculiar silence.

"You still hangin' out at that church?" he asked, while issuing his first puff, as across the way Mac surveyed the dubious prospects on the table.

Mac glanced up and gave a gruff nod; and, in quiet afterthought, as he lined up a shot, "Am now."

Mike watched as his opponent's shot took an unintended direction. "You had your own place?" which Mike found hard to believe.

"Not really my own place," Mac replied with a shrug. "I was jus' kinda stayin' over at their house for a while, until—"

Whose house? Mike paused on the brink of his next shot.

Mac made a vague indication with his pool cue towards the floor above.

Mike hadn't heard of this arrangement. "In their room?" for certainly it couldn't be big enough for three.

"Slept on the couch," said Mac. "Which was cool with me. Sure beats the shelter an' all those people. But then that landlady found out—"

Mike drew rigidly back from the table, his curiosity replaced now by a sneer. "Yeah, I've met her," he snarled, before going on to explain.

"She didn't like that much, either," he remarked, with a snort, of his own appearances at the house. "But, hell, she didn't jus' throw me out—she threw Hank out, too. An' he had a lease! 'course he wasn't payin' his rent," Mike did acknowledge, with a shrug, "so I guess I can't blame her too much for that. But, still, I always thought she was a nasty ol' hag, anyways," and without a trace of remorse in his tone, Mike gladly related to Mac the tale of his and Hank's revenge.

Though Mac was familiar with the anecdote, he allowed Mike his catharsis and listened with a sort of reverent appreciation.

"Well, I ain't gonna do nothin' like that," he declared with a laugh at the story's conclusion. "Besides, your girlfrien' an' Lottie ain't been kicked out. They're still livin' there— kinda; 'cept that Lottie keeps taggin' along with me for some reason an' comes over to stay at the shelter instead—"

His girlfriend? Mike's focus had faltered at this reference and he regarded Mac now with a blank yearning, as the latter continued on in what might as well have been gibberish, for its straying from that allusion to Kate. Why, not even Mike would've made such bold reference to her as his girlfriend. So, upon which basis did Mac?

Could it possibly be that, having roomed with her recently, he may have been privy to her feelings on the subject? But, how incredible—

And how foolish Mike felt that he had not picked up on

the hint, though even now, in reflection, he could recall nothing that should have alerted him to her veiled sentiments . . . except, perhaps, that kiss delivered to his cheek the day on which he moved into his new residence. He had made a conscious effort on that occasion not to read more into her act than he felt likely there. And, consequently, was flabbergasted to learn the truth behind her gesture.

It was not that Mike found such intentions undesirable. Full reconciliation had infiltrated his mind early, but only as a potential and slowly evolving process, not to be subverted by hormonal impetuosity. He had been proud of his restraint and felt safe and comfortable behind it. The thought of now abandoning it frightened him. Though it excited him, as well. And if she were to take the lead . . .

Still, it was all a bit much to comprehend at such notice and, this piece of inside information notwithstanding, Mike was determined not to press the issue. Committed, now, to examining closely her every word and glance, he was quite willing to play docilely into Kate's hand without prematurely tipping his own.

From behind this wondrous preoccupation, Mike was able, momentarily, to pick up Mac's trail and mumble a concurring opinion as to how strange it was that Lottie would forfeit the relative comfort of the McWheeten house for evening stays at the shelter.

Mac had no explanation for it, either, concluding, with a shrug, that, "I wouldn't do it. They got it pretty good there. I figure she mus' be crazy."

Meanwhile, back upstairs, the two seemingly unattached women had unintentionally succeeded in attracting the interest of two similiarly paired men. One of the gentlemen, being quite short—and with a face disproportionately prominent, aligned himself with Lottie; while the other fellow, who was tall and lean with small wire-rimmed glasses and a thin red beard counteracting a prematurely balding scalp, looked actually to be much more in tune with the music than with his new partner.

Kate didn't mind, however, and she and Lottie smiled at

one another somewhat in astonishment.

The shorter man was very talkative and amiable and when, presently, the band took a break, he led his friend in tailing Lottie and Kate over to their table, which tickled the women further.

Lottie, especially, found the attention flattering and blushed intensely when the men extended what sounded to be sincere praise for the ladies' dancing. It was left to Kate to return the compliment.

"We come here almost every Friday night," stated the short man, who had introduced himself as Larry, from his perch atop one of the stools, with his elbows propped forward upon the table. The imparting of this information received a nod of confirmation from his friend, Roger, who remained standing, with his eyes closed—as Kate had observed they had been during nearly his entire stay on the dance floor— and gently swaying to the piped-in music that was being substituted in the band's absence.

"But I don't think I've ever seen the two of you here before," noted Larry.

"Firs' time for me," Lottie answered with a nod she directed at Kate.

He asked whether they were enjoying it.

Lottie again found comfort in making her response to Kate. "It fun, ain't it?"

Kate smiled at her friend's anxiousness before the stranger, and she agreed. "I haven't been here in a while," she remarked. "I'm glad I've made it back."

"Can't beat the price!" crowed Lottie in reference to the free entertainment and reduced beer prices.

Larry concurred with a spirited nod of his own. "Roger and I usually drink up during Happy Hour and then stick around for the headlining band. We know most of the bigger name bands in town—and, also, a lot of the people who work here, so usually we're able to stay and listen to the main act for free."

And, here, Roger poked his small oval face, with eyes finally opened, into their circle and added, "And are able to

Richard Steigelman

get our dates in for free, too."

Roger spoke the truth, Larry eagerly assured the ladies. "Have you ever seen The Disemboweled Rodents?"

The answer seemed to be No; thus, what an opportunity for the men to expose the women to the local music scene!

"Do you like to slam dance?"

"We already here with boys!" Lottie cracked so suddenly as to even startle Kate; but it obviously caused greater surprise among the two men, who simply went dumb.

"They downstairs shootin' pool!" to which Kate felt obliged to provide a corroborating, if somewhat shameful, nod.

"We really did appreciate your dancing with us," she added courteously, "and staying for the main show really does sound like a good time—" but, by now, the men were disappearing through the crowd behind hasty adieus.

Kate turned back round with a sigh and was met by Lottie with a big smile.

"It hard for two women like us to be out alone, ain't it?"

Kate replied that she hoped their feelings had not been hurt. "I realize we didn't ask them to dance with us—or to come join us here at the table, but I just hope we didn't somehow lead them on—"

Definitely not! maintained Lottie. "Ain't our fault men can't control themselves 'round us!" a concept at which Kate could not resist but break into a smile.

"Better not tell those guys," Lottie cautioned her friend against letting on about the episode to their pool-playing companions. "They might get jealous an' start fight!" which, upon a second thought, struck Lottie as a rather romantic notion.

Kate agreed, however, that it should be kept secret; and when the band started its next set, the disengaged pairs made a conscientious effort to stake out opposite corners of the dance floor.

"Hey, you were gettin' better by the end."

Mac nodded, with a skeptical grin, as the two men tossed their pool cues atop the table. "That's only 'cause I couldn't

248

get no worse," he commented near to the truth. "Still didn't come close to winnin' no games."

"Maybe nex' time," suggested Mike.

"Ain't likely," replied the other, though hardly concerned over this prospect of continued futility. "But it still beats the hell outa dancin', that's for sure. Ain't no way they're gettin' me out there to dance—un-uh."

Mike seconded the preference for pool, though they were now making their way back upstairs towards the fray. Observing the active dance floor far across the room, the men assumed the ladies to be a part of it, and to make things easier upon themselves, Mike recommended that they pull up two stools at that end of the bar furthest from the notice and persuasion of their female compatriots.

Mike bought Mac a beer—with a healthy shot of bourbon at is side, as well as an identical round for himself. Together they also shared a few private remarks regarding the attractive face and figure of the female bartender who had served them.

"Hell, we shoulda jus' skipped the pool an' sat up here the whole time," quipped Mike, which would have been fine with Mac.

"I gotta start comin' down here to look for empty bottles," he remarked with a leer.

Mike, giving his bottle a waggle, suggested that the two of them were doing their part this evening in supplying Mac future income. He then asked, "You got any kinda job?" other than collecting returnables, of course.

Mac did not and further replied that he did not want one.

"Neither did I," responded Mike with quiet understanding and he took another sip from his beer. "But I gotta tell ya, man," turning aside in earnest, "I'm glad I finally got one. It gives ya some freedom—"

"Nuh-uh," rejoined Mac in mild dispute. "Ya gotta work when they tell you ya gotta work. That ain't freedom to me. I can go collect bottles whenever I feel like it. An' if I don't feel like it, like today, I ain't gotta go do it. That's freedom."

Mike was not going to quarrel with Mac over his point and, withdrawing a pack of cigarettes from his coat pocket, he first offered one to Mac, which was declined, before lighting one up for himself.

"But, look at it this way," Mike resumed his case, as he reached across Mac to grab an ashtray. "Downstairs, you made it sound like you were tired a stayin' at the shelter now that you've had a chance to stay somewhere else. Well, think about it, then. Wouldn't it be nice to have your own place? Every night, without havin' to worry 'bout bein' kicked out—or not let in—"

"The shelter ain't that bad," Mac now refuted his previous sentiment. "Least it don't cost me nothin'. No rent, no utilities, no phone bill. All the money I make I get to keep for myself. I kinda like that."

"You make decent money collectin' bottles?"

This unexpected inquiry made Mac uneasy, and quietly suspicious of Mike's sudden interest in the bottom line of the bottle collecting business. He merely replied that he did all right.

"Ain't got no costs," he noted, "'cept bags."

"So, what're ya doin' with all this money you're makin'?" Mike had inadvertently flicked some ashes atop the bar and he swiped them off to the floor. "Got it in the bank?"

Mac's resulting glance implied that Mike must be crazy to believe that he might have a bank account. "I keep it hid," Mac asserted.

Mike made a slow nod and, going from his cigarette to his beer, "Let me tell ya, keepin' it in a bank's a hell of a lot safer than keepin' it in your pocket. Hey, it wasn't no different with me," he tried to comfort his visibly agitated comrade, whose reflexive repositioning of his left hand had tipped Mike off as to the whereabouts of his life's savings.

"Didn't think there was nowhere else to put it, either," confided Mike. "Didn't even think of a bank. Wouldna known how to go about it. Wouldna felt safe goin' about it, really. But I got some help, an' I'm glad I did. I know it's safe there. An', hell, ya even make interest on it, which is kinda nice. Makin' money for just havin' it sit there. Can't beat that."

Perhaps not, but Mac more fully empathized with Mike's

prior reluctance to entrust the safekeeping of his money to strangers and, therefore, his expression of gratitude for Mike's offer of assistance in opening up a savings account of his own sounded short on sincerity.

Mike understood Mac's present outlook and would not push the issue. He simply stated that the offer was open-ended, should Mac come to change his mind on the subject, or, for that matter, his feelings towards acquiring a job.

"Just let me—or Timothy—know. Hell, dishwashers get five-fifty an hour where I work. Man, that ain't bad—for washin' dishes? Sometimes we need people," Mike reported with a shrug, as he put his cigarette out in the ashtray. "An' the manager there's pretty cool 'bout hirin' people from the street.

"Hell, they took me. An' Barry. I don't know if you know 'im (Mac did not), he's a friend a mine. You'd prob'bly recognize 'im—big guy. Anyway, I got 'im a job there an' he's workin' out real good, too.

"I'll be honest with ya, washin' dishes ain't the funnest job in the world—but, hey, five-fifty an hour? How many bottles ya gotta collect to make that kinda money? An' I'm up to part-time prep cook already—in just a couple a months! 'course I had a little bit of experience in that back when I was younger. But that's six-fifty an hour. That's pretty good dough. An' even if ya decide to stay at the shelter, think of all the money you could save at them wages. Enough to give ya the option of movin' out if ya wanted. That's freedom. Havin' no options ain't freedom." And feeling decidedly affluent by comparison, Mike hailed the pretty bartender to bring them another round.

The men had hardly completed their renewed appreciation of the pleasant viewing that the bartender's appearance provided them, when Lottie and Kate, on their way downstairs to the restroom, spied them at the end of the bar and teasingly inquired as to why they were hiding out back there, and as to whether or not they felt sufficiently intoxicated to take a spot on the dance floor.

The resounding negative response to the latter question

sent the women down the nearby stairways with a cackle that could be heard till they turned the corner at the bottom.

The men were spared any further attempts to put them on unflattering public display when, shortly after the women returned, the Happy Hour session came to an end.

"Already?" cried a disheartened Lottie. "Why so early? What time is it?"

It was indeed nine o'clock, Mike learned from the pretty bartender. "We didn't get here till after seven—"

"It nine o'clock?"squawked Lottie, flashing a look of alarm at Mac, who was not comprehending. "The shelter already close!"

And whereas Lottie could, of course, return to the McWheeten house, where was Mac to sleep that night?

"I don't care what she say," Lottie proclaimed in a burst of defiance. "I ain't gonna let you freeze to death. You hafta come home with us an' stay," nearly tugging Mac from his bar stool. "There no other way. If she don't like it—too bad. She will hafta kick me out, too."

Kate soberly agreed that there seemed no other options.

"Hell, he can come over an' sleep at my place," shrugged Mike in the face of all the commotion. "I ain't got no couch, but I got a floor. That way, he won't get you two in trouble an' he ain't gotta deal with your landlady again. Hell, my landlord's never aroun'."

Well, it certainly seemed to Kate the preferable solution and she commended Mike on his thoughtfulness—which sent him scrambling for a deeper meaning behind her words— but would Mac mind sleeping on the floor?

"Hell, Barry slept there a couple a nights ago," Mike broke from those other contemplations to interject. "Said it wasn't so bad. I picked up a couple extra blankets this week, jus' so people could stay over if they wanted. An' a pillow, too. Only thing is, I gotta get up early to go to work—"

Mac was quick to remind them of the early waking hour required at the shelter, and very gratefully accepted Mike's offer, with the emphatic declaration that, "I don't wanna go back to that stupid old lady's house if I don't gotta."

And not even Lottie could blame him for that.

And so, with this dilemma successfully resolved, it was happily suggested that no longer were they obligated to make an early night of it.

Mike, however, reiterated his work schedule for the next day and, as it was already nine o'clock, he did not wish to stay out much longer and he certainly desired no more alcohol.

"Them cheap beers go down fast."

"The cheap whiskey, too," added Mac with a sidelong grin for his benefactor.

Mike thought that food, followed by a good night's sleep, would have him adequately revived for his morning shift. With the others admitting to hunger, as well, the two men polished off the remainder of their drinks and all four then joined the other Happy Hour revelers in filing out into the cold night in pursuit of their diverse destinations.

There was a diner just up around the corner, upon which they came into easy agreement. Quaintly housed in what resembled a small converted trailer, the restaurant served round the clock, developing, in that course, the status of favorite to the counter-culture and after-hours crowd; and where the approach of a young waitress with multiple rings gouging nearly every nook and corner of a head whose hair was shaved half off, with the remainder braided in green and purple, did not warrant even a second glance.

She slapped their menus atop the table, with her manner taking them aback until she advised them, "Not to order anything from the grill. The new cook's burning the hell out of everything—again. Besides, meat's not good for you, anyway. I really don't know why we serve it here."

They followed her cue only partially, for the cold sandwiches they ordered did contain meat. Their meal was soon delivered, with no further nutritional commentary nor with any particular care as to whom ordered what.

They managed to sort that out amongst themselves. And the ingesting of the much-needed food helped to rejuvenate the lagging conversation, with Lottie proposing that, perhaps, the Friday Happy Hour could become a regular routine.

But nex' time we make sure Tim'thy can come. An' maybe Jim can take night off a work."

The others thought well of the idea, for all, even Mac, had enjoyed themselves.

" 'cept nex' time you guys gotta dance!" blared Lottie, pulling her sandwich from her mouth. "With each other! Like me 'n Kate did!"

Mike grinned sourly at her frolicsome request, informing her, with an averse shake of his head, that, "Guys don't dance with each other. Only girls do that."

"Uh-huh, yes they do," rejoined Lottie. "Me 'n Kate see two guys dancin' with each other tonight, didn' we?"

Kate nodded uneasily in confirmation, surprised that Lottie would even hint at the subject they had agreed to keep hushed.

Mike simply snorted, as he continued shaking his head. "Well, that don't surprise me none in this town, I guess," he grumbled. "An' it jus' makes me all the more glad we went downstairs to shoot pool. It was bad enough havin' you two after us to dance," and, here, the two men shared a grin, unaware that the women were doing likewise.

Having been the most recent entrants into the tiny restaurant, there had accumulated, in that time since, a fragile surplus of warm air, which was dashed in an instant when the door was presently opened, and spilling in with the bitter waft came two police officers, their hats removed and their eyes fanning about.

They had come only to eat and, though recognizing such, Mike's relief was tenuous, for his slight intoxication now became greatly exaggerated in his own mind. He fell immediately silent, his eyes anxiously following the officers to the table next over but one.

Of all the eateries in town, why would they select an establishment that cast them in such contrast to the clientele? Mike felt certain that he detected, on their part, a perverse enjoyment of the subduing effect that their presence had upon this patronage they seemed to hold in firm contempt.

The waitress heartily recommended the grill to her latest customers.

Kate perceived the change—and its cause—that had come over Mike and she placed a comforting hand atop his and tried to avert his attention.

Mike was oblivious to even such gestures, for he was gaining a strong suspicion that he recognized the officer who more directly faced him as the one who had so callously arrested him for the theft of that bottle of wine back in November. But he could not be absolutely sure, and that uncertainty commanded his gaze.

This attention did not go unnoticed by the thick and youthful officer, though his smirk seemed more of a general response to his scruffy surveyor than any positive identification of some petty thief from a couple of months prior.

Mac, on the other hand, kept his back squared to the policemen and his head low over his plate, for if the officers only knew the number of empty bottles that he had pilfered from the back doorways of area businesses—

Kate, at the next opportunity, flagged down their waitress and requested the check. And though Lottie, alone, was left in confusion over the abruptness of their activity, she put her money on the table with the rest and, fearing that she might be dragged from her plate before she was completely finished, she was thankful for the reprieve granted by Mike's need to visit the restroom downstairs before they departed.

The relief that Mike experienced in locking the door handle behind him was not in the least diminished by his being holed up in a dirty and dank underground room. It had him safely removed from a situation made all the more disconcerting by his own peculiar and irrational fears. He had done nothing wrong or illegal that evening and, regardless of any connection that the officer upstairs may have had with Mike's November arrest, there existed no basis for any reasonable concern tonight.

Able to breathe more freely, as a benefit of these reassuring reflections, Mike was finishing up his business, when he received a deathly start from the sudden rattling of the door handle next to him.

The door fell open and the police officer smiled in, with poorly feigned surprise that the facilities were occupied. "They really oughta get this lock fixed," he wryly observed.

Mike mumbled something about almost being done and tried to swing the door closed, only to be thwarted by the swift imposition of the officer's foot.

"I couldn't help but notice that you seemed a little edgy upstairs," remarked the officer, by way of incidental interrogation. "There isn't anything wrong, is there?"

Answering only with a terse shake of his head, Mike again tried unsuccessfully to close the door.

The officer's grin spread vulturishly, for he interpreted Mike's defensiveness as an unmistakable sign that he was on to something here. He stood fully in the doorway, now, and, taking an exaggerated sniff, wondered aloud whether, amid the foul aroma of the quarters, that was the scent of marijuana he was detecting.

Mike balked, however, in the protestation of his innocence, his tongue tied by his fearful recollection of those dubious figures who, from time to time, had ducked into the unilluminated crevices of the night club's basement to engage, he knew, in the very activity that, having left its fragrant residue upon his own clothing, now directed the officer's suspicion towards him.

Mike pleaded that he had only been playing pool in the vicinity and had not himself indulged. "You can ask the guy I'm with upstairs," his voice quickly succumbing, though, to the realization that he stood alone, backed into the squalid restroom, with no such witness at his beck and call. And the clatter of the pots, pans and dishes from the kitchen at the head of the stairway, long round the corner, ensured that this inquisition would be kept very private.

The officer received Mikes plea of no wrongdoing with an expression of pathetic disbelief. "Listen, do you really expect me to believe that people were smoking pot all around you and you didn't join in?" he asked as he withdrew his flashlight to enhance his examination of Mike's eyes.

Mike flinched under the glare, which further condemned him.

"Empty your pockets," the officer then instructed, slapping his flashlight at the sides of Mike's coat.

Mike was thankful to simply have the harsh light removed from his face and he began readily to comply.

He was proceeding methodically with the officer's request, confident of exoneration, until, with a jolt of supreme horror, he suddenly recalled his postwork smoke with Jerome the previous day. His hands fell desperately still, for he could not remember whether he had pocketed the last fragment, as he sometimes did, for future enjoyment.

The officer's curiosity was whetted by the delay and, having jabbed at it, he trained the flashlight's focus on the pocket in which Mike's hand had arbitrarily paused.

Mike resumed, producing from that pocket a pack of cigarettes, through which the officer zealously sifted, discarding each tobacco product upon the floor in his hunt for the illicit cigarettes he knew must be camouflaged in there somewhere.

The officer was disappointed to discover nothing incriminating in the pack. He demanded that Mike continue.

His apprehension of the unknown still nearly paralyzing, Mike proceeded, though his manner of slowly inventorying the contents of his many pockets before turning them out so grated his antagonist that the young officer threatened to assume the task himself.

Mike accelerated his pace at this prompting, unable to take another full breath until all his pockets were hung out in ridiculous display and he hoped himself cleared.

The officer observed Mike's relief with a wistful smile and, tucking his flashlight away, remarked how odd that Mike should be sweating so in such a cold, damp place.

"Clean up after yourself—or at least I'll get you for littering," the officer quipped, in reference to the cigarettes strewn about the floor. With a pronounced snort of self-satisfaction, as he witnessed Mike's grovelling obedience, the officer made his way upstairs.

Mike retrieved all the cigarettes and, pitching them into the garbage can, he allowed a couple of more minutes to pass before making his own cautious ascent of the stairs.

He avoided making any eye contact with the officer who, from his table, obliged him with ample opportunity, as he moved to rejoin his party, awaiting him now—at Mac's prompting—on the sidewalk out front.

He said nothing of the incident, nor much of anything else, on the walk home. With his residence being the closer, the ladies dropped the two men off at the door to his room.

"You take care a Mac," ordered Lottie in good humor, after reaching up to give her surprised beau a kiss on his cheek.

Mike mustered a weak grin and asked the women, for a second time, whether they would not prefer an escort home.

"We should be fine together," replied Kate, appreciative of the offer, and giving him a tender squeeze on the arm. It was this subtle action that finally succeeded in distracting Mike from his encounter with the officer. Hesitantly, he slipped his hand atop hers.

"Nobody better mess with us!" proclaimed Lottie with such spirit that she seemed hardly ready to call it a night. Nonetheless, the women were soon on their way home.

"Man, thanks a lot for lettin' me stay here tonight," said Mac with a sigh, while Mike began pulling his spare blankets down from the top shelf of his closet. "I really didn't wanna go back there with them. Heck, this even makes me kinda glad I got shut outa the shelter, ya know? It'll be all right, stayin' here," with an approving glance around the place.

Mike said that he was glad to help out and together he and Mac laid the blankets upon the floor next to the bed.

"If ya ever get locked out in the cold like this again—" Mike was interrupted by a knock at his door.

He asked the women what they had forgotten, as he opened the door—to Mr. Broderick?

The cragged landlord smiled, offering, "Good evening," as he peered into the room, with only a passing interest in

Mac.

"Your lady friend is gone?" he asked presumptively.

Mike replied that she was, and his perplexity was only heightened by the portly figure in a brown polyester uniform he noticed lingering in the background.

"Oh, don't mind my brother-in-law," stated Mr. Broderick with a sharp little chuckle, as he turned with a nod of recognition for his smirking second. "I just asked him along for insurance. He works in security."

Security? Insurance against what? "Is there something wrong?" asked Mike.

"Well," replied the landlord, his manner turning falsely humble as his hands went through the motions of wringing together. "It seems as though we might have a problem, yes. May I please see your copy of the lease?"

The lease? But, why—

"Please, if you don't mind," insisted the landlord. "There might be no problem at all, but I do need to see your copy of the lease."

Mike hadn't any idea as to what to make of the request, but felt himself in no position to object. He went over to his dresser and, returning with the document, handed it over to Mr. Broderick, who wasted little time in tearing it into several pieces and stuffing each into his pocket.

Mike was bewildered by the act and when, instinctively, he tried to reach out and stop the destruction, the landlord ducked aside, as his brother-in-law advanced on cue.

Mike was hardly able to ask, "Why—"

"When I was preparing for a trip to the bank the other day, to deposit your lady friend's check," the landlord was relishing the opportunity to explain his deed, "I happened to notice something that had escaped my attention last Sunday, and that was your friend's own personal address, which I recognized as the rental property belonging to a friend— and associate—of mine. Why, yes," grinned Mr. Broderick with dark delight. "I see that you're familiar with Mrs. McWheeten. And having finally gotten through to her this evening, I am now familiar with the terms on which your acquaintance was made. Funny, how you failed to use her as a personal reference, isn't it?

"Mr. Saunders, I expect you out of here by this time tomorrow night, because I plan on showing this room first thing Sunday mornin'. And if you should think of fightin' this in court—be my guest. Because I have the resources— namely, money and attorney friends—to make that a very unpleasant, and expensive, proposition for you.

"And, think about it—who knows this lease ever existed, except for me and two or three street people?" with a mean acknowledgement of Mac, who remained meek and dumb.

"So, really, who do you think the courts are gonna believe?" submitted the landlord with consuming confidence. "Now, if you'll excuse me, I think I'll go home and put this," with a spirited tap at the pocket containing Mike's shredded lease, "into the fireplace, on top of the ashes from your kind lady friend's personal check.

"Mr. Saunders, there is no legal record of this transaction. None. Therefore, if you're not outa here by tomorrow night, I'll have you arrested for breaking and entering, as well as for trespassing. I do hope that I am clearly understood?

"Oh—" Mr. Broderick turned back round with a parting point, "and if you dare to try an' take out your anger on this room—an' I think you know what I'm talkin' about—be forewarned that he," with a nod towards his brother-in-law, "will be staying on the premises until you are gone, and with the authority to implement whatever means necessary to bring any situation under control.

"So, please, enjoy a quiet last evening here," and sharing a grin, and a wink, with his hired hand, Mr. Broderick turned a copy of the master keys over to his brother-in-law, who settled himself into a folding chair at the foot of the stairways with a thermos full of coffee and a very thick newspaper.

Chapter Twenty-Five

It was late in the afternoon and Mrs. McWheeten stood before the stove preparing the pot of soup that would serve as the centerpiece of her and her husband's light evening meal.

She seemed in a pleasant mood, humming a little tune as she stirred the chicken noodle. And that her solitude was interrupted by Zimfou's entrance into the kitchen did not appear to bother her; rather, she welcomed his intrusion graciously, and, learning that the purpose behind his appearance was to fill a water pitcher for his plants, she gaily quipped, "I only hope they don't require a good deal of sunshine, as well!"

Her good-natured African tenant smiled at her jest and agreed that it was fortunate his plants had but a minimal reliance on the sun.

"My, what a dreary contrast to the sort of January to which you must be accustomed," she remarked. "How, may I ask, are you coping?"

"I am getting used to it," he replied with a polite chuckle, while stepping over to the sink, and he mentioned that this was actually his second winter spent in Michigan.

"Oh, I don't think one ever gets totally used to it," rebutted the landlady musingly. "I've been living in the north country all my life and, Lord knows, there are those certain winter days to which I shall never be able to fully acclimate myself.

"I'm not so much concerned for my own well-being, of course—the many trials of my existence have made me quite strong enough to endure anything that life thrusts upon me; but how I do sometimes wish that, for the benefit of my husband's health, we could simply pick up and move to a warmer climate. I really do. Though—" with an abrupt laugh severing her meditative trance, "I'm afraid that your native Nigeria—"

"Kenya."

"—would be a bit of a culture shock for both Mr. McWheeten and I."

Zimfou, too, could appreciate the humor of the notion, probably greater than she, as he played through his mind a vision of the McWheetens—and their dog—straying upon his native continent.

Mrs. McWheeten bid adieu to her tenant and his full pitcher of water and was reflecting upon the enriching qualities of living in such a multi-cultural community, when Lottie entered the kitchen.

The landlady could not help but smile, in declaring that Lottie's being so bundled up in her over-sized robe to be absolutely the cutest thing.

Lottie's reception to this meeting, however, was not nearly so cheery, still being rather sore at Mrs. McWheeten over the subject of Mac; and she was no more false to her heart than an insipid grin.

"I still cold," she explained flatly, and with a shiver.

"Still cold?" replied the landlady, with an uneasy turn of her head. "Why, not from your room, I hope?"

No, it was not from her room, indicated Lottie, shaking her head. "Me, Kate, Tim'thy 'n Jim jus' get back from goin' down to river to feed ducks."

And what a genuine relief to the landlady that Lottie's chill had been caught out of doors. "Well," she rebounded with a chirp, "I trust that, at least, you had a good time?"

Lottie's small nod was sincere, as was the sheepishness of her addendum, "Till I fall in river."

"Until you—fell into the river? Why, dear child, are you all right?"

Lottie nodded, with a weary sigh—and a sniffle. "Long as I don't catch 'monia, I think I be okay. "

"Well—pray tell, how did you manage to fall into the river?"

"Goin' after football."

"Going after—a football?"

Lottie gave a big nod—and a small grin. "Tim'thy throw ball over Jim's head—they ain't very good—an' ball bounce out onto ice over river. I say I go get it, cuz I say I lightest of all four of us. But, when I walk out onto ice on my tippy-toes, ice break. It not very deep where I was," Lottie assured her gaping landlady. "Only got my leg wet up to my knee. But I got ball!"

"Well!" exclaimed Mrs. McWheeten, rather out of sorts, "I think those boys should be ashamed of themselves, allowing you to jeopardize your well-being in order to retrieve their ball, which was out on that ice due only to their own ineptitude! And certainly it should be they who are coming up here to make this soup for you, rather than you trudging up here to make it for them! Why, really, I've half a mind to go down there—"

"Oh, I not makin' soup for them," injected Lottie. "It for Kate 'n me. Kate started not feelin' so good, either."

"Why, good heavens, don't tell me the both of you caught cold? You young people really ought to be more careful—"

"She not catch cold," proclaimed Lottie, vigorously shaking her head; rather, with a perky little grin, "I think maybe baby start kickin'."

"You think—that maybe the baby—what baby? Why, for heavens sake, Lottie, are you telling me that our Kate—that Kate is pregnant? Lottie?"

Lottie's mouth fell open. "You mean you not know?"

"Why, no—I did not know. I didn't even know that she was married, let alone separ—"

"She not married," babbled Lottie.

Divorced?

Lottie shook her head. "I sorry," she lamented, "I thought you know."

Kate had needed to stop off at the restroom before joining up with Lottie in the kitchen and, entering now in her own bathrobe, was thrown immediately into concern by finding her friend in such an agitated state. She was inquiring after the reason—

263

"Kate," Mrs. McWheeten was swiftly gathered up into the portrait of the grave matriarch, "I have just been made aware of your—situation—"

"My situation?" drawing her curiously affected friend close to her.

"Your pregnancy, Kate. You are pregnant, are you not?"

Kate dropped her somber glance upon the head turned reclusively into her chest.

"Yes, ma'am—I am."

"And outside of matrimony?"

That was true, as well.

"Dear child," heaved Mrs. McWheeten, with a pitiable shake of her head. "How could you have allowed this to happen to yourself?"

Kate hadn't any special explanation, and she bowed her head under the landlady's insinuating tone.

"It just happened," she lifted her shoulders into a shrug.

"It just happened? Kate, pregnancies don't just happen. There is a conscious code of conduct involved that leads to a circumstance such as yours. And, as it requires the unleashed yearnings of two, may I inquire after the male figure involved in this—just happening? Do we know his positive identity, for instance—"

"Yes, I—"

"Then he's been notified of the consequences of his actions? And is he prepared to accept the responsibilities he holds towards both this child and yourself? Have you, perhaps, explained to him the many advantages of the child being reared by two parents bound together in the institution of marriage—"

"Mrs. McWheeten," Kate interjected, finally, her patience strained, "if I do decide to keep the baby, then, yes, he has offered to help. As far as marriage goes, both Mike and I know that that would be a mistake—"

"A mistake? Well, good heavens—and just what other insurance do you have against this chap fleeing when the time comes; for, if you don't mind my saying, if I have not seen him on a single occasion in your time here, what sort of attachment could he have truly developed for you that would indicate a conscientiousness to stick by you during the inevitable tribulations of parenthood?"

"Because he told me would," Kate firmly answered, "and I believe him."

"Well—that's all very well and good, I suppose, and I pray that your trust is well placed. And just what does this Mike fellow do for a living that'll enable him to meet his moral obligation of providing for a child—as well as for you, Kate, should you be incapacitated for any length of time due to your pregnancy?"

"He's a dishwasher—and a cook—at the State Street Grill—"

"A dishwasher?" the landlady echoed dismally, "at the State Street Grill. Well, I guess that's better than nothing," if not much, she implied by tone. "Wait a moment—did you say, the State Street Grill? Why, isn't that the place where Timothy works—"

The landlady halted suddenly, one hand now clutched to her breast and her expression cast into the most grotesque contortion, as, breathlessly, she prayed that, "Why, when you say Mike—you cannot mean—"

But, of course, Kate did mean Mike Saunders and plainly acknowledged it.

Lottie had silently cringed when Kate first intimated at the father's identity and had begged with supplicating eyes that she go no further, but, now, with it openly pronounced, she shielded her face again in her friend's embrace.

"Mrs. McWheeten, I know how you feel about Mike," Kate seized upon her landlady's speechlessness, "and I don't blame you. I can't explain my past relationship with him. There's not much from that period of my life that I'm proud of—"

"Of all the appalling concepts to which I've had the misfortune to be exposed," the staggered landlady groped for her wits, "this—the notion that the seed of such a virtueless vagabond as Mike Saunders has launched its perpetuation upon the unsuspecting souls of this planet—

and this household! Good God—"

"Mrs. McWheeten, that's not fair," protested Kate.

"Not fair?" cried the landlady. "Why, good heavens, was it fair of the lot of you in conspiring to conceal from me the true nature of your situation so as not to jeopardize your obtaining residency under my roof?

"And, pray, what is my reward for so charitably taking you in off the streets and giving you respectable shelter, but the opportunity to witness, in my own home, the birth of Mike Saunders, Junior!"

"It inn'cent baby!" Lottie lashed out with tears formed full in her eyes.

"With the bloodlines of Mike Saunders, it shall know no innocence, Lottie—"

"Mrs. McWheeten," objected Kate, "I understand why you feel the way you do about Mike. Honestly, I do. But you have to believe me when I tell you that he's a very different person than the one you remember and the one who fathered this child—"

"Oh—Kate, please! For God's sake, certainly you cannot be naive enough to believe that such a leopard could truly change his spots—and in such a short time, no less! And I suspect you'll discover as much that tragic day when he actually does become a father!"

"Mrs. McWheeten, not only has Mike held his present job for over two months," Kate passionately countered, "but he's already gotten a promotion—and a pay raise! He even saved up enough money and, instead of going out and spending it on booze—like he used to, he's got his own room now!" Honestly, what further proof did the landlady require that Mike had transformed himself into a respectable member of society?

"Ha!" was Mrs. McWheeten's caustic response. "Not any longer does he have his own room! Does the name Mr. Broderick mean anything to you? He owns a rental property out along North Main Street—yes," smiled the landlady sharply, "that Mr. Broderick. Well, he happens to be a friend of mine, you see, and he recognized the address on the check that he said you used to cover Mr. Saunders' initial payment on a room? God, how I pray, dear Kate, that you see that money again—"

Kate informed her landlady that she already had.

"And desiring a reference of any sort on your friend," Mrs. McWheeten continued, "he gave me a call last evening and, naturally, I felt obligated to tell him everything that I knew concerning the party in question, with a particular emphasis placed on a bit of vandalism rendered against a certain rental property of my own.

"The result of our conversation being that Mr. Broderick readily and rightfully decided that it would not be in his best interest to harbor such a volatile temperament, and therefore, as of this very evening, your good Mr. Saunders has been turned out of doors; in time, I do truly hope, to land himself a spot back in the homeless shelter, for I believe the forecast tonight calls for continued cold."

Kate stared in broken disbelief, her anger revealed only by the tears she could not blink away; until, in a voice that no clearing of her throat could steady, "Do you know—how hard he worked--to save up for that room?"

"And do you know how hard," the landlady replied, "that Mr. McWheeten and I worked to save up to buy, and maintain, this house, only to see part of it wantonly destroyed by those two hoodlums?

"And have I heard from either one of them a single word of apology or, more importantly, an offer of compensation? I have not. And until I do, I shall feel no sympathy for their plight. In fact, and you might suggest it, with the rent money that he'll now be saving by staying again at the shelter, perhaps Mr. Saunders would be agreeable to making reparations for his work on apartment two? Though I suspect not, and fully realize that he'll likely be able to secure lodging elsewhere, without my ever gaining knowledge of it. Let him be forewarned, however, that my circle of landlord acquaintances in this town is not inconsiderable and that I shall not hesitate, nor feel the least bit of remorse, in sending him back out onto the streets if it proves to be at all within my power.

"I know that those words do not please you, Kate, and for that I am sorry. But you cannot blame me for having gotten yourself mixed up with such a person in the first place."

The tears fell bitterly now and the lower lip trembled. It was a couple of very long moments before Kate could summon the fortitude to lift her eyes, but having done so, she did not waver while declaring that no longer could she live under the landlady's roof (which drew a tortured squawk from Lottie).

Mrs. McWheeten, too, seemed very much surprised by the announcement, and not necessarily pleased, but yielding a slight and dignified nod, she allowed that she understood. "Perhaps that would be best for all involved," she acknowledged. "May I commend you on the thoughtfulness of your resolution—"

"How come you gotta be so mean!" Lottie uncoiled, to the utter astonishment of the landlady, who was helpless to respond; and between sobs, she begged Kate, "Please, don't move out. I like you for roommate. I don't want you to go— please—"

The watery embrace that the two young women locked into was more than the landlady had stomach to witness. She turned off the stove and, simply leaving her soup behind to be tended to later, marched briskly past them and out of the room.

"God, how damned unfortunate," said Mrs. McWheeten, issuing a distressed sigh, while seated deep in her chair, with her reading glasses folded together in the hand against which she rested her cheek. "She really had been working out quite well," which had been such a source of gratification for the landlady.

"I praised her on her mature decision," Mrs. McWheeten continued her soliliquoy in the presence of her husband, who observed with a special attentiveness from over on the couch, "for, certainly, it would have been quite disruptive to the harmony of this house to witness such a birth.

"God, I simply cannot imagine allowing the filthy paws of that nefarious animal to ever touch my body, let alone—" and, with a silent shudder, she would not permit the horrible thought to pass her lips.

"However," with a settling sigh, "I cannot help but feel what a far different Kate it must have been to yield to such a monster. But, still, how she scares me by rising to his defense, and, by doing so, seemingly leaving open the prospect of reconciliation. Good God, how could she even consider doing such a thing to herself—and to that child who shall have enough working against it!

"Why, I think I could forgive her the circumstances surrounding her pregnancy—and might even be open to allowing her stay on here—if she would simply promise to expunge from her life forever that odius germ who has infected her so.

"Why, really, how so much more beneficial to the welfare of that child should it be molded under the influences of this household as opposed to the environment that would surely result should she take the catastrophic misstep of reconciling with the father!

"I think that it would behoove all the worthy principles involved for me to make the offer," the landlady had worked herself up into such a pitch and was yearning to see her design immediately implemented—with her husband's sincere, if inarticulate, approval—when an urgent knock beat her to the door.

"Why, Timothy—"

"Is it true?"

"I beg your—"

"That Mike's been thrown out of his house—because of you—"

"Well, now," recovered the landlady, with a wicked smile, "I see you've heard the good news—"

"So, then, it is true?"

"Well, only partly," rejoined Mrs. McWheeten. "He was thrown out of Mr. Broderick's house, not so much because of me, but rather for concealing a background that I was only too happy to divulge to my friend and colleague, and for which, incidentally, he was quite grateful.

"Certainly you do not expect me to beg your forgiveness, Timothy, for telling Mr. Broderick the truth? And did you come up here to beg mine for your deceptively incomplete representation of Kate—on Christmas, no less—when you successfully cajoled my goodwill under the guise of the spirit of the day!"

"I'll never apologize for doing what I think is right—"

"Nor shall I, Timothy, my dear fellow; it is simply a difference of perception, is it not?"

Timothy glowered at her, his restraint rapidly deteriorating. "The only apology I'll be issuing," he tersely stated, "will be to Kate, for the role that I played in subjecting her to your hypocritical—and un-Christian-like—whims and beliefs—"

"How dare you! Why, you can go join that rascal Saunders out on the streets—"

"He won't be on the streets for long," snapped Timothy, "so rejoice, while you can, in your little triumph. Just don't be surprised if you live to regret it—"

"Why, is that a threat?" the landlady tried to scoff over the evident unease prompted by her tenant's profoundly uncharacteristic conduct. "Good God, Timothy, listen to yourself—Timothy!"

But he was done listening—and Mrs. McWheeten was left with the empty response of his footsteps trampling down the front stairway.

Lottie could not be consoled. She sat in tearful grief upon the couch in her room, and her few comprehendible utterances indicated that she blamed herself for the turmoil.

"I thought she know," she sobbed over and again.

Kate, with a compassionate, if dispirited, expression, sat next to Lottie and, draping her arm around her friend's heaving shoulders, assured her that it was only a matter of time before the nature of her condition became apparent, and that certainly she would prefer to bear the task of looking for housing early in her pregnancy rather than later. Besides, the impetus behind Kate's action hadn't been Mrs. McWheeten's words regarding her, rather it had been the landlady's inconvertible attitude towards Mike.

But even had Lottie been able to accept her kindhearted friend's absolution—still, she was going to miss Kate terribly—

"We're still going to be friends—and we're still going to be working together," Kate pointed out. "It's not like I'm moving across the country."

But it may as well have been, as far as Lottie was concerned. "I gonna miss havin' you roun' here."

Kate smiled brightly, through a stray tear, and she reminded Lottie that, "It's not like you've been around here a lot yourself lately," a teasing reference to Lottie's attachment to Mac, which succeeded in drawing a faint, though twinkling, smile from her anguished friend. They were tightening their embrace when Timothy returned from his confrontation with Mrs. McWheeten and threw himself darkly into a chair.

The landlady stewed over Timothy's behavior and could hardly touch her soup.

"To speak to me in such a manner—and in my own house!" Her spoon rattled against her saucer, while the fingers of her other hand tapped, in similar agitation, atop the card table that she and her husband had set up in their room. "Why, it certainly does tempt one to employ Mr. Broderick's ingenious tactics to evict—and, at the very least, I've surely every right to revoke the offer of his staying on here with us once his current lease expires! Where does he get off copping such a hostile attitude?

"Why, am I to sit here passively, waiting and wondering whether an apology is forthcoming? He's had nearly two hours to collect himself and return to beg my forgiveness, but I'm beginning to believe that he hasn't any intention of doing so!

"Am I, then, to accommodate my sworn enemy and lay prostrate before his implication of mischief? I should certainly hope not! And, therefore, have I not grounds—with you, Fab McWheeten, as my witness—for immediate eviction!

"Well, let's see how smug he feels now, in the face of my resolve," and the landlady startled her slurping husband with this charge to her feet (causing him to dribble on the napkin tucked into his shirt collar). "If he should apologize," proposed the landlady, "well—fine. If not, he shall discover me both eager and prepared for any skirmish.

"First, however, I think I shall stop by and tend to my business with Kate. You may refrigerate my soup, I shall have it later—in celebration of his humble submission."

Mrs. McWheeten was disappointed that her knocks at Kate's door went unanswered, though the feeling was momentarily supplanted by queer apprehension when she thought she detected the women's voices emanating from Timothy's room down the hall.

Certainly, Mrs. McWheeten would preferred to have handled this case separately, and in an environment unpolluted by the fresh acrimony arisen between herself and Timothy. But there could be no delaying her reckoning with Timothy, and Kate simply must understand.

The landlady's knock at apartment three stilled abruptly all voices therein.

Timothy, alone, seemed to have anticipated the visit and he glanced with quiet foreboding between his stricken visitors, before rising from his chair.

"I am not quite finished with you!" declared Mrs. McWheeten as the door opened before her. "Ladies, you'll have to please pardon me—and, Kate, I'd like a word with you after—why, Good God—what is he doing here?"

Mike had leaned as far forward as he was able in the wicker chair in an effort to conceal himself behind Timothy, though the latter made no conscious attempt to collude in the obstruction.

"He got thrown out of his apartment," Timothy announced with an edge, while gladly standing aside to present Mike to the inquisitor, "and had nowhere else to stay. So, like any good Christian, I offered to shelter him—indefinitely—until he finds—"

"You did—what?" the landlady fell back with a look of the most alien horror for her tenant. "Oh—no, you don't. He is not staying here!" she rebounded with a show of teeth.

"So, this is your little ploy, is it? This is what those threats were all about, eh? Well, I've a threat of my own, buster! He leaves immediately or I call the police! Ha! How's that for a threat? No, I haven't forgotten the nice little unsolicited renovation job you and your pal Klegman did on that room next door! And I shall never forget it for as long as I live! Now, you pick up your things and get your ass out of here right this instant, or I'll—"

"Go ahead and call the police," jeered Timothy. "You repaired the evidence and you have no witnesses—"

"What! no witnesses? Ha! that's where you're wrong, smart guy! Why, Lottie here—"

"I don't 'member nothin'" hissed Lottie.

"What, why—Lottie—"and, naturally, the unuttered blame for Lottie's complicity in this perceived conspiracy fell harshly upon Timothy.

"Mrs. McWheeten," pleaded Kate, finally, "if you just leave us be tonight, I promise you that Mike and I'll be gone tomorrow—"

"Dear Kate, don't do it! Good God, don't do it! Do not be fooled into believing in a false reformation and casting your lot with this reprobate! I don't care if you have risen in life to the illustrious station of pot washer, I know your type—and I pray that this poor child's genetic heritage evolves exclusively in favor of its sweet-tempered mother!

"Kate, I do apologize for my tone taken upstairs earlier today. It was wrong of me and was certainly not meant as an indictment of you. We all occasionally stumble along the tricky path of life and should be judged by an analysis of our overall record. And it is under the influence of such reasoning and reflection that, while I should like to ask you to please reconsider and to stay on with us for as long as you'd like, I simply must demand that this—person here leave the premises at once! and for good!

"For though, on the grounds of vandalism, I may now be without a case," with a glance towards Lottie, "there remains, I believe, a law on the books regarding trespassing—and I shall have it enforced to its fullest extent and presently, should he fail to leave this house—"

"I told ya I shouldna never came here," grumbled Mike, as he pushed angrily to his feet and grabbed his coat off the floor. "Besides, I just as soon stay at the shelter, anyway, than to stay under your goddamn roof!"

"You should be so lucky as to be permitted to stay under this goddamn roof!" retorted Mrs. McWheeten over Timothy's intervening shoulder. "And what a shame, isn't it, that Mr. Broderick found you every bit as unfit for the habitation of a civilized dwelling? Yes—please, go back to the shelter, where such base instincts as yours assimilate more naturally into the fabric of the institution!"

Mike had had enough and, declaring his intention to "get the hell outa here," he broke free of Kate's weak grasp and brushed his way past Timothy, who simmered in his own silent resentment of the landlady.

"And if ever I see you here again—" Mrs. McWheeten was rearing up in crimson deformity as Mike tried to slip past—when, without warning, he turned and burst upon her. Latching onto her lapel with one hand, he clasped his other palm across her face, muffling her horrified scream, and thrust her head, with the savagery of his full momentum, back squarely against the edge of the neighboring door frame.

"Don't worry, I ain't ever comin' back to this dump!" he yelled before discarding her roughly into the corner, where the desperate pleas for intervention gave way to ghastly calls for assistance, as the landlady's body crumpled slowly to the floor, and where, within minutes, she lay still and quiet and unresponsive to the frenzied activity around her.

Chapter Twenty-Six

The delay, while seeming so great, was, in fact, the matter of but a moment, before Timothy could react, pushing Mike away and rushing in to soften the collapse of his landlady.

And it was Timothy, his frantic command having gone unheeded by the two stunned women, who, with the blood of Mrs. McWheeten clinging thick and warm to his hands, sprang back into his room to make the call for an ambulance.

He, then, returned to the landlady's side to provide comfort in her wait for medical assistance. He turned imploringly upon Mike—only to find him having fled, which he had done almost immediately upon Timothy's casting him aside.

Timothy dashed to the front door, left open by the vanished assailant, and, descending out into the street, could detect no signs of Mike in either direction. He sprinted down to the corner for a look. Still, nothing.

Returning to the house, he discovered that the shrieks of the victim, as well as those of the witnesses, had lured a couple of curious persons down the front staircase.

Timothy ignored their inquiries, as, suddenly, he plunged straight through them and scrambled his way up the stairs.

Mr. McWheeten heard the sound of an approaching siren and, unaware of its purpose, was moving with casual interest from the card table over to the window, when Timothy came barging through the door.

The hectoring influence of disease and the deadening edge of its treatment did not dim the landlord's recognition of the urgency in Timothy's expression, rendered all the clearer by the emergency vehicle now pulling up outside the house.

There had been a serious accident, Timothy reported, his

voice halting and his heart loath to reveal Mrs. McWheeten as the victim. Mr. McWheeten, however, appeared to comprehend and allowed Timothy to lead him downstairs, where he broke from his escort and waded into the commotion that accompanied the arrival of the rescue team.

The landlord seemed almost an intruder upon the flurried operation, though, when his wife's body was rushed past atop a stretcher, he was swept right along with it into the waiting ambulance.

Mrs. McWheeten was dead before she ever reached the hospital nearby.

When word of this caught up with Timothy at the police station, he fell silent before his interrogators, his numbed replies needing to be tediously extracted from the inaudible sounds of his anguish. For though he had cradled the limp body that would not respond and still wore drenched upon his shirt the reflection of its broken veins, the notion that she would die from the brief attack had gone completely unexplored.

He did try, as best he could, to cooperate with the authorities, but his patience with what seemed to him a repetitious line of questioning—which was only exacerbated by the frequent introduction of new faces into the circle pressed closely around him— grew thin, and caused him to become irritable and gruff. He was finally dismissed, though not before listing for the police, with a feeling of reluctance he couldn't quite explain, Jerome's apartment as a refuge that Mike might likely seek out.

Lottie, in her statement to the authorities, delved, like Timothy, into the immediate catalyst for the evening's events and that being Mike's controversial eviction from his lodging and, of course, Mrs. McWheeten's role in that. Where their respective testimonies differed slightly was in Lottie's mentioning of Mac as a witness to Mr. Broderick's action, an incidental sidebar that Timothy entirely overlooked.

Naturally, the police were interested in talking with all relevant parties, Mac now included. Lottie pointed the way.

It was disturbing enough for Mac to simply observe the

presence of two police officers within the shelter at Saint Augustine's, but when word quickly spread that it was him for whom they were looking, his heart beat with such fear that his first impulse was to try and outrun them.

Even after the officers had drawn him aside and explained themselves, the crime that had prompted their visit seemed very inconsequential to Mac, in comparison to their request that he accompany them in their police car back to the station.

And why should he have to go with them, for he hadn't done anything! He never touched her! It was her who had almost killed him that one time by sending him out to sleep in the bitter nighttime cold. He had a witness—

The gravity of the situation notwithstanding, the two officers found quiet amusement in the pleas of their fretful charge. Their many assurances that he had nothing to worry about fell hard upon paranoid ears, as they led him out of the building.

Lottie had been excused from her questioning and lingered near the entrance to greet Mac upon his arrival at the station, though the lift that that occasion gave to her spirits was in no way reciprocal. In fact, Mac absorbed her embrace mistrustfully, his own arms remaining steadfast at his side.

And when she informed him that, "Police wanna talk to you 'bout las' night—at Mike's 'partment," his expression hardened all the more at this confirming of his suspicion.

One of the attending officers had been diverted by a passing colleague, and the other policeman bent an ear that way, as well, yielding the two young people a tight realm of semi-privacy.

"Nothin' happened las' night," Mac's growl surprised, and frightened, Lottie. "He got kicked outa his house. Big deal! I didn't have nothin' to do with it! What'd ya have to go 'n bring me into it for? I didn't wanna come down here! I hate this place—"

"But you was there las' night when—"

"Like it ain't bad enough that you always gotta be comin' aroun'. Christ, I can't even ditch you without you come runnin' after me—like las' night. I seen ya comin', that's

277

why I run. But now you're sendin' the cops over, too! Jus' like that firs' time I ever went over to that stupid house. Then they come after me for stealin'—which I didn't do, neither! Jus' leave me alone from now on. I don't want you comin' aroun' an' huggin' me no more. It gives me the creeps. Jus' like your old dead landlady. Why don't ya go fin' someone else to bother for a change—"

The second officer had detected the rising antagonism in the couple's conversation and moving back in, just as his associate was released from his short discussion, they led their sulking witness away and down the hall.

Lottie stared after in dry disbelief. She hadn't any premonition that he harbored such sentiment—why, hadn't they always had fun together? And she had never questioned, until it occurred to her now, that his bottle search was the true and sole reason behind Mac's showing up to the public library at an increasingly later time, if he bothered to appear at all. She knew that she could count on his being there at the shelter in the evening. And that had been plenty good enough for her.

But what possibly could've driven him to rebuff her, and in such a manner? Had she not always been so nice and considerate towards him? Was she not a kind and attentive nurse to him after his accident? Had she not defended him against the antipathy of Mrs. McWheeten? And jeopardized her own living situation in sheltering him against the landlady's wishes? So, how could he treat her in this way? What had she done to deserve it? What more could he have possibly wanted from her? He had communicated no displeasure with her—until now. So, how was she to attempt to modify the behavior that annoyed him when she had not been made aware that any existed?

Lottie made the short trek back home wrapped futiley in this enigmatic speculation, until lifting her eyes, with their tears still not fully developed, up to the sullen silhoutte of the McWheeten home.

And how selfish Lottie then felt for having dwelled thus upon her own misfortune, so faint in the grim shadow of the tragedy that had befallen both Kate and Mr. McWheeten.

She determined to try, as best she could, to conceal her own pain and dedicate all her outward concerns to the consolation of her friend and roommate.

Lottie slipped quietly into her apartment and found not only Kate, but, to her surprise, Reese, as well.

He had been unable, however, to provide any support for Kate, for he mourned, in impotent shock, the death of his landlady, while knowing nothing of Kate's association with her killer.

Kate was visibly relieved by the arrival of somebody sympathetic to her sorrow.

And when Reese rose into a palsied damnation of this shadowy felon, he was met by Lottie, who, with her arms around Kate's slumping figure, quickly took up the task of expounding upon the evening's complete story, antecedents and all.

Reese fell back in chastened silence, his heart turned timidly toward Kate. He had not known, he submitted to her in timorous apology. And while quietly revising to acknowledge that there may have been some provocation on the landlady's part—still, Reese could not fathom striking at another person in such a way—

"He not mean to kill her," Lottie's sharp rejoinder making Reese regret the rash utterance, from which he then retreated into full silence.

Timothy had lost track of Lottie and Kate amid the whirl of his transport from the house to the police station and, wandering into the lobby after his interrogation, he realized he hadn't any idea as to whether they were even still in the building. He did not feel up to a search, and as they all would eventually make their way back to the house, he would meet up with them there.

The porch light illuminated the yellow ribbon that the police had used to cordon off the crime scene. Timothy paused near the driveway, shaken from his thoughts by this stark and concrete symbol of the entire ordeal quavering silently in the night's gentle breeze. How quickly, though, his chill was replaced by a sickened pang over those who would brave the cold to mill about the sidewalk, and across the street, these two or three hours later. And for what? The body had been removed, the killer was long fled. Would a spot of blood satiate them, perhaps? and send them contentedly back to their dinner tables and living rooms with sufficient fodder for their lurid conversation?

Well, then, come on in, Timothy was tempted to beckon, as he marched through their thirsting glances towards the house. Surely there must be some blood left on the premises. And why not scrape up a sample to take for the mantelpiece back home? What a waste it would be to simply sponge away such a juicy story.

Timothy, however, addressed nothing to them, except one last blistering look of disgust from the door, before shutting himself inside the house.

The vultures were forgotten, now, as he pushed himself grudgingly down towards his room. And in what contrast to the obvious interest held by those outside that Timothy wanted no part of the vacant spectacle. But how could he help but look, for it loomed there directly ahead?

And alone in the quiet of that corner, there returned vividly to him now, every syllable of that angry exchange, as well as the poignant distress of Mrs. McWheeten's sinking pleas. Timothy could still feel Mike's brushing past him into the hallway, and recalled the haplessness of his own tardy reflex, as the latter turned on his victim. Too, the heavy, dull crack of the landlady's skull against the door frame—how its echo played so prominently in the bitter stillness of the present.

His head sagged as he turned away, and he tried, without initial success, to catch his key in the lock of his door.

He had hardly collapsed into his chair, when a knock at his door, being so cruelly distorted in his troubled mind to resemble that which had heralded the landlady's fateful visit, nearly raised him, in a start, to his feet. It was a long moment before he could collect himself and welcome Lottie into the room.

"I thought I hear you," she quietly remarked.

"I was going to stop down in a little while," Timothy replied, in acknowledging that he had heard activity in their room. He asked whether Kate, too, had returned from the police station.

Lottie nodded and said that Reese was with her. "She okay," Lottie reported with an ambivalent shrug. "She still cry a lit'le, but not so much any more. I still think she can't believe ev'rythin' that happen."

Nor could Timothy, and, with a sigh, he returned his head into his hands.

Lottie had lingered by the door, apparently waiting for Timothy's typical invitation to sit down, before, presently, taking it upon herself to have a seat on the hassock.

"He gonna go to jail for rest a his life, ain't he?"

Timothy's expression seemed to indicate that he believed so; though he allowed, in a hoarse whisper that, as the attack had been provoked rather than premeditated, perhaps there was some hope of a lesser charge, as well as leniency. He glumly presumed that, regardless, Mike's sentence was likely to keep him in jail for a long while.

"She make 'im do it," Lottie anxiously concurred, though it did not succeed in its intended effect of raising Timothy's spirits.

"We gonna hafta testify, ain't we?" she supposed, after a silence.

Timothy nodded that it were probable, as they were the only witnesses.

"But they ain't gonna believe me, 'cause I retarded, are they?"

It was the first that Timothy had considered the notion, and he could only wonder how badly she might be preyed upon on the witness stand. Gazing up into her wide, susceptible eyes, he nonetheless propounded that, "There were only three witnesses and we all saw the same thing. So, either they'll believe or disbelieve all three of us, and none any more so than the others."

And clearly what a relief to Lottie, for it seemed such a sensible conclusion.

"I saw her make 'im do it," she reiterated, appearing almost eager, now, to present her testimony before the court.

Timothy's face willed a frail smile in honor of her spirit, and he could only hope that the jury would be as convinced.

There came momentarily, against the reflective interlude that followed, a soft knock at the door.

Kate entered the room, a meager smile struggling to allay Timothy's incommunicable concern. She very softly explained that Reese had to go off to work—though he had been unsure as to how he was going to be able to function properly—and that she didn't like the thought of being alone.

She sat herself down on the wicker chair, near to Lottie, and Timothy quickly produced a blanket that she absently allowed to be draped over her shoulders.

She asked if there were any new information. Timothy had none. Mike was still at large.

Kate absorbed the report stoically, and felt certain that he could not long evade capture, for, though she did not expect him to return to the shelter to be so easily apprehended, it was far too cold outside for him not to seek refuge with one of those whose name they had provided the police.

Timothy mumbled a similar sentiment, but was troubled most by his inability to devise the words of solace for his friend that he so plainly desired.

Kate recognized this, with a tender expression of gratitude, but, with a sigh, "I feel so bad for him," she deflected the concern. "He worked so hard—and was doing so well—at turning his life around. I don't know what came over him tonight. I haven't see him lose control like that . . . since I told him I was pregnant.

"Why couldn't she just leave us alone for one night? We would've gone to the shelter tomorrow if we had to—"

"She made me start not wantin' to stay here, either," injected Lottie.

"God, what'll I say to him?" Kate wondered, in turning back to Timothy.

What could any of them say to him? replied his grim glance.

In the desponding silence that ensued, Lottie was

irresistibly compelled to divert, if only temporarily, the anguish of their contemplation by revealing that, "It not good night for me, neither," as a prelude to sharing with them her episode that evening with Mac.

Kate transferred her own sadness so naturally upon her friend and, placing her hand consolingly on Lottie's arm, urged her not to despair, confiding that, "I think having a girlfriend was kind of new to him," and, "I just don't think he was used to having someone around him so much. Before you, the only times I ever saw him he was by himself. I think he was more comfortable that way. Some people are just like that. And there's not much anyone else can do about it."

Lottie listened raptly to her friend's explanation. "An' maybe he jus' don't like girls," she suggested, bringing a small grin to Kate's face.

"Some people are like that, too," Kate acknowledged.

"But maybe, too, he come 'roun' to his senses an' start missin' me," a dubious hope that not even Lottie seemed to believe.

Kate diplomatically conceded the possibility, while advising her friend not to bind herself to the prospect.

"Oh, I begin to look aroun' again," Lottie assured her with an emphatic nod. "I not wait 'roun' for him all my life. He had his chance."

And with a gentle smile, Kate proposed that, at some future time—when their frames of mind permitted, "Maybe we can go out together and see what we can find."

It was a proposition that brought a rosy smile to Lottie's imagination. "But we not jus' settle for anythin'. Like them two guys at bar the other night! They was wierd, dancin' together like that. Only the bes' for us!"

It was a condition to which Kate gladly agreed.

It had crept past midnight, now, and though sleep might not be feasible, the strain of the evening had very much fatigued Kate, and perhaps if she lay down—

Thus, she said good-night to Timothy, with a hug from which neither seemed willing to release, and reassured him that he need not worry for her. She embraced Lottie, as well, though the latter stood ready to accompany her back to their room.

For Timothy, however, there would be no immediate attempt at sleep. He sat back down in his chair, with his head slumped forward into both hands.

Jim sank hard upon the edge of the wicker chair. He had seen the yellow ribbon, of course, on his arrival home from work, but never could he have imagined its tale. The fatal result having been supplied him first, Jim was hard-pressed to follow, now, as Timothy murmured along the tragic sequence of events. Mrs. McWheeten was dead; the details seemed secondary.

"I know that it wasn't his intention," as Jim's foundering concentration came back round to the speaker. "He just lashed out at her. It happened so fast . . . that I didn't have time to react—until it was too late.

"I was so mad at her myself," Timothy quietly confessed, "that I wasn't paying any attention to Mike. I knew that he was angry, but he had every right to be, the way she was ranting. But the thought that he might attack her . . ." had certainly never entered Timothy's mind.

"But, why didn't it occur to me, when I felt so much like slapping her myself? And now, of course, I wish I had. At least she'd still be alive. And Mike wouldn't be out there running—for what? his life? Is that what you call living behind bars?"

And what haunted Timothy most about that notion was that, "I could've prevented it."

But how, responded Jim, if it happened so fast—

"By not bringing him over here in the first place," the brusqueness of Timothy's reply being directly solely at himself, which Jim understood. "He wanted to spend the night at the shelter. This was the last place he wanted to come, because of the chance that he might run into her—which was exactly the reason I persuaded him to come here—

"I wanted to goad her. It's all that I could think about after my confrontation with her upstairs. How to get some sort of revenge. How to make her pay for what she had done to him. And I just knew that eventually she'd come down here tonight to continue the argument. I just knew she would. And was counting on it. And what better way to terrorize her than to have Mike here?

"And to witness her reaction when she saw him . . ." was everything that Timothy had hoped for. "I fantasized about it as I was talking Mike into coming over here. I stood there promising him that I'd take every precaution against his having a run-in with her, while secretly craving just the opposite.

"And it was all working out just perfectly according to plan . . ." Timothy paused, with a sigh, "except that I had gotten so wrapped up in my fabulous scheming that I failed to allow for Mike's response to the entire situation. I never took him into account—except as my bait. Otherwise, maybe I would've forseen the possibility of something like this happening. And prevented it."

Jim tried to assure his friend that nobody could have predicted so dramatic a development, but the consolation hadn't any effect; for Timothy's expression remained distracted by torment, and, hitherto, seemed hardly cognizant of Jim's place in the room.

Chapter Twenty-Seven

Timothy was unable to fall asleep that evening and could only wonder how long he had restlessly lain under the false hope, as he tripped through the darkness to his desk. He dropped himself into his chair and groped along the base of his lamp for its switch.

Reconciled, momentarily, to the light, he removed the hand shielding his eyes and glanced at his clock, which he found rendered illegible by both fatigue and the fact that his eyeglasses had been left back next to his mattress.

Dragging the clock nearer across the desk top, he gradually recognized the approaching hour as that at which he was supposed to be arriving to work. He slumped back in his chair with a miserable sigh. Certainly, he could not chastise himself for overlooking this obligation; nor could he possibly imagine being able to meet it.

Yet, he struggled with the thought of leaving his coworkers understaffed on so little notice. Perhaps if he were allowed to come in late it would permit him enough time to gather himself—but that falsehood was hardly formulated before being dismissed. He would have to call and request the day off from work, and how utterly wrenching the thought of having to break such news to Pam. She had been so supportive and patient at every step of this entire project.

It was probably a little early yet, Timothy realized, for anyone to be at the restaurant, and so he rose from his desk and, with his legs soft beneath him, lumbered across the hallway to the bathroom to try his face in a sinkful of cool water.

It failed to provide the restorative effect to which he had unrealistically assigned it and he transferred his favor to the notion of fresh air.

Dressed for the excursion, he returned to his chair with the telephone receiver viewed as some alien object held at arm's length. The phone number he could not clearly recall and it required a couple of restarts before he sat rigid in dread anticipation, listening to the unsettling pulse of the intended receiver resounding over and over in his ear, several times, until, finally, a voice—

And what a peculiar, though considerable, relief for Timothy to discover that Pam had already learned of the horrible event, just minutes before, from Jerome, whom, of course, the police had visited the night before in accordance with Timothy's lead (which had been to no avail).

They spilled into an instant and affective commiseration, and though Pam's shock was fresh and her comprehension of all the details strained, she did understand, and grant, Timothy's request for an open-ended leave of absence; and expressed a wistful, if powerless, desire to simply close the restaurant down for the day.

Timothy's preoccupation was such that the extreme cold of this morning went unacknowledged. And, if even alerted, he was indifferent, then, to the fact that he had forgotten both hat and scarf. He plodded onward.

The lamp-lighted streets were only beginning to buzz with the earliest risers. And the very few that, like Timothy, were on foot, he found himself beginning to eye intently, in the sudden fear that one should turn to in the mask of Mike Saunders, emerging from his night's hiding to seek out Timothy's help.

That apprehension caused Timothy to jump when, presently, a sharp peripheral movement from up the next driveway produced a hooded figure in his very path!

The young woman who fell under his panicked gape was every bit as alarmed by the encounter, and detoured down into and across the street, with a glance kept over her shoulder, lest this suspicious stranger should turn and follow.

Timothy hadn't any intention of doing so, of course, nor had he meant to frighten her, but he could excuse as logical his trepidation that had triggered their wordless misunderstanding; for whom else might Mike turn to in this time of his most critical need? It had always been Timothy who had lent assistance, whether solicited or not.

But what could Timothy possibly do to help him this time? And what would he be willing to do, if able?

What if Mike were to request his help in fleeing town, which may be very likely once he discovered that Mrs. McWheeten had died? Could Timothy be a party to that? And at what risk could he refuse cooperation, in the face of a desperate, and potentially delirious, fugitive, inclined to stop at nothing to secure his escape?

These pre-dawn phantoms would not dissuade Timothy from his walk, however, though they did alter his steps away from the camouflage lining the narrow sidewalk. Descending into the road near its end, he crossed a by-street and followed a sketchy path down a small decline, over some railroad tracks and through a thin line of trees skirting a riverside park, where, at this hour of the day, he was relying on solitude.

He veered from the frozen prints marking the path's continued direction towards a set of stairs that led up to a street bridge passing over the river, and wandered, instead, towards the water, the icy layering of his course glimmering in the pale light of the retiring moon and cracking gently under his solemn intrusion.

Timothy was grateful for the support of a sturdy old oak, from where he gazed with detachment upon the river, with its stagnant shards of ice carved by the occasional ribbon of dark water snaking bleakly through.

He lowered himself into a crouch, his back propped squarely against the tree. Eastward, as he faced, the first musings of daylight glimpsed through the barren branches of the meandering shoreline.

To the west, with a vacant glance partially obscured by the trunk, he observed the bridge sprinkled with motorists on their way to work; though it appeared, in the case of one, the dash being made a bit too speedily, judging by the stationary flash of a police vehicle glaring starkly against the murky backdrop of the hour.

Timothy sank his stare back into the river, before, shortly, trying to blot out all with the closing of his eyelids, as he rested his head back against the tree.

He discovered his dark thoughts only illuminated by this maneuver, however, and soon reopened his eyes to the hope of distraction. It was through the flesh, though, that he found the most unshakable diversion, for he was discovering it too cold to be simply sitting outdoors.

He would either have to return to the house and retrieve those winter accessories he had forgotten in his urgent exit or, at the very least, keep himself moving to promote the prospect of remaining sufficiently warm.

He pushed to his feet, with a dull ache wound tight in his knees, and, turning full around in surveying his possible route, found muted surprise, and perplexion, in the gathering of so many new emergency flashers upon the bridge, stopping up traffic, Timothy could see, in either direction.

He wondered, now, whether there had been a serious accident and his curiosity led him along the river towards the stairs.

His gaze being fixed on the activity emblazoned upon the nearing bridge, Timothy was startled by a series of flashlight beams jouncing along the wooden walkway that passed beneath the bridge and along the shoreline directly opposite him.

He squinted towards the purveyors of that light, yet they remained but vague silhouettes. Nor were their indecipherable voices made any more coherent by the calculated turns of Timothy's ear.

He proceeded on to the stairway and ascended towards the commotion. Feeling conspicuous as the only pedestrian amid the idling line-up of impatient motorists, Timothy advanced discreetly along the sidewalk, making his way over the bridge till he dared get no closer.

Through the rescue vehicles and many police cars, Timothy could not make out the exact nature of the disturbance. The focal point of the activity, as he could have expected, was centered across the street at the head of the stairs that descended to that walkway beneath the bridge.

Timothy could not repress his impulse to ask a nearby officer what had happened.

The officer, however, appeared engaged at the open window of his parked vehicle and made no acknowledgement of Timothy.

"Seems to be our fella," another policeman passed by with this news for the first officer.

"Any positive identification?" responded the other.

Only that "the description fits, right down to the clothes he was wearing. And we're only a couple of blocks from where that lady was killed last night." And with a shrug that seemed to ask what more evidence was needed, this informer wended his way through the traffic, which was now being allowed to slowly proceed again, along a single lane, under the command of a third officer.

"Say, George, what's the hold up?" one of the motorists, whose turn it was to pass through the bottleneck, had recognized the policeman directing traffic and, defying the brisk permeation of winter air inside his warm vehicle, rolled down his window in sober intrigue.

The officer gave a nod to his acquaintance, and leaning to, "Looks like some homeless guy fell through the ice last night. Managed to pull himself ashore, but froze to death down beneath the bridge."

The motorist's expression contracted into a slight grimace, but he said nothing. Nodding as a sign of appreciation for the officer's time, he rolled his window back up, before moving on, with his glance unsuccessfully resisting the scene that continued to build at the top of the stairways.

It was not long after that a stir was witnessed in that vicinity, and when the contingent from below arrived at street level there was briefly revealed, in the brilliance of the many flashers, a stretcher, fully draped, which was then tucked into a waiting ambulance, with the doors secured behind it.

And when that ambulance rolled slowly away, many of the other emergency vehicles began doing likewise, allowing the traffic to release into an increasingly normal flow.

The bitter cold had subsided, as Timothy turned and began his walk back over the bridge towards home.

Chapter Twenty-Eight

Perhaps it was just as well, was the conclusion that they wanted to make themselves believe; for, really, what could life behind bars for so many years be like and upon completion of that sentence, adjusting to release back into society?

Would they have even known that person? And could they have helped him? Certainly there would have been visits along the way, but what benefit, what strength or hope could Mike have derived to sustain himself from a few minutes interaction every so often?

Gradually, torturously, but almost inevitably, he would've been drawn by his incarceration towards vague recognition and, ultimately, mistrustful rejection of these increasingly distant and inconsequential associations from his past.

They had seen, and lived, the troubled side of his soul, fueled by those years on the street. The imagination shuddered at the monster born of a lenghty prison stay.

And though the embracing of this rationale was perhaps necessary to the healing process, it could not beguile away the grief. Kate's quiet tears, especially, would not cease, and were only encouraged by the contemplation of the suffering and torment of Mike's final hours, laying there alone, a surreal fog rolling slowly over his consciousness, unable to cry out to the motorists whose passing vehicles reverberated through the hollows of the concrete bridge above.

The authorities' request of Kate, later in the day, for assistance in their effort to locate and notify Mike's next of kin renewed in her the instinctive grudge she bore his parents. And though she cooperated with the officials, privately she held that his folks were not worthy to attend to Mike's body.

Nor would she be surprised if they exercised refusal over this responsibility, for, as she remarked to Timothy, it would have been more than they had ever done for him before.

Kate admitted to her friends a sense of shame over the expression of such malice towards these strangers, yet the power to suppress it she also confessed beyond her control. With tears welling in support of this frailty, she cursed the disadvantage into which their disinterest and neglect had thrown their son; for it was the product and personality of this dereliction—and not that of the restaurant worker struggling to overcome—that Mrs. McWheeten had first come to know—and cling to. Kate could forgive Mrs. McWheeten.

Kate, too, became adamant in her vow to remain anonymous to Mike's parents, for fear they learn of her pregnancy and attempt to practice influence over their grandchild, had they the seemingly unlikely predilection to do so.

And from this quiet wrath were sown the seeds that rapidly flourished and led Kate, in those days which followed, to declare herself increasingly disposed towards keeping the child at its birth, in defiance of her previous inclination and despite the difficulties she owned inevitable.

"I kept trying to tell myself before that I was too young to keep it," she explained her shifting intentions one evening to Timothy and Lottie. "And too young to want to be tied down like that. For eighteen years? I talked about having my whole life ahead of me. But what I've come to realize is that I was only being selfish. This baby's the one with his whole life ahead of him.

"And the more I've thought about it the more I've come to think that I can grow at least as much with him as I can on my own. And probably a lot faster, because I'll have to. And I just can't think of anyone who'd be more determined to help him avoid some of the things his parents went through— and some of the mistakes they made.

"I guess what I've come to realize, too," with a soft, reflective sigh, "is that I don't think I could ever give this baby away without spending the rest of my life wondering where it was and how it was doing. To me, that'd be even a worse nightmare than what I've gone through these last few days. I don't think I could handle that. And I don't want to try."

Kate then fell silent, apparently pondering the formidability of the task before her—which, at least, was Lottie's interpretation and prompted her to express both her delight at the news and her very eager willingness to assist in every possible regard.

And what a remarkable tonic this proved for Lottie, enabling her to move her focus sooner and more painlessly from her failed relationship with Mac; for if he did not need her, the baby certainly would. And the latter would probably return her hugs.

They never were to see Mr. McWheeten again. They learned from a hired agent, a well-dressed and somewhat portly gentleman with a red-brown moustache, that he was staying at the home of relatives outside of town, to which neither the address nor phone number were to be given out, and was planning a move to Arizona to be near other family and in a climate more agreeable to the sick.

Still, Timothy kept a very anxious and hopeful eye trained on the activity that began shortly about the house and included not only the somber removal of every last belonging from the McWheeten's two rooms, but, also, the long-needed attention to some of the establishment's more obvious shortcomings. A new stove being shoehorned up the twisting front staircase, better, and sufficient, lighting installed in every hall, new paint being liberally applied and, perhaps most remarkably, the fortification of Jim's dilapidated wall. Yet, no where amid all this did Mr. McWheeten ever appear. Not even briefly.

It fell especially hard on Timothy, that there would come no opportunity to talk with his landlord—to express to this forgotten victim his condolences, his remorse—to apologize, mostly, for the role he had played in the whole damned affair.

And the news that Kate would keep the baby did not

administer to Timothy the same therapeutic effect as it did to the two women. He was pleased for them, of course, but himself remained quiet and introspective, not prone, as formerly, to smile or joke; his new disposition being met with both understanding and concern by those around him.

His return to work, after a week, was a toilsome exercise in going through the motions. Not even Jerome's staged banter could spark a lasting resurrection.

His friends at home, too, were helpless to improve his outlook; and when he began to introduce hints of moving on, they sadly speculated that a move meant at lease's end in August.

They were soon to discover otherwise, however. One evening, with the women, as well as Jim, gathered in his room, Timothy, in a voice weighted with reluctance, informed them that he had given Mr. McWheeten's agent notice that he would be moving out of the house two weeks from that day, disclosing, to their further dismay, that his destination was Kansas City and home.

The reasoning behind such an abrupt departure, he explained to his stunned audience, was so that he would be able to reestablish residency in his home state before resuming his academic pursuits there. In the interim, he would find work, probably in a restaurant, and perhaps, take a course or two at a local community college.

"I've been thinking about this quite a bit lately—and I've talked it over with my parents. I'll be able to stay with them through the summer; so I'll be able to save up some money."

But, of course, there was more to the move than he was letting on; until, momentarily, with a sigh, "I guess—part of it, too—is that I think it probably better that I get away from here. I know that leaving—isn't going to change anything that's happened, and that I'll have to deal with the memories wherever I go. It's just that—the scenery here is such a constant reminder.

"I can't go anywhere in this town without being reminded. There are too many buildings—especially this one, too many streets and parks—and people. Every day they open the wound by recalling some episode or other. And I know that they'll continue to do so for as long as I stay here."

Timothy went on to express how especially difficult this parting was made by their friendship. It was not an easy moment for any of them and prompted Timothy to try and lighten the mood by joking that, though he was sorry he would not be around to help with the baby, even had he stayed he was not sure whether Lottie was prepared to parcel out any share of the paternal role.

They would all stay in touch, of course. And meet up again one day—hopefully soon (they were certainly always welcome to visit him in Kansas City). But the joyful anticipation of any reunion could presently be paid but hollow lip service.

And though each of Timothy's guests were quite likely contemplating various devices of dissuasion concerning his decision to leave, any actual attempt was properly suppressed by the selfishness they were able to perceive in their motives. There arose, instead, quiet murmurings of understanding, followed duly, and sedately, by a discussion of a social itinerary to cover the little time that Timothy had left with them.

The house went up for sale a few days later. It came as no surprise, and had been widely assumed; for the recent repairs certainly could not have come without a purpose. It was sad, nonetheless, to see it made official in the form of a sign out front.

On a day when the long, stern frown of this winter was finally relaxing just a bit, Timothy, upon returning home from an errand, found Lottie sitting bundled up on the steps of the front porch, her empty stare reflecting upon that sobering sign.

The smile with which she greeted his approach was conscious of having been caught in such a trance. "No more M'Wheeten Manor," she weakly quipped.

Timothy sighed, with a passing glance for the realtor's trademark glinting in the bright sunshine of the front yard. "Not for long anyway," he quietly acknowledged as he sat himself next to her on the shaded steps, placing his small grocery bag back round on the porch behind.

"But I can't really blame Mr. McWheeten for trying to sell the place," he added with a shrug. "Instead of hiring someone to run it for him from across the country, it's probably wisest, for a person in his conditon, to just sell it and retire."

Lottie supposed that made sense; besides, "Even if it stay M'Wheeten Manor, I prob'bly move anyway."

And why was that? asked Timothy.

Lottie turned to him. " 'cause me 'n Kate think we will hafta have more space—for two of us plus baby."

Timothy smiled. "That certainly is quite a sacrifice you're making," he made the point proudly. "And quite a responsibility you're assuming. Not many people would give that much of him or herself. I know Kate must be very grateful."

"I will do best I can," Lottie nodded unflinchingly. "An' I don't min' helpin', 'cause I love Kate. She one a my bes' frien's. An' I know I will love baby, too—like my own," which broadened the gleam in Lottie's eye, though how swiftly it faltered when, "I jus' wish—I jus' wish you was gonna be 'roun' to help us, too. I know you gotta do what bes' for you, but I gonna miss you—a lot. 'cause you one a my bes' frien's, too," and her smile, though it struggled, was so big and genuine—and congruous with the tear that welled in her eye.

It was a moment before Timothy was able to compose himself to reply, and, with his smile breaking tenderly over her bowed head, he assured her that the feelings were mutual.

"You were the first friend I made here," he reminded her. "And there's always something special about that first friendship when you're new to a place. It makes you feel welcome and at home. Without the friendships I made, this would've been nothing more than a big old house—with a little tiny room in it for me. And this For Sale sign out here wouldn't mean a thing.

"You were the first step in making this place something special for me. And I won't forgive either one of us if we permit a few miles to deprive us of this friendship. It doesn't cost much to send a card or a letter. And what's the price of a phone call when measured against the value of all the experiences, the laughs—and tears—that we've shared? We've been through quite a bit here together, haven't we? Unfortunately, a little too much recently, but—we've always been there for one another, like the times—"

"Like that first time when we don't even know each other yet an' you give me your only light bulb an' hafta use candles for your own room," she called up fondly.

"And all those times," he countered, his smile tempered some by the pain of the subject, "that you helped cover for me when I had guests here of whom Mrs. McWheeten would never have approved. We seem like such old friends," he marvelled, "that it's hard to believe we've known each other only three months.

"And you do know," he remarked, momentarily, in an optimistic turn, "that even without me around, you'll still have plenty of good friends here in town. Kate, of course— and the baby. Jim will still be here. Reese. And Hilgen."

"I lucky to have so many frien's now," Lottie did recognize. "But you was the first an' that makes you extra special. When I really don't have nobody else my own age in whole world, you was nice to me. An' like havin' me 'roun', 'cause you don't min' I han'cap. That 'portant to me an' I not forget that. An' I not forget how bein' 'roun' you make it easier for me to meet more people 'cause you not ashame to take me places an' introduce me. I like bein' 'roun' you. But even when I can't be 'roun' you no more, we still call an' talk to each other on phone, right?"

It sounded to Timothy so much like a plea that, while it saddened his heart, it also provided added vigor to the recital of his devotion in maintaining their friendship from afar.

But until then, he gladly took to remind her, they still had a few days yet in which to enjoy one another's company, and what was the point in delaying the fun?

Pleased to discover that Lottie hadn't any plans for the day, Timothy withdrew from his grocery bag a loaf of bread, with the cheerful suggestion that there was a much better use for it than his own personal consumption.

Lottie quickly caught on and, though her enthusiasm was slow in building to match his, she very willingly fell in behind him as he started them along the snowy sidewalks, on toward the island park where the ducks liked to congregate.

As the disheartening thought of her good friend's departure began to lift and she was increasingly able to appreciate the present, Lottie reverted back towards her old self. And things stood where they always had, when, shortly, she scooped up that first handful of snow and, tittering with a glee that threatened to betray her maneuver, pelted it across the back of her unsuspecting companion. She then collapsed, giggling, onto a snow bank, in happy defenseless against Timothy's spirited retaliation.

About the Author

Born in the Lake Michigan shoreline town of Muskegon, Rick left home to attend The University of Michigan in ann Arbor. Receiving his BA in communications, he set about putting it to use tending bar while he worked on his writing. This is his first published novel. Rick and his wife, Donna, reside in ann Arbor under the command of their cat Keiko, the calico princess.